EXTINCT

IVY CARTER ADVENTURE SERIES
BOOK TWO

HAYLEY CAMILLE

For my children.

Finn, Orrin and Ivy.

PART I
CLADOGENESIS

CHAPTER 1

IVY

Somehow, whatever it takes, I'm going to save them.

Ivy's emerald eyes were hard and resolute in the face of the impossible challenge she had set herself.

And then I'm going to save myself, too.

She grit her teeth, willing her brain to come up with something miraculous. To defy evolution. To outwit the laws of physics. But there was no epiphany. Ivy sighed in frustration. Something soft dusted Ivy's cheek and stuck there. She rubbed it away, then looked down at her fingers. *Dark grey powder. Ash.* Ivy turned her eyes up to the large, crooked branches of the Rosewood copse that sheltered her. Volcanic ash was drifting in the morning sky, finding gaps in the canopy. *Oh no. Not again.*

Ivy scrambled to her feet, heart hammering, as the earth suddenly rumbled deep within its bowels. The branches above began to shake. There was a thunderous *crack!* as one came crashing down only meters away, tearing off others on its path. Arms flailing for balance, Ivy froze against the tree behind her, unsure what to do.

"Kyah!"

There was a terrified shriek above her. Kyah was already moving. Ivy's constant companion, a ten-year-old bonobo, dropped to the ground. Long, black arms encircled Ivy's neck as the creature climbed up into a hug, burying her face against Ivy's neck like an overgrown child. With her intelligent eyes, high forehead and gracile build, Kyah was smaller than a common chimpanzee. Normally bright with curiosity, those eyes were now filled with fear.

"Shhh. We're okay." Ivy hugged her tight. The adrenaline shooting through her own veins wasn't convinced it was the truth.

Rii-iip.

The earth jolted again, instigating a screeching cacophony of bird flight. Not ten meters from her feet, the earth ripped open in a jagged line. Ivy stumbled, throwing an arm out to the tree behind her. A shower of leathery leaves joined a new onslaught of falling ash. A foul smell, like rotten eggs, filled the air.

Another one.

Ivy was backed up to the base of the gigantic rosewood she had been sitting under, hoping its roots were strong enough to withstand the rumbling. There was no point running. The forest stretched as far as she could see. She'd be as likely hit by falling branches if she ran than stayed still.

Kyah lifted Ivy's right hand from the tree, placing it gently against her own cheek. Her deep brown eyes locked onto Ivy's green ones, searching for a moment as they waited, wide-eyed, for the quake to pass.

"I think it's nearly over," Ivy said.

It wasn't the first time they'd been caught out as the earth tore apart around them. In fact, it was becoming terrifyingly familiar. The tectonic plates under the jungle island of Flores, in the Indonesian archipelago, were shifting. Long dormant volcanos were waking up. In her old life, Ivy had seen what these earthquakes were leading to. An archaeologists' delight. Layers of volcanic ash that divided one stratigraphic layer from another like a perfect cream cake of geology. An extinction-level event.

Fifty-thousand years in the future, Ivy had stared down a microscope, poring over the prehistoric stone artefacts that lay underneath this layer of ash. It had been so simple then. So academic. One species of human had lived, then a more advanced one had killed them off, aided by the volcanic apocalypse that tore apart the island. *Homo sapiens* had thrived in Flores after the ash settled. Natural selection and environmental ruin had joined forces to doom the old species to nothing but bones in the dust.

The stratigraphy, and future, was clear.

Until Ivy Carter, molecular archaeologist and full-time recluse, had been ruthlessly and painfully hurled back in time, and implored to save the dying species from extinction. Now Ivy was living an archaeologist's dream. And any sane person's nightmare. She was trapped fifty-thousand years in the past. On the wrong side of the ash, trying to prevent the extinction of a species of human that was in every way doomed.

A new wave of rumbling began. The sky darkened under belching grey dust.

Ivy shuddered, then set Kyah gently onto her feet, keeping one hand clasped tightly between them. She stroked Kyah's fine black hair with the other hand, picking flecks of leaf litter from the neat part in the middle of her head.

"I think the earthquake is done." Ivy looked around.

Prehistoric Flores was magnificent. But the island was a death trap.

And it was time to find a way out.

Ivy sat back down and leant against the Rosewood trunk. Kyah picked at a spot on her chest. It was a nervous habit the bonobo had left behind in the past month they'd been living with the tribe of tiny humans at Liang Bua cave. Picking, meant Kyah was anxious. It was a ghost of the trauma she'd once suffered in a pharmaceutical laboratory.

"You're safe now, honey."

Ivy gently took Kyah's fingers and redirected them into the soft peat. She cleared the leaf litter a bit, then dragged Kyah's index finger across the soil in the shape of a symbol. *Play.* Kyah hooted softly and began to dig into the forest floor with her toes instead, making a game of fishing out leaves with her toes.

"Good girl."

The disturbed earth caught Ivy's attention. Almost hidden in a moist cradle of soil, dwarfed by the archaic biosphere around it, a tiny seedling reached green arms up to find light. Ivy couldn't help but be impressed. Against all odds, the shoot had pushed through the crowded forest floor. Minuscule roots would eventually grow thick and deep to find nutrients. The fragile stem would one day be strong and powerful.

It just needs time.

Time.

"I need more time," Ivy said aloud. She glanced out at the drifting ash. A stick was poking into her back and the ash floating in the air made her eyes sting. Ivy felt dislocated in every conceivable way. She shifted, then settled again.

Okay, she thought, *so they need more time. To adapt. To learn everything I can teach them.*

"But if I'm right about the full moon being necessary for the Time Shift," she glanced at Kyah, "it means we only have one month to work this out. By then Orrin might have figured out a way to get us home." Kyah grunted, though she didn't sound impressed. Ivy knew the bonobo loved her new life in prehistoric Flores. In modern Melbourne, freedom was impossible. Kyah was owned by the university. She was a resource in the Behavioural Research Laboratory. The bonobo was *property*. But still, wherever Ivy went, Kyah followed. And Ivy wanted to go back home. *If it's even possible.* Ivy pushed on, clearing her thoughts as she spoke aloud. "But if we leave the tribe here as they are, it's a death sentence. And I just can't do that either."

She knew Kyah loved her new adoptive family as much as Ivy did herself. Loved them so much it hurt. Ivy smiled at the thought of Api, the tiny baby whose harrowing birth she witnessed and whose life she had saved from the ravages of a cave fire. His soft, downy hair smelled of coconut. He was only a few weeks old, but already astonished her with intelligence behind his shining eyes and those five perfect little fingers that reached up to tug on her flyaway red hair.

I suppose, in the jungle, it pays to grow up fast.

The *Homo floresiensis* tribe, or *hobbits*, as Ivy had referred to them from modern-day popular culture, were critically aware of their impending extinction. The *Karathah*, those prehistoric *Homo sapiens* that had shared their volcanic island for centuries now, had recently become relentless in their efforts to eradicate them. They had poisoned, hunted down and slaughtered the hobbits, and then set fire to their Home Cave. Something had triggered the violence, though Ivy didn't know what it was. The Karathah would show no hesitation in killing baby Api if given the chance. They would slaughter little Trahg, or his cousin Filhia and any of the others that Ivy adored. The Karathah were set on genocide, there was no doubt of that. And Ivy refused to let it happen.

Ivy knew that natural selection *should* dictate the fate of the hobbits. But the modern variation on that law, the relentless domination of all other species by modern *Homo sapiens*, was the hand in play now. The tides had shifted. *Anthropogenic selection* had taken over. And this time, Ivy decided that card could be played by both sides. The hobbits deserved the right to fight for their own survival.

"I need more time," she said aloud again, as if the statement might somehow allow it.

Only a few days ago, Ivy thought she had a lifetime ahead of her in Liang Bua cave. That she would live and die with the other fossils buried there.

But Orrin's voice had reached her through fifty thousand years of time. He was trying to bring her back. To defy the laws of physics or manipulate the hands of time or whatever he had to do to save her. And if a return to her old life was possible, however improbable, Ivy was determined to make it happen.

There was a chance that she could return to the modern world - to her university, to old books and her beloved cello, to blessed soap and hot coffee and the internet. And if it was there, Ivy would embrace it.

Memories rushed behind her closed eyes and bit her heart.

Tom, her elderly landlord, tending his beloved daisies in a tartan hat.

Liam's rebellious heart and boundless energy propelling her to take up banners and march in the streets.

Late night conversation with Jayne over a microscope littered with old stones.

The archaeology lab.

The purple veil of jacarandas in summer flower.

The beating heart of Melbourne city.

Heat flooded her every cell. Orrin's face was still vivid in her mind. His voice fresh in her memory. Ivy trailed her fingertips across her thigh beside the medicinal poultice that Shahn had put on. She was left with a tingling whisper across her skin and a deep ache that didn't feel like it belonged to the wound.

"Time has already stolen too much from me," Ivy muttered. *No more.*

The tiniest inkling of an idea suddenly occurred to her.

Would it be possible? Could I even find them?

"I'm an archaeologist for God's sake," she said to Kyah. "If I can't find them, no one can."

Ivy stood up abruptly.

And if I do find them, will they come?

There was only one way to find out.

She dusted herself as she ran, knowing Kyah would be close behind.

CHAPTER 2

IVY

*J*vy's plan was rough and hinged on a good deal of luck. Every moment that passed counted urgently. So far, it wasn't looking good. She pressed the amulet hanging from her wrist into Xiou's hand and held it between them to speak. Her thoughts, rather than her words, translated through the stone.

"Any luck, Xiou?"

"I'm sorry, Hiranah. I returned to the site of the stegodon hunt. There was no sign of your drawings. Either the Karathah stole them, or they are lost." His words out loud, in that foreign, whispered tongue, were harsh and truncated, but those in Ivy's mind were whole. A repaired translation.

"I definitely had my journal at the riverbank for the hunt," Ivy said. "It was in the folds of my skirt." She flattened the leather wrap around her hips and bit back a pang of disappointment. "It must have fallen out when that red-beaded hunter attacked me. I don't understand why he would take it though. That book is useless to the Karathah. They can't understand it. It means nothing to them." Now more than ever, Ivy needed her journal, with all the maps she had drawn on quiet days in the archaeology laboratory. Though it was a day's journey there and back, Xiou had returned to the ill-fated riverbank to search for it but had no luck.

"Who knows what twisted plans that Karathah has in his mind," Xiou said. "He means to see us all dead, that is the only thing I know for sure. I have never seen a man's eyes so full of dark plans."

"He is behind all of this violence," Ivy agreed. "I just don't know why. I do know one thing though – he was trying to steal my amulet. Perhaps he knows the power within it and sees some way to use it for himself?"

The same Karathah hunter who had sliced her thigh with his stone knife only a week prior at the stegodon hunt, had also laced the hobbit's waterhole with the poisoned red seeds he wore in his hair. Twice now, Ivy had felt his muscles and fury bear down upon her. Twice she'd wished she had the physical strength and courage to kill him. She had caught him poisoning their water red-handed. To ingest the toxin of the Rosary Pea seed, Abrin, was to trigger a debilitating breakdown of every cell in a person's body, as each was stripped in turn of its cardinal ability for protein synthesis. The bloody vomiting and diarrhea, seizures, hallucinations and fluid within the victims' lungs would begin after a single day. Within a week, the liver, kidneys, and spleen would shut down. There was no antidote and no way back from the pain. There was only death to hope for. A Swift Death. The poison had taken many of their hunters, those who had frequented the remote waterhole on hunting trails before Ivy had uncovered the insidious plot. She had put an end to it, but the damage had already been done.

Over the past month, the hobbit tribe had suffered beyond measure.

"It was he who led the fire attack in the dead of night," Xiou said, quietly. "Only a man like that would target sleeping women and children."

"I think you are right," Ivy said. Her heart ached with the

injustice. The grief of the Swift Death had been followed by arson of their Home Cave in the dead of night. Another seven had died. Among them was Turi, the glowing and perfect dusty-haired little cousin to Trahg. Ivy had screamed for him amongst the flames, but hadn't noticed him curled, hiding from the barrage of feet and smoke. She had found him too late. He was barely past toddlerhood. His mother, Floni, had become a shell of a women in her grief. Her son, life, and breath, had been stolen from her.

But it was the stegodon hunt that had brought the final strike from which Ivy feared the tribe could never recover. Fifteen hunters had been murdered in cold blood. It had been an ambush. A bloodbath. Ivy had fought alongside them. And failed. It was only after she'd delivered the unconscious body of Leihna to the girl's grandmother that Ivy had succumbed to the infection growing in her wound. The red-beaded hunter had stabbed her. Done his best to murder her to steal the amulet. But Ivy had refused to die.

Instead, she was fighting back.

"I'll have to rely on my memory then," Ivy sighed. "Are we all here?"

"All that there is left of us," said Xiou. He looked out across the tribe gathered in the bamboo copse on the western side of the mountain. A few stragglers were just arriving. In all, perhaps seventy people were left, many of them elderly. With Krue murdered in the ambush, Xiou was now head hunter of the tribe. His deeply scarred face attested to his experience to lead, but his kind heart and courage had proven it. He had been a friend and ally to Ivy since she had arrived. From the end of the stone land-ing, Xiou's mate, Shahn, watched them gravely, small hands encircling her distended belly. Ivy shot her a grim smile.

"Then let us not waste any more time. Gihn – when you are ready."

Ivy turned away from the milling crowd to the wall of the

limestone shelter behind her. The smooth rock housed the beginnings of *Homo floresiensis* cave art.

The golden handprint she had left only two weeks prior was still there. Beside it was a smaller handprint, like that of a child. It belonged to Gihn – the elderly spiritual leader of the tribe, and Xiou's father. It was he who had called Ivy back fifty thousand years through time and compelled her to stay and save them from extinction.

He was watching her now in that quiet, dignified way he often did. Gihn's eyes appraised her with piercing intelligence. He alone understood the insurmountable task ahead of them. Ivy smiled at him as he made his way over to her. For a moment, Ivy tried to see him again as she had that first time. Gihn was a man in miniature, like all the others of his species. Not one of the hobbit tribe stood higher than Ivy's chest. They were oddly proportioned with slightly-too-long arms, strong sinuous muscles, and a thickly shaped body. Their features were every bit as human as her own, but not human at all. Dark tangles of hair framed the coffee-coloured faces around her. Pronounced brow ridges shadowed broad flat noses and wide cheekbones. When Gihn had recovered Ivy from the jungle after her violent shift through time, she had been terrified to see him. Back then, these hominids had seemed like fossils refleshed. Now, the faces were of family.

A dish of soapy oleos pulp had been placed at the base of the rock wall, along with fresh bowls of sienna, umber, and ochre paint. Gihn had ground the coloured clays to a fine powder, then mixed each with animal fat to form a thick paste. Though Gihn had created the recipe for cave paint alone, Ivy felt responsible for it. It was she who had painted Emiri's hands with turmeric after she had died. The ritual had inspired Gihn's discovery of *art*. It was a golden rule of ethnography broken – Ivy had biased the tribe's behaviour with her own. She had never meant to influence their culture in such a profound way. But she was about to be responsible for something with far greater consequence. Their very survival.

"I have made my hand mark on this rock," Gihn said, his voice raised to address the crowd. "So the earth will carry our story – that we have lived here and will be remembered by those who come after us. The Karathah may be intent on killing us, but we must make sure it is our own people that live on. We must show the Karathah that we intend to survive!" The faces that looked back at Gihn seemed to have lost all hope. Ivy didn't blame them. Shadowed by the towering bamboo stalks, the tribe, and indeed Ivy's task, seemed ill-fated.

"Every one of you must come forward and leave your hand-print on this stone," Gihn urged. "This is your promise to be counted. We must all fight together."

"But we cannot win," cried a woman. "The Karathah are relentless. They have murdered so many."

"You are right, Cachi, they have murdered our most precious ones," Ivy said, taking Gihn's hand with her amulet to translate for her. Ivy stepped backward and picked up a small piece of hide that was soaking in the oleos soap. Very gently, she rubbed away one finger of her own handprint. It was a lament to Rinap, the hobbit-sister she couldn't save. Ivy returned to Gihn's side. "And we will never, *ever* forget them. Those we have lost are our missing parts. None of us are whole anymore. But still, our hands remain strong, and we must use them to save ourselves."

"Please Cachi," Gihn urged the young woman. "Come up here first. Put your handprint on this wall. Lend our family your strength."

The woman stood for a moment; eyes downcast. Ivy knew she was grieving for her mate Ziku, who had been killed in the stegodon ambush. Cachi had already lost two children to the Slow Death before Ivy had arrived. With a deep breath, Cachi took her remaining daughter's hand and led her up to the stone shelter.

"We will be counted, Hiranah," Cachi said, resolutely. The woman bent down and flattened her hand on the bone bowl, letting red ochre paint cover her palm. She pushed it onto the wall of the limestone shelter.

"Well done, Tiki," Gihn smiled as Cachi's eight-year-old daughter did the same.

"You could not stop me, Hiranah," said Setian. "We will win this fight."

"Of course we will," added his mate Kora. They were both good hunters and allies.

Shahn stepped forward and added her handprint, followed by her five-year-old son Trahg, who insisted that Kyah should leave an imprint as well. He and the bonobo took great delight in painting one another's hands. One by one, each member of the tribe hesitantly stepped forward, until the wall was bright with handprints in shades of gold, red and brown.

When they had all taken their turn, a nervous energy filled the air. It was time to set Ivy's plan into action. She held up one hand asking for their attention.

"Then it is time to begin. This isn't a fight of weapons, but one of strategy," Ivy said. "And there's something very important you need to understand first–" she took a deep breath. "–I alone, cannot save you."

Panic scattered across the faces in front of her. Gihn's brows furrowed. Ivy held up her free hand once more. "But..." she continued, "I *can* teach you to save yourselves. You called me here because you thought I had some special power. But I do not. The only power I have is knowledge of what your future holds if you do nothing."

With sudden clarity, Ivy realized that from the moment her amulet was torn from her through time, landing at the feet of these people countless generations before she herself would arrive, her own fate had been sealed. The residual energy it carried from Ivy's thoughts, the image of *her* it forced into the mind of the hobbit woman that found it, began a self-fulfilling prophesy that led her to be here, now. Ivy didn't simply want to save this species, she had to.

"The Karathah want you dead," Ivy said, grimly. "We all know this. I've seen the future of your species – of *your people*. In my time, many, many generations from now, all my people ever found of you were bones in the dust. Your tribe, *your people*, were extinct, entirely and irreversibly. None of you survived beyond now."

Whispers pitted the tribe. Though they all knew Ivy had Fallen from the sky, but only Gihn truly understood not where, but *when*, she had Fallen from.

"It's clear to me now *why* your tribe did not survive," Ivy continued. "The Karathah have been poisoning your water, setting fire to your home, stealing your hunting grounds and even murdering you in cold blood." *It was genocide. Unnatural selection.* "That future – a future without you – is being created *now*. It is nearly too late."

"Then there is no hope," someone cried out.

"Please – don't give up, Buchi." Ivy braced herself for a very uncomfortable truth. "You called me here because you thought I had the power to save your people. And I have always said that you were wrong. That there was nothing I could do." Her chest was tight. "But it wasn't true."

"You lied to us!" shouted a young man from the back. "You let people die!"

"There was no lie," Ivy insisted. "I simply did not know how to help. But now – *I understand*."

Kari's eyes lifted. He was pure rage. "You could have saved us sooner! Rinap didn't need to die! None of them did. If you had the power to stop the Karathah, you should have done something sooner."

"No, please…" Ivy stammered, imploring Gihn for support. "I would never have let Rinap die if I could help it! I tried to save her; you know I did! The Karathah that attacked her was too strong for me. I loved her as much as you did, Kari."

"No one loved her as I did!" Kari spat back.

Memories of the young man sobbing over his sweetheart's body stabbed at Ivy's heart.

"I didn't just let Rinap die!" Ivy shot a desperate look at Filhia, imploring innocence in the death of the girl's sister. But Filhia's eyes were glazed, staring into the trees. "You misunderstand me, Kari," Ivy said, turning back to the young hunter. "Please let me explain. What I mean is, that I have only now realised that my power lies in my *knowledge*. What *I know* could help you survive."

"Then why did you not tell us before?" someone yelled.

"Because I wasn't sure I could do it!" replied Ivy. "Or even if I should. I still don't know if what I'm planning to do is the right thing for your people. Please understand; this has never been done before." Ivy's breath came fast. This wasn't going as well as she'd hoped. "You want me to save your people from *extinction*. I must teach you what I know about the laws of nature to do that. You are forcing me to play God!"

Gihn's eyes shot up. "What do you mean? *Play God?* What is this game, of *God?*"

A manic hiccup caught under Ivy's breath. *Oh no.* Nothing good would come of telling them more than what was necessary to survive. And religion was definitely one of those things. "Gihn, I can't explain it, because that's exactly my point," she sighed. "By giving you my knowledge, by potentially *saving you* with it, I could be leading you into an entirely different kind of fatality to the one you are already faced with." *But it's not a fair fight*, Ivy reminded herself. *This current fate is based on genocide. No matter what their future might be, they deserve the right to fight for one.* Ivy sucked in her breath and tried to regain her resolve.

"Kari, I'm so desperately sorry," she said. "I didn't know *how* to help you. This new plan I have still might not work, but it is the only option you've got left. So I'm giving you a choice – either help me or watch more of your tribe be murdered every day."

Kari's chin trembled. He met Ivy's eyes for a moment, searching for truth in her apology, then gave a slight nod and looked away.

"Please. Listen to me," Ivy addressed the tribe. "If you want my help, I will give it, but you need to fully understand what that means for you all. What I do could change the course of future humanity." *For the better*, Ivy tried to convince herself, but her stomach wouldn't swallow the omission. "I can't guarantee that future humans will treat you well. In the time I come from, forests are burnt to the ground and many animals are hunted until there are none left on the land. The Karathah in the future can be ruthless and cruel and selfish and you will have to continue to share the earth with them as you do now. They may not treat you well. In fact, I fear they may treat you just as badly in the future as they do here and now."

On the end of the stone landing, Kyah sat with the little boy Trahg and his mother Shahn. While the mass of people broke into anxious conversation, the pregnant woman smiled across at her. Filhia was now curled despondently with her head resting on Shahn's lap. She was still staring off into the trees. Since Rinap's murder, the ten-year-old had been mute with grief. With both parents already dead from the Swift Death, Shahn had stepped in as Filhia's surrogate mother. The girl now dogged the pregnant woman's steps with hollow eyes. Nothing seemed to reach her.

"The Karathah can also be kind and courageous and selfless, Hiranah," countered Shahn, smoothing Filhia's hair as she spoke. "I refuse to believe you are the only one. You said that the Karathah woman with the blue feathers in her hair saved Filhia when she was being attacked by the hunters. I know the woman you speak of – I have seen her at the trade offering. She has a gentle heart. So, there must be others like you and her –

Karathah people who see us differently and are willing to fight for us. We must trust in that."

"But I can't guarantee it–" Ivy began, but she was cut off.

"I want to live," called a voice from the crowd.

"I want to live too!" yelled another.

The chant swelled through the remains of the tribe. Ivy knew there was no turning back.

She raised her voice over the clamour.

"Then I will do everything I can." She turned to Gihn. "But I will need your help."

The old man nodded graciously. "I am yours, Hiranah."

"And Xiou, Setian, Kora and Guntah, I'll need your help too."

The sea of bodies shifted and without hesitation, each of the hunters stepped forward. Ivy held her breath for a moment, wondering if they would be so willing to co-operate once they knew what she needed them for.

Ivy had chosen those that she trusted the most and, apart from Gihn, were capable of the fastest travel.

Still, she felt guilty. It was likely that Xiou would still be absent when his mate Shahn gave birth. If Xiou didn't survive the journey, or if the baby or Shahn herself did not survive the birth, the family would be irreparably broken. But without this journey, none would survive anyway. Ivy took a deep breath and addressed the four hunters that had stepped up beside Gihn.

"We are going to travel across the land," Ivy said to them. "I have chosen you because we will have the hardest route. It will be difficult, and I can't guarantee that you will all return. Gihn, it will be hardest for you, but I'll carry you if I have to." Ivy looked apologetic but Gihn simply nodded.

She turned back to the group at large. "There are less than seventy of us left, including children and elders. So I am going to divide the rest of you into four groups. Three of the groups, led by our strongest remaining hunters will travel across the land to places I will describe to you. The remaining group, the largest, with our young mothers, all the children and all our elders, will slowly travel east to the Falling Place. We will all meet there one week before the next full moon."

Ivy closed her eyes for a moment, imagining the monumental task she had only three weeks to see done. She pushed down the feeling of dread that threatened to overwhelm her.

"Where are we going, Hiranah?" asked Kora, jolting her back.

"Each group has a specific task and will travel in different directions to achieve it," Ivy explained. She steadied her voice, wondering how much of her plan she should reveal. "I believe that more of your people still exist," Ivy declared. "They are out there, somewhere. I'm sure of it." She flexed her fingers, curling and uncurling them together. A moment passed and a tremor of uncertainty hit her gut. *I can do this. They need me to do this.* Ivy took a deep breath, plastered a grim smile on her face and straightened her shoulders, pulling herself up tall. "We are going to find them."

The hum of surprise became a torrent of disbelief.

"But we haven't seen any others like us for generations," Phren spoke up. The old woman was the keeper of stories. She knew the oral history of the tribe better than anyone. "Not since the ancients left The Three Sister Lakes."

Phren referred to a story that Ivy had heard her tell before. *The Three Sisters* were the tri-coloured lakes of Kelimutu mountain. Even in modern times, their volcanic beauty was legendary. Ivy had seen them herself at the Falling Place when she had awoken in this prehistoric world. Ivy still remembered the way Phren had described them in her story.

One lake was bright blue, like the great sea that gives Life to the fish that swim. The second lake was green, like the forest that gives Life to the animals and plants born to earth. And the last lake was red, like the blood that gives Life to our bodies.

In the story Phren had told, The Three Sisters were considered the ancestral home of the *Homo floresiensis* species. Many generations past, in a time of massive volcanic upheaval, the once prolific tribe had been fragmented. Their cave in the mountains of Kelimutu had been destroyed in an earthquake as the volcano erupted, leaving them homeless as the sky rained down ash and fire.

The ancestral tribe had broken apart, terrified for their lives and fractured in leadership. They split into groups, each searching the jungle island for a new place to call home.

The ancestors of the tribe that had settled in Liang Bua cave in the far west had never seen another of their own species since. But stratigraphic layers of ash and stone in Ivy's modern-day laboratory had her told the story on a prehistoric scale. Ivy guessed it may have been ten thousand years since the ancestral tribe had left Kelimutu. Finding other descendants of those lost tribes in the jungles of Flores, was like searching for a needle in a haystack that spanned tens of thousands of square kilometers.

"Your people are still out there," Ivy insisted. "In *my* time, a long time from now, we found the knives and spearpoints of your people, long after they died. Their weapons, their *bones*." She shifted uncomfortably. "We found them in caves across this island and I spent a long time learning about them. To try to understand what these people were." Ivy looked at the faces around her. "I mean, *who* these people were. I know where to search for them and if you find them, you have a chance of surviving the Karathah together."

"What if they are no longer there?" Kora asked.

"It's true, we risk finding nothing," Ivy conceded. "Or worse, we could find Karathah living in those caves instead. It will be a dangerous journey. If we do find others, it may not be easy to convince them to join us. But the fact of the matter is, if they want to survive then they have no choice – and neither do you."

Ivy looked at the faces of the people she had grown to love. She hated to be so brutally honest with them. From the end of the stone landing, Shahn gave her an encouraging smile.

"This Slow Death is killing your people," Ivy said. "Each year less children are born to your tribe. Women do not grow babies as often as they used to, and those that do are born too soon or have deformities and cannot thrive. There are simply not enough left of your people to continue beyond a few generations. I cannot explain to you why this happens because I've already told you too much. But I *can* make this promise; unless we unite all of the lost tribes, soon your people will be gone forever."

Ivy paused to let her words sink in. "The Karathah are strong. They have more deadly weapons and more hunters to use them against you. They will expand into your territory, and they will find ways of using the forest to their advantage. There will be no stopping their progress and I do not recommend that you try to fight them because they *will win*. But you *can* save yourselves. The faster and better you can change to suit this new world and use your advantages, the greater chance you have to survive."

There was a moment of silence.

Xiou spoke up. "Where will we travel?"

"You, Setian, Kora, Guntah, Gihn and I will head east. There are many caves that once sheltered people in those mountains." The jigsawed grasslands of the Soa Basin would prove difficult terrain, but Ivy had studied the stone tools from at least six archaeological sites there. Though the makers of those tools may have left them thousands of years before now, a little hope was worth trying. "After that, we will turn south to follow the coast. There are more caves by the sea. We travel east, then turn north again to the meet the others at the Three Sister Lakes."

Ivy looked out into the crowd to find the young hunter that grieved for Rinap. "Kari," she called, "will you join Chiri and Sira to search as far east beyond the Falling Place as you can go? Search all mountains and caves you pass and you may find some of your own still there. Anywhere that looks safe enough to live, but beware in case the Karathah are living there instead." Kari nodded, a glimmer of purpose returning to his eyes. He stepped forward, along with the bird hunter Chiri, and his sister Sira. The three of them had strong, young legs and would make good time travelling the furthest distance across the land. "You'll have to backtrack to the Falling Place when you are done."

"Shia, Sholon and Buchi," Ivy said, as the three men stepped forward, "I need you to travel to the northern sea, then follow the mountains as far east as you can go. Search the caves along the coastline. Boru, Shashi and Ren, you will do the same to the west until you reach the beaches where the Komodo dragons gather. Whether you find others or not, you need to return by the full moon to The Falling Place."

Xiou stepped forward. "When do we leave on our journey, Hiranah?"

A familiar screech cut across Ivy's response. Kyah jumped to her feet and stared intently to the sky. The bonobo's nostrils flared as she tasted the delicate shift of chemicals in the air, then she rushed toward Ivy.

"Fire – Dirt – Broken." The bonobo signed.

Her forewarning of danger had saved lives in the cave fire. No one doubted her now. The tribe dove into action. Kyah rushed back to Trahg, scooping him onto her back like an infant. The bonobo looked to Shahn, who nodded, then Kyah leapt into the nearest tree, heading back for Home Cave. Shahn stood at once, following them on foot as fast as her pregnancy would allow, sheltering Filhia in her arms.

With shouts of alarm, the others funneled behind, jostling those carrying children into the middle of the group. Perimeter eyes raked the forest for signs of danger and those who held spears raised them warningly to the unseen threat.

Within a minute, only Ivy, Gihn and Xiou remained.

A menacing shadow clawed across the sky, stealing the sun. Ivy shivered. Under her feet, the earth shifted violently. A grinding shudder sent scatters of rock down the limestone terrace. Gihn staggered and fell. Xiou pulled his elderly father to his feet then turned to Ivy who was still frozen in place, eyes turned upward. The easterly wind swirled heavy and dark with a new wave of volcanic ash. Her eyes stung as the stench of sulphur assaulted the air. In the distance, great sparks of red shot through the sky. Another shatter of rocks crashed behind her and Ivy stumbled, grasping for surface against the limestone wall. Where Shahn had stood only moments before, a tree split and splintered as it fell with a loud *crack!*

The landscape to the east was growing deadlier by the day. *Volcanos. Earthquakes. Karathah. Death.* The very direction in which she was about to embark.

There's no choice. I have to get to Kelimutu. Hidden away inside her mind, was a more desperate reason to reach the Falling Place, and it had nothing to do with saving the tribe. *The Three Sister Lakes. The place where I Fell from the sky. The place that could take me back home.*

Adrenaline surged through her muscles and Ivy turned to Xiou to finally answer his question.

"We leave now."

CHAPTER 3

NEIL

Day 6 in Liang Bua, Flores
~50,000 years BP ????

Dear Journal,

Apparently, my life exists now only as a means to ensure the survival of this tribe. These people hold such naïve faith in my ability to save them. Of course, they don't understand the gravity of what they are asking me to do. Change the course of human evolution? I feel like I'm losing my mind. I'm entirely out of my depth here. I just wish this had never happened. I'm so desperate to go home.

One thing is obvious to me - this species is dying out, and fast. There's an awful wasting sickness in some of the hunters. They call it the "Swift

Death". Gihn said that none have survived it so far. The symptoms are horrifying, and they don't know what has caused it.

The other problem seems even more sinister and complex - I suspect the "Slow Death" that they refer to, is a result of infertility through inbreeding. Women aren't having as many babies as previous generations, and man infants are lost to deformity or miscarriage. I suspect the tribe has been isolated for too long and their gene pool is too limited. Their ability to expand, as a population, has become unviable. Unless there are more of them out there somewhere, they'll be extinct within a few generations at most.

Life here seems surreal. I feel like a giant towering over them all. Some of them don't want me here, that's clear, but most have been kind. They seem a peaceful tribe - primitive, obviously, but there's an intelligence about them that is entirely humanistic. Upper Paleolithic technology- but that much, at least, I expected. From what I gather, they have no art, but they do have an oral tradition passed down many generations. Phren tells beautiful stories to the children.

These little people may not be the type of human I'm used to, but the humanity of Homo floresiensis is undeniable. No doubt any other archaeologist would dream to be in my shoes - to live with them and see the world through their eyes. But, right now, all I want to do is find a way home.

How does this work? How am I here? Why am I here? I've stared at the excavation maps and photos of Liang Bua cave in this very journal until my eyes can't take it anymore. There's no mistake.

There are no piles of sediment here. No signs of a modern excavation. The cave mouth is taller than modern photographs show it to be. The massive stalactites that are burned into my memory from hours of study now hang above me from the domed roof of the cave. But they look different. They're at least two meters higher than they should be. Oddly shaped. Because the mineral deposits need to drip for longer to create them. Fifty thousand years longer.

I've dug down into the cave mouth until my fingernails bled. I can see how it should be in my mind. Somewhere, there should be that single strati-graphic layer in the cave floor that would save my sanity. A geological footprint to tell me that I'm still on the civilised side of the fine, white volcanic ash that suffocated so many of the species on this island fifty thousand years before archaeologists would come and dig them up again.

But no matter how far I dig, there's no bed of white tuffaceous silt. The layer of ash hasn't fallen.

Because those volcanic eruptions haven't happened yet. Extinction, by whatever hand, hasn't happened yet. It is happening now.

But I do recognise the stratigraphy that is under my feet. The subtle differences in colour and texture of my makeshift excavation pit screams out to me. So do the stone tools of the people around me now. Their food. Their bones. I recognise it all.

These are the living floors of Liang Bua cave in the prehistoric past. From a time before volcanos suffocated the island in synchronous eruptions.

This living floor was buried fifty thousand years before I was born.

Whatever disaster of physics threw me back here must have been a terrible mistake. I've landed on the knife edge of extinction in a volatile land. I'm terrified.

I don't know what my future holds - but I know I've lost the future I once had. I never realised how desperately I'd wanted it until now.

Perhaps there's no point to this, but I'm going to keep writing in my journal. I suppose now, it's become a field journal, of sorts, instead. I'll record everything I can and maybe it'll keep me sane.

At least until I run out of paper.

~ Ivy.

*D*r. Neil Crawford flipped through the pages of Ivy's journal, reading and re-reading every entry for the past month. It was clear that the redhead, who he now knew was called Ivy Carter, still had no idea he was here with her. She had not seen him in the physics laboratory when she had entered with the chimp. At the time, he'd been doing a little 'reconnaissance work' of his own. They were up to something in that lab, he knew it. Something to do with the fluctuations of the lunar energy field he'd been monitoring over the university. So Neil had left his useless underlings from the CSIRO Division for Astronomy and Space out at The Dish to continue crunching numbers, and he had flown to Melbourne University to poke about. It was that poking that had landed him in the fetid mess he was currently trying to get out of.

The instant the redhead had entered the physics laboratory, there had been a blinding flash of electric blue and swirling grey. Lightning had filled the room. Neil had been swallowed by excruciating pain and the swirling black of nothingness. Terrified, furious, he had awoken in this hellhole of a jungle and had spent the better part of the last month spying on her trying to figure out what she knew. Initially, Neil had wanted to face the redhead down and have it out with her for leaving him stranded and unconscious on the side of a fucking volcano, but by the time he tracked her down to the river cave, he realised things weren't quite what they seemed. The little ape-men followed Ivy everywhere. They were heavily armed with spears and Neil was at an obvious disadvantage. So instead, he watched, and waited.

Lady Luck had found him by means of an alliance with the so-called 'Karathah' tribe. These were true humans, *Homo sapiens*. A primitive Stone Age tribe, sure, but tall and strong with a plethora of weapons and enough superstition that Neil soon had them eating out of the palm of his hand. Which is how Ivy's journal had come into his possession. Starting a war was surprisingly easy when you were dealing with fools and animals.

He flicked through the journal once more. Labelled scientific sketches filled the pages – stone tools, bone utensils, woven bags and weapons. There was even an illustrated layout of the living hearths within the cave although some names had been crossed off – the cave fire fatalities, Neil assumed with a slight satisfaction. An elaborate kinship map detailed the relationships of every 'hobbit' creature, as the redhead referred to them, as well as endless illustrations and lists of plants and animals they used for food or medicine. The book might prove very useful, if he ended up ditching the cavemen.

The redhead, Ivy, was relentless with detail. Prior to the last month, there hadn't been anything particularly useful in the journal, which was a frustratingly eclectic mix of vain reflections on her own life and archaeological notes from her work at the university. During his days watching her by the river, Neil became infuriated trying to decipher her motives for indulging the hobbits' affections. Now that he had a direct line to her innermost thoughts, Neil realised how severely he'd underestimated her. Ivy had real power here and the potential to change the course of humanity. The creatures wanted her to save them from extinction. And what's worse – her latest entries suggested she thought she was justified in doing it.

Reading further, it seemed the Karathah hunter, Charat, had been on his grisly mission of killing hobbits for some time. Going by the account in Ivy's journal of their altercation by the poisoned waterhole, and his angry, rather than surprised, reaction to a photograph of the redhead that Neil showed him, the situation now made much more sense. 'Swift Death' indeed. Neil made a mental note to steer clear of the strings of red seeds the man wore so shamelessly in his hair.

It was, however, an entry dated five days prior to the time shift that had legitimate potential to change Neil's fortune.

... I ran into Eli today at the refectory and he offered to take a closer look at the amulet Tom gave me. It's odd – the stone always feels warm, even when it's cold outside. The scientist in me can't help but be curious as to why. The geology lab was buzzing with grad students of course, so he didn't have much time, but confirmed it's probably an iron ore of volcanic magnetite. When Eli compared it to his comparative post-doc analysis from South East Asia, he suggested a Floresian origin, or at least one of the volcanic islands of Nusa Tengarra. Apparently, the tri-coloured crater lakes of Kelimutu volcano have a similar geology. Imagine the chances of that; here I am working on the Flores dig stone tools, and this amulet falls into my lap. It almost seems like fate. It was lovely to catch up with Eli again and nice to know I'm not the only workaholic around this place. Anyway, regardless of where it came from, I'll wear it for Tom. I know how much it means to him.

Neil stopped reading. The rest of that entry was just an emotive guilt vomit about the old man and his apparent decline in health. But Neil had what he needed to know – the amulet probably came from Flores and was likely dug from near crater lakes near a volcano. Three differently coloured lakes within the craters of a volcano – the description was practically a gift. Neil recognised it – he'd been there before. She was describing the place that he'd awoken after the accident in the lab. He'd found himself there with a dislocated shoulder, covered in cuts and bruises. The redhead, he now realised, had awoken first and begun walking. Ivy obviously hadn't seen him lying unconscious in the rocky crevice he'd fallen into. If she had, her chronic martyrdom would have forced her to help him. In any case, it didn't matter now.

Back to the volcano then, Neil decided. Given he had a willing band of hunters at his command, surely such a place wouldn't be too hard to find again. He left the cave to seek out Charat. He didn't have to look far.

The young woman with the turquoise blue feathers in her hair, whose name Neil had finally determined to be Atasi, was cowering at Charat's feet near the entrance to the cave. Spilled in the dirt around her was, apparently, Neil's lunch. Charat hissed a rebuke, roughly clipping the side of her face with his hand. A few shouts of indignation came from the women cooking nearby, but no one stepped forward to counter him. Neil frowned. As little as he cared for these cavemen and their daily trivialities, Charat's treatment of Atasi grated him.

In fact, if he were honest with himself, Neil considered Atasi's near constant presence to be the least repellent aspect of this entire situation. Beneath the fear in her eyes, the young woman was extraordinarily kind. And beautiful.

Since Charat and his band of idiots had returned from the stegodon hunt with only Ivy's journal in their hands, the hunter's treatment of Atasi had become more belligerent than ever. He seemed to delight in using his new-found status in the tribe to humiliate her. Having read Ivy's account of the trade offering and the apparent fondness the "blue-feathered" woman had for the hobbit girls, Neil suspected Charat was openly punishing her for something. Right now, Charat was leering at her as she quickly gathered up the mollusk shells strewn around. Neil's fingers twitched.

"Charat!" Neil strode forward to stand beside him. "Come. Talk." Neil jutted his chin toward the low stretch of rock wall past the trees that he now regularly used for mapping out his strategies. It was a slow means of communication, and frustrating, but better than none.

Charat gave Atasi another instruction. She flinched and the hunter smirked. Charat turned and walked toward the drawing wall. Neil turned to leave, but hesitated. The woman was still shaking at his feet. Brusquely, Neil reached down, offering her his hand. Her eyes widened with shock. After a moment she took his hand, gracefully rising to her feet. She hesitated for a moment, caught somewhere between fright and confusion. Someone inside the cave mouth murmured and Neil realised he had an audience. He dropped Atasi's hand a little too roughly, then cleared his throat, and strode away.

"Your men," Neil said. "We travel here." He stubbed his index finger on the rock wall. "This volcano with three lakes in it. One. Two. Three."

Charat studied the diagram thoughtfully while Neil wiped his ochre covered fingers down his filthy trousers. Neil knew it wasn't ideal; he'd never been much of an artist. But he'd already managed to convey the meaning of his volcano drawing quite well due to a conveniently timed drift of grey ash and established the name for a volcano as *berap*, or something similar. The concept of the tri-coloured lakes were proving a little more difficult. Neil had gouged out three small concaves in the top of his sketch and coloured them with different shades of ochre paint. When that didn't work, Neil had taken three bone plates from a cooking hearth and stained some water inside them with ochre instead. He could see Charat struggling to relate the task to the image Neil was desperately trying to convey.

"Okay, what about this..." Neil strode a few paces to his left where the dirt underfoot was looser and began to scrape it into a mound with his hands. After a few minutes, while Charat simply sat back and watched with an amused smirk on his face, Neil dribbled water down the sides of the mound from a bladder he always kept in his belt. He compacted the shape as best as he could to resemble a volcano.

"Berap," Neil said. "This volcano – berap. And these," he gently placed each of the three small bowls on top. "Lakes. Water. One. Two . Three – all different colours."

Charat's eyes tightened with interest and understanding flickered. Then he shook his head. *No.*

"God damn it!" Neil turned away, furious and ranting, even though he knew Charat couldn't understand a word. "This whole fucking escapade is a joke! If I had the damned stone already, I'd just talk to you through it like the bloody redhead does with her little apes. No, forget that, if I can get here," he hit his fist against the painted volcano on the wall, "I can just get a bloody stone myself and go home."

Charat's eyebrow raised and he stepped forward to meet Neil at the rock wall. He was relaxed but curious, entirely unconcerned by Neil's outburst. Where the others still avoided and feared Neil, Charat was arrogant. He knew the truth. Neil was no real God. He was all magic tricks and intimidation. The superstitious sapien tribe believed Neil could lock their mortal soul away in a photograph on his strange glass rock, or create fire with a flick of his fingers. They understood neither mobile phone, nor cigarette lighter, nor any of the other modern illusions that Neil used to keep their weapons at bay. But Charat had witnessed Neil's desperation. He knew Neil was simply a man lost in the jungle – a bizarre white-skinned man from goodness knows where, but still, a mere mortal. And his growing complacency toward Neil's authority had only served to elevate Charat's status within the tribe even further.

Charat said something, touching the painting on the rock wall then opening his palms to the sky. *Why?*

"The stone," Neil said. He shuffled through and found a sketch of it in Ivy's journal. "To get this stone. To help us kill *Ebu gogo*." Neil drew his hand across his throat. "The black stone kills Ebu gogo." Neil's gut twisted at the lie. *I'll be gone before he figures that one out.*

Charat's eyes danced with dark interest. He held a hand up, signaling for Neil to wait, then jogged back toward the cave. He returned a few minutes later with a handful of elders. Charat described the model to them, indicating the three coloured lakes on top. There was a murmur of discussion, but all eyes, with the exception of Charat, shied away from Neil.

"Mutu," said an old woman over the other voices. She recounted something and Neil listened eagerly, wishing he could understand what she was saying. She nodded as she finished, pointing off toward the south-east then dragging the ochre water through her fingers. "Mutu."

A heated discussion quickly followed. Two men argued, apparently opposed to whatever Charat was saying. The hunter stood tall, raising his voice. The elders growled and tried to wave him off, clearly unconvinced at whatever plan Charat was pushing for. Neil stepped forward. He pulled out his mobile and held it up to their faces. With angry whispers, they shuffled back. No one met his eye. The threat was enough. They had conceded.

Charat turned abruptly and strode toward the cave, gesturing over his shoulder as he went. Neil quickly joined him, trying to maintain his illusion of supremacy over the cocky hunter. At the front of cave, Charat began to shout orders. Eight of his syco-phants jumped up to join him. His usual hunting gang.

"Atasi!" Charat shouted.

The young woman hurried forward at his request. He pulled her roughly to stand beside him. "Tipun! Martu!" Two more women joined her. Neil noticed they were slightly younger than Atasi. They looked terrified at being singled out. Charat began growling instructions to them.

"No," Neil interjected, shaking his head. "No women. No Atasi. We don't need them."

Charat lifted his jaw. It was set tight and his eyes flashed dangerously. He glanced sideways to see which of the other hunters were watching. They all were.

"Atasi," Charat repeated, his voice hard. The young woman wilted beneath the grip he had on her arm. His meaning was clear. *She's coming with us.*

Atasi dropped her eyes to the ground. She barely breathed.

"No," Neil shook his head, dismissively. "We don't need her, Charat. Just the men." He pursed his lips and turned away, feigning a new interest in the gathering of supplies.

Charat rounded on him, dragging Atasi along for the ride. His words were cold and deliberate. Jerky hand movements gave weight to their meaning.

Charat stabbed the woman's bare skin with his index finger then brought his hand to his mouth. *Cook food.* Atasi flinched, anticipating his next move. He grabbed her chin with one hand, letting the other fall to squeeze her backside, pulling her against his leg.

Neil's eyes followed the lewd gesture back up to the challenge in Charat's face.

Charat lowered his voice dangerously. He brought his hand up slowly and stubbed his finger, this time, at Neil.

You. "Berap." *Volcano.* "Mutu." *Coloured lakes.* He brought his finger back to his own chest. *Me.* Then Charat extended it to the row of sycophants standing behind him. *My hunters.* "Atasi." He tightened his grip on the young woman's arm. She winced in pain. Neil realised that there were other bruises under Charat's grip. Old bruises. Atasi's eyes brimmed and her bottom lip was almost white as she clamped it between her teeth to keep from crying out. But she made no move to pull away. Charat's glare said it all. *Me.*

Shrinking away, the wretched look in the woman's eyes left no room for doubt.

Neil stepped back, disgusted. *He rapes her.* There wasn't a chance she would go to Charat willingly. The glimmer of barbarism that Neil had been ignoring for weeks suddenly wrenched his insides. *You filthy little bastard.* He covered his mouth with his hand, sealing the unspoken words inside his lips. It would take nothing for Charat to kill him if he chose to. The younger man was lethal. When the girl brought Neil's breakfast each day with a tapestry of new bruises, Neil had assumed that was the worst of it. Charat was a brute and apparently enjoying his newfound authority in the worst way possible. But Neil had not considered where else his powerlust was being directed. In retrospect, it was obvious.

Beyond the red beaded hunter, a few others were smirking at their exchange. *Are they all involved?* He had no idea. They were certainly aware of it. A seething disgust settled in Neil's chest. *No, this isn't my problem*, Neil pushed the thought down until he felt it settle, angry and churning, in his gut. *I just need to get the hell home.* Every fibre of his being urged Neil to smack Charat across the jaw. In another time and place, Neil could have skinned him alive with words and intimidation, leaving a cowering mess of man on the boardroom floor. But here, Neil was trapped. Charat was the stronger player and had an army of muscle to follow him. *I play his game, or the game is up. I have to give the little bastard what he wants.* Charat loosened his grip on Atasi's arm, leaving finger prints to fade slowly like the burn of sun in Neil's eyes.

"I'm getting my stuff," Neil said, unnecessarily, nodding toward the cave. He didn't have much to pack, just the redhead's journal and his make-shift phone charging kit. Still, that wasn't the point. If he stayed any longer, he'd punch the smirk off Charat's face. As Neil turned away, Atasi shifted ever so slightly. He looked over to her. Their eyes connected. Neil's jaw slackened and he almost stumbled at the expression she gave him.

Pity. For me. She actually pities *me.*

For the first time in over a month of bitterness, loneliness and physical pain, Neil felt his eyes burn.

Within an hour, the traveling party had set off to find the three coloured lakes of Kelimutu.

Neil walked with tense shoulders and dark thoughts. He spat

the sour taste in his mouth onto the ground. He carried only a hide bag. It was big enough to carry his collection of ripening fruit and the set of marsupial skulls, his stripped USB cord and pieces of the copper bracelet and zinc alloy watch band that he used daily to recharge his mobile phone. His jacket was tied around his waist by the arms. Though it was far too humid to wear, he felt obliged to carry it. He had so few possessions.

Charat had taken the lead, insisting Atasi follow him closely, burdened under a heavy load of supplies. The other hunters trailed single file behind, sparking to attention whenever Charat barked orders back to them. The man was insufferable.

Neil walked last, gruffly ushering the two other women before him. He watched them sway as they walked, laden with bags and baskets but for once, there was no lust in his gaze. He looked ahead and saw Atasi stumble. Charat ignored her. Neil ground his teeth and looked away.

I don't need anyone's pity.

He pulled his lighter from his pocket and began to spin it slowly in his fingers, tracing the minuscule grooves of the etching under his thumb. *Benjamin would know I was missing by now.* An uncomfortable ache settled in his neck and he rolled it back, looking up to the canopy. *Would he care? I've been gone too long. Years. The whole damn time he needed me. The kid barely knows me. My own son.*

The urgency to fix him, to prove to the boy that his father would bend time to make him well, compounded in Neil's veins every day. *This is my chance*, he muttered as he walked. *My chance to give him more time. My time. I'll fucking control time when I'm done here.*

That black stone Ivy wore was a gift. A gift that was being wasted and misused to save a bunch of animals. There was no place in the future for the little ape-men; at least, not in the future Neil was planning to create when he returned.

His eyes flicked once more to the young woman with blue

feathers in her hair. Despite the bruises and brutality Atasi suffered, she actually pitied *him*. An angry flush crept up the back of Neil's neck. His stomach twisted with a sudden guilty thought. Neil had told Charat he needed the black stone to kill hobbits. But it was a lie. He simply needed it to facilitate his own escape from this suffocating green hellscape he was in. But without Neil as a false God to lord all over his tribe, Charat's newfound authority might falter. Neil knew he was walking a tightrope with the red-beaded hunter. Their interdependency was sickeningly fragile.

When Charat finds out I've gone, he'll be humiliated. His power over them all will disappear. Will he take that out on her too? Neil watched the woman's back as she walked. He pushed the thought away, but once there, it lodged hard within his chest. *Of course he will.*

Neil kicked the leaves, sending a shower of dirt into the undergrowth. *Ridiculous fucking nightmare,* he thought. *If I have to dig the whole damn volcano up with my bare hands, I'm getting out of this place.*

CHAPTER 4

ORRIN

*D*ale rushed up to the plastic table, knocking over an empty chair. Dr. Orrin James startled, scowling as he grabbed the papers he had been scribbling equations on, now stained with coffee.

"What the hell?"

"Sorry," Dale said. "But you need to get to the lab. Now!"

"What's going on?" He rubbed his eyes beneath his glasses.

"It's bad."

Orrin scraped the plastic chair back and quickly gathered his belongings. Dale Brennan was his most dedicated post-doctoral student, and one of only two staff in the physics laboratory aware of the mess Orrin's life, and lab, were currently in. Orrin's second PhD research student, Phil Chan, the yin to Dale's yang, was prone to dramatic statements. Dale was not.

"The Chancellor is there with some Government officials," Dale puffed as he turned back to accompany Orrin. "CSIRO, I think. They're asking questions."

"Shite! Where's Phil? Is he talking?"

"No, he hasn't been in all day and he's not answering his mobile."

"Bloody hell! He's always late! Of all the days to sleep in, and full of guff when he finally turns up–"

Orrin's gut twisted as he paced toward the Physics building. Neither Dale nor Phil knew yet about his midnight communication with Ivy. He had been alone last night when he'd heard her voice in the lab. Alone as he'd clung to the intimacy of every word they'd shared. And alone, as he waited hours for her voice to return. The thrill and triumph that Orrin now carried from actually *talking with her across fifty-thousand years of time* overrode the disappointment of losing her again, and Orrin wasn't ready to share that yet with anyone. The cynicism he knew he'd get from Phil could wait, and frankly, Dale seemed too burdened already for the update.

Chancellor Thandi's eyes narrowed as Orrin walked into the room. She was bristling with authority.

"Doctor James, how fortuitous that we've found you." Her eyes flicked briefly across his ironed shirt and clean-shaven face before she continued with a small smile. "I have just reiterated to our visitors here, that no unauthorised experimentation is taking place in this laboratory that would place the staff and students of Melbourne University in danger, or interfere with the natural energy resources of our wider community. Isn't that so?" Her set jaw and critical eye left no room for opposition.

"Of course," Orrin stammered, "I mean, of course *not*. I wouldn't–"

"Let's not play games here, people." A grey-suited woman stepped forward. Her tone was icy. She was tall and slender, with thick black hair piled elegantly at the nape of her neck. Her blue eyes challenged Orrin.

With a jolt of recognition, Orrin struggled to defer his panic. It wasn't the woman who shook his confidence. It was the man standing beside her. *Dimi.* Orrin's oldest friend caught his eye with the tiniest shake of his head and briefly pleading eyes, then stepped back minutely, fixing his stare onto the floor.

The black haired woman raised an eyebrow, demanding his full attention.

"We've picked up massive energy fluctuations streaming from this location, into and out of our magnetosphere, Doctor James. Frankly, you are the only person who has the resources required to be involved. As I have just informed Chancellor Thandi, any scientific experimentation that directly impacts the safety and resource capability of the greater public, automatically falls under the jurisdiction of the Department of Natural Resources." The woman lifted her chin, surveying the room decisively. "That being the case, such jurisdiction would then include your equipment, research notes and any and *all* experimental results that you have collected in these experiments."

Orrin's hand tightened imperceptibly around the papers he still carried. He drew himself tall, calling her bluff.

"The Department of Natural Resources. And that's you, is it?" Judging by Dimi's presence, Orrin already knew the answer.

"No, it isn't." She glanced briefly toward Dale, who shrank back. The woman looked slightly amused, although her tone didn't change. "My name is Cassandra Chevallier, and I am the Director of the Division of Space and Astronomy for the CSIRO. However, you can be assured *Doctor* James, that I have the full co-operation of any relevant Government Departments in my investigation here, as well as federal law enforcement if necessary." She paused for effect. "So I strongly suggest you assist me with my enquiries."

"One moment Director," Chancellor Thandi interceded, facing Cassandra squarely. Orrin suddenly appreciated how formidable the older woman was, even though she stood a clear head shorter. "Irrespective of the *alleged* legality and wider implications of any experimentation currently being undertaken by Doctor James," Thandi shot Orrin an accusatory look before continuing, "I would like it noted that *any and all* results from his energy-field experimentation remains the intellectual prop-

45

erty of this university. That includes any *commercial implications* of his discoveries."

Cassandra's lips momentarily lost their smile, confirming Orrin's suspicions. This was about *money*.

"That remains to be seen Chancellor, depending on how much assistance Dr. James is willing to provide me. My department anticipates devastating environmental ramifications if the current situation is not resolved immediately, and if your university is in any way responsible, well, I assure you that intellectual property rights will be your least concern. The Australian Government, *or in fact, the United Nations as a whole,* do not look very kindly upon interference with critical natural resources."

Chancellor Thandi blanched. Her shoulders tightened.

Orrin watched their exchange mutely as he raced through his options. He was painfully aware of his best friend's efforts to avoid eye contact. It seemed that Cassandra was oblivious to the men's familiarity with each other, and apparently Dimi wanted it to stay that way. A sickening wave of betrayal hit him.

Cassandra stepped closer. Her voice and smile were beguiling but laced with danger. "I understand your hesitation in revealing your *situation*, Doctor James, so I would like you to be absolutely clear of what's at stake." She tilted her head to the side, scrutinising his face for any reaction. Her breath hit Orrin's lips as she spoke. "If intellectual property really is your concern, I may be willing to negotiate in light of what you can provide me. I am not an entirely unreasonable woman." She paused, turning briefly to Dimi, who returned her unspoken demand with a small nod. "However, if you make this difficult for me, I will return with a warrant, and my colleague Dimitri here will obtain your experimental data and equipment for me regardless."

Behind him, Orrin felt Dale retreat. Cassandra's eyes followed the postgrad to his desk and watched him for a moment as he shifted uncomfortably. With a hint of a smile, she stepped back away from Orrin and once again addressed the room.

"Dr. James, given you've obviously kept your own superiors in the dark," she raised a perfect eyebrow at Chancellor Thandi, "it seems this decision rests entirely upon your shoulders."

Orrin drew a calculated breath. He turned and walked slowly to the door, delaying the moment of decision as he gathered his wits. When he turned back to face her, Cassandra was watching him with a self-satisfied smile; it was clear she was never denied what she demanded.

Until today.

"I'm afraid I can't help you Director." Orrin's answer came like a slap in the face. Cassandra looked stunned, then instantly livid. Beside her, Dimi's eyes were wide with disbelief. Within a few seconds Cassandra's cloak of cool authority was back.

Orrin plastered his most insincere smile on his face. "I have no information for you and I deny any involvement in whatever *energy-field* concerns you're investigating. I was completely unaware of the situation. Sounds like someone's having a bit of a craic at your expense, if you ask me. Nothing to do with this lab though. If you don't believe me, then I'm afraid you'll have to do whatever you feel necessary to confirm that." Orrin took a deep breath, holding the door deliberately wide. "Now if you'll excuse me, my assistant Dale and I have work to do."

Cassandra's eyes flashed. "You do realise what you are doing here, don't you, Doctor James? I *strongly* urge you to reconsider your position." There was not a touch of warmth to her civility. Orrin knew she had underestimated him. She wouldn't let it happen again.

"My research is entirely benign, Director," said Orrin. "I have *no involvement whatsoever* in your current concerns." The lie hung between them like electricity. "Now, if you will kindly leave."

With a graceful stride, Cassandra swept by, her eyes never leaving Orrin's until she passed. A step behind her, Dimi caught

Orrin's gaze for a split second. His own blazed with warning. And then they were gone.

Chancellor Thandi paused in the doorway. "You'd damn-well better know what you're doing," she said. Orrin nodded grimly as he shut the door behind her.

Only Dale, with eyes downcast and mouth set tight, was left to witness Orrin's weakness as he slumped into the nearest chair.

Jaysus, he thought. *What* am *I doing?*

"Where the hell have you been, O? I've been calling you for a month!"

Orrin had never heard his sister so upset. *I shouldn't have picked up the damn phone.* He offered his most conciliate tone.

"Rach, I'm really sorry. Look, this just isn't a good time–"

"Again?! What on earth is going on with you? First, you're a no-show at the barbeque – and you stood up Renee, by the way – who was humiliated! There I was, talking you up at work for weeks and you don't even call to warn me you're not coming. You don't answer your phone, I even called in to your apartment a few times and you're never home – I thought you'd died!"

"Look, I'm sorry Rach, things have been a bit hectic that's all." Orrin pictured Rachael on the other end of the phone with maternal concern fraying her usually even temper. The barbeque invitation and even the prospect of contacting his family, his *altered-reality* family, hadn't even nudged at his subconscious. As far as he was concerned, this wasn't home. Of course, to everyone else on the planet, including his sister, it most certainly was.

"I've been worried about you, O. Every day, I've been waiting for a call from the morgue or something for god's sake."

Orrin allowed himself a grin. Of all his sisters, Rachael had always had a flair for the dramatic.

"Look, I can't explain it now but I'm sorry I haven't called. There's a... *situation* at the university that I have to keep a close eye on. I've been sleeping there most nights – just give me a few more weeks and I'll come visit. I promise." Orrin pushed his thumb and forefinger into the ache beneath his glasses. *A few more weeks and I'd better be back where I started.* Ivy's voice was still clear in his head. Orrin's determination flared. Failure wasn't an option.

Rachael gave a disappointed sigh.

"Well, make sure you do, or I'll damn well chase you down. We've missed you, especially Jess. She was so disappointed you didn't turn up a few weeks ago. She's been bursting with excitement – her pet hobbit had just started walking and she wants to show you–"

"Her pet what!?" Orrin's voice nearly exploded down the phone line.

"H-hobbit. What's the matter? You sound crazy. What's going on?"

"I sound crazy because I'm going bloody crazy! Since when does a child get given another person as a pet? What the hell are you thinking?"

"Another person? No, it's just a hobbit."

"*Just* a hobbit?!"

"Well, yes, from the exotic pet breeder. I mean, I suppose it's a bit over the top, but you know how much Jess loves animals and she's actually very responsible. She hasn't missed a feeding and she baths it everyday–" Rachael's voice faltered as tried to justify her purchase. Orrin's breathing grew heavier. "It was her birthday, O, *remember, you were supposed to be there*. Besides, it was all above board. I got an exotic animal license and all the bits and pieces to look after it. Immunisations, breeding certificate...it was bloody expensive actually."

Orrin was reeling. "Exotic pet breeder –"

"Of course!" She sounded offended. "You know I'd never buy from one of those backyard breeders. This place had a licence. I mean, I would have preferred a capuchin because they don't get as big, and the marmosets and macaques are too noisy. Obviously, the squirrel monkeys are just too messy, and we wanted an indoor pet, at least until it gets too much for Jess to manage."

Orrin was incensed. He bit back the string of profanities that threatened to foam out. *It just took a license and some cash to buy, no, to own, another human being.* He tried to calm his breathing. "I can't believe you did this. Jess is a kid; she can barely tie her own shoelaces! How on earth could she understand the responsibility involved–" Orrin stopped short. Rachael's words suddenly caught him on a jagged edge. "Wait – you said it was just starting to walk–?"

"Well of course. I can't have an untrained fully-grown primate in the house. But it's weaned and we keep a nappy on it. Jess loves dressing it up. I've never seen her so happy, O. She treats it like a real baby – you know how she dotes on the boys–"

"It *is* a real baby, GOD DAMN IT!" Orrin exploded. "Jesus, Rachael, it should be with its mother! They should all be with their bloody mothers. You have no idea what that hobbit is capable of. I know it seems like a furry little toy, but it's *not*! It's just not, Rachael." Orrin's voice cracked under the weight of pent-up emotion. There seemed no end to the insanity of this new world. *Exotic pet breeder. A baby...*

Pushing away his overwhelming disgust, Orrin slammed the phone down.

The half-crescent moon was past midnight. Orrin paused in the shadows, pressing back against the sandstone wall of the Biology building. He held his breath. Once again, the sound of shuffling leaves ahead amplified in the silence. *Closer this time.* At any moment, he expected a security guard to appear on the dark path and catch him prowling. Instead, a possum did. Twigs snapped as it dropped from a Callistemon shrub and scuttled across his path. Orrin relaxed. He followed the base of the building into darkness, skirting the security cameras he knew were perched high on the external walls.

He threw himself up and over the barbed wire topped fence, tearing his shirt and hands.

"Feckin' hell." Orrin rubbed his bloody palms down the legs of his jeans, trying to dull the sting where barbs had caught his skin. With a furtive glance around, he navigated the inside perimeter of the fence to bypass the security monitored laneway outside Behavioural Laboratory Six.

He pulled keys from his pocket, quickly muting the jingling noise in his fist. *This was it.* Of all of the things Orrin knew he was capable of; he'd never considered he had the capacity for this. *Well, I'm a criminal now.*

But he couldn't wait any longer. He needed help. Cassandra could be back any day with a warrant to tear his laboratory apart. His data wasn't safe, and Ivy wasn't safe. The amulet was important. Ivy had mentioned it before their connection was lost when she had managed to somehow reach him across time. But Orrin had no idea *why* the amulet was important. Right now, he could only think of one person that might be able to help him. Specifically, *one hobbit.*

Under the guise of visiting for an update on her progress tonight, Orrin had stolen Jayne's laboratory keys from her handbag. His duplicity left a bad taste in his mouth, but he couldn't bring himself to deliberately involve her in a break and enter. Both now and before the time-shift, Jayne Williams was the archaeology department's newest postgraduate. After graduating, she had been bounced around by overworked staff and had finally landed under Ivy's wing in the Molecular Archaeology laboratory. When Orrin had first met her, she was in Ivy's company at an interfaculty mixer, which is to say, in return for her help wading through Ivy's PhD experiments, Jayne had insisted Ivy accompany her to rub shoulders with the other staff. Where Ivy was quiet and reclusive, Jayne was bubbly and outgoing. But like cheese and crackers, they worked together perfectly. She was the first person Orrin had turned to when he'd suddenly found himself in a broken world of missing pieces.

But Jayne had no memory of ever knowing Ivy Carter. She belonged to this new version of the world, in which Ivy had never existed. Now, Jayne was working on the Liang Bua excavation alone and it had taken a lot of effort to convince her that a Time Shift had somehow thrown Ivy into prehistory. Finally though, the archaeological clues became too obvious to ignore. When Orrin had called in to steal her keys, Jayne was still working on DNA identification of the latest remains from Liang Bua cave. Her worried voice rung in Orrin's ears.

"An almost complete skeleton dated to fifty thousand years before present – on the same stratigraphic level as previous hobbit finds. The skeleton is a modern Homo sapien. It's not a hobbit, it's one of us. And it's female. It's a modern Homo sapien woman."

Jayne thought the skeleton was Ivy. Now, she was working hard to disprove the possibility. Running the analysis over and again. Looking for mistakes.

Cold dread filled Orrin's gut. He refused to believe it. If Ivy was already dead, how could he bring her back? The thought made him hollow. He couldn't allow his mind to entertain it, not now, when he needed every drop of optimism he could scrape together. He pushed the thought out of his head as he clutched Jayne's stolen keys in the dark.

Holding a penlight torch between his teeth, Orrin pushed the keys sequentially into the steel door until he found the right one. He cringed at the heavy screech as the door swung back on its hinges, then stepped in and pushed it closed from the inside. As he moved forward, the flashlight pinpointed scattered papers and feeding equipment. A row of illuminated road studs were glued along the linoleum floor track. Silhouettes of mice shot back and forth in their cages, disturbed in their nocturnal pursuits. Orrin reached the concreted viewing area, beyond which the room gave way to a vast wire cage exposed to the elements. He flicked the torch light across the floor.

"Hello? Are you in there? I'm not going to hurt you – I need your help." Orrin knew that the hobbit woman wouldn't understand his words, but he tried anyway. He spoke gently, coercively, his ears straining for the slightest movement.

Silence.

I need your help, he thought. *Please be here.* Orrin moved to the wire door in the cage wall. Again, he tried each key until he heard a satisfying click. He pushed the door open and walked into the enclosure. Shadows from overhanging trees patched the cement. *There must be at least six hobbits here, somewhere in this dark.* He made his way warily around the perimeter. Until that moment, Orrin never considered what he would do if they chose to attack him. They may be small, but they were far stronger than they looked. He fought back a shiver.

There you are! Orrin's torch caught two bright eyes staring back at him from the darkness. He rushed toward them and heard a body recoil against the wire mesh. Realising his mistake, Orrin froze. He crouched low and let seconds tick by. Softly, he spoke into the darkness.

"I'm not here to hurt any of you. I just need your help. Please."

He inched forward keeping low, anticipating an attack from the darkness. If they'd already surrounded him he wouldn't even know.

"Please. I just need your help. Then I'll go away," he whispered.

When Orrin reached the creature's hiding place without

being attacked, he breathed a sigh of relief. He propped the torch between them so its light illuminated his own face, then realised why he had not been surrounded.

They were all gone.

Only the tiny mother remained, bundling a sleeping ball of skin and hair to her breast. The others – the other young ones – were all gone. Her children had been taken from her. *Oh, God no. That bastard, Nerov.* The professor had taken over as Head of the Behavioural Research lab after Liam Kent got himself arrested. Orrin had tried and failed at stopping him from taking one of the juveniles before to transport to a pharmaceutical laboratory for research.

Orrin saw piteous defeat in the woman's face. Her eyes were hollow with grief. She clung to her baby as if its existence was the only thing keeping her alive. She was emaciated. Her hair hung dull and listless across her shoulders. There was no pleading in her eyes this time. No rebellion or even resentment. She had given up.

Of all the emotions that swept through him, shame pitted itself as the strongest against his conscience. *I came here to ask for her help... her help me... without a second thought to her own suffering. How dare I expect anything from her?* He felt sick to his stomach.

Orrin made a decision. He'd already stolen one thing tonight. He'd steal again. Only this time, not only Ivy's life was at stake.

Now there were two more lives in his hands.

Each step sparked panic in Orrin's heart. Tiny creaks in the dark became minefields of fear. Fear of being caught... but worse still; fear of what might befall his charges should he fail. Orrin crept slowly toward the physics building, his hand gently enclosing the delicate fingers of the child-sized woman. She seemed acutely aware of the danger.

At first, he didn't think he could convince her to come. After trying unsuccessfully to coerce her, Orrin considered simply picking her up and carrying her. But all she would have to do was scream and security would swarm. The hobbit woman had no reason to trust him, so Orrin knew it would have to be earned. He pulled the wire cage door as wide as he could. And waited. Orrin guessed that it must already be nearing sunrise. The instant the sun spilt over the university grounds; his chance would be gone. Finally, the tiny woman decided.

With the little bundle gathered tight in her arms, she crept toward him. She cowered back when Orrin drew up to his full height, it seemed that the indomitable spirit she'd once shown had all but left her. He dropped to a crouch.

Orrin gently extended his hand to her and she had hesitantly taken it, and now they dashed across the mosaic of shadow to the safety of his physics laboratory. As he closed the door behind him, he heard the early shift janitors arriving. *There's no leaving now, I'll have to hide them again until nightfall. God damn it.* During his waiting, Orrin had hoped to get them to his car and back to his apartment before sunrise. From there, he had no plan at all – other than to keep her out of Nerov's hands.

He led the hobbit into the retired radioactivity room within the lab that served as his office. Its lead-lined walls had protected him once before. He prayed they would serve him again as he switched on the external warning light and shut the door. He quickly planted himself out in the main laboratory.

Greetings of early-birds and cleaners unlocking class-rooms filtered in from the corridor. A key twisted in the lock and a bleary-eyed janitor pushed the laboratory door open. Orrin flattened down his shirt.

"Morning!" He greeted the woman a little too enthusiastically from behind a computer monitor.

"Morning love," she replied, entirely unsurprised to see him there.

"You're off the hook today, Jean." Orrin pointed to the red radioactive sign above his closed office door. "New project."

She looked a little confused but nodded. "What about the rest of it?" Jean eyed the empty food containers on Orrin's bench dubiously.

"Uh no, residual.. photochemical.. radiation," Orrin said, lamely. "I need everything to stay as is. For measurements and um, data integrity. So, no cleaning in here for at least a week. Less work for you though, huh?" Orrin grinned and winked at her, guessing he looked a little less dashing than he hoped.

Jean sighed. "Righto love. Don't let it build up too much. My back can't take what it used to."

"I'll take care of it, don't worry," said Orrin. The cleaner nodded and left, a little lighter with notion of less work ahead. Orrin ducked back into his small office, locking the door behind him.

Under the harsh artificial globes he could finally see the hobbit clearly. She had ignored the swivel chair and cowered in the corner instead. Orrin joined her on the floor for the second time that night. He'd never been so close to something so strange and different before. The baby had woken under the glare and now struggled in her arms. Orrin tried not to stare, but he hated what he saw. Not her, but her *condition*. She was in worse shape than he'd thought. The woman looked at him beneath a veil of filthy hair, with dark, round eyes that drew pity from his soul. She was naked. Her ribs protruded sharply and a burning red lesion had swollen the skin below her left breast. *Nerov's tranquiliser dart.* Orrin remember the callous way the man had immobilised her when she fought to protect her children from being taken.

"Well, maybe she'll be a little more cooperative next time," Nerov had said.

What chance had this tiny woman ever had to protect her family? She was no match for a gun aimed from behind the safety of steel bars.

More for his own modesty than hers, Orrin pulled off his jacket and offered it to her. Dismissively, she lay it across her lap, then rested the wriggling boy on top of it. The child stretched out with wide eyes and little balled fists.

Orrin pushed a half-empty water bottle and a bag with yesterday's remaining doughnut toward her. Without hesitation, she took them both, first mashing the doughnut in her mouth, then retrieving it again to push into her baby's mouth. There was none left when the baby seemed sated, and Orrin resolved to buy proper food as soon as the cafeteria opened. The woman herself must be starving.

The hobbits face was wide but not altogether unpleasant. Her eyes were rounded with heavy ridges that swept to a rather flat nose. A strong jaw framed a delicate mouth with no distinctive chin. Coffee coloured skin and a fine layer of hair softened her legs and slightly too-long arms. Although she looked distinctly primitive, perhaps even animalistic to some, there was no mistaking the intelligence in her eyes. She watched silently as Orrin appraised her, quite aware of his assessment. There was no self-consciousness in her returning gaze, just utter misery.

With the immediate concern for her safety at bay, Orrin couldn't repress his need for information anymore.

The concept of *Hiranah* seemed inexplicably tied to the five stars of the Southern Cross he'd found engraved on Ivy's amulet. When he'd last sought out her help, the hobbit woman had drawn an Ivy leaf and connected it too, to the five stars on the amulet. Given Ivy's mention of the amulet, it was the obvious place to start.

If she can show me the meaning of those symbols... it might give me a clue where to start.

Orrin unlocked the cold steel drawer of his desk, picking up the stone. He sat back down. Once again, the hobbit recognised the amulet immediately. She reached for it. And as Orrin placed it in her hand, something incredible happened.

He heard her speak.

CHAPTER 5

IVY

*T*he party of seven had travelled east for two days. The first couple of hours had been easy, with rolling hills and a meandering river to follow, but they soon left it behind to face the razor-blade valleys that footed the dormant volcano of Ranaka.

Kari, Chiri and Sira had travelled with them for the first few hours, then split off to follow a hunting trail. They would skirt around the northern part of the Soa Basin as they made their way as far east as they could walk in three weeks, searching caves and mountains as they went. Ivy had made it very clear, that whether they succeeded in finding other tribes or not, they had to return to the Falling Place at least two days before the next full moon. The other travelling groups – Shia, Sholon and Buchi together, and Boru, Shashi and Ren – would travel along the north ocean coast as far east, and west, respectively, as they could go. Each route came with its own inherent dangers, not least of which were high exposed cliffs, nesting Komodo dragons and the unfamiliar sea faring Karathah tribes.

Cresting the volcanic ridge of Ranaka had taken Ivy's party

until nightfall. They had camped on the eastern face of it, leaving their steep decent to the following morning. Ivy passed the time learning new words as they trekked. Shahn had begun teaching her when she had first joined the tribe, but now that they were travelling, Setian had picked up the job. The hunter was surprisingly good teacher. Ivy found herself to be a surprisingly good student.

"Jiran-shi-suapu-karid?" Ivy asked. Setian passed her his spear. A few moments later, Ivy handed it back, asking for his water bladder instead.

"You are getting better," Setian grinned. "Soon, you won't need the amulet to translate at all."

"Hirep-cathu-masi-rua," Ivy replied, feeling extraordinarily pleased with herself. Her survival skills had also improved. Each day, Kora helped her identify edible plants as they travelled. The prior night, their meal had been entirely gathered and prepared by Ivy alone.

As the sun fell behind the mountains each night, the hobbits raised their voices together in harmony, honouring the beauty of the land with a Dusk Song. Afterward, evenings passed in quiet conversation.

Xiou led them down into the valleys below at dawn, where they had to skirt another ridge and navigate their way across two rivers. The water was shallow and neither Kyah, nor the hobbits, had needed help to swim across. They made good progress and camped on the far side of the second river overnight, discussing the journey ahead.

"The ridges and thick jungle will slow us down," Ivy said. "So, once we have thoroughly searched the Soa Basin, we should head south to the coastline that borders the Savu Sea. From there we can trail East Nusa Tenggara's flank. When our time is up, we'll turn north-east again, to come up to the Three Sister Lakes of Kelimutu from the south." It was a different route than that which Ivy had first taken to reach Liang Bua Cave. Without the maps in her journal, she could only remember major landmarks and the general direction they would need to take across the long, narrow island. Gihn's old bones were already struggling with the mountainous terrain. By following the flatter coastline, Ivy hoped the route would be less challenging for him.

She had scrutinised maps of Flores during her old life in the lab, back when the harsh geography represented only archaeological sites to her – plotted points on a flat page. This journey, however, felt anything but theoretical. Ivy guessed they had climbed as high as sixteen hundred feet above sea level on their first day. The air felt thinner in her lungs and Ivy had slowed the group down as she struggled to adjust. She pushed herself relentlessly, critically aware of the hourglass that had lodged firmly in the back of her mind. They had only three weeks to gather as many hobbits as possible. In this volatile landscape, at the final stage in their evolutionary demise, Ivy knew they'd have more luck finding needles in a prehistoric haystack. Her gut twisted and she tried to push away her foreboding sense of failure.

Ivy wasn't even sure if hobbit tribes still existed in those caves that their future bones had told her they once had. The displacement of time and fossils could differ by thousands of years. In archaeological terms, it was considered the blink of an eye. In real terms though, she may very well be searching for people who were no longer there. It felt like a fool's errand. But still, she had to try.

"Ouch! Damn it." Ivy picked her way through the undergrowth, feeling too big and awkward. Kora brushed past vines and branches ahead of her with barely a scratch. Ivy was red raw from scraping thorns and rough bark. Swatting away a fly, she anxiously fixated on her chance of success.

As a scientist, she knew that the likelihood of a single bone being successfully fossilised was one in a billion. First, that bone would have to survive the environmental stress of burial itself. Rain and wind erosion might scatter the creature's remains, animals could scavenge and eat its flesh, then microbes would break down whatever was left. The grand archaeological prize – immediate burial and preservation – was infinitesimally rare.

The probability of that same bone then being discovered, thousands or perhaps millions of years later by modern scientists, was even less likely. It was a big earth.

A single bone might be the only morsel left to represent an entire species, while the ten thousand other species that may have lived alongside it would never be discovered. Many of Ivy's colleagues had spent the better part of their lives constructing a timeline of evolution out of these minuscule jigsaw puzzle pieces. But the complete picture would always be elusive. Over its four and a half billion-year prehistory, 99.9% of the teeming life of planet Earth had already been reduced to compost.

As she put one foot in front of the other, Ivy hoped against hope that the statistics that plagued her in the lab might work in reverse. That the fragmentary fossil record of the future might conceal an abundant population of *Homo floresiensis*, still living in the caves she sought. And with those people, a chance for the tribes to reunify and *survive*.

After their third gruelling twelve-hour day, Ivy had barely eaten the food she was carrying before falling soundly asleep. The next morning, as they closed in on the savannah grasslands of the Soa Basin, the energy of the travellers picked up. In this huge expanse of ridges, well over a dozen fossil sites had been recorded by modern archaeologists, spanning a timeline of possible hominid occupation over one million years. If there were any other hobbits still living on Flores, Ivy felt sure they would be here.

"Let's camp on the eastern side of Inielika tonight," she suggested, nodding toward the dormant volcano. "We'll begin to search the Soa Basin tomorrow."

"Suppose we do find more of our people–" began Setian, who had slowed to fall in step with her so he could reach the amulet at her wrist.

"We *will* find them," Ivy assured him.

"–so, *when* we find them," he continued, "How do we convince them to leave their home and join us at The Falling Place? I would not leave mine on the word of strangers."

"If Hiranah says they will join us, then they will." Kora waved him off, though her eyes didn't seem entirely convinced. "She has the Life Stone." She nodded toward the amulet. Most of their travel passed in silence – it was difficult terrain – but at times like this, when conversation was easier, the hobbits took turns walking beside Ivy to share her amulet and allow her to join their discussions.

"No, Setian is right," said Ivy. "They probably won't come on my word, in fact, if anything, the sight of me will terrify them. Your Beginning story says your ancestors found the amulet after the tribe had already split. It's possible that other groups never knew of the Life Stone. Even if they remember, it only infers the stone would protect your people when they needed it. Not what it would protect them from. The other tribes have no reason to believe us."

The others exchanged glances.

"Then how will you convince them?" asked Xiou.

"I won't." She turned back to look at Gihn who was trailing behind. The old man looked up warily. "Gihn will."

"I assumed that was why you asked me to come," Gihn sighed. "It certainly wasn't for my speed." He stretched, wincing. Ivy heard his old bones click. "I will try my best." Kyah dropped down from the trees above and settled beside the old man.

"They'll see me as an outsider," Ivy said. "You called me here, Gihn, so when we find the others, make sure they understand why."

"Setian is right," Gihn said. "It won't be easy to convince them to leave their homes."

"Tell them the Beginning story. Tell them about the three coloured lakes and how the Life Stone led me to you."

Ivy disconnected from Setian and looked at the amulet hanging from her wrist, wondering at the paradox of its double life. Perhaps she hadn't brought it with her at all when she Fell, but rather, like Gihn had said, that the hobbits had had it for generations before she had arrived. Perhaps it had fallen further through time than she, to wait for her thousands of years before she would come to reclaim it. Eons of slumber, so the hobbits could find it first, and keep it as a talisman for the day she'd come. Ivy frowned. Until she could figure out how the amulet worked, there would be no answers.

"You'll need to show them your own memory I think, Gihn," Ivy continued, stepping back to him. "Your Dusk Song on the night I Fell. Even your memories of tracking me in the forest if that helps." She looked around. It felt like her own memories of those events were years old, not only five weeks. As if she'd lived an entire life here already and that the modern world, the one she was planning on returning to, was only half-real.

Her chest burned at the thought of reclaiming her old life. Every morning Ivy replayed her conversation with Orrin as she trekked, hoping his voice would somehow lead her home.

Kora had been quiet, listening with a grim expression. Ivy knew her friend well enough to know that her mind was never still. She was a hunter. One of their best. Strategy was second nature. Finally, Kora spoke up.

"If they refuse to join us, do we take them by force?"

Ivy thought on that that for a moment. "No. There's no point. The young ones can't be forced to find mates outside their cave, any more than we can force the older ones to believe our story. There aren't enough of us to overpower them, and if we tried, we would be no better than the Karathah. *So no violence.* They must be convinced with our words alone. They have to understand what's at stake. They'll just have to trust us. Or at very least, trust Gihn."

"And if we fail?" Kora's eyes narrowed. "If Gihn can't gain their trust?"

Ivy looked to over the old man. His shoulders were bent, as if the weight of their survival pressed them to the ground.

"We will not fail."

Aching muscles woke Ivy early on her fourth day travelling. The sun was barely peeking across the savannah ahead, baking its silhouette in an orange glow. Behind her, Inielika volcano slumbered in the dark like a giant beast.

"I feel like we have some good fortune coming today," Xiou said, passing her some water. He was still sitting by the hearth, the last to take sentry during the night.

"Me too," Ivy smiled. "We have a lot of ground to cover." A blinding sun broke over the edges of the horizon. It spilled across the dark shadows of the landscape below them, flooding in like a spreading lake. The scene was breathtaking. Soa Basin had been shaped in sharp relief over millennia by volcanic eruptions and violent tectonic up-lifts. Prehistoric coral reefs had been hoisted onto exposed mountain tops. Rivers were blocked and forged anew as lava flow plugged their paths. The vast basin ahead of them now was built on a plateau of valleys and deeply incised gorges surrounded by a ring of distant volcanos. Once a great lake itself, the Soa Basin was furnished with dry grassland and deep pockets of greenery surrounding the veined tributaries of the AeSissa River.

As they set off, rested and comfortably full of food, spirits were high.

Their optimism didn't last long.

"We are being tracked," Xiou said, slipping into place beside Ivy. He had been leading the group east toward the first of the fossil sites Ivy thought had potential to be inhabited.

Ivy's neck stiffened, but she kept walking. "By whom?" There were only two possibilities that really frightened her. Komodo dragons, or...

"Karathah," Xiou muttered.

Fear twisted her gut. "How many are there?"

"Only two I think. I caught a glimpse of them in the trees as we passed the hot spring."

Ivy's muscles urged her to spin around and look, but she kept her eyes firmly ahead. "What should we do?"

The lead hunter was silent for a moment. "Nothing yet," he said. "I think the sight of you will be enough to keep them from attacking us immediately." As he caught her expression, he added, "Sorry, Hiranah, but it's true. Pale skin and hair the colour of fire. They will never have seen such a creature before."

"I remember the way the Karathah women looked at me at the trade offering," Ivy frowned. "They ran away screaming."

Xiou grinned. "And they did not even know you yet." Ivy gave him a sharp nudge with her elbow and he stepped aside, chuckling, as it missed. "But even two Karathah are big trouble," Xiou continued. "If they choose not to attack us now, they could alert others that we are here. They will be wary of Kyah too," he added, nodding to the bonobo who was knuckle-walking ahead of Kora. "She is also aware of their presence, I think." As if on cue, Kyah looked back at Ivy, an undercurrent of anxiety in her eyes.

"Oh yes, she knows." Ivy watched her best friend turn away again. The bonobo was always hyper-aware of impending danger, even as Ivy naively marched headfirst into it. Ivy knew that Kyah was stronger than a fully-grown human man, her muscles far denser, despite being significantly smaller in stature. In a bare-knuckle fight, she could win in an instant. But bonobos as a species rarely fought, living a more peaceful and altruistic life than their chimpanzee cousins. Ivy couldn't bear the thought of Kyah having to defend herself against spears and blades.

"I don't like the idea of leaving this tree cover," Kora said, eyeing the open grassland they were about to step into. "We cannot climb to escape them if they attack."

"Hiranah cannot climb to save her life anyway," Setian smirked. But his joke was tainted by the concern in his eyes. "I think we should continue as we planned. In the open valley we will see them easily if they decide to follow. They cannot hide out there."

"Setian is right," Xiou looked behind them into the shadows of undergrowth, then at the open expanse ahead. "But if the Karathah do choose to follow us onto the grassland we will have to fight. Be wary as you walk – they have the advantage of knowing this land's hiding places – we do not." With a determined step, he left the cover of foliage and strode onto the plain.

Ivy threw a furtive glance over her shoulder before she joined him. After a few minutes, the Karathah hadn't appeared, so she assumed their pursuers were hesitant to expose themselves. As they put distance between themselves and the danger behind them, Ivy felt little comfort. *Why did they give up so easily? Where did they go?* It didn't seem likely that Karathah hunters would simply let five hobbits, one bizarre, white-skinned woman and a ground-walking black ape enter their territory without consequence. But there was no time to dwell any further on it. Because they had finally reached the first archaeological site.

And found nothing.

The archaeological dig of Mata Menge had been Ivy's first choice to try. In modern times, the rocky outcrop had borne fruits of fossilised animal bones, a potluck of stegodon, crocodile, giant rat, Komodo dragon and bird bones scattered amongst stone tools from the ancient hominids that had butchered them. The remains were closer in time to a million years before Ivy found herself standing there – a massive temporal displacement. The location had offered shelter, water and fertile hunting ground to possible predecessors of *Homo floresiensis*, rather than the descendant species she travelled with now. But Ivy had hoped the location itself might have kept its domestic appeal across generations. Apparently not.

"Let's split into pairs and scout the ridges," suggested Setian.

"Those Karathah may still be about, so be careful." Kora directed her warning to Ivy, knowing full well the others would blend seamlessly into any environment they entered.

But after half an hour of searching, Ivy had to declare defeat. There was no sign of anyone using the terrace at all. No fresh butchering. No living floor. Nothing to indicate it was used for anything more than passing through.

Her disappointment was visceral.

"There are other places near here." Ivy tried to keep her voice buoyant. "Let's keep going."

One of many tendrils of the AeSissa River was close by, so they followed it north-east. High gorges rose into the air on either side of deeply incised gullies that drained into the river when it rained. Thick patches of greenery were mottled by dusty sandstone.

"If anyone is here, they will live close to the river." Gihn looked around, shading his eyes from the morning sun. Caves were dotted into the high ridges. They didn't look particularly habitable.

Kora and Guntah kept a sharp lookout as they walked on. But there was nothing to see.

The group doubled-back to Kobatuwa then continued east to

Lumbar Menge and Boa Leza. All three archaeological sites were as dry and lifeless as they would be fifty thousand years on.

"North then," Ivy decided. "It looks greener where those ridges meet the river. Maybe there's a cave hidden in the side of that mountain."

The disappointment was beginning to grind. Another two hours of trekking revealed nothing.

"Hiranah!" Xiou called. "Come quickly!" Ivy turned, her heart leaping. He was halfway up a ridge shrouded in leafy shrubs. She climbed up to meet him. It didn't take long to see what had caught his attention.

"Oh no." Dropping to her knees beside him, Ivy stared at skeletal remains that spread from Xiou's feet into the opening of a small hillside cave a few meters ahead. The bones were almost clean. Traces of desiccated musculature remained on the long bones and ribs. The rest of the soft tissue had either rotted away or been picked off by small animals. Ivy guessed that at least fifteen hobbits had died here. Their bodies were piled and arranged awkwardly, as if they'd been dragged into a heap and discarded. It was a macabre sight.

Ivy sniffed and looked around. The slight outcrop above her and the shallow cave ahead, gave the ridge some degree of protection from the elements. By the degree of decomposition, she guessed they may have been dead anything from a few months to a few years. Murdered in their own home. The thought made her nauseous. Because these people most certainly *were* victims of some violent attack. There was enough evidence of that.

Very gently, Ivy picked up a small skull and turned it over in her hands. It was tiny, not yet an adult. The left temporal bone was shattered, likely from a heavy blow. She ran a careful finger across the fracture. Despite the damage, the features of these bones were undeniable. The *size* was undeniable.

"These were some of our people," Xiou said quietly from beside her.

"Yes, they were." Ivy's heart was breaking for him.

"And this," he knelt, retrieving something from within the rubble, "Is a Karathah blade."

A chill prickled Ivy's spine, giving her goose flesh.

"Yes, it is."

CHAPTER 6

NEIL

*N*eil spun his silver lighter between his fingers, watching the activity around him. The stone wall of a cave was at his back. Ahead of him, at the mouth of it, the three women, Atasi, Martu and Tipun were preparing food over a small fire while the men stood around discussing their journey. Charat's band of hunters had come across the shallow cave at sunset the previous night and it had proven to be a good shelter. A small stream close by had allowed them to refill their water bladders and wash before sleeping. They'd awoken refreshed. Luck was still on their side.

Or so it had seemed. A couple of Charat's men had been sent to scout ahead at dawn and bring back some fresh meat. They still hadn't returned.

Charat turned and caught Neil's eye. His mouth was sour and his shoulders tight. As the morning hours ticked on the hunter's mood was fouling.

"We should leave them," Neil said. He drew his arms out to indicate the reminder of the group as he got to his feet. "They can return home on their own." Though his words weren't understood, his body language was clear. There was no point wasting more daylight on a couple of extras.

Charat shook his head and turned his back on Neil, waving him off. Apparently, he was going to wait for them.

With a frustrated groan, Neil sat back down. He closed his eyes, spinning the smooth metal of the lighter under his thumb again. He let his thoughts drift toward a hazy irritation that had been gnawing at his brain since they'd left. He was travelling to Kelimutu to search for a stone made of the same volcanic magnetite as Ivy's amulet. The geology should match – her journal notes had suggested it. But there was something else. *What would he do with the stone when he found it?*

"It's not going to just zap me back home right then and there," Neil muttered to himself, eyes still closed and head resting back against the stone wall. "Ivy's been carrying that thing around for weeks and it hasn't zapped her back. There must be more to it."

The energy fields Dimi had been tracking from The Dish before this happened had been fluctuating wildly. They'd been increasing day by day. Neil had already figured out that the amulet had somehow reacted with the lunar energy field. It wasn't the physics lab itself that was drawing the energy field toward the earth – *it was Ivy.* More specifically, it was her amulet. But the lab must have amplified the frequency of the electromagnetic fields, distorting and fracturing them somehow. *They had the gear. All those damn machines.*

Behind his closed eyelids, Neil replayed the moment he had been stolen from that physics lab at the university.

"No, it's someone here," he had insisted. *"They are conducting their experiments here, now!" Neil had been rewarded with an antagonistic smirk from the Chancellor and a closed door.*

Laboratory 179. He'd let himself in. The silver door handle had clicked softly behind him. Once again, Neil was faced with the sterile white walls of a laboratory. But this time, they were plastered with high resolution screens. Patterns flickered on them enticingly. Suspicious; that's a bloody understatement, *he thought.* Energy measurements, wavelength frequency, sound and light monitors – something isn't right here. Even the effing plants are hooked up. *Neil had crossed the room silently.*

Behind a closed door on the back wall, he had heard quiet conversation. In the furthest corner, an impressive arrangement of spectrographic equipment was set up. A tesla coil took centre stage. Neil could tell that it was highly powered enough to provide a significant pulse of ionized voltage within the room. This was a lightning laboratory. Neil was only slightly surprised by its presence in the lab. He had scanned the room again. A Faraday cage made of conductive mesh screening was against the back wall near the servers, just large enough to protect one or two men inside from the electrostatic charges released from the Tesla coil. But why protect the men, and not the equipment? *Intrigued, Neil had looked closer. Bizarre. A silver trolley of labelled samples stood nearby. Cobalt. Iron. Nickel. Magnetic elements. The whir of server fans had smothered his clicks on the keyboard nearest to him. Huge screens betrayed his prying fingers as he ran a search of the computer's data log.* What are they up to? *He'd reached into his pocket, searching for the usb cable he always carried. If I can just steal another minute to download the data into my phone...*

Suddenly, Neil had heard the main door handle twist. Someone was coming in. There was no time to hide. Neil threw his shoulders back, preparing to greet the newcomer with his usual serve of intimidation.

A woman had walked in. Long red hair. His scowl froze. She was carrying a monkey? A fucking big one. *Its long black fingers were gripping the dark cardigan she wore, pulling it down from her neck. Neil saw a flash of black stone against the white skin on her throat –* the amulet – *before it pulsed electric blue like a neon light, stunning his eyes. Lightning crackled all around. Then the room drained of colour.*

The walls caved in around him. Screams followed him as he collapsed. He was falling.

And then there was nothing but pain.

Neil opened his eyes. The brightness of the cave surprised him. Something felt clearer, as if he was on the edge of remembering.

There was lightning all around, he replayed again. *Lightning all around. Was it that Tesla coil I saw in the corner of the laboratory? Did it discharge? It must have. How else would a damn room suddenly be filled with lightning?* Neil had seen it himself; the laboratory had a built-in faraday cage at the back. Whatever experiments were being done in that room clearly involved releasing ionised voltage into the lab. Were they measuring the effect on all those labelled samples he'd seen on the trolleys? Samples were hooked up in various configurations, even the plants. So why hadn't the electricity killed him when it struck? It should have stopped his heart. *No. There must be more to it.*

Neil closed his eyes again. *Because it didn't strike me directly,* he realised. Neil jolted forward; his eyes wide open. *The lightning struck the amulet. It reacted to the amulet being in the room and struck the amulet directly – not me. Not the woman or she would have died as well – just the amulet. That's when the world around us disappeared and woke up on the other side of this Time Shift.* Neil could barely breathe. Answers were finally unravelling thick and fast. The lunar energy field reacted with the amulet somehow, but until the lightning struck it, nothing happened. *So the amulet needs lightning to react to the lunar energy field to make the time shift occur. It's a combination of events. Lunar energy field fluctuations – amulet – lightning. Is that it? Is that all? What if there's something else?* But nothing else seemed as obvious as those three elements combined.

"Yes!" Neil hissed. A dozen eyes spun around to look at him. Neil couldn't wipe the grin off his face. "I need lightning," he declared to no one in particular. Though he knew none of them understood it, he felt the discovery was worthy of announcement. Charat frowned. He opened his mouth to speak, but a shout in the forest behind them stole his attention.

"Charat! Charat!" A string of incoherency was hurled toward the group by the two missing hunters, who had finally appeared and were running toward the cave. As they approached, breathless, Neil only caught two recognisable words. *Ebu Gogo.* Charat and the others strode to the cave mouth to meet them. After listening to their story, Charat turned and strode back toward Neil. He gestured to the mobile at Neil's feet and Neil quickly swooped it up. Although their translations were becoming a little easier as familiar words lodged themselves in Neil's subconscious, his gallery of photos still aided complex conversation.

"Eye-veee." Charat said, pointing to Neil's last image of the redhead. "Ebu Gogo." He held up five fingers. "Cheeemp." Neil was impressed by the hunter's recall of names as he waded through the language barrier. Charat turned and gestured toward the north, then east. He reiterated with a line in the dirt at their feet. "Nee-el." A smudge to indicate their own position at the cave. "Ebu Gogo," to the north of them, following a line east. Charat indicated his own group of travellers and walked his fingers through the air. It was crude, but enough. Neil understood. Ivy and the Chimp, along with five hobbits were north of them and travelling east.

Charat spoke quickly, his expression dark. He wanted to know why.

Neil frowned. *How the hell am I supposed to know what the little bastards are doing?* He picked up Ivy's journal and flicked through the pages. To be fair, he had more than an inkling of what the redhead might be doing. She was probably moving ahead with the plan that her bleeding-heart journal entries had been hinting at in the final pages she had written. *Looking for more hobbits.* It was clear she felt justified in trying to save them from extinction.

She'd even begun a list of places to search. Old archaeological sites. The last thing Neil wanted was to join her wild goose chase across the mountains. Then again, he needed to keep his pretense for needing an amulet alive. Charat was desperate to kill the hobbits. He was always searching for an advantage over them. Perhaps this was a new flame to fan.

"Nee-el!" Charat's tone was sharp.

"An army." The words were out of Neil's mouth before he even knew where he was going with them. "She's searching for more Ebu Gogo. Ivy – she's building an army of them to fight against you." Realising his words meant nothing, he dropped the journal and phone in his bag. He led Charat over to the mouth of the cave. He squatted down, collecting pebbles to use as counters. They'd played this game before. Neil drew a line in the dirt. A map to lay the counters across. Bit by bit, he played out the story of hobbits gathering, more and more of them, until a mass of pebbles on the ground loomed like a threat. The sapiens were bigger, faster and had better weapons, but hobbits, despite their size, were built with a brute strength far superior to a human man. United, it was quite possible the creatures could fight back against Charat and his sycophants. Charat was furious. In a move that mimicked one Neil had made in the past, he drew his own hand across his throat. *I'll kill them.*

Neil stubbed his thumb against his own chest. "No. I'll kill them," he lied. "If you help me find that stone. The stone comes first!" He stood up, looking down on Charat. *"Stone, first. Then Ebu Gogo."*

Charat didn't have time to respond. Neil's army of pebbles skittered across the ground at their feet. Far below the ground, a deep rumble began to build. Neil felt the vibrations move up his legs and he shot a look back into the cave, where he had left his bag with its precious contents of survival. The journal, his battery recharging fruit and skulls, the USB cord. A shower of dirt rained off the cave face above them, coating him in filth.

Charat shouted something to his men as the rocky ground shifted and lurched underfoot. Charat dove for the forest cover below. A host of cries sounded as everybody flew to save themselves.

"Get away from the edge!" Neil yelled as they scattered to the forest. He skidded down the embankment, struggling to find purchase on the disintegrating terrain.

With a wrenching twist, the limestone roof of the cave shattered behind him. It collapsed inward. Great gashes of rock were clawed from the cave walls, and rubble filled the floor where Neil had been sitting only minutes before. Boughs cracked and trunks split. Neil's arms flew out, he grabbed a tree, clutching it for balance. With a dawning look of horror, he pushed away again, ducking as a branch came crashing down to land where he had just stood. Somewhere nearby, there was a scream.

"Atasi!" Neil lurched forward. He grabbed the woman as she stumbled, then wrenched her sideways to miss a crumble of boulders that slipped from the hillside above them to come crashing down. With wide eyes, they stood staring at one another, frozen in place, ready to leap again. The earth rumbled like thunder beneath their feet. It shuddered a few times, then went still.

Coughing through a thick waft of sulphurous gas, Neil came to his senses. He was still holding Atasi's arm. He quickly let her go, looking her over to make sure she wasn't injured. Her eyes were terrified, but her face unscathed. Neil turned away at Charat's call. The others were appearing out of the ravaged greenery one by one.

A cry went up. It was Tipun, the youngest of the women. She was calling for help. Neil pushed through the undergrowth. She was standing beside one of the hunters, a twenty-something year old man with red-stained teeth from chewing Betel nuts. *Kechu*, Neil thought he might be called. A broken branch had skewered him through the middle. He was already dead. Neil grimaced. It was a grisly sight. As some of the hunters rushed forward, Neil turned and walked back to the cave. He scrambled up the rubble toward the mouth of it.

Neil carefully picked his way through the fallen rocks to where his bag still lay. It was obscured by a mound of broken earth and fallen rocks.

"Damn it, my phone!" Stones and rubble were thrown out of the way, until enough of it was cleared to drag his hide bag out from underneath. Desperately, Neil rummaged inside, assessing the damage. His mobile phone screen was cracked, but it was still working. "Small mercies," he muttered, as he pocketed it, delving back into the bag. His heart sank when he found the ten tiny rat skulls he'd so meticulously collected and cleaned. They were crushed. They had been an integral component of the primitive battery charger he'd created. Neil relied on it. He'd created the battery charger out of an alternating linkage of malleable copper and zinc alloy pieces, each only a couple of centimetres long. The short metal wedges dipped along the connecting edges of a horseshoe row of tiny, upturned skulls like makeshift bowls; *zinc, copper, zinc, copper...* until he'd had a line of ten. Each skullcap was full to the brim with pulpy, under-ripe fruit. Each end of metal arched between two skulls, dipping down into the mashed fruit cupped inside. *Ten perfect battery cells, about half a volt each.*

He had stripped the plastic coating from one end of the USB cable he carried for transferring files, and left the other end jacked for his mobile. The first time he had pushed the long delicate wires into the first and last of his line of pulpy skulls and plugged his dead mobile into the jack, he had felt nauseous with the anticipation of whether it might work. His mobile was a lifeline to sanity in this place. There was no internet of course, and no one to call, but he still had the functionality of the camera, dictation, stellar map and torch, among other things. It meant *control*. A scrap of reality in an unreal world. He needed to replace those skulls as soon as possible.

It'll take a few days to catch another ten rats. Neil's shoulders sank. The skulls had been crushed like eggshells. It had been a good setup, and he had better things to do right now than trap vermin. *If only I had something a little less fragile to use,* he thought. *Has to be small though, with thin walls between chambers.* The links of zinc and copper were short. He looked around but nothing sprang to mind.

Neil got to his feet, shaking dirt off his bag, and tucked the journal and USB cable inside. He left the shattered rat skulls in the rubble. Musty, earthen air filled his lungs. Stepping away from the wall, Neil surveyed the damage. The inner walls of the shallow cave around him were cracked. Striations of newly exposed rock stared back at him. The dull mottle of grey limestone intercalated with volcanic breccia was unremarkable. *But this* – Neil stepped closer to the wall, balancing on rocks and uneven earth. His fingertips ran cautiously along a distinctive reddish-orange strip of rock. It was thick, more than a finger-width and over a meter long before it disappeared back under layers of unbroken earth. Neil held his breath. *It can't be.* Fumbling in the dim light, he flicked on the torch of his mobile phone. Metallic red shone back at him. Neil brushed away loose earth, following the shimmering line along the wall again. His thoughts were scrambling. He forced himself to focus, to glean reason in what he was seeing. *But it is. Copper. Native copper.*

Potential was zipping through his head. In modern times, *Neil's time,* pure copper was rarely found. It had been already mined out over ten thousand years of prehistoric metallurgy, eventually giving way to mineral ores instead which were extracted and refined to produce the lustrous metal. *But this – pure native copper in abundance.* Neil couldn't help but *whoop* in delight. This was the answer to one of his most pressing problems.

The lightning.

Copper conducts electricity. It was, in fact, the most efficient conductor of electricity ever known. Which made it the perfect material to use to create *a lightning rod.*

With ideas spinning in his head, Neil rushed back out of the cave.

"Charat!" He shouted. "Charat!" A moment later, the red-beaded hunter appeared out of the forest. Behind him, two men were dragging the body of their fallen comrade. "Come here!" Sensing Neil's urgency, Charat left his hunters and strode up the uneven entrance to the cave. Neil grabbed his wrist and pulled the other man over to the crumbling wall. He ran his palm across the copper strip embedded in the limestone. "This," he said jabbing it with his finger. "We need to cut this out. I need to use it." It may have been forty thousand years before it was due, but the Stone Age hunter was about to get a lesson in Bronze Age smelting. Neil bent down and grabbed a sharp rock to illustrate his intention. He scratched and scraped the edge of the metallic strip, shearing limestone off from around it like dust.

"All the men," he said, gesturing to those still outside the cave. "We're going to get this red stuff out together."

"Ebu gogo," Charat growled. Though he didn't immediately understand Neil's intentions, he could see there was a new priority being suggested.

Neil shook his head. "Change of plans," he said. "We're staying here for now. *I need that copper.*"

CHAPTER 7

ORRIN

*I*t was surreal. The conversation was taking place entirely within Orrin's mind, like a shared translation for both the hobbit's voice and his own. He understood her, in her own words. Her memories appeared like images in his mind as she offered them in answer to his questions.

They had been talking for the better part of an hour. Orrin was still astonished by the clarity of her words, delivered to him in the same gentle, husky tone that she spoke aloud simultaneously, in her native language.

One thing had become abundantly clear to him. *This was definitely a human.* And her name was Indah.

Ivy *was* Hiranah, of that fact Orrin was now entirely convinced. Indah had obliged his endless questions and recounted stories that had been passed down through countless generations. To Indah, these were simply old fairytales she had been told as a child, almost forgotten now as they distorted and lost relevance in the changing cultural landscape of her people over time. But the bare bones of them were still buried underneath, strong, and timeless, in slumber beneath the dust. The *truth* of Hiranah's story could be recovered, he was sure of it.

And with each new layer of understanding, Orrin's heart thrummed faster.

"She was simply a woman," Indah confirmed.

The importance of getting this singular point correct, drove Orrin to ask again.

"So, she's not a deity of some kind?" At the look on Indah's face, he tried again. "I mean, Hiranah wasn't special in some way. She was mortal – just a normal woman that could live and die like the rest of us."

"That's right," Indah said. "Just a woman. She was one of your type though, not ours."

Orrin had to hold back on fist-pumping the air. Hiranah was no deity. Which meant potentially, she was all the more real. The interpretation made by those original ethnographers was quite wrong. She had not been worshipped or idealised in any way by the tribes. Simply remembered.

"What do you mean *my type?*"

"The stories say that Hiranah had pale skin like the moon," Indah said, "and blazing red hair like the sun. This is why they call her *Hiranah*, you see. It means *fire-hair.*"

Orrin laughed out loud. He felt like he could have danced on a cloud.

"She looked different, but Hiranah was family. She became one of our people. That is in *all* the stories."

"And I can easily believe it," Orrin said. It didn't surprise him that Ivy was remembered simply as kin. *Family.* She was willing to sacrifice her life to save them. That is was what family did. He had heard her say it when he'd connected, so briefly, across time that night. The determination in her voice still rung in his ears.

"You shouldn't be there," Orrin had said. "It's all a terrible mistake."

"But that's just the thing, I think I should be here," Ivy had implored. "I don't know how to explain it, and I resisted it at first. But now I think

– that I'm meant to be here. I always was. I'm meant to help them survive. That's why they called me here. There's no other explanation – as crazy as it sounds."

"No!" Orrin's voice was shaking. "Their survival is not your problem Ivy–"

"But it is! It's everybody's problem!" Ivy had cried out. "They don't deserve this, Orrin. This isn't natural selection. It's genocide. It's deliberate and cruel and fuelled by greed alone! I can't just sit back and let it happen. These people are smart and kind and yes, different – but they have a right to fight back!"

Orrin had sighed, his heart so elated to have heard her voice now threatening to drown him in grief. "But why do you have to be the one to fight for them?"

It had been a moment before she had answered. "I think – because no one else will."

With a little encouragement, Indah recounted the stories for him again. Orrin tried to glean what he could from them. Like all fairytales, they were moralistic and vague.

There was an underlying theme. Hiranah had taught the 'ancient ones' to save themselves against some force that had bound them to death. The 'death' Indah referred to was not defined, but the implication was clear. *Ivy had saved them from something.*

Orrin thought back to the fierce intensity of Ivy's conviction at that rally. What better champion could these people have asked for? It was inevitable that she had channeled her passion into their cause.

She did it then, he realised. *She must have succeeded in overcoming whatever was against them. Otherwise, they wouldn't even be here, would they?* For a moment Orrin was awed by the sheer force of her will. Even trapped within time itself, Ivy was formidable.

"What about the stone?" Orrin asked. "You recognised it."

"I never saw the stone itself before you showed it to me."

"Then how did you recognise it?"

"This shape is in our paintings. It is described in many of the stories, too. *The talking stone*, they sometimes call it. *The Key*, in some other stories. Mostly though, it is called *The Life Stone*.

Orrin dragged his hands over his head, as if they might keep the jumble of thoughts from spilling out.

It was all interconnected; the cave painting Jayne had found with phases of the moon arcing the Southern Cross; the stellar map illustrating the position of the Southern Cross constellation the night Ivy had disappeared, and apparently, reappeared in prehistoric Flores; that same constellation marked into the back of the amulet. Each new scrap of understanding came as a revelation as Orrin began to connect the dots.

The amulet – *the Life Stone* – seemed to represent the ancient *Homo floresiensis* people at the time Hiranah was with them. The constellation of the Southern Cross marked the time of Hiranah's arrival as well as the ancient tribes that she somehow saved. Hiranah herself was symbolised by a crude five-pointed shape, drawn across the stars of the Southern Cross and connecting at each star to shape the terminal and lateral points of a five lobed leaf, finishing with a star at its petiole node. *The shape of an ivy leaf.* The symbology was there, but it was confusing.

Somehow, long ago, Ivy had kept this species from extinction. They remembered her with their symbols and stories. There was logic beneath the madness – it all finally made sense. Orrin was pumped with vindication. A final anxious question broke through. Orrin hesitated. He wasn't sure he wanted to know the answer.

"Indah?" Orrin asked, "What happened to Hiranah in the stories? Did she – *die?*"

Indah's face was drawn and the baby was beginning to fuss. But Orrin couldn't help but implore for something more concrete. He needed to know how the stories ended. *The Homo sapien skeletal remains in the cave. European ancestry...* as much as he hated to consider it, that body could still be Ivy's. If she had died there, fifty thousand years in the past, it meant he was destined to fail. He'd never brought her home.

"How do the stories end, Indah? What happened to Hiranah?" But Indah had no resolution for him.

"We lost her," the tiny woman said. "The stories say that we lost her one day. That is all I know."

The tiny woman, clearly exhausted, broke the connection between them and sunk back against the concrete wall to pacify her baby.

Orrin clutched the black stone, critically aware of the warmth it bore into his skin. *Why the hell didn't I realise before?* This amulet was the only connection between Ivy's past and present. It wouldn't have taken long for Ivy to discover the translation it created between minds.

He turned it over slowly in his fingers. Clearly the stone was unique, but *why?* It was nicely shaped and held his gaze, but otherwise looked like any other stone. *What the hell is this thing made of? If I have any hope of recreating the Time Shift, I need to know how it works.* Orrin got to his feet.

"I'm going to get you some food, Indah," he said. But she was already asleep, with the baby tucked in her arms. Orrin let himself out of the office quietly and made a quick trip to the refectory. He left a bag of fresh food and a water bottle by the sleeping hobbit, then left again, locking the office and laboratory doors behind him. It was still very early. Phil was always late in and Dale wasn't due for a while yet. They'd be safe until he returned.

Orrin turned the amulet over in his palm as he strode through the campus.

I need a geologist.

"Interesting." A quizzical smile settled on the man's mouth and he looked up with slightly knitted eyebrows. "Are you sure we haven't met before, Dr James?"

"Orrin, please. And, I'm positive." As Orrin had scoured the geology lab for early risers, this man was the only one to be found already working. "Why do you ask?"

"No reason, I suppose. This stone just seems oddly familiar, that's all." Dr Elijah Nnamani, a senior researcher in the Geology department turned his attention back to the amulet in his hand. "Trust me, I see a lot of rocks so I don't know why it stands out. Déjà vu." He shrugged. "Anyway, I can tell you it's igneous – volcanic. You can see by this smooth, black, opaque luster. At a glance, I'd say it's magnetite."

"Magnetite?"

"An iron-ore, usually mined to make steel. It's ferromagnetic. When you place it in a magnetic field it remains magnetic, even after the external field has been removed. The most magnetic of all naturally occurring minerals, bar one very rare deposit. Highly commercially useful."

"Right." Orrin muttered, but his mind was leaping ahead, considering the potential reactions created by his experimental magnetic fields. The time shift itself, obviously. *But what's the catalyst?* The stone had remained passive since Ivy had disappeared, except for that brief period that he had heard her voice. None of his equipment had been turned on at the time though.

Dr Nnamani continued, unaware of Orrin's distraction. "Let's have a closer look." He moved across the partitioned room to a workbench where an impressive microscope sat surrounded by slides and trays of broken stone. The geologist spent a minute adjusting the focus, bringing the lens close to the narrowest edge of the amulet. On a screen in front of him, a dark crystalline pattern swam into view.

Dr Nnamani flicked a diffuser on the side of the microscope. A stunning kaleidoscope of bright purple, aqua, fuscia and orange appeared, highlighting the structure of the mineral.

"Okay, so we've got an octahedral system of crystallisation here, typical of magnetite. The absence of tabular crystals tells me it's definitely not hematite, although that doesn't rule out volcanic origin – both hematite and magnetite can be formed by the rapid cooling of lava or mineral hot springs. Where did you say this came from?"

"Flores – Indonesia, I think." Orrin watched his work, impressed by his quick assessment.

"That makes sense." The geologist nodded slowly. "The Indonesian Archipelago is a melting pot of volcanic activity, stunning geomorphology. I've been working in that area for a while now. Big business going on over there. I'm actually heading back over to Flores in a couple of weeks, consulting on a geological survey for a mining company. All *hush hush* though." He winked, his teeth shining beneath a wide smile.

"My lips are sealed."

Dr Nnamani continued chatting as he shifted the stone slowly under the lens. "Lovely sample. Look at this edge – uneven fracture, indistinct cleavage, hard and brittle..." he picked up the stone and carried it to another machine to continue his analysis, "specific gravity of about 5.17..." He placed the amulet under a multi-focal torch beam. Prisms of iridescent light split across its surface.

"Is that normal?" Orrin asked, intrigued by the stunning display of colour.

"Normal for magnetite, yes," Dr Nnamani answered over his shoulder. He placed the amulet back under the polarized microscope. "The colour of the mineral changes with the angle of incident light. It's typical for this type of–" He paused. "Hmmm. Hang on, *that's* not typical."

After a frustrating silence, Orrin leant forward. "What's not typical? Dr Nnamani?"

"Call me Eli," the man said vaguely. He frowned and then transferred the amulet to a scanning electron microscope instead. He carefully focused. On the screen above, clusters of octahedral crystals appeared, some joined on one edge by an identical twin, like microscopic flowers billowing out from one another. The effect was striking. Ribbons of black material snaked between the clusters, pushing them apart. So intent was Eli in his analysis, he startled when Orrin spoke once again behind his chair.

"What's not typical?" Orrin pressed, failing to keep the urgency out of his voice.

Eli glanced up, then gazed once again into the eyepiece. "*That.* The black material there between the magnetite crystals. I don't know what that is." He looked put out. "It might be some sort of metallic intrusion, I suppose. But it must have been made when the crystals themselves formed to create this effect, which in this case, would have been millions of years ago when the tectonic plate itself formed. It's extremely unusual – I've never seen anything like it."

"What does it mean?"

The geologist hesitated. "Well, I suppose it means that without knowing what that substance is exactly, I can't tell you what properties it will embed into the magnetite. It might affect its magnetivity; although this is already the most magnetic of all the naturally occurring minerals on earth."

An uncomfortable feeling solidified in the pit of Orrin's stomach. *I know the effect that substance has on the magnetite,* he thought. *It shifts time.* The black material was yet another unknown in this puzzle. He had enough of those already. Orrin watched as Eli tried unsuccessfully to magnify the unknown substance more highly. After a few minutes, he gave up.

"Without sectioning some off to analyse, there's no way to tell what that intrusion is, or the implications of it being there. It might have no effect at all." Eli looked somewhat unconvinced at his own words.

"But you've never seen something like this before?"

"No," Eli said. "But intrusions aren't entirely uncommon. I just can't identify what it is right off, that's all."

He placed the amulet back into Orrin's hand and Orrin felt a flicker of regret in his mind as their fingers touched. *It shares emotions as well.*

"Let me know if you want me to look into it further for you," said Eli. "I'd be happy to."

Eli reached out to shake Orrin's hand. Out of curiosity, Orrin took it, keeping the amulet in his palm, as if by accident.

"Thanks, I'll keep that in mind," Orrin smiled.

Loneliness – He's searching for something –

Eli's head tilted and he frowned. "What was –?"

"It was great to meet you, Eli," Orrin said, quickly pocketing the amulet.

Eli followed him to the door, still frowning. "If there's anything else I can do–"

"I'm pretty sure I'll need your help again soon, actually," Orrin said. "If you don't mind."

Eli's frown settled into an easy smile. "My door is always open."

Orrin returned to the physics laboratory, readying his key for the door he had left locked. With a shot of panic, he realised it was slightly ajar.

Shit! He ran in, slamming the door shut behind him. Standing by the open internal office door, Phil spun around to him, accusation and anger spilling from his face.

Dale was frozen, a few steps back and staring into the open office, pale with shock. As Orrin strode toward them, heart hammering and terrified for the damage they may have caused, he threw his hands up in surrender. His mind drew a blank. He had no explanation prepared. No excuse ready to offer. Orrin hadn't expected Phil and Dale to arrive before he could get Indah out of the laboratory and off somewhere safe. He cursed himself inwardly. He'd made no plan to ensure her safety. Too caught up in his desperation to have his questions about Hiranah answered. And it was Indah who was about to pay the price.

Behind Phil, cowering in the corner of the messy office stood the tiny hobbit woman, clutching her baby tight, with tears streaming down her face.

CHAPTER 8

IVY

*T*orrential rain fell hard onto their faces as they searched the Soa Basin for the second day. It was a perilous trek. They'd fallen into single file, each lost in their own thoughts as they scoured the landscape with sharp eyes.

Ivy's mind flicked between Orrin and her current challenge. Finding more hobbits, those that hadn't been murdered by the Karathah, was only the beginning of this impossibility. Convincing any survivors to leave their homes would be another thing altogether. As far as the tribes were concerned, Ivy was a Karathah herself. After years of persecution, distrust was woven into their DNA.

Picking her way along slippery rocks, Ivy took advantage of her momentary privacy. Sharing the amulet and her thoughts with the others, sometimes felt invasive. Not that she was trying to hide anything, but some ideas were better left unspoken. She never talked of her plans beyond uniting the tribes, but Ivy knew Xiou had his suspicions. The man was unnervingly intuitive at times.

If I give them a chance to survive together, I can go home. The more the decision had settled inside her, the more it gave purpose to her steps. Ivy wanted to return to her own future life, the one that had been ripped so violently from her.

It was for this reason she had to reunite the *Homo floresiensis* tribes where the Three Sister crater lakes met at Kelimutu, rather than back at Liang Bua Cave. Kelimutu was the *Falling Place*. And if Ivy had Fallen through time there once before, perhaps she could Fall again. Only this time, she needed that Shift to take her home.

Ivy couldn't think of a single good reason why her plan might work, and she could think of plenty of reasons why it might not. Not least of which was the fact that she still didn't know *how* to make it work. Ivy replayed her conversation with Orrin in her head as she walked. He had been convinced that there was a catalyst. Something they hadn't thought of yet, that had reacted with her amulet to incite its change. When they'd connected again that night only a week ago, just long enough to hear each other's voice, the amulet had grown so hot in her hand that it had almost burned her skin. But still, it hadn't reacted enough to send her back home. Something was missing.

Ivy turned the puzzles over in her mind, trying to piece together everything she knew so far.

As I stepped into the physics lab, there was a flash of blue light and all that lightning... Orrin had said that his Tesla coil malfunctioned. Which meant there had been electricity loose in the laboratory. Ivy knew enough about Tesla coils to know that there was usually a safe place to stand while they were live. Apparently, she hadn't been in a safe place. But if it had been *only* lightning that was necessary to Fall, then why would Orrin still be searching for an answer? He had access to her amulet in the future, he had been holding it when he spoke to her. He had access to the Tesla Coil. Clearly whatever experiments he was doing had not managed to recreate the Time Shift with lightning alone.

And then there was that noise – *the singing*. She didn't know why, but Ivy just knew music had something to do with her Time

Shift. The hobbits had admitted they had been calling out for help – singing their harmonic Dusk Song, which they did every night, but especially during the full moon. They had sung it again when Shimma was giving birth to bring her strength and good luck. It was an eerily beautiful sound. Each adult within the tribe held a single harmonic note, long and clear, that floated through the night like the undercurrent of a dream. They had seen Ivy Fall from the sky as they sang, like a streak of lightning, to the earth. Ivy was convinced their song had influenced her Fall somehow, but *how?*

I'm a scientist, she chided herself as she sank ankle deep in mud. She scowled, shook off her foot and kept walking. *There must be a logical explanation. Singing alone can't shift time.*

Perhaps the moon? The bright full moon was as vivid now in her mind's eye as it had been that night. It was just beginning to rise as she had walked with Kyah into Orrin's laboratory. The night after she had awoken, bruised and bleary on the edge of Kelimutu volcano, the moon's face had already lost a sliver of its glow.

There are just over three weeks until the next full moon. I'm running out of time.

This morning they had scoured another two archaeological sites, or at least, the general area where Ivy expected they would be found in the future. She might have been off by a kilometre or two, but if there had been any hobbits living nearby, Xiou, Setian and Kora's eagled-eyed scouting would have discovered them. With the exception of Gihn, they all took turns scuttling up the steep gully walls to poke into caves and thickets of trees, but there was nothing to be found but the nests of giant rats. Kora swiftly skewered a few for their evening meal.

The sites of Boa Leza and Ola Bula bore nothing but mud, and Wolo Milo, a wide sandstone platform that would in the future bear fossils of large stegodon and a scatter of stone arte-facts, lay bereft. With each hour that passed, Ivy's expression dropped further into grim disappointment. A downpour washed mud into her eyes, and she rubbed her forehead. She was the first to the site of Tangi Talo. Dogged determination faltered as she was faced with failure once more. Tangi Talo was the oldest site that future archaeologists would claim for the Basin. In itself, the stratigraphy was a polaroid of mass death. Beneath Ivy's feet, impoverished fauna lay waiting to be sifted out of the layers, the victims of a massive volcanic eruption almost one million years before. Ivy closed her eyes against the pelting rain. She could almost feel the bones beneath her feet calling up to her. They were as trapped here as she was herself.

The smell of sulphur in the air twined headily with the petrichor of wet earth. Volcanic groaning underfoot threatened again to tear the island apart. With a deep breath, Ivy lifted her chin and kept walking.

"Ouch!" A slippery rock brought Ivy heavily onto the mud.

"Are you alright?" Kora's hand closed over her wrist.

Ivy pulled herself up, rubbing a sharp pain on her shin. "I'm fine." The skin was heavily grazed and bleeding. Rivulets of mud ran from her hairline down her pale face. Every inch of her body was streaked with filth. Another day had passed with nothing to show for it but aching bones. Ivy pushed the pain out of her mind. It was nothing in the face of failure. Each day the full moon drew closer. Desperation to save her friends weighed as heavily as the guilt at wanting to leave. Ahead of her, Kyah paused, then came loping back to Ivy's side, her brows furrowed in concern.

"Can you walk?" Kora asked.

Kyah pulled her friend up. Ivy tested her injured leg. The pain wasn't too bad.

"No problem." She gave a rousing grin. "Let's keep going." Before she could take a step, Kyah's hands touched Ivy's shin. Her bottom lip stuck out thoughtfully.

"Hurt?" She signed as her index fingers pointed together with a quick twist.

"No, honey." Ivy shook her head. "I'm okay." With curious fingertips, Kyah assessed the injury for herself. Seemingly appeased, she hooted and turned away again.

"If you're sure, Hiranah?" Xiou asked.

"Really, it is nothing," she reassured him. With a nod, he turned away to continue on. Kyah followed Xiou, picking her way carefully across the wet rocks. One by one, Setian, Gihn, Guntah and Kora followed.

The volcanic rift they trailed slowly widened and turned from rock to trees. Kyah was the first to disengage from their single file descent. Unlike the two species of human, Kyah's physiology had not evolved to accommodate long distance walking. She leapt into the branches, glad to be rid of the precarious knuckle walking the morning had insisted of her. Setian and Guntah were engaged in quiet conversation up ahead. The drizzle of rain had finally eased into a steamy afternoon that felt as thick as soup.

Xiou dropped back beside Ivy, studying Kyah through squinted eyes, apparently lost in thought. Eventually, he wrapped his hand around the amulet on her wrist and spoke.

"There are stories of others like Kyah you know. The Ancients tell of people that were seen during the great Beginning journey. When our people crossed the sea."

"You mean the Karathah?"

"No, not Karathah. There are plenty of stories about them, of course, but there were different people as well." Xiou nodded toward Kyah. "Like the *Hiranthah*."

"Hiranthah?"

"'Fire people'," he explained, "because their hair is coloured red like the setting sun. Like yours, Hiranah. *Fire-hair*." Xiou grinned, reaching high to flick the bedraggled red hair strewn across Ivy's shoulders. "The stories say they lived in the trees. Like our Kyah."

'When our people crossed the sea?' Ivy wondered. *Migration? Could their oral traditions really extend back that far?* Ivy reflected on the tutorials she used to run at the university. It seemed like a lifetime ago. *Xiou must be referring to leaving the Indonesian mainland to cross the Indonesian Archipelago,* she realised. Ivy's curiosity burned. She wondered what other secrets their stories might reveal. Human colonisation across the string of Pacific Islands was an endlessly debatable topic.

Kora slowed down to join their conversation. Xiou adjusted the utility hide strapped to his waist. Inside small folds, his stone knives and dried food were easily accessible. Aside from his spear, the hunter's hands were free to keep the connection with Ivy's amulet as they walked.

"The Hiranthah aren't in many stories," Xiou added. "Only the oldest ones."

"What do the stories say about them?" Ivy was intrigued at the thought of another hominid in the distant past of *Homo floresiensis*, especially if they had crossed paths often enough to become inducted into sacred stories. Ivy's mind flew to potential species – the Denisovans, *Homo erectus*, or even the newest discovery, *Homo luzonensis*.

"They lived alone, and slept high in the trees like Kyah," Xiou recounted. "There were many of them in the forest. Many more than our people anyway."

"Oh." *Red hair, solitary tree-dwellers.* Ivy's heart burned. "Yes, I know of those creatures. Very well. They still live in the forests in the time I come from." *What's left of them anyway.*

Ivy remembered her satchel, burnt in the cave fire. Inside, along with her research notes and a few belongings, had been the bright orange rally leaflet. 'Palm Oil Murders' had blazoned across the top of the page. Xiou frowned at the image her mind inadvertently shared, not understanding.

"In my time, they are called 'Orang-utan'," Ivy explained to him. "It means 'Person of the Forest'".

Kora nodded, as if the name designation were self-explanatory.

"Person of the Forest," she repeated. "Like us."

"Well, yes, but no," Ivy hesitated, wondering how to explain. "They are not considered people like us, Kora. They are considered animals, like the birds and Komodo dragons – the *shirakan*. But I'm afraid there aren't many Hiranthah left in the forest in my time." Ivy wished she could save Kora from the insight she was seeking. It felt a little too close to home.

Xiou sensed Ivy's hesitance. "We are hunters too, Hiranah," he said. "You keep forgetting that what we fear most, will always find us. You cannot hide the truth from us forever."

Ivy sighed. The man was too perceptive.

"Soon after the time I come from, the Hiranthah will probably all be gone." Ivy admitted. "*Extinct.*"

"Another People of the Forest extinct?" Xiou repeated. "Like us again." His mouth twisted into a frown. "And why is that?"

Ivy struggled with an explanation. "It's very complicated. Things are very different in the future; there are many Karathah. More than you could ever imagine, all across the earth. The trees have to be cut down so the Karathah can grow other plants that can make the food we eat." Ivy edged around the concept of agriculture; again the contradiction of interfering in certain aspects of this hunter gatherer society but not others, seemed absurd. Especially now that she was committed to keeping them alive. Everything Ivy told them had the potential to break down their way of life irreparably, or build it into something entirely new. "When the trees are taken away, the Hiranthah lose their homes," she continued. "On the ground they have no place to hide from Karathah and so they are killed." Ivy watched Xiou and Kora's faces closely, waiting for a reaction. She refused to let her own memory wander to the images that haunted her, of orange corpses on bare, scorched earth that stretched as far as the eye could see.

"Surely not so many trees are cut down?" countered Kora. "There is no sense in that; animals need trees. The earth needs trees. Even the Karathah need the earth to survive." Guntah and Setian slowed down to join the conversation.

"There is not much sense in any of it," Ivy admitted. "But the Karathah have other things that are more important to them than trees and animals." *Money*. Ivy dismissed the thought immediately. Explaining even the broadest points of economics definitely fell into the category of 'too far'.

"Still, if these trees are cut down, why kill the Hiranthah? The Karathah must simply find them new homes." Guntah nodded sagely, as if his own logic was impenetrable. "They are people after all. *People of the forest.*"

Ivy sighed. "Do the Karathah care about finding you a new home, Guntah? Or do they simply want you gone so they can take what you have?" The hunter's shoulders tensed. "The Karathah want the land but not the animals who live on it," Ivy continued. "Animals are not hunted to be eaten for food, nor are they spared because they are so much like us. By many, the Hiranthah are seen as pests. With the trees gone, they become hungry, so they eat Karathah food instead. Because of that, they are killed. I wish it wasn't so."

Ivy suddenly felt bone-achingly tired. Somehow, she was here, with people long lost in her own time, discussing the fate of a species that would follow them to extinction fifty thousand years later.

Homo floresiensis. Orangutans. Ivy could name two dozen other species without even trying. How many countless more? All lost to the insatiable appetite of *Homo sapiens.* Hungry for land, food, money, power.

Xiou had fallen silent, his scarred face jigsawed with grief. "Who will fight for them?"

Ivy squeezed his hand. "I tried, Xiou. Many others are trying and will always do so. Not all of the Karathah consider them worthless. I know some people who will fight for them to the very end of their lives." Liam Kent's face flashed before Ivy's eyes. She felt a lonely rush of affection. It seemed a lifetime ago that he had stood with her at rallies as she painted the horrors of environmental destruction to a swelling crowd. Ages since Liam had led the marching protestors through the streets of Melbourne. It had been barely a month ago.

This time, Kora spoke up. "Hope is not lost for the Hiranthah then, if there are people willing to fight."

"Perhaps," said Ivy.

"You fought for them. Now fight for us. We will survive," Kora said, resolutely. "The Hiranthah will survive too."

Ivy couldn't reconcile such blind faith. "You know I will try to save you, Kora, but you can't have hope in me alone. You need to learn to save yourselves. You need to fight back."

"I am always ready to fight," Kora grinned.

"Good," said Ivy. "Never underestimate your strength to change the ways things are. Your size may be small compared to the Karathah, but if you fight together you are large. You don't have to fight with spears to survive, but with your decisions. Be clever about it. Never give up." Ivy looked between Xiou and Kora, two of the best hunters the tribe had. They were invaluable to Ivy's plans. "Even when it feels impossible," Ivy said, "You have to trust that these struggles do make a difference. Otherwise, you invite a more dangerous enemy than the Karathah into your lives."

"And what is that?"

Ivy stopped walking and turned to face them. "Apathy." Her eyes flashed. "The people who do nothing – who just accept cruelty and embrace ignorance because the struggle doesn't affect their own lives – they are really your worst enemy. Indifference affects everyone, eventually. Cruelty multiplies under a blind eye. The people that do nothing hold real power in the world. So they are the ones you need to prove your humanity to. Stir them up. Ignite their hearts. Make them act." Ivy squeezed Kora's hand in solidarity, then turned, to continue walking. "Fight against apathy. That is how you change the world."

They continued in silence for several minutes.

With an almighty screech, Kyah suddenly dropped from above.

Broken, her hands signalled urgently. *Ground broken.*

The hobbits froze, passing a critical look between them. Instinctively they backed together, each facing outward to greet potential danger. Ivy's grip tightened on her own spear.

"I smell it," Setian whispered.

"Move!"

The ground shuddered beneath their feet, groaning as foundations shifted deep under the earth. Chunks of rock split from the ridge above and smashed down, splintering into shards that tore at Ivy's bare legs. She leapt away, into the tree beside her and clung to its trunk. The hobbits dissolved into the trees as a cacophony of birds screeched to the sky. Distant bellows echoed across the broken land as stegodon rose in fear.

Ivy tried climbing higher but her toes slipped on the smooth trunk. She slid painfully back. Splinters stabbed beneath her nails as she grappled for friction, heaving herself into the first junction of branches. Leaves and sticks rained to the ground. Kyah was already high above, screeching and pointing to the south. The branch cracked as the bonobo jumped. She was clearly desperate to tell Ivy what she saw. Kyah curled her strong toes around the branch leaving her arms free, then quickly brought her fists together, snapping them apart again. She repeated the sign over and over until she was sure Ivy understood.

Broken. Broken. It was an earthquake like Ivy had never experienced.

She sucked in her breath, terrified, then forced herself further upward into thinner branches. Stretching out onto the limb that already held Kyah, Ivy ripped leaves from her view. A massive chasm had split the valley below like a wound. It ran north toward their ridge, then doglegged east in the direction they were traveling. Its gaping centre was black. From above, the forest was a picture of devastation. The wretched stench of sulphur stung Ivy's eyes. She doubled over in a fit of coughing, clinging to the overburdened branch.

The sky grew dark as if a blanket had been cast over the sun. Beyond the chasm, the volcano Inielika spewed black smoke and ash into the sky. Rivers of molten lava gushed from the crown of the volcano and disappeared down into the chasm the earthquake had borne at its feet. Ivy crawled backward, choking. For a few minutes, she clung to Kyah in the knot of branches as the earth rumbled and belched. Finally, the aftershocks settled. She was still alive.

"This place is a nightmare." Ivy dropped heavily to the ground. Kyah and the others were already waiting for her.

"The earth speaks louder every day," Gihn said. He gingerly lowered himself onto a fallen rock and rubbed his face in his hands. Blood dribbled down the side of his arm. Ivy could tell the old man was exhausted. Although he brushed off her concern, she had noticed the grimace of pain and stiffness his bones carried whenever they stopped and started.

"The earth is split in two, ahead of us," Ivy said. "But we have to pass through that valley to reach the coloured lakes. Or at least, what's left of it."

"It will be more dangerous now," Setian said. "It's going to slow us down." Ivy's heart sank. This was the last thing they needed.

"Come on then." With a resigned sigh, the group of travellers began to pick their way through the mess of undergrowth. They descended east from their rifted trail, and set out into the southern forest valley. As they grew closer to the chasm, the smell of sulphur intensified. Broken trees littered the ground and an unnatural silence hung in the air. After an hour, the tail end of the massive tear in the earth was ahead of them, snaking its way across the valley toward Inielika volcano.

Kora shivered and Ivy offered her a falsely confident smile.

"I think we're safe," Ivy said, taking her hand.

Kora reflexively turned away from the broken earth. "It smells like death," she said, with a grim expression.

Ivy knew it wasn't death itself that had Kora anxious. The woman was a hunter – death was a daily part of her life. This was something else altogether. A sense of foreboding, perhaps.

Ivy squeezed Kora's hand, then let go. She picked her way toward the chasm, determined to look inside. Her companions stayed behind, content to wait in the forest fringe away from the carnage. Only Kyah was beside Ivy, picking her way carefully through the rubble.

"Holy–" Ivy clamped her hand over her nose to diffuse the wretched smell. "Wow," she said against the muffle. "So many dead things." The very tip of the chasm tail at her feet was only about six foot deep, but tumbled with loose rocks and branches. Further ahead, the back fill disappeared and there seemed to be nothing but dark, empty space inside. Beneath the debris, the earth was littered with dead birds, snakes and marsupials that had been crushed by falling rocks and branches. In the corner of her eye, Ivy noticed a flutter.

"Oh no, poor baby." A small bird was trapped under a heavy rock, the right side of its body crushed. It was golden orange across the chest, with sky blue wings and a saffron coloured head banded with a black line beneath its eye. The little creature was stunning.

Cinnamon-banded Kingfisher, Ivy guessed, recalling the classification chart she'd once created, now lost inside her journal. Microscopic bits of feather were often recovered from archaeological digs, either bound to prehistoric quivers or scraped across butchering tools. For the most part, Ivy could identify them to genus level at least under her microscope. But that was in a cold, sterile laboratory. Here, with the little bird's heart pulsing in its soft feathered chest, species made no difference.

Its left wing trembled. The poor creature flapped in a pitiful attempt to free itself.

With utmost care, Ivy removed the rock. The right wing was badly broken and there was a deep gash into its ribcage. It simply couldn't survive. The twig-like toes of both feet skewed off at unnatural angles.

Ivy gently picked the bird up and cradled it in her palm, like a tiny pile of warm, breathing satin. It blinked terrified eyes, panting with pain. The bird lifted its head ever so slightly and let out a shrill call.

"I'm so sorry sweetheart," Ivy whispered. She gently stroked the feathered chest with her thumb. A tear dropped onto the amulet at Ivy's wrist. "Some things I just can't fix." She took a deep breath and closed her eyes, but try as she might, Ivy's hands just wouldn't work. She took another breath, watching it struggle for its own. There was nothing humane in watching it suffer. With the weight of guilt in her gut, Ivy quickly snapped the little bird's neck.

With a shriek, Kyah fell upon her from behind, knocking Ivy roughly onto the chasm's edge. The dead bird flung from her hand into the rubble.

"What the hell–" Ivy began, but the words caught in her throat. From the tattered west edge of the forest, a dozen enormous birds were bolting toward them, screeching. Each one spread its nine-foot wings menacingly. Bald heads and legs were flecked with blood. Tatters of flesh hung from their beaks. Even together, she and Kyah were no match for the beaks and claws.

"Find Xiou!" Ivy pushed Kyah back toward the forest where she hoped the hunters were paying attention. She spun back around, alone. *Not anymore.* She was surrounded. "Get away!" Ivy screamed, flapping her arms wide, hoping she looked more imposing than she felt. She grappled for the spear tied behind her shoulder. The giant storks leered over her, lurching forward in bursts, as if trying to decide how much of a threat she really was. They were deadly opportunists. Carnivorous. But Ivy was larger than their usual fare. The closest stork cocked its head to the side, staring down at her with an unblinking eye for what seemed eternity. Then its head dropped to the ground and reappeared with the limp body of the little Kingfisher clutched in its beak.

Ivy felt an insane urge to protect the tiny, feathered body, then thought better of it. All at once, the thick legs of the storks began to claw the upturned soil around her. *They want carrion,* Ivy realised. Fresh meat littered the valley. This lot were claiming their prize. The thief with its Kingfisher quarry turned and bolted. The remaining five storks clattered their beaks in warning, jabbing toward Ivy. Strips of fabric tore from her clothes, shredding her singlet. Ivy threw her hands in the air.

"You idiots!" Ivy yelled. "I'll be naked!"

Ivy lunged for one of the birds with her spear. A beak tore at her arm as she missed. "Get away!" She spun around, spraying blood. The giant birds scuffled and circled in tighter.

"I'm not trying to steal your damned food!" Ivy screamed.

Ivy felt a *whoosh* of air behind her. A heavy *thud.* She swung back to see one of the birds crashing to the ground. A spear through its heart. In a mayhem of footfall, the other birds hissed and scattered, bounding for cover. One stork remained, rearing back to unfurl its wings over Kora. The tiny hunter fell under its shadow. A black eye glared down at Kora, now left defenceless but for her breathless, predatory glare. At only three-foot-tall, the hobbit woman was far easier prey than Ivy. Its beak clattered in macabre warning, then opened wide. It lunged. Kora ducked, grabbed a heavy rock from beside her feet and smashed it into the attacking bird's head. The stork dropped, stunned, in a crash of feathers.

"We'll leave this one," Kora said. "It deserves the headache it will have when it wakes up." She stepped around it, then clambered over the slain bird and used her foot to steady its chest. With a grunt, Kora retrieved her spear. "And I suppose this is dinner."

CHAPTER 9

NEIL

"*H*ere," Neil dragged a heavy pointed stick along the entrance to the cave. They'd cleared the rubble and flattened out the ground. It was a semi-sheltered cave was elevated and drier than the vegetation in the rainforest below. Six of Charat's men were waiting for instruction. Neil hoped actions would speak for themselves. He drew a large rectangle, a meter and a half across, then two lines radiating from one end in parallel strips. "This bit," he stood inside the rectangle and gestured with his hands. "We dig this out." He held his hands up, about thirty centimetres apart. "This deep. Nice and flat on the bottom." He knelt, picking up one of the rocks the men had been using to mine the copper. It was as big as his fist, with a nice point shaped into one end. Neil began to beat at the ground within the rectangle, chipping bits of the limestone and earth floor away and brushing it clean with his fingers. He looked up. "Come on then," he barked, "let's get it done!"

When the six had begun to carve out his fire pit, Neil left them to it. He would return to help soon, but first, there was something more important to do.

So far, Charat's men had proven strong and useful. Whether

they were too scared to disobey, or whether Charat had made a threat or promise on his behalf, Neil didn't know or care. In three days, they'd made huge progress. And tonight, on the eve of the fourth day, Neil hoped to solve not just one of his problems, but two.

"Atasi?" Neil was almost surprised at how gentle his voice sounded as he approached the young woman. A pang of guilt hit him as she jumped to her feet, lowering her eyes. He frowned. There were dark circles under her eyes and Neil had seen her startle like a frightened bird whenever Charat was nearby. Though the two other young women still laughed and joined the conversations of the party, Atasi was increasingly silent. Even the bright blue feathers in her hair seemed lifeless. "Will you help me?" Neil asked. He gestured to her to follow him. Atasi didn't move.

With wide eyes, she scanned the area for something, or *someone.*

"He's not here," Neil said, shaking his head. "Charat is gone. He's out hunting." His hand skittered across the air, trying to illustrate distance between himself and the red-beaded hunter. Atasi rarely did anything without Charat's approval. She didn't dare.

Her shoulders relaxed as she realised he was nowhere to be seen. She gave Neil a small nod. He gestured again for her to follow.

"Kalim," Neil explained as he walked. Whether the word meant *river* or *water* he still wasn't sure, but he'd been trying to pick up a few useful words every day to bridge the language divide between them. Atasi simply nodded and continued walking toward the river that lay a few hundred meters from their temporary camp. Neil surveyed the riverbank, then proceeded to pick his way across the water to a muddy bank further downstream. He gestured for her to follow. It had taken him an hour yesterday to find what he needed. Now, he was returning to claim his prize. "Here." Neil pointed to the clean mud. "Let me show you." Pushing the sleeves of his filthy business shirt up to his elbows, Neil crouched down. He'd left his shoes and socks at the cave. Though still felt tender-footed without them, his soles were toughening up. Every so often he took the opportunity to wash his shirt, but not often enough. He knew he stank. Humidity seemed to suck the sweat right out of his pores. Neil guessed he'd lost at least fifteen kilograms over the past month. He was hungry, but he felt stronger. Better balanced. He'd purged more than overhanging gut. Alcohol had long burned from his system and his head was clearer than it had been in years.

Barefoot and graceful, Atasi joined him at the edge of the river. Neil sank his fingers into the thick grey clay at his feet. He was just above the waterline, where the clay was still wet enough to make the ceramic dish he needed.

"Like this." Neil drew a large handful of clay from the edge of the river. He placed it on a rock by his feet and carefully began to smooth it out. "You see, we're going to make a few cups and maybe some bowls," he said, looking up at her. Atasi was watching him with a concerned look on her face. "I probably look infantile right now," Neil said, deciding to speak aloud for the sake of it. "But you'll see why I'm doing this in a few minutes." It was the closest to a normal conversation he could get with anyone given the language barrier, so Neil decided he may as well just talk to himself. His pretense of being a dangerous and intimidating God wasn't necessary with Atasi. He knew that *she knew*. She'd figured him out quickly. He was just a man. A lost, desperate one at that. She even pitied him for it. With no witnesses, Neil decided to drop the act. He was left with a vulnerability that made his skin feel too hot. He hadn't felt that since he was a child.

Neil fumbled with the clay, pushing his fingers inside to form a concave shape while keeping the base flat on the rock.

"If we just add some water," he dipped his fingers in the river and the cool grey clay slipped and reformed beneath them, "it's easier to shape. This isn't really my thing – pottery – but I thought you might like doing it. You can make some cups or something to use instead of those filthy bladders we drink out of." Neil held up the finished cup. It was basic, slightly misshapen, but it would work. He held it carefully in his hand, supporting the base, then dipped it into the river to scoop up water. It held. Neil let it tip back out. He repeated the action, pretending to tip the water into his mouth. "You see – *a cup.* I'll fire it in the pit. We'll make it nice and hard so it will hold water for longer without collapsing. But for now, you just make a few more of these and we'll take them with us." He looked up.

Wonder shone in the young woman's eyes. Her hesitant fingers rose toward the cup, and she met Neil's eyes with a question.

"Yes, you can touch it," he nodded. He placed the clay cup in her hand. Atasi held it almost reverently, her face lit with a genuine smile. Neil had never seen her smile like that. It was breathtaking.

"*Acup,*" she repeated quietly.

"That's right. I shouldn't be showing you this of course," Neil frowned. "Your lot aren't meant to make these for another forty thousand years or something. But I need a new container for my battery charger – all those little skulls broke – so I thought I may as well show you while I was at it." He pointed to the long strings of blue feathers that hung from her hair. "You like making nice things. I thought you might like the artistry of it, you know." He shrugged, nodding at cup, "I mean, they're not much to look at, but they're usable."

Atasi held her free hand out and carefully, gently, touched Neil's arm. He froze, surprised. No one had touched him in months, other than to threaten his life.

"Shivu," she said. Still smiling.

Neil couldn't help the rush of warmth to his chest. That rare smile was for him.

"You're welcome."

With a quick grin and a nod, Neil set about gathering more clay. He would need a few big handfuls for himself this time. Lumping them in front of his feet, he began to shape out his idea. He needed something to replace the crushed rat skulls, and it had occurred to him that if he could shape what he needed out of clay, it would be sturdier, more compact, and easier to travel with. He began with a rectangular shape, bringing the sides of the bowl up a few centimetres to hold the mashed fruit he used to conduct voltage.

Surreptitiously, he watched Atasi gather her own lump of clay, experimenting with shaping it, as Neil had done. She had placed his cup back on the flat rock and was trying to replicate it. The corner of her lips were turned up in a small, distracted smile as she worked. Her eyes were shining.

Good. She deserves a few moments of happiness, Neil thought. *Barely ever smiles anymore. Not since Charat's been lording it all over her.* Anger set solidly in Neil's gut. *Vile bastard. If I didn't need him so much...* A pang of guilt hit him as he thought of the daily abuse Atasi was subjected to by the red-beaded hunter. Gnawing frustration settled deep inside. Charat was ruthless. A rapist. A killer. Neil knew he was good as dead himself, the moment he lost his usefulness to the hunter. Neil dropped his gaze and got back to work.

Lumping more clay beside him, Neil began to smooth a series of dividers inside the rectangular bowl. Two rows of five chambers apiece, like something akin to a ceramic egg carton. He found a stick and pressed it on flat on the top of the narrow dividing walls between the chambers, forming grooves for his zinc alloy watch links and copper bracelet chunks to hang over. Each metal connection would touch the fruity mash either side of its divider. The ten chambers would then serve as a series of battery cells. The citric acid of the fruit he had brought with him provided just enough electric current to keep the phone charged. Like everything else, it wasn't perfect, but it worked. By the time he had finished moulding his battery bowl, Atasi had made a handful of cups. They were much better than Neil's had been.

"Great work," Neil nodded. "I knew you'd have a knack for it. Artists hands." The woman glowed under his praise. Though she could not have understood, Neil's encouragement was clear.

"Let's make a couple of bigger ones too, what do you think?" Neil set his finished charging bowl aside and reached for some more clay. "I need a big bowl, to squash my battery fruit in. And something for you to cook those soups in that you like so much, hey?" With a wink, Neil began to shape out a replica of his cup, only bigger and wider. Quickly assessing his intentions, Atasi gathered some more clay and followed suit. Her neat bowl was finished first.

Stacking up their collection of soft pottery, Neil and Atasi picked their way back across the river and through the forest.

It was time to build a kiln.

The fire pit was deep and long, just as Neil had ordered. While the men stood back, Neil got on his hands and knees in the dirt. He needed moulds for the melted copper to fill. Moulds for his lightning rods.

He scraped at the earth with a sharpened rock, digging two long parallel lines from the edge of the pit along the rocky ledge of the cave mouth. The further away, the lower each strip ran into the earth and the wider it flared. At its widest point, each rod was no more than two centimetres, but each was two meters long.

If his plan worked, he could cut each of the two thin copper rods into half, each section a metre long. Neil had decided that it would be impossible to travel the thick jungle with anything longer, so he would create four seperate lengths instead, and strap them together while he walked, carrying them like a walking stick in his fist. Once the metal was cast, Neil planned to thin one end of each rod by beating it, and hollow out the other, slightly thicker end, so that they would fit inside one another like nesting pegs. When the time came, he could then connect them one on top of the other to form a lightning rod that would rise 4 meters into the air. Neil had no idea when or *how* he might create the opportunity to use it, but he did know he couldn't get home without lightning, or an amulet. So he had to be prepared.

It had taken Neil three full days to figure out how to not only smelt the copper he needed, but to then shape its liquid form into rods. Finally, he had engineered a structure that he thought might just work. It was a gamble, and the extreme temperature he needed to melt the copper *and* fire the pottery could combust the very materials supporting them in the flames. He could lose his hard-won copper by attempting to melt it. But he had no choice. He was about to succeed or fail on a spectacular scale.

Over the prior three days, Charat's men had gone from hunters to miners. From dawn until dusk, they had hacked and scraped at the limestone cradling the native copper, digging the metal out in strips and chunks with stone mauls. They had done well and there was plenty. Enough to fill the moulds as well as a bit left over.

Charat annoyed at their delay. He was still edgy, watching the proceedings with a suspicious eye. He didn't understand exactly what Neil was up to, and his cooperation had come at a price. Neil had promised Charat a new weapon. But with the plentiful supply of copper Neil now had at his disposal, it was a price he was willing and able to pay. Neil was about to bring Bronze Age technology to a Stone Age tribe.

While the men had mined, Neil had crafted a bellows. He'd

sacrificed his sleeping hide to craft the soft leather casing, which was a risk that left him cold and exposed at night. But there was no other way. The potential benefit far outweighed the loss.

Thin leather strips, sewn into punctured holes, bound the hide tightly to two flat boards. He stripped lengths of a branch back to create the two crude boards, shaped like long paddles, with enough length to leave short handles beyond the hide bag itself. Neil had fashioned a rudimentary valve into one of the paddles by grinding a coin-sized hole into it. He stitched his leather hide to its inner surface, leaving one side open. The remainder of the hide was then shaped, wrapped, and stitched by thin hide strips sewn into punctured holes. Neil sewed the hide between the two paddles, with enough material to allow them to be pulled apart and pushed back together by the handles. As the paddles of his hide bag were pulled open, air was sucked inside the make-shift valve, filling the bellows up like a balloon. As he forced the paddles to collapse together again, the inner valve would close and flatten out, the leather flap compressed against the inside of the board with the pressure of the air rushing past it, forcing a gust of air through a front hole instead. Fitting the leather around the backside of the bellows was difficult. Neil folded and stitched the thick material until it was as airtight as possible. His fingers were bruised and calloused and hurt like hell. Neil looked at the crude instrument with pride. The bellows had taken him the best part of three days to build, and while it was primitive and ugly, the contraption was critical. Without the ability to fuel the base of the bonfire with oxygen, there was no way he would get it hot enough to melt the copper. Like every-thing else he had made, it wasn't perfect, but it would work.

With the long, thin moulds for his lightning rods etched into the rock, Neil set about building a kiln.

"Atasi." He called her over, gesturing to the pile of pottery. "We're putting this in first, down the bottom of the pit, see? It will cook under the fire and get nice and hard so it will hold the water." Neil knew he was wasting his breath by explaining but spoke anyway. On some level, she might understand his intentions. That was enough.

"Here, help me," he gestured. Together, they layered the soft pottery in the empty space of the pit. "Now our base boards. You," he gestured to one of the men, "come with me." Neil backed off, stepping into the hollow of the cave and re-emerging holding one end of a nearly flat slab of rock. Together, they placed it across the width of the pit, then returned for another. Soon, there was a serviceable floor for the bonfire. Underneath, the kiln pit would be protected from shifting wood.

Half an hour later, a pile of kindling and solid, slow-burn branches nearly reached his own height.

"Right, you lot, let's get some wood." He led the men down into the forest.

Neil pulled his silver lighter from his pocket. It licked into flame.

"And now, *the fire.*"

"More oil!" Neil shouted above the roar. "It needs more oil!"

With raw skin and stinging eyes, Neil dashed forward to throw lashings of oil from a bladder onto the huge bonfire at the cave mouth. His eyes danced in the orange flames. With each flick, the fire roared. The oil was highly flammable with a pungent scent. Neil had seen the women making it back at their cave, though he didn't know what plant supplied it. They had crushed pale green berry-sized nuts, pressing them until the oil within leached out in quantities high enough to store. Each night, one of Charat's men would soak plant fibres in the stuff to wrap around a palm frond, then set it alight. It made a good torch. But Neil needed something much bigger than a torch tonight. He needed a miracle of pure destruction. A fire hot enough to melt metal. This oil was precious stuff, apparently, and Neil was using far more than their daily ration. But the result was magic.

Flames clawed fiercely around the great skull sitting on a platform of rock to one side of the bonfire. The skull was inverted, turned upside down like a bowl. Neil guessed it had once been the cranium of a stegodon. The women used the skull daily for cooking, but Neil had seen its potential for a different use. Bright copper chunks were now piled high on top of the bone above the heart of the fire. It was all of the copper that they had recovered from the cave wall.

Neil knew he could get the bone to 1100 degrees delicious before it charred and disintegrated. The native copper would melt only slightly below that heat. The difference could be a matter of minutes. *I've gotta make this work.* The dread of failure urged Neil to rid his mind of the possibility. *It has to work.* Smokey, putrid air filled his lungs. *I need that lightning rod. I want that battery bowl.* His white shirt was tied tight around his nose and mouth as he darted, bare chested in front of the flames. *Lightning rod. Battery bowl.* The objects he desired felt sacred. *This is creation.* Sweat stung his eyes. But Neil couldn't look away.

On the forest edge below, Charat and his men hollered and danced, drawing energy from the chaos. They had full bellies and superstitious hearts. Red sparks and pulsing heat flicked up into the air around them. Neil hoped whatever God they prayed to might hear his own desperation above the discord – *I need this to work. Make it work. Please –*

Neil's plan was simple. Melt and shape the copper, before the skull bowl was destroyed losing its precious contents to the flames. With a wheezing hiss that he could barely hear over the roar, Neil fanned the fiery heart with his bellows. Smokey air sucked inside the leather bag. He squeezed the handles shut again and again, forcing oxygen into the birthing centre of flames. A bud of iridescent blue emerged inside a nest of pure white flames. Neil whooped with joy. It was hot enough. But he couldn't get close to it. Walls of yellow, orange, and red wheeled and stabbed the night air. He stared, piercing the flames with an agonising gaze that left his eyeballs dry. After minutes that felt like eternity, a single drop of liquid copper dripped from the hole he had drilled in the base of the skull. Sizzling, it was joined by another, and another, until a thin trickle of red snaked its way down the first of the long thin moulds that Neil had carved into the rock. It grew longer as it filled, like a ray of sunshine bleeding out of the sun. Gravity led the liquid to the deepest point in the strip, then it backfilled as it cooled and hardened, inch by inch, drawing its way back home to the flames. Neil's heart hammered. His blood pressure soared. *The bloody thing is working.*

The liquid began to pool at the top point, then finding its path now blocked, spilled across into the second hollow strip instead. Bit by bit, the copper crawled into line again, filling up the second groove just as Neil had planned. Soon it was full, a second thin, glowing line of metal.

One by one, two more moulds were thrust under the skull's drainage hole before it emptied. The shallow shape of two small, pointed daggers carved out of flat bedrock. Charat's payment. Above them, the skull blackened with char, its powdery edges breaking away as the last drops of copper drained from its belly. With a crack and sigh, the bone collapsed into the ash below, finally engulfed by the fire's heart. It had disintegrated, but not before giving Neil the prize he craved.

Liquid, malleable metal. Shaped.

His way home forged.

The lightning rods were cast.

CHAPTER 10

ORRIN

"*W*hat the hell is this, Orrin? Are you out of your god-damned mind? Do you want to get us all fired? And ARRESTED?"

Phil stood over Indah, who cradled baby Bala in the corner of Orrin's office. As Orrin approached the doorway, Indah screeched to him. Tears shone in the hobbit's eyes. Orrin could see her thin muscles ready to spring. Even in her wretched state, she could probably make short work of Phil. Bala's tiny face crumpled and he began a high-pitched wail, burying himself into his mother's hair.

"That's enough!" Orrin rushed between them, his hands open. "Step away, Phil. She's been through enough!"

Phil glowered but stepped back.

"What the fuck, Orrin?"

"Of all the bloody days to turn up early!" Orrin fumed, glaring at Phil. "I had to do it! They've all been taken by Nerov– the other hobbits, all of her children. This baby is all she has left, and they'll be back for it next, you know they will! You know as well as I do what they do to them in the pharmaceutical labs, Phil. I had to get her out of there." Orrin lowered his voice and hands carefully. "I just – I didn't expect you here so early. I was going to explain."

"You'd better damn well explain or I'm calling Thandi right now. What the hell were you thinking? They're university property. You can't just steal them!"

"You shouldn't have done this Orrin," Dale whispered from the doorway. "*Really*. It was a bad move." His face was paler than usual with dark rings under his eyes. Orrin turned to face him, guarding Indah defensively.

"How can you say that Dale? You know better than anyone that these hobbits shouldn't even be here, *now, on this earth*, let alone being used as lab rats under the management of someone like Nerov. They're sitting ducks in that biology lab – it's only a matter of time until he sells them to the highest bidder." Behind Orrin, Indah relaxed her stance slightly. She sat, cautiously, pulling Bala down to rest on her lap. "Look at her," Orrin said. "She's not an animal and you know it!"

Dale dropped his eyes to the floor. "Maybe." He turned and sat in a swivel chair, rubbing at an imaginary spot on his knee. "But they're not our responsibility. I've been telling you that all along. This situation is so much bigger than all of us, it's bigger than you and it's sure as hell bigger than me. There's a lot a stake here, Orrin." Dale's eyes flicked over the whiteboard and lab equipment but refused to meet Orrin's.

"What do mean, *there's a lot at stake?*" Orrin's voice cut like ice. His heart skipped a beat. He'd heard that phrase before.

Dale frowned. "Nothing, it's nothing Orrin – I just mean we can't go all vigilante and start saving these hobbits one by one. Please, just listen to me for once. We need to fix the entire situation – recreate the time vortex and then put things right. That's all I meant."

The lump in Orrin's throat refused to go away. Phil stepped away from the hobbit woman and Orrin held out his hand, helping her up from the ground. "It's okay Indah, they won't tell anyone you're here." He shot a reproach to each man in turn. "I can't move her in daylight. It's too risky. But they'll be gone at nightfall, so if you can manage to shut up about it until then there's no problem, is there?"

Dale hunched in front of his computer under a cloud of disapproval. He didn't touch the keyboard, but instead watched intently as Phil continued to berate Orrin.

"You're losing your mind." Phil moved away from the office door, where the hobbit woman had settled in her usual corner. Orrin was handing her a new bag of food from the cafeteria. Indah pulled the sandwiches and fruit out the bag carefully before peeling the orange rind. She began to feed the pulp to her baby.

"Phil, I need you to trust me. There's more to this than you understand."

"Why the hell should I trust you, Orrin?" Phil was furious. "You've just stolen lab animals from the university! You've almost had me fired already for teaching your bloody undergrad classes with no qualifications and you've lied outright to the Chancellor, the CSIRO, and the Australian Government. If we've truly created the energy surges within this laboratory and *if* we've screwed with the evolutionary history of the earth, then why, *why* on earth, shouldn't I tell the authorities? This situation is way bigger than we can handle. If I told the CSIRO what was really going on, I'd be doing you a damn favour! You obviously can't handle this!"

"No, Phil! Jaysus, we'd lose it all, wouldn't we!? The laboratory, the equipment, Ivy – and this woman–" Orrin gestured to Indah. "She'd lose her baby, Phil. She'd lose her *life*. Those experimental animals never survive! If she isn't kept alive for years for drug testing, she'll have some god-awful medical procedure done on her. The best she can hope for is to be euthanised sooner rather than later. I just couldn't leave them there, man. I just couldn't." Orrin sunk to the ground, shaking with emotion. He *hated* that he needed to justify his actions, he hated that he needed help. Saving Ivy – and now saving this woman and her baby, grew more dangerous with every person he confided in.

Phil's bottom lip curled in disgust. "She's an animal Orrin! You're risking everything for an animal. You're risking *my* god-damned job for that creature. You're a selfish son-of-a-bitch, you know that?"

Orrin knew he had no choice. Indah was human, but Phil couldn't see it. And why should he? Phil's entire life up to this point had led him to believe the woman in front of him had no humanity. No soul. No intelligence other than an instinctive need to consume, procreate and survive. *But she was so much more.* Orrin pulled the amulet out of his pocket and took a step forward, placing it solidly in the palm of Phil's hand. Behind him, Dale watched every move. *I need to trust them.* Orrin wished he could convince himself that his trust was well placed.

"Phil, please – come and meet Indah and her son Bala. Talk to her. I mean *really* talk to her."

Orrin's plans to take Indah and her baby home with him at nightfall were soon impossible. By mid-morning, the campus was crawling with security guards and Jayne phoned him to say she'd already been questioned. He stepped outside to take the call.

"They're watching me Orrin." Jayne's voice was low and Orrin could barely hear her over the noise of passing cars. It seemed she had left the residue lab to make the call. "Nerov suspects me. I can't see you anymore – at least not here; I don't want you involved." Orrin sighed. He was more than involved already. "There's another thing," Jayne hesitated. "My key is missing."

"Jayne, I–"

"No, *stop* – I don't want to know. If I don't know anything, then I can't tell them anything. As far as I'm concerned, I lost the key."

"Thank you."

"Also – *just in case you needed to know*–" Orrin noticed three security guards buying a coffee from the cafeteria. He turned away, pretending to watch the cascading glass fountain as he waited for Jayne to continue, his fingers sweaty around the mobile phone.

"Yes?"

"Well, the thing is that Liam's posted bail. Actually, *I* posted Liam's bail. He's been fired from the university of course, for what he did to that pharmaceutical building. But in case you need to contact him about – anything – I'm going to leave his phone number on your home phone answering machine, okay? I figured you could access that from here?"

"Of course. I appreciate that Jayne. And I'm really sorry you're implicated." Orrin sighed. "I didn't want that."

"I can handle it. And I should have confirmation of the skeletal DNA origin in the next 48 hours as well."

"Great, thanks. I'll talk to you soon."

The following five days dragged like an iron chain. He hadn't heard from Jayne and suspected she was being watched too closely to risk contact. To house Indah and Bala, he had refurbished his tiny lead-lined office with a makeshift toilet bucket and bed. It was little more than a jail cell despite his intention to give them freedom, but it had been too dangerous to move the hobbits again, even at night. Security personnel had doubled on campus. Additional cameras had been installed on the low lit walkways joining buildings. Although no one within the physics department were questioned about the theft, police notices requesting information had been emailed to all faculty staff and the gossip line buzzed. The more normal Orrin tried to behave, the more conspicuous he felt.

To her credit, Indah did not complain once and had been nothing but grateful for Orrin's attempts to provide comfort. She didn't speak unless necessary. Thankfully Phil had cooled, and his treatment of Indah seemed almost kind. He preferred not to speak directly with her, but on the occasions Orrin had insisted, Phil seemed respectful, even gentle. On their third night of hiding, Orrin had been surprised when Phil had even offered to take his place sleeping in the laboratory, a necessity Orrin had undertaken to keep the early-morning janitors at bay. Since then, Phil had also taken on the task of bringing food.

Orrin continued his data analysis by day, tracking the movement of the stars by night. If he was correct in his calculations, and he was sure he was, the lunar alignment predicted by the Floresian cave paintings would occur in less than two weeks. Only two weeks remaining until his final chance to save Ivy. The amulet was clearly important. He still didn't know why. Orrin had momentarily considered just placing the amulet within the strongest area of electromagnetic field and hoping for the best, but his scientific mind just couldn't reconcile not understanding the process. If it didn't work and he could have prevented it by understanding – *no*, that simply wasn't an option. That black elemental substance within the crystalline magnetite needed to be identified. To this end, Elijah Nnamani would be waiting for him in the geology department tomorrow morning at nine. Orrin fervently hoped that removing a tiny sliver of the stone for analysis wouldn't affect its abilities.

The laboratory felt claustrophobic and smelled like sweat and human waste. Everyone's nerves were frayed. Dale's mood began to ride the swinging tension in the room. None of the men were at ease with conspiracy. At times, Orrin could taste stress on his tongue, acrid and sharp. The three men arrived early and left after dark, feigning casual busyness when questioned by colleagues. The dark rings under their eyes told otherwise. The previous night, Phil had once again offered to stay as guard. Now, he looked worse for it.

"You're treating her like a pet." Dale tone was resentful.

"I am not. And at least I am acknowledging her Dale. You won't even look at her." Phil shut the inner office door behind him, leaving Indah in privacy to feed her baby one last time before the transfer. "I'm treating her the same way I treat you."

"With barely concealed intolerance?"

"With *respect*, you puerile pain in the arse."

"Yeah, right." Dale turned back to his screen. "Since when did you ever give a shit about hobbits? I know what you're doing. And I doubt she'll fall for it."

Phil towered over Dale's monitor, but Dale, refusing to acknowledge him, kept typing. Orrin looked up from the over-sized silver case he was gutting. Pieces of hard foam and telescopic equipment lay on the tables around him. He momentarily considered interceding, but the two men had been at each other for days now. Given the situation, Orrin himself was not sure he could interject without losing his temper again.

Phil wouldn't let it go. "In case you hadn't noticed Dale, Jayne's not even here. Christ dude, maybe if you pulled your head out of your arse, you might realise that the reason she doesn't see you, is because all you see is your own pathetic ego."

"And what's that supposed to mean?"

"It means what it means Dale, figure it out."

Orrin sighed. "Both of you give it a rest. It's nearly time. *Please* just hold it together. I know it this is a shite situation and we're all tired, but in a couple of hours Indah will be safely in Liam's hands and we can get back to business."

Phil sat heavily in his chair. "Maybe we shouldn't move them. What if Liam doesn't show?"

"He'll show." That was the only thing Orrin was convinced of at this point. "Liam said he has a contact that can transfer them to a sanctuary, no questions asked. He'd risk everything for them, I mean; he already has, hasn't he? That's why he can't come here."

"But moving them in broad daylight? Nope. I don't like it."

"That was your idea, Phil. And a bloody good one too." Orrin had drilled a series of air holes in the telescopic travel case on wheels he had just emptied. It was large enough for Indah and her baby to fit inside, albeit uncomfortably. Indah was feeding the baby now in anticipation of their move, hoping a full stomach would help keep him quiet. It wasn't a perfect plan but moving them during the day concealed in a telescopic case might just be bold enough to work. Phil had reasoned that the more obvious their movements, the less suspicions they would arouse. To add to the ruse, Orrin had brought in his largest computerized telescope from his personal collection at home. He had made a point of showing the instrument to some colleagues under the pretence of a new lunar study, making sure the large silver travel case he had now gutted was a familiar sight over the preceding days. "It's a good plan Phil. They'll only be in the case for fifteen minutes, twenty max. As soon as they're off campus, they'll be safe."

Dale left to get a round of coffees and Phil busied himself checking the astronomical data from the previous night. Another hour passed. It was finally time. All three men looked up at the sound of the inner office door opening. With a little trepidation, Indah entered the bright laboratory carrying Bala on her hip. She looked at each of them in turn. There was no smile on her face, Orrin thought, but there seemed to be a little hope. Perhaps she had saved her last child from the horrors of experimentation after all.

With the amulet between their palms, Indah said goodbye to Phil and then Orrin, while Dale looked on. Shushing her baby, she stepped into the open case and curled down, arranging their petite bodies in the most comfortable way she could. Her arms were wrapped tight around Bala's back and his little body clung to her chest. He looked up at Orrin standing over them with wide eyes. *Good luck, little one.* Orrin turned the metal lid over, preparing to latch it on.

The entrance door slammed back against the wall. Two men burst into the room.

Stepping past them, Nerov motioned grimly to Orrin.

"Step away from the case, Dr. James." Terror rose in Orrin's chest. Behind Nerov, more uniforms crowded the hallway.

"You can't take her Nerov." Orrin laced his voice with as much conviction as he could find. "I won't let you." His fist gripped the metal lid tightly. He couldn't fight them all, but he considered trying. "This woman is not an animal. Her name is Indah and she understands what you're doing. She deserves better than this!"

"What she deserves is irrelevant! I've explained this before. She has no rights, Dr. James." Nerov didn't move, but his intentions were clear. He was here to do a job, regardless of how it got done. "This female and her offspring are no longer university property. They belong to Cosmitech. Now move away."

"No."

Without hesitation, two security guards and a uniformed officer pushed past Nerov into the laboratory. Orrin planted himself between Indah and the men and was momentarily buoyed to find Phil stepping in beside him. The burly officer forced Orrin out of the way as the guards pushed past Phil. They seized Indah under the arms, lifting her out of the metal case with Bala still clinging to her belly. Indah screamed, writhing under their tight grip as fright and anger exploded within her. She ripped one arm free from the police officer. With her free arm supporting her baby, she lashed out, biting the man's wrist. He fell back, clamping the parabolic stem of blood that sprung from his skin.

Phil lurched forward, trying to pull the second officer away as Indah swung wildly. Although she was no taller than a five-year-old child, her strength was formidable. Wasted muscles on her arms flexed and the officer stumbled, losing grip. It was clear she could have handled one of the men on her own. But not three. Phil threw himself into the fray. With white knuckles, he broke the guards grip from the hobbit's arm, throwing the man onto a desk. With a solid punch, Phil's fist caught the guards' face.

"Run Indah!" yelled Phil, although Indah could neither have understood, nor complied. She was surrounded and the doorway was blocked.

The tremulous hope Orrin had built up in her over the previous five days disintegrated, cascading into violent grief. Orrin pushed the bitten officer away as he regained his footing, but the second security guard had already leapt past, pulling Indah's free hand aside, leaving Bala hanging. They brought their own arms high, pulling Indah's feet from the ground. With no stability or power, she screeched as the bitten guard pulled shrieking Bala from her chest. The infant boy wailed, reaching for his mother as she struggled. Orrin and Phil shouted furiously as they tried to free her. For a moment, Indah caught Orrin's eye. Pure desperation fuelled her struggle to reach her stolen baby.

A tranquilliser dart landed squarely in her middle. Indah crumpled, gasping on the linoleum amongst a sea of boots. Bala wailed pitifully, and the bleeding officer who held him passed him to the nearest guard. The man pushed his way out of the room clutching the infant around the waist, holding him away from his own body. Little arms grappled at air as the baby twisted, shrieking, searching for the safety of his mother's arms.

Nerov lowered the dart gun and handed it to the second guard. Without a word, he stepped forward, removed the empty dart from Indah's belly, then picked her up. As he turned to leave the room, he stopped before Orrin, who sank into a chair, breathing pained stabs of despair.

"I hope you understand what you've done here, Dr James," Nerov said. "All you've accomplished, is to make it that much harder for the female. Separation would have been easier without the theatrics, for me, for you and for her."

"You can't do this." Orrin pleaded. "It's not right. You *know* that."

"*I'm* not doing it." Nerov shifted the weight of Indah's unconscious body in his arms. "Your government is. *The people are.*"

And he left.

CHAPTER 11

IVY

"They've been murdered in their cave, just like the others." Ivy took a deep breath and squeezed her eyes shut, forcing back tears. It was horrible, *terrible* to imagine how this poor tribe had come to such a grisly end, but more than that – Ivy's own disappointment was palpable. She was losing hope.

They had scoured the Soa Basin for a week, to no avail. And this – the area surrounding the archaeological site of Dozu Dhalu, had held the final promise of finding *Homo floresiensis* people alive in the area. They had found first a short spear in some shrubs to the north as they travelled toward it. Then scattered stone tools by the riverbed below the cave. Above, nestled amongst shrubbery was the telltale shadow of a cave mouth. The sun was fading. Buoyant with hope, the travellers had nearly raced up the side of the mountain.

And found genocide.

"*The Karathah,*" Guntah spat. His mouth was twisted in anger. He crouched down, reverently touching the side of a face that looked so similar to his own but was entirely unfamiliar. "This can't have been more than three days past. We were so close."

Ivy's mouth trembled. This was much worse than the dry

bones they had found north of Boa Leza. These corpses still had faces, almost three dozen of them. Men and women. The attack must have caught them by surprise, as only a few had taken up arms, their plentiful weapons still stowed at hearths within the confines of their cave. Those that had held weapons were the furthest from the cave mouth. Lookouts, perhaps, that had not made it back with enough time to raise the alarm.

For long minutes, the travellers sat in devastation, staring at the bodies of those they had been searching for.

"Why?" Kora whispered. "What could possibly justify such horror?"

Ivy looked at her, unable to offer an answer. *It might have been retribution for something they did,* she thought, *or simply because their territory infringed on the hunting trails of the bigger species.* The population of modern sapiens on the island was expanding. More people meant more food needed to feed them. Perhaps this hobbit tribe had simply found themselves in the way of the Karathah once too often.

Ivy looked across at Gihn. The old man did not wipe away his tears, but rather, let them fall as he moved resolutely to stand amidst the dead. He held out his arms and began a quiet chant.

It was Xiou who joined first, a low bass note, held long and steady against the still afternoon air. Guntah joined him, then Setian, their voices sliding into the harmonic clefts that Ivy hadn't realised were empty until they were filled. With a gentle sweeping release of his hands, Xiou raised his voice, a rich baritone that seemed to echo from deep inside. Kora, eyes closed, heart broken, joined the Dusk Song in an unwavering soprano. Their lungs emptied and refilled barely breaking note, the sound rolling from the earth to the sky in unending waves of grief. Ivy couldn't bear it. It was too beautiful to hear. Wretched with the loss of more lives and their unfulfilled potential, Ivy got to her her feet and began the only thing she could think of doing. One by one, she gathered up the bodies and carried them back into their cave. She lay the hobbits close beside one another, sheltered along the back of the cave, each head beside the next until a rainbow arc of souls lay at rest.

When she was done, Ivy left the mountain. Only Kyah followed her down the shrubbery and loose rocks, a silent sentinel by her side. After a short while, the bonobo disappeared into the forested gully at the base of the mountain. Ivy supposed she had gone in search of food. She had no appetite herself. Ivy sat by the river instead, letting grief wash her face as the water washed her feet, and the Dusk Song continued into the night.

Belching grey ash forced them onward the following morning as the ground once again began to rumble. Ivy had been up and ready to leave at sunrise. Kyah paced, anxious to find tree cover beyond the slated gullies. She had not returned until daybreak, so Ivy had spent a restless night by the river alone, as the hobbits kept their vigil. Now, Ivy wanted nothing more than to put the sadness and disappointment of Dozu Dhalu behind her and push on.

"Do we head south?" Kora asked. She turned away from the rising sun as it split across her face.

"Yes. I think it's best we leave this area," Ivy replied. "The Karathah that attacked them must be living nearby. Let's head further east, then turn south to look for the sea caves."

"The earth is more unsettled the further east we go," Gihn frowned. He pulled himself up straighter against his walking stick. Xiou had broken it off an uprooted tree the day before to aid his father's old bones on the difficult terrain. Gihn was finding the trek more tiring than Ivy had hoped.

"Yes, it is, and there are more mountains to pass before we get to the coast," Ivy said. *More volcanoes.* "But this is the way we must go. The caves by the sea might hide more of your people. We have no choice but to search them. Especially now." She threw a look over her shoulder at the hint of a shadow in the mountain. The loss of life stung, but it was anger, now, that settled within. These people were fighting a losing battle on so many fronts. If the hostile land didn't take them first, the Karathah would certainly do the job. Ivy took a resolute step. If they were going to all die, it wasn't going to be because she hadn't tried hard enough to save them. "Let's go."

"We're being tracked." It was Setian this time, who slid in beside Ivy as she walked.

"Is it the Karathah again?" She stiffened. Suddenly, the threat felt palpable.

"I don't know. They are keeping to the bushes." Setian's eyes were tight as he glanced back, considering the new threat. His fingers flexed around his bow.

Ivy chanced a look over her shoulder. She saw nothing but the tangle of vegetation that lined either side of the ravine. At its highest point, Ivy could have stood behind it, hunched and concealed. A Karathah hunter, trained from childhood to blend seamlessly into the environment, could have managed it more easily.

"There is no escape from this ravine but to continue forward or turn back," Setian murmured. "We will have to fight."

"I see." Adrenaline pooled in Ivy's veins. Setian was right, they were trapped. The sides of the ravine were far too steep to climb. The landscape had channelled them into a trap.

"Do the others know?" Each step Ivy took suddenly felt unnatural and stiff, despite her best efforts to appear unaffected.

"Of course," Setian said.

Ivy nodded. As always, she was the last to become aware of danger. Though her senses had improved, she had none of the instinctive intuition of her friends.

"Kyah," Ivy beckoned quietly, trying to keep the fear from her voice. But the bonobo was ahead of her, knuckle walking over sharp rocks with intense concentration. Kyah was finding the terrain as difficult as Gihn, and whenever the ground allowed it, Ivy carried her instead, to give Kyah's knuckles a chance to heal. Though she could travel across land, the bonobo was evolution-arily adapted to the trees. "Kyah!" Ivy called again, little louder. Her companion looked back at her expectantly. Ivy made the sign for *wait* and the bonobo complied, rising to her feet. *Danger*, Ivy signed, bringing her index fingers to the sky in a slight wave.

The bonobo snapped her fingers shut then copied Ivy's sign. *No – danger –*. She turned and continued on.

Ivy stumbled, a little stunned. Kyah had never ignored her directions before. It was usually the bonobo who sensed trouble first. But now she nonchalantly continued on her way, picking along the base of the ravine.

"Kyah!" Ivy dropped Setian's hand. "Come back!" She chased the bonobo, as fast as the uneven ground would allow. Behind her, Ivy heard the others call to one another. They had broken formation, no doubt reaching for their weapons. Whoever was watching them would plainly see now that they'd taken up arms.

Ivy grabbed Kyah's hand. "Danger!" She signed again. Kyah flicked her head to the side, brushing Ivy's hand away. *No – danger –* the bonobo signed.

Ivy couldn't hide her panic. Xiou, Setian, Kora and Guntah formed a tight half-circle around herself, Kyah and Gihn. The hunters' backs were to their friends, each holding a weapon raised to the path behind. Gihn took Ivy's wrist. His eyes were wary as he scanned the ravine.

"This is a bad place to fight," he muttered. "There is no cover. We need to continue further on to have a chance."

"Kyah won't stop moving," Ivy said. Again, the bonobo had pushed onward, ignoring the danger behind her.

"Then I suggest we keep moving with her."

"Go then," Xiou called over his shoulder. "We will follow you."

Ivy took a tentative step. A rustle in the bushes only meters behind, froze her feet. She spun back around. Someone was close. Far closer than she had expected. With narrowed eyes, Kora lifted her spear as Setian raised his bow, an arrow pulled taut in its sinewy string.

For a moment, only silence held it in place.

Kyah gave a sharp screech. Suddenly, the bonobo spun back, all nonchalance lost as she raced toward Ivy, her knuckles raw as she skidded across the sharp rocks. But protecting her friends was not Kyah's intention. She knocked Ivy and Gihn aside as she passed, then grabbed Setian's arrow, just as he was about to let it fly. The bonobo's strength and speed caught the others by surprise. Kora fell aside, her spear thudding mutely off course into the rock beyond them. She looked up at the bonobo in shock.

"Kyah!" Ivy rushed forward. Though Kyah was no taller than a child herself, the bonobo had four times the brute strength of a human man. And the hobbits, though far stronger than Ivy, were no match for her either.

With a shrill bark of anger, Kyah lifted her hand. *No – danger* – she signed again. Her head twitched sharply to the left, a nervous habit she had developed in her solitary infancy, that now only reared its head when she was stressed.

With years of abuse still etched in her memory, Ivy had earned Kyah's trust painfully slowly over many years in the behavioural research laboratory at the university. But now – it seemed the bonobo was angry with her. Kyah scratched her own chest, drawing blood from skin above her heart. Ivy didn't understand. They were in danger. Weren't they?

Kyah pushed past the hunters, her back to the wall of the

ravine. She seemed impervious to the threat of attack that grew each moment they hesitated.

No. Kyah's fingers flew through the scatter of dirt at Ivy's feet, tracing the lexicon Ivy had taught her years ago. *No.* She stood up, repeating the sign with her fingers. *No – danger –*

"What do you mean?" Ivy asked. Her heart was racing. There was another rustle in the bushes, this time further back. More than one person was trailing them. "We're being followed, Ky!" Ivy took a step away. Between them, Kora was scrambling to her feet. Her spear was just out of reach, laying against the cliff wall in a narrow break of vegetation. She slipped a knife from her travelling hide instead.

Kyah twisted toward Kora and barked a screech. A warning.

"Kyah!" Ivy growled. The bonobo's behaviour was beyond comprehension. She had never shown aggression to the hobbits. Ivy's gut twisted in concern. Something didn't sit right. Terrified of both their impending attackers and Kyah's unexplained behaviour, Ivy pushed her own fear down. She stepped forward, trying to allay the rising anger in her best friend.

"Put your weapons down," Ivy begged her travelling companions. "Please. Put them down now. We need to trust her." After a moment of hesitation, Xiou and Guntah lowered their spears. Setian let his bow hang by his side. With a scowl, Kora slipped her knife back into her belt. "Tell me, Ky," Ivy pleaded. "What's going on? Tell me what it is."

Kyah took a step back. She cast a suspicious look over each of her travelling companions, apparently to make sure none were about to strike. Then she turned and slipped back toward the bushes. She crouched at the edge of the foliage, hooting softly, one arm held out. For a moment, there was nothing.

Then wide, fearful eyes appeared between the leaves. Kyah hooted again, high and soft, as if coaxing someone out to join her. After a few moments of hesitation, a tiny hand took the bonobo's own, then the arm followed. Finally, the infantile body it belonged to, was revealed. It was a child – a *Homo floresiensis* child. A girl perhaps only five or six years old, the same size as Xiou's son Trahg, whom Kyah had grown so attached to back at Home Cave. The child's face was sallow and thin. Her eyes were framed with dark rings as if she'd had no sleep for days. Ivy felt Gihn's fingers close around the amulet on her wrist. The old man looked to her, clearly as astonished by the turn of events as Ivy was herself.

Ivy's breath caught in her throat. The girl wasn't alone. At the insistent, gentle encouragement of Kyah, at least a dozen more children appeared from behind various bushes trailing the ravine. They shuffled in close to Kyah, filling the spaces around her with tiny bodies. The girl who had appeared first twisted her fingers gently through the fine black hair on Kyah's head as she stood staring up at Ivy with scared eyes. She looked skittish, like a rabbit about to scarper, and only anchored to the spot by the presence of her new friend.

Kyah looked at Ivy, her head flicking reflexively to the left. Her muscles were relaxing, the anxiety slipping away. Kyah's long fingers lifted to her chest. *Baby,* she signed. *No – danger –*

"So that's where you disappeared to last night," Ivy said. Fear was rushing out of her, quickly replaced by wonder and a glimpse of understanding. "You found these children somewhere near the cave." Ivy did a quick headcount. There were sixteen of them, none more than two and a half feet tall, ranging from what she guessed were toddlers through to Leihna's age of perhaps twelve years. The oldest child, a dark-eyed girl with thick, wiry hair was holding a baby. Her childish figure suggested it was not her own. "Or maybe they found you?"

"These children must belong to the cave we found," Kora said. Her hand was well clear of her hunting knife now, all thoughts of an attack flown from her mind. The hobbit woman stepped forward with slow movements, her empty hands held aloft. "Where are your family, children?" She directed her question at the oldest girl. The girl's eyes flared in fright and she stepped back, dropping her eyes and adjusting the bundle in her arms. It was Kyah's little friend who spoke instead.

"Our family is dead," the girl said. The words aloud were punctuated, as if some nuance was missing in translation. Even without speaking the language of Gihn's tribe, Ivy could tell that this dialect was different to the one she was familiar with hearing. Kora and the others seemed to be having some trouble understanding the girl. Ivy's amulet allowed her the insight of the girl's thoughts, rather than relying only on the words themselves. "She says *our family are dead*," Ivy repeated, for the benefit of the other travellers. With startled whispers, the children shuffled back, as if the strange, tall, white woman might eat them after she spoke. Ivy crouched to the ground, realising once again how enormous and frightening she must look.

"I understood enough," Kora breathed in reply. "*Family. Dead.* Some of their words are different to ours, and the way she says them are different, but still close enough for us to guess what's missing." She directed another question to the little girl. "Where do you live?"

No doubt Kora has already guessed that answer, Ivy thought. But she too, wanted to confirm her suspicions. The girl next to Kyah, who, though very young, seemed to be the boldest of the group, spoke up again.

"Home Cave, back that way." She pointed to the mountain behind them. The travellers turned. It was indeed the direction from which they'd come, in the vicinity of the archaeological site of Dozu Dhalu. In their desire to put as much distance between themselves and the mausoleum Ivy had found the day before, the mountain itself was now small in the distance.

"How did your family die?" Ivy asked gently. Her words made no sense to the girl. With a meaningful look at Gihn, he translated her words to the children.

"The giants," the little girl said. "They killed them. We saw them pass us in the forest. We were hiding." She took a deep breath, her mouth twisting downward and tiny lip quivering. Her ribcage stuck out in stark relief. Ivy realised they must be starving. "Some of the giants followed our hunters back to Home Cave moons ago. Since then, they have come many times. They steal food and cause trouble if we don't give it to them."

"You were hiding when they came?" Ivy asked. Gihn repeated for her.

"My mother sent me to the forest." She looked around for support, but the other children stared back at her, apparently too scared to speak. "Our mothers always do if they are worried the giants will come. There is a place we can wait."

"How do you know it is safe?"

"Because the giants are too big to fit inside." She looked Ivy up and down critically. "You would not fit."

"Your mother left you there?" Ivy prompted.

"Yes. All our mothers did. But they didn't come to fetch us at nightfall. Nobody came." She looked at her companions. "We waited two more nights. Everybody was very hungry, so we decided to return home by ourselves. But when we got there, we found them." The little girl's face looked as if it were about to crumple. "We didn't know what to do, so we went back to the hiding place." The hobbit child buried her face in the soft hair on Kyah's arm.

Ivy's eyes stung. She couldn't imagine the horror and grief of discovering a dead mother, not to mention every other adult they knew and loved. Somehow, the children had still had the presence of mind to stay together. Ivy shot a quizzical look at Kyah.

"And then you found this new friend?" Ivy gestured toward Kyah. Gihn translated.

"She came into the hiding place. She is small, like us." The girl looked at Kyah as if the sun shone from the bonobo's face. "Then she went away again and brought us back food."

Ivy's heart swelled. *Of course she did.* No wonder Kyah hadn't returned to the river until sunrise. She hadn't been eating and nesting as Ivy had assumed. She'd been taking care of her newfound charges. And when she'd returned to Ivy and the hobbits, ready to continue their journey, she must have brought them to follow along too.

"We will bring them with us," Xiou announced. Until that moment, he had been listening to the children's story in grim silence. "They are lucky to be alive. They have no guardians now, and we are bound to our mission to find as many of our own people as we can. These poor children need to be taken care of, so they should come with us. We are their family now."

Ivy looked to Gihn, who nodded. In turn, each of the travellers agreed. No one would question that the responsibility was now theirs to carry.

"They will slow us down though," Setian said, not unkindly. "So many extra mouths to feed, and such small steps to walk a long distance. We need to reconsider this journey." He looked at the children thoughtfully. "These little ones could not make it all the way to the southern sea. They look barely strong enough to make it out of this ravine."

There were a few moments of silence while they each considered this unexpected turn of events. Finally, Kora spoke up.

"You and I will continue on to the Sister Lakes with the children then." She looked over to her mate for his agreement. At Setian's slight nod, she continued. "We will spend some time hunting to feed them first, and then cut across the east mountains. That way, we will not delay the journey. Besides, if we go directly east from here, we will arrive first and can prepare for our own tribe of young ones join us."

"You continue our journey as it was planned." Setian looked resolutely at Ivy, then the others in turn. "After we all pass through these mountains, you turn south and search the sea caves. We will continue east and meet you at the Sister Lakes before the full moon."

"Are you sure?" Ivy's heart sank at the thought of losing Kora and Setian so early in the journey. They still had another two weeks of searching ahead of them before they began their trek to the Sister Lakes. She would miss their company, as much as the food and protection they both provided. Already, their little band of travellers was breaking apart.

"This is the best way." Kora turned to the children. "They have no one else and there are few enough of our people already. We must keep them safe from the Karathah."

Ivy hid her worry behind a warm smile. Only two adults to feed and protect sixteen orphaned children. *But if anybody could get them safely to Kelimutu,* she decided, *it was Kora.* The woman had nerves of steel.

"Then let us begin together," Gihn said. He raised an arm toward the newcomers, ushering them forward. "We have far to go."

CHAPTER 12

NEIL

The forge had burned down to cinders. Neil sat beside it, the radiating glow warming his leg as he hammered at each of the two copper daggers in turn. The sun had risen a few hours ago, but the fire was still too hot to touch. Underneath the rock plate, he hoped his pottery bowls were still in one piece. He'd never tried firing pottery before, or even making it for that matter, but he knew it was temperamental.

Neil shot a look at Atasi. She was grinding something on a bone plate a few meters to his left. Food probably. She was always making food of one kind or another. Good food too, as far as the bizarre concoctions of plant and animal parts went that he'd suffered through so far. Atasi was artful in her cooking. Though he noticed she didn't seem to find as much joy in it as she used to. Back at the cave, Neil had watched her prepare meals with her family and friends. A tinkling laugh had never been far from her lips. But now, after weeks of daily torment from Charat, the young woman rarely spoke, let alone laugh. It was as if the joy that had once shone from the very pores of her skin was now sucked dry and lifeless. On the rare occasions that Neil had been able to make her smile, it was restrained and careful. As if Charat might witness it and punish her simply for enjoying herself. *He probably would.*

Neil struck the copper knife hard with his rock. The flat plane of the stone hit the metal with a dull thud, shaping it against the larger slab of rock underneath. As he worked on it, the copper knife hardened. The more he hammered, the harder and stronger it got. He had already made his own knife. The fact that he was making this one for Charat irked him. The red-beaded hunter was arrogant, power-hungry, and cruel. Even worse, Neil had handed Charat his newfound power on a plate the day they'd made their unspoken agreement. Neil would play God with his magic fire tricks, soul-stealing photographs and daily dose of intimidation and threats. Charat would act as the mortal bridge of communication that kept the superstitious tribe on the right side of Neil's potential wrath. Neil offered ingenuity and knowledge about the hobbits from Ivy's journal. Charat offered Neil the security of survival – at least while he was still useful. But Neil hated him.

Neil put down his hammering stone and ran his finger along the edge of the copper blade. *Sharp. But not sharp enough.* It needed more work. A shadow fell over him as he picked it up once again.

"Nee-el." Charat crouched down. He leaned forward and copied Neil's movement, dragging a finger along the blade of the knife. He pushed the pad of his index finger into the end point, then gave an appreciative grunt as a prick of red blood appeared on the end of it. He held out his hand expectantly.

"Not yet," Neil said. He shook his head. "It needs more work." Carefully, he picked up the knife again, and turned to blade edge toward Charat. With his hammering rock, Neil made a couple of motions to infer his meaning. "I'm still working on it. It's not sharp enough." To force the point, Neil set the blade flat against the slab of rock and began to hammer it. In his peripheral vision, he saw Charat scowl. The man didn't like to wait. Neil paused and pointed up to the sun. "A few hours," he said, arcing his arm across the sky until it was directly overhead. "I'll have it finished by noon." With a dismissive nod he turned back to his ministration with the hammer stone, ignoring Charat. Neil knew he was pushing his luck, but he hated giving the hunter the satisfaction of getting what he wanted as soon as he asked. The unfamiliarity around what Neil was doing with the copper was one of the few advantages he still had over him.

"Atasi!" Charat's bark nearly made Neil jump. He watched as the disgruntled man stepped away, changing tack. The young woman had startled too, and was now frozen in place, eyes wide. *"Ashana-gatu ma shivale'! Aja!"* Another barked order saw Atasi place what she was doing down on the bone plate. With a nervous frown, Tipun stepped in to take her place. With a stiff jaw and dead eyes, Atasi followed Charat away from the mouth of the cave. As she walked, delicate shoulders slumped, she chanced a look back at Neil. A flicker of desperation lit her face. Then they were around the corner and out of sight.

With an angry growl, Neil took up again with his hammering. The malleable copper grew harder in the hands of his anger.

"Damn it!" Neil's fist paused in mid-air. With a curse, he threw the hammer stone to the dirt. A hair-line crack had spoiled the blade. *Too much.* Sighing, he picked up the copper knife and shuffled closer to the glowing forge, resting the imperfect side of the knife against the blistering-hot rock plate. After a few minutes, Neil lifted it out again with his makeshift tongs. The cracked metal had brightened and re-softened enough. He would be able to repair the crack and re-strengthen the blade. Picking up his discarded hammer stone, Neil began his labour again.

The sun rose above him. Before Charat had returned with his plunderage, the edge of the knife was sharp.

Neil thrust it into the cold river to set.

"Thanks." Neil took the proffered clay bowl and leaned back against the wall of the shelter. "See? You did well," he added, offering Atasi a small smile. "Didn't I say you'd be good at making these?" Though his words meant nothing, Neil complimented her anyway. His demeanour was enough to soften the misery in her eyes. With a couple of fingers, he began to scoop out the stew inside her new pottery bowl and eat it. Beside him, his own battery charging bowl was working beautifully, currently filled to the brim with mashed, underripe fruit acting as individual battery cells for the simple circuit of alternating copper and zinc that ran through it and connected to the stripped USB cable that charged his phone. All but one of the pottery bowls had survived – the first one he had made cracked in two. When he had pulled them out of the cooled kiln to show Atasi, she had been astonished. Her soft clay bowls were now strong and hard enough to cook and serve food in. She had said something to Neil, that he assumed was some sort of thanks, but her words were meaningless compared to the gentle touch she gave his hand. That was the only thanks he had needed.

As the days passed, Neil realised he leered less at Atasi's body. Instead, his eyes were drawn at the way she stiffened anxiously when Charat was near, and the way she seemed to shrink under the man's gaze. When Neil had first arrived, it was easy to objectify her. She was barely twenty, lithe, beautiful. The sort of creature he had always devoured with greedy eyes even if he couldn't get his hands dirty. In the old days, the fact that a young woman like her wouldn't look sideways at a paunchy businessman had never dampened his ego. Or his efforts. On the odd occasion, he'd even stacked his odds, won the hand and lured one to his bed. What they'd thought after they'd left it, didn't concern him at all.

But this was different. *Something* inside him was different. As Atasi slipped away, leaving Neil to his dinner, he watched the blue feathers in her hair float behind her with a gnawing worry in his gut. She was fading. Her laugh gone. Her eyes dull.

He wanted to get her away from Charat. But not to take her for himself. Possibly, just – to keep her safe? It was a surprising realisation.

I can't even protect myself for God's sake. And what the hell can I offer a young woman like that? Nothing. She's stuck here. She's going to live her life at the mercy of that bastard and there's nothing I can do about it. Neil ate some more food. It suddenly tasted bitter on his tongue. *What do I care anyway? As soon as I get that amulet, I'm going home and leaving her here. Fifty thousand years in the past.* Neil shivered, despite the humid air pressing in on him. *And eventually she'll be buried in the dust, like all the others.* From the side of the shelter, Neil watched Atasi serve up bowls of food. Charat took a bowl from her with greedy eyes. Neil put his food down. He'd lost his appetite. *That's her fate,* he forced his mind to hear the words. *There's nothing I can do. I don't need to do anything.* An impotent frustration settled in his chest. The thought of leaving Atasi to such a miserable fate didn't sit right in him. The obnoxious, arrogant and unscrupulously ruthless version of himself that existed before the Time Shift would never have accepted a result he wasn't happy with. He would have knocked as many heads together as he needed to get his way. But now he wasn't so sure. *There's nothing I can do,* he decided again, trying hard to convince himself of it.

I can't protect her from him. Neil's jaw clenched as he saw Charat push the young woman ahead of himself, forcing her away from the eyes of the group. *Can I?*

Hours of trudging through tangled forest brought Neil and the band of hunters onto the razors edge of a volcanic rift. Charat stopped first, laying aside his spear and taking a seat on the rocky outcrop. As Neil caught up, the others had already begun to rest, laying their meagre belongings on the ground and shuffling over to the edge to take in the view. The three women were busy unloading the vegetation they'd collected as they travelled. With a digging stick in one hand and hide bags draped over the opposite shoulder, they had lost little time collecting food as they trekked. Now, they began to process what they'd found, preparing to cook.

"Holy mother of–" The air rushed from his lungs as Neil stepped up to join them. Stunned, he looked around, trying to take it all in.

The view was magnificent. Charat had set up camp on the very pinnacle of a mountain's edge. Ahead of them, the island stretched in untamed, majestic splendour. The landscape screamed prehistoric. To the east, a sliver of glistening blue on the horizon told him the ocean was there. Black clouds of ash swirled above a volcano in the distant north and blanketed the land for miles, casting a filthy shadow across the afternoon sky. Down below, shreds of broken earth were sliced into the forest below like colossal scratches from a raptor's claws. The gaping wounds of black soil were edged with felled and shattered trees. The smell escaping from the fissure was putrid, even high above it. Like rotten eggs. Neil knew it was hydrogen sulfide gas escaping from the bowels of the earth, mingled with the acrid, smoky odour of volcanic ash.

Neil sat down a few feet from the edge of the precipice. He chanced a look down. His stomach gave a lurch. The cliff face dropped over one hundred meters onto a rocky outcrop, then another hundred into forest. There was no surviving a fall like that. He shuffled back a few meters and took a deep breath. His limbs ached from a full day of hard walking. The group had left the copper shelter and his makeshift furnace behind that morning, to continue their journey to Kelimutu. His possessions felt heavier. The hide bag was carefully packed with his clay battery bowl, Ivy's journal, stripped phone charging cable, metal links and what fruit he had remaining to mash for the battery. He had strapped the large bellows to his back with vines in case he needed it again and, in his fist, bound tightly together, was a walking stick made of the four meter-length copper rods he had smelted. His new copper knife was tucked in his belt. His silver lighter was in his right-side pocket and in his left, was a small gift – one he had yet to find the opportunity to give. Around his waist, his filthy jacket flapped as he walked. The bright blue logo embroidered on the pocket – a sphere encircling a silhouette of the Australian continent, sliced by seven parallel pinstripes – had faded and was beginning to unravel.

Neil was proud of what he had created. They may not be much to look at, but all his worldly possessions were invaluable to him. When he considered the modern glass and expensive, stylish decor his life had once been furnished in, he was irritated by the uselessness of it all. His life had changed. And he was changing with it.

For a solid half hour, Neil simply sat and stared at the green abyss ahead of him. Daily, he was suffused by the minutia of surviving in the jungle. Heat and humidity by day. The sudden drop in temperature at night. The possibility of starvation or animal attack or infection. The politics of simply staying alive. But seeing the island laid out before him on such imposing scale sent a chill up Neil's spine. The desolation was terrifying.

I gotta get out of here.

As if to solidify his sudden feeling of insignificance, the ground beneath him suddenly groaned and stretched, sending a tumble of rocks sliding over the face of the ridge. Neil stumbled backward and crouched, splaying his hands flat on the ground for support. Around him, others did the same, shouts of fright barely audible over the grating tectonic plates.

"Karachu? Figunva!" The scream was almost lost in the noise. One of Charat's hunters was swinging his head wildly back and forth, searching for something and trying to maintain his balance at the same time. *"Ais hin Karachu marvu-kasha!"* Neil held his head up just high enough to see the commotion. Others were shouting too now. To his right, near the tree line, he could see Atasi, Martu and Tipun lying together on the ground, their backs to the trees swaying precariously above them. Neil's neck twisted too far. A sharp pain shot through it. He dropped his head, squeezing his eyes shut. Violent jolts rattled his body against the earth. *Just get through it. Just get through it.* He was chanting inside his mind, clenching his teeth together so tight he thought they might crack. *Just get through it.* In the forest behind them, deafening cracks joined the cacophony of birds screeching as trees split in half and upended.

Long minutes passed before the earth settled.

Another minute passed before Neil dared to move.

Slowly, the party rose to their feet, wide-eyed and shaken. Charat was unharmed, much to Neil's chagrin. The women, thankfully, were also safe. But it seemed not all their party had been so lucky.

"Ais hin Karachu marvu-kasha!" A flurry of conversation followed and anguished eyes cast toward the edge of the rift. It seemed two of the hunters, Karachu and Figunva had been knocked from their feet as the tremor hit the mountain. They had been too close to the edge. No one dared get close enough to look down after them. There would be nothing left of them to see anyway.

With soulful lament, the others shook their heads and cried out in disbelief. Neil felt a twinge of sympathy. Though they had been loyal to Charat, whom Neil despised, the two hunters had been decent enough men and good diggers for his forge. He took no joy in seeing them die. With the earlier loss of one impaled by a tree, Charat's party of sycophants had now fallen from eight to five.

With a shout of fury, Charat made his displeasure known.

"Nee-el!" Waiting a beat before he answered, Neil turned to him.

"Yes, Charat?"

"Ebu gogo!" The red-beaded hunter shouted into his face. He let a string of incomprehensible words fly from his mouth as he pointed east. *"Carni-xio furon mach ura dana..!"*

"I need the stone first," Neil replied gruffly, refusing to back away. He pulled Ivy's journal from his bag and flipped through the pages until he found the diagram of the amulet. "Eye-vee. Stone. Then – stone–" he swiped the blade of his hand across his throat to simulate death. "Stone kill Ebu gogo." Neil's heart raced at the lie but he kept his mouth in a hard line. He could not show weakness at any cost. "Stone first! *Then* kill Ebu gogo." The red-beaded hunter's single-mindedness at wiping the little creatures off the planet was infuriating. There was a dangerous look in Charat's eyes. Neil wasn't sure how much time he would have after he found the stone to make his own escape. There was nothing the stone itself could do to help Charat kill the hobbits. But the charade had to continue. Neil couldn't make this journey on his own. "The stone," Neil repeated. "We need to get to Kelimutu first. *Berap – Mutu.*" He held up a finger. *"Mutu."* He added another finger. *"Stone."* Finally, a third. *"Then, Ebu gogo!"*

With a hiss, Charat turned and stalked away. He shouted orders and shoved the women back to their work. Neil darkened at the sight of Charat's rough hand on Atasi's arm. His remaining sycophants scattered, rushing into the forest to retrieve firewood and anything else that might prove useful. Neil turned away and settled himself down with Ivy's journal.

He'd read it through, but opened it again, desperate for more knowledge on how he might manipulate his way into surviving this unpredictable hellhole. Charat was becoming more irrational. Time was running out.

Day 24 - Liang Bua Cave

Today we journeyed to the oleos grove again. There is talk of stegodon somewhere to the south. I don't dare to hope I get to see them myself...

Neil blinked up at the dark sky. He rubbed his eyes. They were itchy and sore, inflamed from a new influx of volcanic ash in the air. Around him, soft snores and snuffles filled the quiet. The camp was asleep. A brush of wind caught his ankle, and Neil's eyes followed a pair of bare feet close by. They made their way past, stopping at the edge of the rift. Too close to the edge of the rift. Neil's heart missed a beat.

"Atasi!" The woman was standing, staring, her slender figure silhouetted in the moonlight. Her toes curled over the edge of the rocky outcrop. She didn't respond.

"Atasi!" Neil sat up, throwing a glance behind him. No one else was awake. It must have been past midnight. "You need to step back." His voice was gruff from being silent so long. Neil quickly adjusted his tone. "Atasi, step back." He was pleading now. *She's going to jump,* Neil realised, his heart shuddering into action. He leapt to his feet and crossed the distance between them faster than he thought possible. He slipped his hand around her wrist, then pulled her gently back away from the edge. She resisted, pulling against him. The young woman looked up at Neil, tears shining in her eyes.

"Please, no." Neil said gently. "You don't want to do that."

Atasi's eyes countered him. The pain within was almost unbearable. The heavy burden of guilt rose within him. He had given Charat the opportunity to take on this new mantle of power. By collaborating with the red-beaded hunter to save his own life, Neil had elevated the man's authority far beyond what he deserved. Charat was ambitious, vengeful and had illusions of himself as a great leader. But he had none of the wisdom or empathy required of the job. He ruled with intimidation. The recognition of that trait within himself gnawed at Neil's gut. *But he's worse than me*, Neil reasoned. Intimidation was only the beginning of Charat's abuse of power. The man was violent. Obsessive. Cruel.

More than anything, Neil wanted to be rid of him. Watching Charat's brutal domination over Atasi was almost worse than witnessing the bloodlust with which he killed the hobbits. He suddenly felt nauseous.

"He torments you because he's a power-hungry bastard," Neil said quietly to her. "And you don't deserve it. Charat needs the sharp end of a spear." Neil's harsh words meant nothing to her, and he knew it, but they were soft-spoken and kind. "You've got to hang in there for me, Atasi. Please? I'm going to–" Neil looked around. He was on the top of a mountain, in a prehistoric jungle with only a glimpse of hope to survive. Despite it, a rush of optimism filled his chest. "I'm going to figure out how to get you away from him, okay? I swear it." He fumbled in his pocket and brought out the small gift he had been carrying for the past two days. Waiting for an opportunity to give it to her. Neil put a shining object in her hand. "For you." It was roughly shaped like a feather, with a small hole in one end, and engraved striations that radiated out from the centre line to the edges. An ornamental bird feather, shaped from beaten copper, for her to tie into her hair. "To go with your blue feathers there." He shifted one to show her. "You can tie it on the end, see?"

Atasi's lip trembled. Overwhelmed, she crumbled down onto the rock. Neil sat beside her, letting her cry it out.

After a few minutes, she met his eyes. There were questions there. Confusion. Concern. She lifted his hand and brought it carefully to her breast.

"No," Neil shook his head, pulling his hand away quickly. "No. That's not what this is. You don't owe me anything." In a rare moment of honesty that made him tremble inside, Neil gave her a sad smile. "This is all my fault, what's happening to you. And I'm sorry for it." Neil didn't want to admit he had looked at her the way Charat did, not that long ago. Now, seeing how she recoiled from the other man, he felt ashamed. "You deserve better than this," he said. "And I wish to God I could make you smile again."

CHAPTER 13

ORRIN

*T*he police officer turned back at the doorway. "Would you like to lay charges on these two, Chancellor?"

Chancellor Thandi now stood where Nerov had been. Behind her, Cassandra and Dimitri fronted a crowd of onlookers in the corridor including Jayne, who was ashen faced.

For a moment the Chancellor considered. She glared at Orrin with steely condemnation before averting her attention back to the policeman. "We've recovered the stolen property it seems, so for now – *no*. I will speak to the Board of Directors about further action that will need to be taken. I'll be in touch with the authorities then. However, Officer, I would like you to remain here while Dr James and Mr Chan gather their personal effects." The Chancellor turned back to Orrin and Phil. Orrin looked up from the chair. Phil stood staring, mesmerised, by the metal box at his feet.

"I must say Dr James," Chancellor Thandi said. "I am deeply disappointed. Your involvement in this travesty and your reluctance to confide in me has not only just ended your employment and likely led to a criminal charge, but it has seriously damaged this university's reputation. Whatever work you were doing here is now entirely out of our control, thanks to you. The authorities have granted full access to this laboratory and all of your data and equipment to the Department of Natural Resources and the CSIRO."

"No! Chancellor, you can't let that happen! There are things, issues that I need to fix. This is bigger than the university, so much bigger–"

"That's right. It is, Dr James." Cassandra stepped forward, a shrewd smile on her lips. "And I must say, thank you for making your laboratory so accessible." She gestured to Dimitri, who stood behind her, grim-faced. "My team will ensure all of your files are thoroughly researched and the situation you have created here will be resolved in a way that reflects the government's best interests."

"You mean *your* best interests!" Orrin yelled. The energy fields would be manipulated for the benefit of those few with the power to control them. The potential for corruption was omnipotent. And then there was Ivy – she was lost to him now. Irretrievably, devastatingly lost. A new kind of anger fell over him. Betrayal, worse than he ever thought possible. Beside Cassandra, Dimi had his hand drawn across his mouth. Orrin stared in disbelief at his oldest friend, then rushed forward, ready to unleash a tirade of accusations. But before he could, another man stepped into his path.

"It was me."

"What?" Orrin froze, dumbfounded. *Dale?* It was wrong, all wrong. "What do you mean?"

"I'm sorry Orrin, but I'm so sick and tired of playing second fiddle in *every single thing* that I do. I'm an afterthought! I'm a – a – a dogsbody that just sits and takes whatever you give me – scraps of nothing! And I try so God-damn-hard! It's never enough for you. The hobbits, the experiments, the Shift – I don't even care what version of reality this is anymore! It's good enough for me. I don't want to go back."

Cassandra interjected. "Version of reality? Dale, it seems we have more to discuss."

Orrin's heart thumped. So, Cassandra didn't know about the time shift. *Yet.* It was little consolation. Without the laboratory, all hope for fixing it was now gone.

"But it's *not* good enough, Dale!" Orrin growled. "Of all people, you know that! You know how this world is supposed to be!" He was gutted. *"Indah! Ivy!* Think what you've done!"

Dale's face flushed with anger. "Ivy. Indah. Yeah, everybody *but me!* To hell with the hobbits and to hell with your obsessions! You never saw it Orrin, you never saw *me!* I was *always* here! Even when I was the only person who believed you, and the only one who stood by you, you still valued *him* and his opinion over mine. *Phil.* Every. Single. Time. I'm so sick of the crap I put up with here, the disregard from you and everyone else in this god-damned place." Dale looked away, breathing hard. "I had information that they wanted," he said stiffly. He glanced at Cassandra who nodded. Dale took a deep breath and continued, "and they were willing to acknowledge me and give me the credit I deserve."

"As we will, Dale," Cassandra purred. "You see, *I* value my employees, Dr. James. Clearly you have little interest in the ambitions of your students. Dale has provided me with most interesting information over the past week, and unlike you, I fully intend to reward his loyalty."

Orrin was speechless. He knew Dale resented Phil's popularity and confidence, but this – it was *vindictive.* Orrin turned on him, his voice tight with emotion. "Do you understand what you've done here? Do you *really* understand? Oh my God, how can you even begin to justify this after everything we've been through?"

Dale turned away and sank behind his desk, stony faced. He stared at his monitor, unseeing.

"It seems Dale has outlived his usefulness to you Dr James, as

I'm sure you are now critically aware. No doubt, his use to me is limited as well, but at least I can recognise job dissatisfaction when I see it. Apparently, you either lack the skill to read your staff, or you were so blinded by opportunity, you lost control of the resources you needed to reach it. Now that resource is mine, along with all your data." Cassandra stepped forward, considering the vast array of equipment astutely. "That being the case, Dr. James, Mr. Chan, kindly leave *our* laboratory. It seems we have a mess to clean up. Dimitri, please begin copying the data from the main servers."

En queue, Dimi stepped forward, pulling a laptop from his briefcase. Within a moment, he was connecting it to the first of the data servers. Orrin rushed toward him.

"Please. Dimitri is it?" Orrin feigned unfamiliarity with the man he had known for so many years. "I have sensitive data here, if it gets into the wrong hands…"

Dimi looked to Cassandra momentarily before replying. "I'm sorry Dr James, but it seems you've put your faith in the wrong people. Your data now belongs to the government. I intend to do my job." There was no trace of recognition in his eyes, and no hint of support.

Orrin turned away, gutted. "Chancellor, please! You can't let this happen. It's imperative that I finish these experiments!"

Chancellor Thandi was furious. The situation had deteriorated beyond her control, and she clearly resented Orrin for her enforced subordination. "Gather your effects gentlemen. You are both dismissed from the university, effective immediately. You will give me all your laboratory keys and swipecards before you leave. Rest assured; all security access codes will be changed upon your departure. Do not, I repeat, *do not*, even consider returning to this university again or I will have you arrested."

Phil picked up the metal lid and placed it gently onto the empty case. He was grey with shock as he gathered his bag and keys from his desk. He reached to fold up his laptop.

"The computer stays." Cassandra placed a manicured hand on it. "I have provided the Chancellor with a search warrant, Mr Chan. All equipment, including personal computers will be analysed by my team. If there is nothing of interest, it may be returned to you at a later date." She scowled at him. "If I were you though, I wouldn't hold my breath."

Phil nodded vaguely and looked to Orrin, devastated. "I'm sorry man, I tried." He stepped toward the Chancellor and dropped his keys and swipe card in her hand. When he reached the doorway, Jayne put a consolatory arm around his shoulders. They disappeared down the hallway.

"My bag and keys are in the back office." Orrin addressed the Chancellor. Beside her, the uniformed officer still waited. Orrin needed a plan and some time, even just a minute to gather his wits.

"Then I suggest you retrieve them Dr James. And quickly. This officer will be escorting you to your car to ensure we have no further incidents today."

Orrin walked into his office, pushing the door mostly closed behind him. Through the crack he left open, he heard Cassandra continue passing orders to Dimi.

Her words spiralled in his head. *Apparently, you either lack the skill to read your staff, or you were so blinded by opportunity that you lost control of the resources you needed to reach it.* Orrin despised the term. *A human being was not a resource.* Hobbit or sapien, Orrin would never have considered his friend – and Dale *had* been his friend – as a mere resource to be exploited. Used and discarded. A true friendship was not defined by utility or convenience.

But was he the only one who had assumed staff loyalty where it didn't exist? *Dimi hadn't actually betrayed him. Yet.* For some reason, despite refusing to acknowledge Orrin and following Cassandra's instructions to the letter, Dimi had kept his secret. Cassandra knew about the energy fluctuations; she knew Orrin had somehow caused them and understood all of their potential exploitations and threats. *But Dimi hasn't told her about the Time Shift, about this evolutionary holocaust I caused, or about... Ivy.* With a burst of adrenaline, Orrin knew what he had to do. He ripped a page from the closest book and scrawled as fast as he could across the top.

Dimi —Amulet is the catalyst —? black elemental intrusion within magnetite – must analyse. Contact Elijah Nnamani – Geology Dept. PLEASE. I need to save her – HELP ME. O.

But where could he hide it? If Cassandra got hold of the note instead of Dimi the consequences were unthinkable. Orrin's eyes darted around the small office, suddenly so small and limited. The shelves, books, equipment – nothing would be safe from Cassandra's shrewd eye. *Of course! The Tek!* Orrin knocked layers of books and articles off the vintage Tektronic Oscilloscope under his desk. It was approximately the size of a microwave, analog, and so ancient and clearly unused that no one would give it a second thought. Its glass display screen was cracked, and the trigger control knobs were missing. It had travelled from office to office with him, a piece of sentimental rubbish used most often as a bookshelf. *But Dimi would recognize it.* He and Orrin had resurrected that machine more times than he cared to remember during their undergraduate days, attacking it with amplifiers and filters with zealous enthusiasm to expand its limited capabilities. He slipped the note inside its metal shell. Orrin piled the papers back on top, letting them spill across with an air of neglect.

He heard Cassandra's voice outside the door raise. Chancellor Thandi responded with restrained fury. It seemed she resented the loss of commercial control as much as Cassandra relished gaining it. Time was running out. *Dimi needs to find that note – but how?* Although Dimi would recognize the old oscilloscope, he had no reason to pull it apart. *Unless – yes!*

With a flash of inspiration Orrin opened his email calendar. *New appointment today. DON'T FORGET – 4pm catch up with old Tek.* Orrin knew it was a long shot, but it was the best he could do. He set the reminder to repeat at five-minute intervals. If anyone else opened his email they'd dismiss it, undoubtedly irritated by the insistent pestering. He could only hope that Dimi would understand its true meaning.

Devastation welled inside him. He'd failed Ivy, and now he'd failed Indah and her baby. Orrin knew that any hope he now had, rested on the uncertain friendship he held with a man who refused to acknowledge him. *If I'm wrong, God help us all.* Orrin shoved his hand into his pocket to check the amulet was still there. He closed his fist around it. *Please Dimi, don't let me down.* All it needed was a handshake to pass it on; a show of goodwill to the astrophysicist, now busy copying all of his files, that could-be his downfall. *Or his saviour.* Orrin took a deep breath, preparing to face Dimi, then the Chancellor and Cassandra Chevallier with his most sobering, apologetic, and humble mask of defeat.

In his spare hand, he grabbed his bag and left his lead-lined office for the last time.

Orrin walked slowly and deliberately to Dimi, who was crouching at the back of the laboratory behind the rack server to access its cable ports. Leaning down, he offered his hand. "I had the best intentions; I assure you Dimitri. I'm sorry it's come to this. When you analyse my data, I hope you understand the position I was in." Dimi looked stunned at the gesture. With a glance to Cassandra who watched from the middle of the room, he slowly took Orrin's hand and shook it. For an infinitesimal moment, Orrin thought Dimi would give him away, rejecting the black stone he passed between their hands. But he didn't. *Please Dimi. Find. That. Note.* Dimi's eyes widened in shock. Orrin's face implored in silent communication. Finally, with an infinitesimal nod, Dimi closed his hand around the stone and returned to his work.

Orrin repeated the false gesture with Cassandra, who looked slightly amused and not remotely affected by his words. The Chancellor refused outright to shake his hand. "You'll be hearing from me, Dr James. Believe me; this university doesn't take theft of property lightly, not to mention this debacle you've created within our department. This officer will escort you from university grounds and I strongly suggest you do not return." The police officer fell in beside him and they stepped toward the door.

"Orrin, wait." Dale pushed away from the desk where he sat. His face was desolate. "You asked me how I can justify what I did after everything we've been through." Dale paused, looking briefly at Cassandra. She'd used him herself, as callously as he'd betrayed Orrin. "Well. I just – I can't justify it."

Dale navigated the desk, passing Orrin. He placed his laboratory keys and swipe card on the shelves by the door. He turned back to face Orrin from the doorway. "I'm sorry. I didn't know what they would do to the hobbits; that they would take Indah like that. They promised me she'd be looked after." Dale's eyes were hollow with regret and something more. *Loneliness.* "I looked up to you so much. For the past four years I've tried so hard to win your approval. You have no idea how important it was to me. And no matter what I did, it could never compete with your other students, with Phil, this Ivy woman – even Jayne. I'm sorry, but I just couldn't do it anymore." Orrin swallowed hard. Dale's familiar face suddenly seemed more wretched than Orrin remembered it. His eyes were shadowed and the frown lines on his face seemed out of place considering his youth. Bitter disappointment clung to Dale's shoulders as he offered a sad smile. "I wanted you to regret passing me over for so long. So you'd see I was worth something after all."

Despite his betrayal, Orrin felt responsible for the veil of sadness hanging over his student. Dale had been through the same devastating change of reality as he had been himself. But the younger man's struggles had been overlooked as a by-product of his own chronic under-confidence and Orrin's singular focus to save Ivy. *He was right,* Orrin thought. *No matter the cause, Dale was an invisible man.*

"I really *am* sorry Orrin." Dale turned to Cassandra. "Screw your job. I don't want it." He pushed through the crowd and was gone.

CHAPTER 14

IVY

"Are you sure you will be alright?" Ivy returned Kora's spear, concern in her eyes. The hobbit woman adjusted the orphaned baby who was now strapped solidly to her front. She carried another small child on her back. Her mate, Setian, was similarly burdened. The two eldest orphans held their next youngest cousins by the hand and the remaining eight huddled together. Wide eyes and sad little mouths suggested that although they trusted their new guides, they were deeply traumatised by the murders of their parents. Ivy doubted the haunted look would ever quite leave them.

"We are all fed well and strong," Setian said, with a rousing smile, "aren't we children? We will make it there in no time at all."

He received only a few shy nods in reply.

"We'll travel directly east to the Sister Lakes from here," Kora said. "So, it is likely we will reach them before the other travellers. I imagine that our own elders and children are preparing to leave Home Cave now."

"If you do get there first, find a good place to camp," Xiou said. "Somewhere that everybody will be safe. And with some protection if the Karathah should attack."

"I know, friend." Kora pressed her forehead against Xiou's. "You just worry about getting to the south sea. We will take care of these precious ones," she nodded at the children around her. "Perhaps when you reach the lakes, Shahn may be ready to deliver your own new baby to the world."

Xiou offered Kora a smile, but his eyes betrayed him. He was worried about Shahn, far more than he had let on. Ivy felt again, the burden on her shoulders. Xiou's mate was nearly full term in her pregnancy. She and Xiou adored one another, along with their first born, little Trahg. If something happened to Xiou while he was travelling, or to Shahn herself, on her journey to meet them, Ivy would never forgive herself. It was she, after all, who insisted that Xiou accompany her on such a dangerous mission. But Ivy knew she would be lost, or dead, without him.

"Keep together then, little ones," Ivy said, crouching low to take Kyah's new friend by the hand. "And we will see you again soon." She had begun to get to know the children the night before, as they ate by the hearth. Quiet, solemn little creatures that barely spoke, with the exception of Kyah's new friend, who seemed content to speak enough for all of them. That girl's name was Jindi, Ivy had discovered.

"Off we go then," Setian said, nodding to Kora. His voice was far too jovial for the task ahead of him. Both had taken on this journey with full knowledge it could cost their lives. Either would sacrifice themselves to save these children. These were not just innocents, but also their tribe's future.

With a wave, Kora turned and began the trek up and out of the gully they had been camped in overnight. From here, Ivy would head south with Gihn, Guntah and Xiou. She watched as the group of tiny children, some no taller than her own knee, followed their new carers toward an unknown fate.

"Kyah?" Ivy called. The bonobo was still loping alongside her tiny friend Jindi. "We're going this way, hon." Ivy pointed to the south. "The children will be fine. Come on."

Kyah paused. Her dark, intelligent eyes surveyed the group around her. With swift and gentle movements, she lifted her hand to sign. *Baby.*

"The babies will stay with Kora," Ivy tried to explain with intermittent signs. "You stay with me. This way." Ivy turned her back on her best friend, and took a step away, hoping the movement would clarify her intentions. When Ivy looked back over her shoulder, Kyah hadn't moved. She wasn't following. Ivy's heart missed a beat. "Please. Kyah." She motioned to the bonobo once more. "Come with me. We need to go."

Me. Baby. Stay. As each simple gesture whispered through the air under Kyah's fingertips, Ivy felt breath leave her lungs. She was blindsided. Kyah was choosing to stay with the children.

"Ky-" Ivy heard the pleading in her own voice. She couldn't hide it. Kyah had been her constant companion, her *sister*, for much longer than the past month of this terrifying adventure. They had spent years by each other's side at the university. Ivy was the bonobo's greatest champion and protector – the only person able to reach her after the decade of abuse and neglect she had suffered as an experimental test animal. And Kyah, for her part, held the deepest part of Ivy's heart. There had never been a time that Ivy had considered her friend may prefer someone else. Kyah was always *simply there*, a faithful and protective shadow by her side.

With a look down at Jindi, Kyah dropped the child's hand and loped slowly back to Ivy. A twinge of guilt hit Ivy despite the rush of relief. Kyah lifted Ivy's hand to her own chest. The bonobo pressed it against the scars of scratches she had inflicted on herself over so many years. Ivy felt them under her fingertips, another remnant of Kyah's past suffering.

Baby. Hurt. Kyah's own hands flew to the lexicons Ivy had taught her back in the behavioural research laboratory. Countless hours together, learning to bridge the worlds between them. *Me.*

Baby. Stay. She waited a moment, as if to add meaning to her final word. *Baby. Danger.*

As if it were a glass ornament in her chest, Ivy felt her heart crack. *This is it then.* She would never force Kyah to follow her. This journey was one they had been thrown into together and had precious little control over. They'd survived it so far hand in hand and were as much alive by Kyah's cleverness and fighting skills as anything Ivy had offered in return. Kyah deserved a choice. And she had chosen to leave her.

Ivy nodded. Tears welled as she pulled her best friend into a tight hug.

"Please be careful," she whispered into Kyah neck. "I'll see you again soon." Desperation to make those words come true choked her up. Muffled goodbyes were barely audible as Ivy tried to keep the emotion from overwhelming her. "You look after the babies, Ky. I *will* see you soon."

The bonobo gave a soft grunt in reply and touched Ivy's cheek. She turned and loped back up the gully to re-join the other party. Kora watched the exchange with solemn eyes and offered Ivy a silent promise. She would protect Kyah as selflessly as she would protect the children. Ivy knew Kyah would return the favour.

With a shuddering breath, Ivy squeezed her eyes shut, then turned her back on her best friend. One foot in front of the other, she forced herself south, until the razored landscape between them hid the bonobo from her sight.

Days grew oppressively humid. By the end of the second week of their journey, the air seemed as much liquid as gas. Ivy struggled under the harsh sun whenever their feet forced them out of tree cover. She could feel herself burning day by day, porcelain skin turning beetroot red under the rays. She fashioned a makeshift hat out of giant leaves strapped down with vine, but it did little to quell the radiating heat.

I'm failing. A steady stream of sweat ran into her eyes. No more hobbits had been unearthed. Not even a whiff of another tribe. But they weren't alone on their trail. The evidence of Karathah was everywhere. Xiou and Guntah could pick it easily, pointing out broken leaves on the path, trodden trails that were only visible to a hunters' trained eye. Occasionally, they saw large groups travelling in the distance and Ivy hid until they had passed.

Every so often, Xiou came across middens of animal bones; hunted, butchered, and discarded. Once he drew her attention to them, Ivy recognised them for what they were. She had seen enough of the tell-tale marks in the archaeology laboratory to recognise patterns. The distinctive cut marks of stone tools etched onto the bones were clear. No animal, other than the human kind, used a stone knife to butcher its prey. What they represented though, was more worrying to her companions. The middens were evidence of an ever-expanding hunting territory by the Karathah. An urgent need to satisfy the stomachs of a swelling human population.

I'm fighting the inevitable, Ivy thought. *And there will be others.* She wondered how many more hominins would pass through Flores in the fifty thousand years between now and her own time. How many more battles would the hobbits have to fight to keep extinction at bay? Would they encounter the Denisovans perhaps? – that elusive species of human that left their DNA in modern populations throughout the Pacific?

There would be more modern *Homo sapiens*, certainly, as they dispersed through Southeast Asia to populate and dominate future earth. Modern humans were a*daptable. Inventive. Prolific.* With an ability to claim and conquer even the harshest land-scapes. This jungle island, with its exotic resources and ash-filled skies, was merely a steppingstone across the string of volcanic islands of the Indonesian Archipelago. The first sapien sea farers had already crossed this ocean to reach the Sahul continental shelf, then continued down to Papua New Guinea and on to Western Australia. Even now, fifty thousand years before her own time, indigenous Australians had long settled across the great continent Ivy would one day be born to. The hobbits were hopelessly outnumbered. Was this war that Ivy insisted they could fight, simply the beginning of an endless tide of attacks? *Am I forcing them into a more violent struggle than the one they already face?* Each day, the question of culpability sank heavier in her chest.

Ivy had seen no sign of another *Homo floresiensis* tribe since the cave massacre near Dozu Dhalu. It seemed whatever hobbits may have once lived here, had already been hunted out by the Karathah.

"Probech." Xiou called over his shoulder. Ivy snapped out of her reverie. She didn't need an interpreter for that word. Only a few weeks prior she had seen the prehistoric stegodon for herself. *Stegodon florensis insularis.* Each beast was a spectacular illustration of island dwarfism. Over forty thousand generations of isolation and adaptation on Flores had reduced the once gargantuan creatures to a weight of barely six hundred kilograms. Additional molar ridges had evolved to chew the coarse island vegetation and the stegodon had flourished with no apex predators to limit their population. Until now.

Krue had orchestrated a hunt to replenish the food they lost in the Karathah arson attack. Xiou and his fellow hunters had slipped around a matriarchal herd, silent in their deadly choreography as they chose an outlier as their prey. The single young bull had fought valiantly, and finally succumbed. The hobbits only took what the stegodon family could afford to lose. But Karathah hunters had set an ambush to steal their prize. Fifteen hobbits had been murdered that day, Ivy's diary had been stolen, and her thigh still bore the wound of the red-beaded hunter's knife.

"Why are there so many –?" Ivy clamped a hand over her mouth and nose as she came to Xiou's side, staring at the spectacle he had come across. *Rotting corpses. Four of them.* Piled in the grass like an enormous blight in the green. The skeletons had been stripped of their flesh. What remained, an ugly trophy of sinew and buzzing flies, was being torn apart by carrion scavengers. Massive ivory tusks still protruded from each bulbous, double-domed skull. The dead straight tusks were each nearly two meters long, and heavy; apparently not worth carrying the distance home. Each of the great tusks flared out at its' end, chipped, and rubbed worn over decades of use. Ivy leant forward, reaching into a cavity beneath the ribcage of one closest to her. Shifting her wrist to manage the awkward angle, she pulled out a fist-sized hand-axe. It was bifacial flint, with percussive chips taken off both sides with a stone hammer to form a sharp edge around an egg-shaped border. The stone tool was easy to grip and perfect for hacking through bone, tendons, and muscle. In her old life, Ivy would have relished the idea of finding such an iconic Palaeolithic tool *in situ* – but now she shuddered at how close its makers could be at using the weapon on her instead.

"All male," Xiou frowned, surveying the stegodon remains. "This was a bachelor herd."

"But why would they kill so many at once?"

Guntah frowned, kneeling beside her. "They must have many mouths to feed, Hiranah."

"Which means there are many Karathah in this territory." She stood up, shaking off the feeling of disquiet. The smell of rotting flesh was nauseating. And she was not the only one who had noticed.

"We have company." Ivy nodded toward the tree line behind them. Familiar shapes were appearing from the shadow, drawn by the promise of food. Giant storks, the six-foot tall, flightless terrors with their clattering beaks and soulless eyes. The birds began to stalk the distance between them. Heads bobbing as they strode, clawed toes ready to tear shreds off the carrion - or anyone that got in their way.

"Don't run," Xiou warned. "It will draw more attention to us." He gripped his spear, lending his father the support of his shoulder. Gratefully, Gihn took it.

"Together we look bigger," Guntah added. He turned and walked backward behind the pair, his own spear at the ready. The three hobbit men, and Ivy, quietly slipped away, across the remainder of the plain and breathed a sigh of relief when they hit forest cover once more.

As the afternoon sun wore down, they began looking for a good place to camp for the night. Ivy watched the outline of another great volcano grow larger as they approached it from the north. A constant haze of steam and magmatic gas hung above it. A steady layer of ash rained from the south-west as they travelled. Rumbles occasionally knocked her off her feet. Xiou, Gihn and Guntah inevitably sensed them and took to the trees, but Ivy; with her evolutionarily dulled sapien instincts, had no warning. After each rumble, Ivy's mind mulled over their precognition. If it were, as she was now almost certain it was, drawn from a sensitivity to the magnetic field variations around them, Ivy wondered when *Homo sapiens* had lost that ability. Because it *was* a loss, in every sense of the word.

Modern technology could compensate for some of it, but still, the ability to sense minute electromagnetic changes in their environment was an extraordinary gift that many animals took for granted. The hobbits, it seemed, were not only self-aware of their advantage, but used it to great effect. Countless times, it had saved their lives.

"It is strange," said Gihn as he took Ivy's wrist for support, "that the closer we get to the coloured lakes, the more I feel I am returning home, rather than being away from it."

"What do you mean?" asked Ivy.

Gihn's mouth set in a quiet line as he considered. "The part of my mind that always knows where Home Cave is, knows this place too. I feel it calling to me inside. We are travelling with the rising sun to our left hand, so I know Home Cave is to our right. Not simply because of the sun's path, but because I feel something pulling me to the left. I imagine it is the Sister Lakes calling us back home. It's always been there, but never as strongly as I feel it now. Normally, when we hunt, we simply navigate this feeling to find our home," said Gihn. "It may pull greater, or less."

"Like a divining rod," Ivy smiled. She recalled Trahg and little Turi being able to navigate the forest simply on instinct alone. They had told her once that they always knew how to get home, no matter where they were. That they just pushed away from the rising sun to find Home Cave. Gihn shot her a quizzical look. Of course, he had no idea what a divining rod was. "Sorry – I mean, that is why you weren't worried that Trahg and Turi would get lost on the hunting trails." Her heart wrenched at the memory of the dusty-haired little boy who died in the fire. Another life stolen by the Karathah.

"Yes," Gihn frowned. "We all feel the pull of it. Our children can use this feeling to find their way home. It is very rare for a child of our tribe to get lost. They are more likely to get taken by the Shirakan if they wander." Ivy shuddered at the thought of becoming dinner to a vicious Komodo. "But the closer we get to the Sister Lakes," Gihn continued, "the stronger I *feel* it pulling me in. I felt it draw me when we travelled to the Falling Place to find you." The old man stopped for a moment to consider his thoughts. "That is how I knew you were the one. We were drawn to you. I've known the story of our Beginning since I was a child, but I think I understand it now, for the first time." He touched the amulet reverently. "The Life Stone was born there, at the Falling Place near the Sister Lakes. That is where our ancestors found it. In your time, it found you and brought you to us. Now it is leading us home to the Sister Lakes, through you. I believe this."

Ivy pushed her hair from her eyes, considering. "I think you're right Gihn. But not because of the amulet. I think you have something in your body, or your brain that is telling you which way is home. Maybe the amulet has it inside too. I know there are other creatures that carry something within them, that helps them follow the trails of seasons to find food and mates or warm weather." The more she considered the likeness of their behaviour to other animals that sensed the Earth's magnetic field, the more the idea made sense. It was not the Falling Place itself that drew the hobbits, it was whatever was *in* the earth at that place. Perhaps – whatever was also in the amulet that *came* from that place in the Earth.

Ivy felt sure of it now. Given their ability to predict earthquakes, and this sense of 'direction' that oriented them within their land, the hobbits were clearly sensitive to changes in the earth around them. Ivy guessed that they must have a hypersensitivity to the magnetic field poles of the earth, the same as those found in homing pigeons, sea turtles and migratory herds.

Like a magnet, Ivy realised. Something was drawing these hobbits to Kelimutu *specifically*. If their brains did have significantly more magnetite or some other physical adaptation within its chemistry, then it could certainly increase their ability to sense changes in the earth's magnetic fields, like any other animal. It also made sense that such sensitivity could be used to orient themselves and 'feel' direction, as it were. *But why Kelimutu?* Gihn was insistent that the Falling Place was the centre of the pull. If this instinct was the same as other migratory animals, there would be no single point of condensed magnetic focus. They should simply have patterns based on a sense of the magnetic poles of the earth.

As they camped against the wall of another ridge for the night, Ivy's mind couldn't help but puzzle over the idea. She struck her flint rocks together over a tinder of shredded oleos-soaked bamboo. It took longer than usual to catch fire. The air was almost dripping with humidity. Finally, a spark caught, and Ivy blew it into flame. She added some more kindling, stuffing her flint back into the folds of her hide skirt. Soon enough, a decent-sized fire was burning on the hearth.

Kelimutu is just another volcano, isn't it? Ivy pondered, as she stared into the flames. Certainly, the Three Sister Lakes that sat atop it were a geological marvel. She had read many research articles about them. Each crater lake was a different colour and temperature, changing over time as the fluid flux from vents at the bottom of the lakes triggered chemical reactions within the water. The volcano was still active in modern day, and in a constant state of change. Beautiful and unpredictable.

But it was also the home of the Falling Place. The barren shelf where she had found herself after she had fallen through time and landed fifty thousand years in the past. *Why that place?* Ivy wondered. *Why not in the forest? Or at Home Cave? What was it about Kelimutu that drew her amulet, and herself, back into its own heart?*

Ivy searched her mind, desperately trying to recall the geology of the volcano itself. It had been a long time since she had studied it, and only within the context of the archaeology of the island itself. *Is there something unique about this volcano?* Ivy wondered. *Something in its creation that has influenced the evolution of the hobbits.* Their species had, after all, spent nearly a million years isolated on the island.

Whatever chemistry that drove the hobbits' adaptation to feel a 'pull' toward Kelimutu, must surely have a corresponding 'pull' from the volcano itself. Like two opposite poles of a magnet, each drawing the other in.

So, what's down there? What lies within the volcano itself, to create such a powerful attraction? Ivy wondered. *Is it the same thing that dragged me here, through space and time?* The sheer power of such a force made her shiver. Ivy turned the amulet over in her hand. As always, it was warm to touch and seemed to draw her gaze. She didn't know what mysterious element was hiding within it, or within the hobbits' brains, or inside Kelimutu itself for that matter, but Ivy knew it must be something extraordinary.

Something powerful. And dangerous.

Something the modern world had not yet discovered.

CHAPTER 15

NEIL

"What the hell is that?" Neil moved aside as one of Charat's hunters dragged something enormous across the forest floor and rolled it in front of him. A swarm of flies were hovering around the man's face. He waved them away unconcerned, as he stood back and grinned over the body of what turned out to be a gargantuan flower of some sort. It was at least a meter across. "Christ, that's stinks!" Neil whisked his arms in front of his face, trying to shoo the flies, but had to retreat to be clear of them. The hunter who had delivered it, a man named Gori, fell back in a betel-juiced, red-mouthed cackle. He had been scouting off to the side somewhere, hunting as they travelled, and had just returned. Two giant rats were tied around his waist, hanging limp as they slapped heavily into his legs as he walked. Gori shouted something to the other hunters, then waved ecstatically for Charat to come join them. At the sound of his name, the red-beaded hunter, who had been leading the trek down the side of the mountain paused, looked back, and retraced his steps. At the sight of what Gori had presented him with, he too threw his head back in peals of laughter, then shouted something to the women.

Neil could tell by the sexually explicit gestures that accompanied Charat's words, and the tinkling of laughter from Martu and Tipun in response, that his words were suggestive. Atasi remained stone-faced at their mirth, then turned quickly away. The other two women continued the conversation for a few moments as they teased the men who had crowded around. An uproar of laughter took hold and Gori began to slice one of the enormous red warty petals from the body of the flower. A fresh wave of putrid stench hit the air. It was like rotten fish. Neil swallowed hard, hand over his mouth and nose, trying not to gag. It was the most bizarre and foul-smelling plant Neil had ever seen.

He peered at it from a safe distance. It was a fleshy-looking thing, almost four feet across, and shaped like an enormous petaled flower. It was fungoid in texture, with the rubber consistency of a mushroom and heavily mottled in brownish pink warts. Inside the circlet of petals was a large bowl-shaped cavity, which seemed to be drawing the haze of flies.

"Nee-el!" Charat called out to him, a wicked grin spreading across his face. *"Karan-it-al-chira!"* Charat pointed to the plant, then his mouth in a simulation of eating. *"Karuna-martu-los-ora!"* This was followed by a lewd gesture toward the women. Martu's eyes shot wide, and she stepped back nervously, laughter suddenly gone. Apparently, Charat's innuendo was as unwelcome by the young woman as it was to Neil. Though he had no idea what the plant was, Neil could only imagine it was used by the tribe as some kind of aphrodisiac or philtre. He gave a tight smile, then turned away, resentful of the humiliation Charat was directing toward him. The hunter's facade of respect for Neil's supposed *omnipotence* was slipping as his arrogance grew.

He didn't dare rebut it though. Neil already walked on dangerous ground. He was only untouchable at the hunter's demand. Without Charat's cooperation, he was worse than lost in the woods. He was a dead man.

Think... As Neil turned away from those who were now laughing again at their putrid prize, he willed himself to come up with a solution to Charat's increasing disrespect. *Maybe if I give him taste of what he wants. Throw him a bone, so to speak... he'll reconsider my worth.* An idea was forming in Neil's head. Something that might buy him a little more time.

"Aaaarghh!" Screams sliced his musing. Terrified shouts and – something else – *a low and eerie hissing noise.* Neil spun back to see the group scattering in all directions. A creature had burst into their midst as they were gathered around the vulgar flower. A massive lizard, almost three metres long and heavy, heisted up on legs like tree-trunks with thick, curved claws at each finger. Neil scrambled for the name of it as he dashed backward, tripping over branches in his haste to put distance between himself and the thing. *Komodo dragon.* He'd only ever seen one on a documentary channel, a lifetime ago. An apex predator, he knew. It wasn't hard to see why. Most of the men took off downhill, the way they had been travelling. Neil would have to circle around the creature to follow them, leaving Charat and Gori alone to face the most terrifying creature Neil had seen.

He hoisted his hide bag higher over his shoulder, gripped the copper rods tightly. *I can pass behind it,* he thought, keeping his eyes fixed to its muscular shoulders as he moved. *If I'm slow, it might not notice me.* His optimism was shot down before Neil had a chance to believe it. The Komodo twisted toward him, its eyeball, forest-green and disturbingly human-like, tracking each step he took. It hissed at Neil, strings of bloody saliva dripping from its gums from the wear and tear of razor teeth constantly shearing the inside of its own mouth. Neil stopped dead still. He was too close. He couldn't outrun it – the thing looked like a dead weight, but it moved like lightning.

Charat was as far from the Komodo as Neil was. But while Neil was desperate to escape, the other man's mouth was twisted into a grimace of silent ecstasy. One fist was slowly rising, his spear clenched within it. He looked tense, muscles coiled and tight, as if he were about to spring.

The Komodo's eye slid back to appraise the hunter. But if it realised what his intentions were, it thought little of it. The Komodo instead swung back to Gori and took a few slow steps, its head shifting from side to side as its shoulders moved. A long, yellow, forked tongue flicked out with each step, tasting the air then retreating to the roof of its mouth to analyse it. The scent of warm-blooded animals was in the air. Apparently, the creature liked what it tasted. Gori's eyes were darting wildly, looking for escape. *The rats.* Dead rats, each as big as a domestic cat, coated in drying blood, tied to his waist. There was no hiding that scent. Nor his own. Gori backed up. Hit a tree. His hands held only the stone knife he had been using to slice the putrid flower. It would not make a dent on the Komodo's armoured skin. The rats made him too heavy to climb, even if he'd had the skill, which Neil doubted. Neil met Gori's terrified eyes.

Then it happened.

The Komodo lunged, jaws twisted open with razor-sharp teeth. They clamped around the giant rat, dragging Gori tethered to the dead thing as he scrambled to get away. The Komodo lunged again, intent on claiming a live meal. This time, rows of teeth caught Gori's legs. His flesh split like ripe fruit. Gori screamed in agony as Charat's spear found its mark in the reptile's back. Even with the force of Charat's weight behind it, the spear slipped on the layered bone plates of its skin, only puncturing a couple of centimetres. Enough to infuriate the beast. *Another bite.* Screaming. *And another.* Neil was rooted to the spot as Gori's left leg was torn away. Charat was dancing around the Komodo, madness in his eyes, as he jerked his spear from its puncture marks and thrust it down again, higher into the back of the beast. The creature writhed up, almost pulling to full height, then collapsed onto Gori. Its jaws were working madly, trying to bite the man with the spear. But Gori's blood curdling screams said it was he that bore the brunt of its retaliation. His right leg was pouring blood, soft tissue torn away. Gori's face paled. His voice gone. Poison from the venom glands were pumping into his heart. His eyes rolled wildly. Grave injuries were amplified with anti-coagulant in the Komodo's saliva. His body was being forced to bleed itself out.

Once more, Charat's spear shuddered from the Komodo's back. He was standing behind it now, practically *on* the huge creature as his wrenched his arm back again, then forced it down hard, higher still. This time through its thick skin above its heart.

Finally, *finally*, the Komodo, slowed and swayed, collapsing again on Gori's waist. The hunter's right leg was still hanging between its teeth. His left leg, a metre away.

Gori's eyes were wide, his mouth open as he blinked. There was no screaming now. Just eyes. Neil stared back at him.

Then once more, Charat's spear was wrenched from the back of the reptile. Thrust one last time.

Into Gori's chest. The hunter's agony brought to a violent crescendo.

His hopeless battle was lost.

It was a chilling walk from the site of the Komodo attack. Charat had left Gori beneath the tree under which he died, his body scattered with leaves, legs replaced. There was no funeral pyre this time, as there had been back at their Home Cave. Death while travelling meant being left behind.

Charat had dragged the Komodo as far as he could from Gori's body. Neil had helped him, his fingers chaffed raw by the bony, rough skin. He wasn't exactly sure why Charat had wanted it moved. But when the red-beaded hunter had grabbed the Komodo by the tail and begun to heave it backward, Neil stepped forward to help. They worked in silence. Charat was seething. Neil assumed by the loss of yet another of his hunters, or perhaps at the fact that those remaining had scarpered to save themselves and left their comrade to die. Either way, the man was mercurial with his temper, and Neil didn't want to see the blame turned onto himself.

As they followed the others that had run ahead, the back of Neil's neck prickled. There weren't many left, he realised. Which meant less protection for him, and less hands to help find an amulet when they reached Kelimutu. They had lost one hunter, Kechu, in the earthquake at the copper cave when he had been skewered by a fallen tree. Another two, Karachu and Figunva, had fallen over the cliff when the mountain shook. Now Gori was gone. That left only four hunters remaining, as well as Neil himself, Charat, and the three women, Tipun, Martu and Atasi. The travellers were falling like flies. Neil tried to shake off the fatalistic gloom that followed him down the mountain.

When at last they found the others, nervously waiting within a fractured copse of bamboo, Charat still said nothing. He simply scowled at them, and continued walking. As they fell into line behind their leader, each cast a glance at Neil, then further up the mountain to look for Gori behind him. The loss registered as a murmur or a whimper and downcast eyes. One of the remaining hunters looked to Neil with an accusatory stare, then turned his back and stepped in line.

So, I'm to blame, am I? Neil shook his head, but the pit of his stomach churned guilt. *This farce is my doing. They wouldn't be out here exposed, if not for my need to find that stone.* He glanced ahead. Charat was now out of sight. *And they're going to want recompense from me sooner than I can give it.*

As his feet fell into a monotone, Neil's mind whirred.

"Nee-el," growled Charat.

Neil noted the hunters' narrowed eyes and pursed lips as he walked toward him. Charat crouched, his chin jutting out imperiously and he flicked through Neil's belongings on the ground with a suspicious air.

Neil ignored him, turning back to his work. The hunters' foul mood could wait. Due to the declining number of fruit trees as they travelled into drier territory, Neil had had to become a little more resourceful to keep his mobile phone working. They'd passed a fumarole field the day before, on the western plains of a volcano. The field had seemed innocuous enough, despite the patterned bursts of steam and mud that littered the barren stretch of land. Regardless, Charat had insisted they travel south around it, bypassing the faster route in favour of a safer one. Neil had called a halt though. Gingerly stepping onto the caked mud, he'd scraped off as much of the yellow sulphur coating the rocks around the vents as he could without losing his skin in burns. He scooped it into one of larger bowls Atasi had made. Neil was high on the heady thrill of his own ingenuity. This supply would last days, maybe even a couple of weeks if he stretched it out. It was an ideal replacement to the dwindling fruit that usually powered his cell battery charger.

Neil's gratification had only lasted another few hours. Charat had called a stop and they'd set up camp early. Given their proximity to volcanic rock, Neil decided it was as good a time as any to begin searching for a black stone like the one Ivy wore. With the aid of his dying phone, Neil had gestured instructions for the party to search for one like the amulet she wore in his photographs.

They had all swept and dug bare-knuckled in the rubble of the volcanos' sweeping neck until darkness fell. No luck. At daybreak the next morning, Neil had enlisted them to continue their search through a sudden deluge of rain that lasted hours. By lunchtime, drenched and furious, fingers were bruised and bleeding. The rain had finally stopped, but the party were still empty-handed. And angry.

Desperately frustrated by his continued failure, Neil instead turned his attention to his second priority. To maintain his status as a God, and for access to the compass, notes and camera that were so integral to his survival, he needed a new way to recharge his phone.

It was early afternoon now. Under the western shadow of the volcano, he tipped a portion of yellow sulphur into one of Atasi's smaller bowls. Smoothing his thumb over the engraving on his polished silver lighter, he flicked and then lowered the flame carefully into the powder. The fire caught, springing up in iridescent blue flames filling the bowl.

Neil sliced four strips from a hide Atasi had given him, then emptied his bladder of travelling water onto them, soaking them through. Using two large sticks as tongs, he held each dripping rag above the blue flames one by one. The white sulphur dioxide gas that escaped the flames was quickly absorbed into the water, turning the rags acidic. He spun them slowly, watching the flames dance underneath like blue demons.

After what he hoped was an insulting enough delay, he looked up at Charat.

"What?" Neil said.

Although his scowl was still set in place, Charat had been watching Neil's activity closely. *He trusts me as much as I trust him,* Neil thought. Though the hunter had no idea why Neil did the things he did, he wasn't to be underestimated. Neil was sick to death of their game of cat-and-mouse.

Charat gestured to where three of the remaining men were sitting through the scattering of trees. One was missing. Neil assumed he was hunting dinner. The remaining hunters, Keron, Ubyes and Agung, were grim-faced, silent, and stiff-jawed. One stubbed the ball of his foot into the mud repeatedly. Another flicked a stone knife across a stick of bamboo, sharpening it to no end. The last, the one that seemed Charat's most enthusiastic sycophant muttered something under his breath, eliciting a challenging bite back from the first. Even from a distance, Neil could feel their agitation. The men were restless. And that meant danger. Words were unnecessary; a clear warning was reflected in Charat's eyes.

Neil nodded, grunting in acknowledgement. With a last look at the odd set up Neil hovered over, Charat returned to his men. Neil sighed. He'd promised them that a black stone buried somewhere beneath them would enable the death of more hobbits. Charat had convinced his tribe that the little creatures were at fault for their bad luck. The loss of their cave, the earthquakes, restricted hunting territory and goodness knows what else. Their superstitions had been whipped into a need for action. Fools' gold, of course. The creatures were irrelevant, and Neil knew it. But he needed a black stone, and his lies were the only way to facilitate their labour in searching for one. The men were on a dangerous journey and had already faced heavy losses. Now, they were at a loose end.

I need to distract them until I find that stone.

Once he had the stone, Neil would use it to ditch this prehistoric hell and leave Charat and his lot to their own violent pursuits. A twinge of guilt twisted inside him. Atasi didn't deserve that fate though.

Yes, she does. Simply because she belongs here.

The truth of it only made Neil resent them more. He took a deep breath. He brought his hand to the back of his neck, rubbing tense muscles. His mouth twisted in consideration. *I need to distract them.* He chanced a look at the bickering hunters and found no improvement. *The fools are itching for a fight.*

Neil lay down the tongs. Carefully, he opened his hide bag and pulled out the interlinked clay bowls that were his new prized possession. *This stuff is stronger than the fruit,* he thought, *I won't need as many cells to get the right voltage.* He stuffed the four rags, each now an electrolytic cell of sulphuric acid, into its own bowl segment. Ever so carefully, Neil connected one to the next with alternating links from his broken zinc watch band and the chopped copper bracelet he had once begrudgingly worn to waylay arthritic pain. It had never worked then, but now it was worth its weight in gold. Neil pulled his de-threaded usb cable from the bag as well, plugging his mobile phone into the jack on one end and laying it on the ground. He connected the other end – the split, exposed wires that had once plugged into a computer – to the bowls, one on each end of the row.

Once the circuit was complete, Neil sat back, relaxing while his phone charged, with a smug expression. His thoughts flicked over to the precarious footing of his position at the CSIRO. *Past my used-by date, was I? Every self-important jerk on that bloody board of directors would be dead by now if they were in my shoes.* The ever-present vehemence to escape, to re-write history and trump the power play he'd been too long denied, flared up again, burning hard and bright in his chest. *This isn't my fate,* Neil reassured himself. *I'm going to get out of here. No matter what I have to do.*

PART II
ADAPTATION

CHAPTER 16

ORRIN

Tick. Tick. Tick.
     Nothing.
Tick. Tick. Tick.
Again, nothing.

Time progressed mercilessly, tempting Orrin to desperation. He had heard nothing. *Nothing from Dimi, nothing from Jayne. Phil had disappeared.* One week had passed since he had been escorted off the university grounds; his laboratory keys, swipe card and career stripped away.

Orrin drew his head into his hands and then pushed away, standing up from his study desk. His eyes strained to adjust to the change in focus and light. An old laptop had been dragged out of his study to replace the one confiscated at work. He'd been staring at it for hours. A stream of media releases had dominated his research today.

"More extinctions to come: Migratory patterns scrambled, burgeoning environmental collapse"

"CSIRO launches emergency energy facility at Melbourne University"

"Government addresses radiation concerns; Massive signalling disruptions anticipated"

The Earth's magnetosphere was weakening day by day, with record high levels of radiation breaking through the shield that had protected the planet for millennia. The repercussions were devastatingly visible. But it wasn't the beginning of the end. *No, that had started long ago,* Orrin knew. *We were just too stupid to recognise it. And somehow, we did this to ourselves.* As Orrin had scoured the internet, retrospective forewarning of the situation was heartbreakingly obvious. It had begun so slowly. First came the deforestation, mass cultivation and waste, *oh, so much waste.* Fossil fuels were burnt, and natural resources were squandered. Strip mining had intensified. The earth's innards being shucked out and pulled apart like carrion by scavengers.

Then the planet's natural shields against the sun's radiation had broken down, frayed apart, faltering in key places across the globe. Individual species had disappeared, along with their habitats; most slipping away silently, without drawing grief or concern, others with public remonstration by their advocates, but neglected by the distracted masses. They were tiny losses, one by one, each impacting little on the earth. But the sinister implications of each loss grew like a tumour, silent and deadly. Tiny threads broken, leaving those around to cling on until they too, snapped and fell away.

Now, a self-perpetuating spiral of destruction was crippling the Earth. *Now, the masses noticed.*

Orrin had read news article after article. Scientific journals had become harbingers of trouble. The damage was too much. A cascade of devastation followed. As each ecosystemic process was drawn in, repercussions spread like wildfire. Every species of plant and animal was intimately entangled in the destruction, including the human communities that had exploited them. Interdependence was lifeblood, and that linkage, so long ignored by the arrogance of humanity, had finally become their own Achilles heel.

The highest rung on the food chain only held supreme when that ladder was unbroken.

Now, finally, humankind was suffering like never before.

The rippling of fear that Orrin had felt when he had first discovered the magnetospheric anomaly in his own version of the earth before the Time Shift – *the real version* – had amplified in this new reality. The magnetic compounds he had identified within the Earth's core had reacted horrifically to increased solar radiation.

Inside the Earth's core, the thermal convection of the liquid iron had maintained a magnetic field over astronomical time. Now, this geodynamo of the magnetic core of the Earth was in a state of flux, destabilizing the convection current it naturally generated and in turn disintegrating the protective force field around the earth created by it.

This new earth was already too damaged. The balance had shifted too far.

Something had happened on this new version of the earth, Orrin reasoned, *that had triggered the cascade of environmental destruction.* He couldn't help but think that the hobbits were somehow involved. The creatures themselves were benign but their *survival* had made a critical difference. *But why?*

Orrin sat down again at his laptop. He scrolled through the day's news for what seemed like the hundredth time. One article suggested that Cassandra's CSIRO team had abandoned Orrin's laboratory in favour of the penthouse auditorium in his building. The penthouse was a prestigious new facility within the physics department. The ceiling to floor glass walls gave an impressive view of the campus. It was usually reserved for impressing dignitaries. No doubt the room was now crawling with experts, fancy laboratory equipment and tight security. He felt relieved to think they were out of his own lab, no doubt now gutted and stripped of his research.

To distract himself from clawing frustration, Orrin navigated the mess in his kitchen searching for some food. A week of empty takeaway containers were stacked on the bench. With a growl of irritation, he realised a trip to the supermarket was necessary. Orrin grabbed his keys and phone, then drove to the nearest store. He dropped a loaf of bread into his basket, still churning over unresolved questions. His mobile rang as he was shoving groceries into his car. He nearly dropped it in his hurry to answer.

"Jayne?"

"Yeah, it's me."

"What the hell is going on?" Orrin's breath came all at once. He couldn't help the anger in his voice. "I haven't heard anything."

"It's been difficult for me to contact you. Long story. Look, I have some news – can you meet me?"

"Where?"

"I'm leaving the residue lab now," her voice wavered, and she quickly cleared her throat. "You can't come here though, security are everywhere..."

"I know somewhere nearby." As he gave Jayne the address, he felt a familiar chill running up his spine.

"Okay, give me fifteen minutes."

*

Orrin didn't know why he felt compelled to return to that place. It was pure masochism to go where the ghost of Ivy's presence felt so achingly close. It was the way that she *should* be there, but *wasn't*, that felt like a fist to his stomach. As he pulled up under the barren jacaranda only a few blocks from the university, Orrin felt even worse. The last time he'd been here, he'd been greeted with a crumbling apartment block and a demolition crew. But regardless, he had *felt* her there. The old building had resonated with loss. It had seemed as if it knew that Ivy was missing in this world and echoed that emptiness within its walls and windows, willing someone to notice. *Willing him to notice.* But now it was completely different. The old building was gone entirely, and the shell of a modern apartment complex was being pieced together in its place. A bright jigsaw of steel framing and neatly rendered bricks gleamed in the sunlight. A handful of labourers were scurrying around. The lawns had been stripped back to bare soil in preparation for landscaping and there was no sign of the vibrant white daisies that had crowned the entrance before. These new apartments would be sleek and attractive. It felt dismally empty. Even Ivy's echo had disappeared. Orrin swallowed hard, fighting the sting that rose behind his eyes. He'd done this to himself.

Within minutes, a yellow smart car was pulling up. Jayne got out, a zipped satchel over her shoulder.

"Thanks for meeting me here."

"No problem." She looked around critically but didn't ask where *here* was. Jayne leant back against Orrin's car, taking a few deep breaths, and smoothing the fabric of her shirt absently. "I'm sorry I haven't contacted you."

She looked sincerely apologetic. Orrin still felt a little annoyed. He tried to keep it from his voice. "I'm guessing there's a reason why you didn't?"

Jayne hesitated, looking away. "A few reasons. Bad ones."

After another hesitation, Orrin prompted her again. "Yeah?"

"So–" She sighed. "Apparently, some of the equipment from your lab has disappeared. Also, from some of the other physics laboratories as well. Expensive stuff. The Chancellor thought I was involved. Security searched my lab and office; they've just put my research on suspension until further notice. It's all very courteous and official of course, but basically, I've been kicked out of the archaeology lab."

Orrin's breath escaped through his teeth. "Jeez Jayne, I'm so sorry." He felt compelled to ask. "*Were* you involved?"

"Of course not. Apparently, it's tens of thousands of dollars worth of equipment. I mean, I wouldn't know what to do with it if I had. I'm not a bloody physicist, am I? They haven't located it all yet, but they've recovered one of the machines."

"Where was it?"

"Oh man, I don't know how to tell you this–" Jayne gritted her jaw and blinked furiously, holding back tears. Orrin's annoyance at her lack of communication dissolved. Although Jayne looked as strikingly confident as always, she was clearly scared. She rubbed her palms down her jeans and took a deep breath as Orrin waited for her to finish. "It's Phil. Security caught him on the university grounds after hours a few days ago. He was stealing one of the machines, a specto, skepto–"

"An audio spectrum analyser?" Orrin offered.

"Right. That's the one. It's the only piece they've recovered so far, but they're charging him with the theft of the others as well. They arrested him on the spot, and he's been in a holding cell ever since. He's in serious trouble."

"Jaysus!" Orrin punched the roof of his car with his fist, drawing startled looks from the labourers across the road. He lowered his voice to a hiss. "What the hell was he thinking?" A sickening guilt rose from Orrin's gut. *He was trying to help me, that's what.* "He should have talked to me first – that should have been me stealing the lab equipment! Damn it, why would Phil do something like that?" He threw his face to the sky, willing some sort of retribution to smack him down. "This is all my fault."

"It's absolutely not your fault, Orrin! Phil does what he wants. I don't know why he did it, but I bet he had some sort of stupid plan in his head." Despite her words, Jayne looked mildly impressed. "There's a hearing tomorrow. If they let me, I'm going to bail him out."

"No, I need to fix this. I'll go."

"If you go anywhere near him, it'll just make him look more guilty. Seriously, I'll do it."

Orrin scowled. "Fine. Then I'll pay for it."

Jayne raised an eyebrow. "I'm not going to argue on that one. Posting Liam's bail last week already cleared me out. I'll let you know how much it is."

"Good. Thanks." Orrin's nerves felt held together by glue. He turned away. "I've only got two and half weeks left until the next full moon, Jayne. What the hell am I going to do?"

Jayne lay her hand on his arm. "Perhaps there *is* nothing you can do, Orrin. I'm usually the first to see the glass as half full, but at the moment..." She dropped her hand, focused on some distant object, refusing to finish her own sentence. Orrin checked his watch. Again, the hands pushed relentlessly on.

"You said there were other reasons you couldn't contact me?"

Jayne looked back at him. Her eyes brightened and she stood up straight. "Yes! Sorry, yes of course. I have other news."

"Please let it be good."

"Actually, it *is*." With renewed clarity, Jayne pulled an envelope from her satchel and handed it to him. "The results from the DNA tests on the latest skeletal remains from Liang Bua. Undoubtedly a modern female Homo sapien, fifty thousand years old, but..." she grinned, and Orrin's heart positively leapt in anticipation, "*not* of European origin. It seems that the first results were subject to contamination, possibly at the dig site. The remains are Austronesian in origin, most likely from one of the indigenous tribes present on the island at the same time as our hobbit remains. How they ended up in the cave with the hobbit bones is anyone's guess, but still – *it's not Ivy*. I ran two confirmation analyses to be sure before I felt confident enough to let you know."

"Oh, thank God!" For the first time in what seemed like weeks, Orrin laughed. The implications of Ivy's supposed death in prehistory were still unclear. Only two and a half weeks remained until the next full moon, and assuming his calculations were correct, *which they were*, his final chance to recover her. If she was already dead, now, in the past, would there be no one left to recover? Orrin was desperately glad he could throw that jumble of unknowns far from his mind. Those skeletal remains *were not* Ivy. So he had to assume she had survived long enough to escape. The thought she might be buried elsewhere was too much to consider. *There was hope. I still have a chance.* "Jayne, you're the best!" With renewed conviction, Orrin grabbed Jayne by the shoulders and kissed her cheek with a *smack*. He dashed to the driver's side door.

"Orrin! Wait, there's more!"

"More what?"

"More news! Hang on, I have something." Jayne pulled a pair of latex gloves from her satchel and flicked her fingers into them with practiced efficiency. She bent back down and retrieved a scuffed book wrapped in a plastic sleeve. She slipped it out of its protective cover and held it gingerly, flipping through the pages. About three quarters of the way through, a scrap of paper that had been serving as a bookmark fluttered out. Jayne walked to him and lay the open book on its plastic sleeve on the bonnet of Orrin's car. Orrin read the title across the top of the open pages. *Ethnographic recollections of the Homo floresiensis sub-human primates, by Eugene Devonet.* Before he could ask, Jayne hurried to explain.

"I have a friend that volunteers at the Melbourne Museum, cataloguing Aboriginal stone artefacts after hours. I thought there might be something useful in the literature archives on *Homo floresiensis*, so I called in a favour. A big one. Their archive library is restricted for good reason; usually the books and historical documents are one-offs or original research papers and they're often in pretty bad shape. They're just as fragile as the archaeological artefacts themselves, some more so." Jayne seemed intent to impress upon him the delicate nature of the book they had in front of them. Orrin nodded in understanding, noting the yellowed pages and worn fabric binding. Gummy yellow glue stained the edges, and threads of cotton frayed in places, leaving the pages hanging precariously. Jayne turned to look at him, a slight blush creeping up her neck. "Now strictly speaking, this book isn't allowed off the premises–"

"You *stole* the book?" Orrin raised an eyebrow at her, trying to keep the grin from his lips.

Jayne's face flushed. "I prefer *borrowed*, thank you very much. And given my current competition for criminality, it doesn't even rate." Orrin considered his own impending charges for stealing Indah and her baby and Phil's recent arrest for stealing equipment. Liam was still pending on charges for Nerov's assault, as well as the arson of Cosmitech. Orrin's humour left him completely.

"Fair call. So, what did you find?"

"This." Jayne's index finger skimmed an illustration within the text. It was a simple line drawing that lacked any detail whatsoever but was the precise shape of Ivy's amulet. Underneath were the words. *The Key.*

"The Key? What is that supposed to mean?"

"It's hard to tell. The symbol is intrinsically linked to the word Hiranah, that's the first obvious point."

"Of course it is, it's the amulet–"

"*And,*" Jayne ignored his interjection. "the only cultural reference to this in the text suggests that the Hiranah deity–"

"*Ivy–*"

"Yes, we'll assume Ivy," Jayne continued again, looking sternly at him for interrupting, "anyway, the books suggests that the Hiranah deity, *Ivy,* referred to this particular symbol as *'The Key'.* This reference was then passed through oral tradition until historical times and finally recorded here, by the ethnographer, *Devonet*, over two hundred years ago."

"Right," Orrin said. "So – what does that mean?"

"Well, the weird thing is that the hobbit reference to this word is pronounced *'th-kee'*, an almost exact replication of the English pronunciation. Phonetically, that is quite unusual for their language system. The translation of the meaning could have varied over time of course. I mean, a stone age tribe had no literal use for the word 'key' as there were no locks, as such. So, a metaphorical meaning is assumed – perhaps they are referring to a solution, an answer, a secret of some kind? 'Th-kee' does seem a rather pointed inference though if you ask me."

"I think I see where this is going." Orrin looked at her for confirmation. "You think Ivy named the symbol 'The Key' and then ensured it was passed on that way?"

"Yes, I think so. There was a single account of this symbology by the original ethnographer – *here*," Jayne slid her gloved finger across a paragraph highlighting words. She read aloud. "'*And the primates revered a symbol crudely outlined in ochre on a stone wall during a ceremonial display. This coincided with a full moon and included oral and physical exaltations as a form of primitive lunar worship. The symbol (sketched above) was inferred to represent time or a state of transition that the Hiranah deity had conferred upon the moon. A protracted harmonic display of vocalisation followed, after which the brutality of primitive life was resumed... It occurs to me that this proto-humanistic connection between the concept of time and the movement of stellar bodies may be relevant to understanding our own supreme transition from brutality to civilised behaviour...*'"

Orrin sucked his breath through his teeth. "So patronising..."

"I know," she smiled. "It grates, doesn't it. But you've got to consider the social context of when this was written. The colonisation of places like Flores represented an opportunity to civilise and exploit a previously 'undiscovered' part of the world for western civilisation. This was a matter of *conquer, classify, and concrete* in that order. The hobbits were seen as an archaic species that didn't belong to the modern human family tree at all. At least, no more than a chimp or a lemur or any other species of primate. For the conquerors, our world was created by God's design and humans were the supreme creation within that environment. The fact that hobbits were perfectly adapted, physically and socially, to their environment was irrelevant. They were an animal, like all other animals."

"You only have to look at them to see they're not like any other animal—"

Jayne shrugged. "Science dictates that we deny animals any emotions or descriptions that might anthropomorphise them. In other words, we deliberately de-humanise them so we don't inflict any human qualities on them that they might not possess. We emphasise *instinct* rather than *intelligence*. We take away references to any social culture, grief, empathy, love."

"There's no way Indah could be described like that."

"I know that. You know that," Jayne said. "But traditional science dictates that animals are no more than biological machines." She tapped the ancient book. "It helped perpetuate the absurd notion that humans have reached the pinnacle of evolutionary perfection and intelligence on earth. Top of the food chain." She frowned. "I'd like to think our understanding has improved in the last few hundred years, but lately I just don't know."

Orrin studied the picture again, ignoring the ethnographers' notes. *Time. The Key.* After a few minutes, he shared his thoughts with Jayne. "The thing is – I think I already knew this. If Ivy wanted me to learn about this symbol – if she wanted me to know that the amulet is *the key* to the Time Shift, then I don't think this book is of much more use. Because I *do* know the amulet is the key. I just don't know *how* or *why*."

"What do you mean?"

"I took the amulet to the Geology lab and spoke with a senior researcher called Elijah Nnamani."

"And?"

"The stone is magnetite," Orrin said, "he was pretty sure about that. But then this guy – Eli – looked at the crystalline properties of the magnetite under a scanning-electron microscope, he found something else. Intrusions – he called them. He said it was some kind of metallic material between the magnetite crystals that looked like black ribbons pushing the clusters apart. He couldn't identify it, but he was convinced it had to have been as old as the crystals themselves, pushed together millions of years ago when the tectonic plates formed."

"So, he didn't know what the black ribbon things were?"

"No idea. But he thought it might embed unusual properties into the naturally magnetic magnetite."

"Like what?"

Orrin shot her a sardonic look. "Unfortunately, I didn't give him time to work it out. But I think we can assume *time-travel* is one of them."

"That's insane," Jayne breathed.

"And that's not all," Orrin said. He explained how he had been able to communicate with Indah directly through the stone, and how their linked thoughts allowed images and memories to be shared. "So, you see," he finished, "the amulet *is* the key to the time shift and the link to understanding the hobbits. That black ribbon stuff inside the magnetite must be the key to how it all works. I've never been surer of anything in my life. I just don't know what it is, or how to *use* it to recreate the time shift to get Ivy back."

"Okay, so we need to find out what that black stuff is then, right?" Jayne said triumphantly. "I mean, knowledge is power. We find out what we're dealing with and then… do something with it…" Jayne trailed off feebly.

"Do something with it?" Orrin wanted to laugh but didn't have it

in him. "Yeah, well, that's what I've been trying to do. But I've lost access to my lab, the whole campus in fact –"

"Me too," Jayne said, dejectedly. "But maybe we can get the amulet back to the Geology lab some other way? To that Eli guy –"

"It's too late," Orrin frowned. "I've already given the amulet to Dimi."

"Dimi who?" Jayne's pallor passed from pale to ashen as Orrin explained what he'd done.

"So, you've put all your trust – *and our only hope in fixing this mess* – in some CSIRO dude you went to uni with a million years ago and now you're hoping he finds a note you left him in a broken machine in your old office that's been ransacked and gutted!?"

"Pretty much."

"And this guy – *this Dimi guy* – has he come through with the goods?" Jayne held her breath.

Orrin's shoulders sank. "He said outright he wanted nothing to do with it all. Then he told me I was on my own. When I was fired he wouldn't even acknowledge my existence in front of his boss. And I haven't heard from him since."

"Urgh!!!" Jayne threw her back against the car dramatically. "For a moment there I thought we had some hope. *Damn it, Orrin.* First Dale turns on you and now this Dimi guy? You *really* need to learn not to trust people."

Orrin frowned. "I trust you. Don't I?"

"Yeah, well. I'm not much help either." Jayne slid the book back into its plastic cover. She slipped it into her satchel with a sigh. "I suppose if anything, at least we have affirmation that we're on the right track." She pulled off the latex gloves and threw them on the backseat of her car. "That amulet has the answers we need."

"Yeah," Orrin said, bitterly. "Unfortunately, I trusted it to someone I don't know if I can trust."

Jayne couldn't offer him anything but a hug.

"Go home," she said. "No offence, but you look like you could do with a sleep and a shower."

"I know."

After Jayne had driven away, promising to contact him again with any new information, Orrin sat in his car for a long time.

Ivy left that clue for me – another attempt to reach me across fifty thousand years of time. And somehow, despite the myriad of opportunities where it could have been lost, she managed to tell me what I needed to know. 'The amulet is the key'. The most critical piece of this puzzle.

And I gave the damn thing away.

Orrin slumped into his seat, feeling more hopeless than ever. He couldn't bring himself to start the engine. Dusk settled on the quiet street. House cats began prowling their picket fences. He didn't notice what time the school buses dropped off their scatter of children, or when the construction workers across the road packed up and left, but when his empty stomach finally prompted him to gather his wits and drive home in the dark, Orrin's face was still wet with tears.

CHAPTER 17

IVY

"*L*et me help you." Ivy took Gihn's arm as he struggled over the fallen trunk of a tree. It had likely come down in a recent earthquake and was still sporting green branches and moist upturned roots. While Xiou and Guntah could easily traverse the obstruction as high as their own chests, the elderly man was having more difficulty. Ivy clambered over, then lay aside her spear to lend her arms to Xiou to grasp onto from the other side. Though he was still more strong and capable than he looked, Gihn's vitality had declined over the past weeks. Worry and grief had taken its toll on all of them, but none more so than the elderly spiritual leader of the Liang Bua tribe.

"You are kind, Hiranah," Gihn settled on his feet again and began to walk, leaning heavily on his stick. The raucous din of squabbling parrots rained a shower of tree nuts on their heads. Ivy threw her eyes up to the canopy admiring the rainbow of feathers.

"You must miss them, Gihn." She retrieved her spear and walked slowly, keeping the connection of the amulet between her palm and Gihn's. She knew Gihn's mate, Rahn, had died four summers past. Truen, the youngest son of his mate had died of the Swift Death the night after Ivy had arrived. He was poisoned by Karathah hunters. Truen had been a hunter too, Gihn had told her proudly, he was the best with arrows. But the loss of a family member far outweighed Truen's loss as a hunter. The young man's mate, Juni, still grieved terribly. She had stayed behind at Home Cave to travel with the children and elders to Kelimutu. Gihn's only daughter, Rashi, had also died a year past. In her case, it was the Slow Death that stole not only her life and that of her unborn child but was diminishing the future of the tribe through miscarriage, stillbirth and difficult pregnancies. Still, the old man pushed on, doggedly determined to ensure the fate of his only surviving son, Xiou, and the rest of his tribe, was assured.

"Grief is always the heaviest burden to carry," Gihn said. "Because you can never put it down. Not even for a moment." They continued walking for a few minutes in silence. "You would have liked Rhan," he finally said, a smile on his lips. "She had a temper, like you."

"I'm sure she was a wonderful woman," Ivy laughed.

"The Karathah killed her." Gihn's sudden admission came as a shock. Though Ivy had said nothing aloud, Gihn had felt the question form in her mind before she could consider whether to voice it. The amulet often brought an uncomfortable exposure of private thoughts into conversation. Ivy felt it was sometimes better to hide the truth. Perhaps only because she kept so many secrets.

Ivy stopped walking. "How?" Fresh grief filled his face.

"She was gathering Oleos fruit with Lahstri and Bosxoi," Xiou said, stepping back to join them. "Three Karathah hunters came across them near the grove and tried to scare them away. When my mother refused to leave, one of them hit her with his club. Lahstri did what she could, but even a medicine woman cannot heal a broken skull."

"They brought Rhan home," Gihn finished, his voice wavering. "But she did not survive the night."

"Was it the red-beaded hunter?" Ivy asked. Despite the years since it had happened, she was suddenly desperate to put blame to a face. That Karathah hunter had seemed to be at the centre of the genocide she had witnessed so far. She had seen his massacre of Emiri, the arson of their Home Cave and poison of their waterholes. There seemed no depth to the inhumanity he would sink to, in his efforts to exterminate the smaller species.

"No, it was not him," Xiou said. "Lahstri said it was an older man. My mother was furious the men were in the grove at all – it is a women's place. That is why she refused to leave. The Karathah trade us for oleos because it is in our territory. That was one of the first times they deliberately invaded our part of the forest. Since then, they have done it frequently. When my mother was alive, only four summers past, there were twice as many in our tribe as we have now."

"Time is running out for us." Gihn squeezed Ivy's hand. "But now we have you."

The burden of responsibility to save an entire species from extinction felt suffocating. Ivy took a deep breath. Instead of sinking beneath the weight of it, Ivy did the only thing she could; she straightened her shoulders, gave a bolstering smile to her friends, and squeezed his hand back.

"Yes, you do," she said, stepping forward. "So, we'd better keep moving."

A vast plain at the base of a rifted valley greeted the travellers the following morning. Along the west side of it, rocky ridges ran southward toward the sea. On the opposite side, the grassland was bordered by the dense forest that curved behind them and from which they'd just emerged.

"We are not far from the sea now, I think," Guntah said, with a wide grin. "Can you smell it, Hiranah?" Ivy sniffed at the air but found no noticeable difference. She shook her head. "I think we will find the ocean beyond this plain." Ivy looked ahead, but the slight rise in topography hid what was ahead. "I have only been to the edge of the land three times," Guntah continued, leading her out of the tree cover and onto a grassy plain. "But every time was an adventure." Long yellow stalks of grass brushed past the top of Ivy's thighs as she pushed through them. Only her companions' heads and shoulders were visible above the grass line.

"A good adventure, I hope?" Ivy asked.

"Of course," Guntah replied. "The first time I was chased by a Shirakan up a tree. The second time, I nearly fell off a cliff. And the third—"

"Let me guess," Ivy interrupted, laughing, "You nearly died?"

Guntah shook his head. "I got bitten by a turtle." He laughed. "But then I ate him, so all was well."

"You have a strange sense of adventure," Ivy grinned. "I think I'll stick to walking – *very safely* – across this grass."

Guntah's good-natured response was interrupted by a gruff hiss from Xiou.

"Ficharu!" Ivy dropped immediately to her knees. She recognised the instruction without need for translation. *Get down!* There was danger ahead.

Xiou slipped back to them, now moving low through the long grass without breaking its uniformity from above. She still marvelled at the hobbits' ability to move seamlessly through their environment. Xiou lay his palm over Ivy's amulet, giving Gihn, who was behind them, a moment to catch up.

"We are not alone." He nodded his head toward the southeast. "Near the forest edge, a herd of Probech are grazing. Twelve of them – a matriarch herd."

"Can't we go around them?" Ivy asked.

"It is not the Probech I am concerned about," Xiou said. As he spoke, Guntah's head popped up just above the cover of grass, scanning the landscape with an eagle eye.

"Karathah." Guntah spat. He ducked back down.

"More hunting?" Gihn looked dismayed. "They took the four bachelors only days ago. How many more animals do they need?"

"They must have a far bigger tribe near here than we thought." Ivy's heart sank. "To need so much food, there must be many." She recalled the distant travellers they had encountered during their journey.

"Your adventure through the grass will not be as safe as you had hoped, Hiranah," sighed Guntah.

"What if we move closer to the mountain?" Ivy suggested. "Follow those ridges south. That way we can put more distance between us."

"Yes," Xiou said. "I think that is the only way. But keep low, Hiranah. Your hair is like a fire in the grass – easy to see." Ivy nodded, pulled out the thin strip of leather binding her hair, then re-tied it tighter, trying to drag more of her unruly red curls into submission. "Let's go." With a signal to the others, Xiou took off ahead again, moving through the grass like an arrow, barely shifting the carpet above. Ivy followed, as low and carefully as she could, her heart thumping. Her fiery hair, her pale skin, her height – were all liabilities here.

Across the plain, Ivy could hear the Karathah's ambush launch into action. *The hunt was on.* Trumpeting screams split the air. Shouts of instruction. Bellows of rage.

Pounding footsteps and the thud of one massive body colliding against another. The pandemonium drew closer.

"Shisa!" Xiou urged her. *Faster!*

Ivy dared a glance above the grass cover. They were almost at the rocky ridges of the western line of mountains.

"Shisa!" Xiou urged again. He was on Ivy's tail as she bolted, doubled over through the grass, clutching her spear. She stumbled and fell onto her hands, terrified of lifting her face above the

cover. Bellows of rage were almost up on her. The stegodon were stampeding. Toward Ivy. And bringing the Karathah hunters with them.

In an instant, her hope of escape was lost. The long grass split apart, and a quartet of enormous legs caged her; the matriarch stegodon and her sisters were surrounded by spears, pounding their fury into the soil. Ivy ducked and rolled, dodging the legs as they came crashing down.

At least two dozen hunters closed in around the stegodon, trapping them both in a ring of spears. The stegodon bellowed and bucked. Her sisters and daughters pushed through, scattering men, and snapping bones. The animals screamed as sharpened flint pierced their hides. As if in sympathy, the earth itself began to rage.

From deep underground, the matriarch's footfalls were answered by a primeval growl that rattled the land above. Monumental jolts knocked the hunters off their feet. Ivy grabbed the earth for stability as the matriarch shifted aside to swipe an assailant. *I'll get trampled. I need to run.* Ivy scrambled to her feet, pushing up from the ground with her spear. Her head swivelled wildly, searching for a clear path ahead. But the sudden appearance of a woman with a spear, with pale skin and bright red tangle of hair above the yellowing grass, could not go unnoticed. Screams of surprise amplified the aching groans of the earth.

A battle cry broke from the mouth of a Karathah hunter, his lips twisted in horror at the aberration of Ivy's face suddenly emerging from between the legs of the great beast. The fallout was instant. The chaos, spectacular.

All weapons turned on Ivy. A dozen spears at her neck. The Karathah hunter moved forward, tall, and dark with sinewy muscles that moved beneath his skin. He called out in a language Ivy didn't understand – then gave a battlecry that hollowed her bones.

EXTINCT

I'm about to die. The truth of it froze her in place. Xiou and Guntah appeared beside her, urging Ivy to run.

Thunk! The Karathah hunter fell, mouth twisted in shock as the blood drained from his face. Xiou's spear stuck in his neck.

Thunk! A second Karathah keeled over, his own spear scraping from Ivy's ear down to her chest as he fell with it in hand.

"Hiranah!" Xiou was shouting, but Ivy's reactions weren't fast enough. Her friends grabbed at her wrists, trying to drag her away, one hand each now brandishing a knife to replace their lost spears.

"Ebu gogo!" The cry went up. "Ebu gogo!" Astonishment at the sudden materialisation of the hobbits dove into uproar as their alliance with the bizarre woman became apparent. Cries of alarm became hisses of fury. Ivy did not need to a translation to understand the Karathah's hatred and fear.

"Ebu gogo!" Animals that infested their hunting territory.

"Ebu gogo!" Wretches that wasted caves and prey.

"Ebu gogo!" Pests that refused to be exterminated.

A pandemonium of confusion offered the stegodon a thunderous chance to escape. *Thunk!* A Karathah spear missed Ivy's leg by an inch as Mother Earth ripped herself open and shuddered, sending everybody sprawling once more.

Ivy scrambled to her feet. Her fist sweaty, spear slipping. Rough skin grated Ivy's face. The old matriarch's eye met her own as Ivy rose to her feet. Beneath the long lashes, Ivy witnessed exhaustion and frustration amassing inside. The stegodon's feet had detected the seismic vibrations growing in the earth long before the earthquake hit. Her efforts to lead her family to safety had been thwarted by the hunters that threatened them with violence. She'd had enough.

The matriarch tossed her head, storing each attacker's face to memory. Then she lifted her front legs together and *Crash!* descended upon two Karathah, her weight crushing them down into the tremoring ground. She lifted her trunk in a scream of fury, urging her herd to fight. Sisters and daughters alike leaned back on their hind legs, then heaved forward together, crushing the Karathah in a scatter of bones and split of skulls. Ivy's breath was strangled.

Run. Run. Run.

Her spear-tip got caught in the grass. She tried tearing it away, but it wouldn't come. Ivy had no choice but to relinquish the spear. She dragged the hobbits with her instead, but each in turn slipped from her grasp. She felt a hand push her forward through the wall of bodies.

"Tarup!" Xiou's voice broke over the din. *Run!*

"No!" She cried back, trying to drag him along.

"Tarup! Tarup!" He pushed her hard.

So, Ivy ran. Faster than she had ever run in her life. Away from the bellowing stegodon, and the Karathah hunters falling to pieces beneath their feet. Away from her friends as they faced the sapien predators alone. With an immense groan that split the air and earth alike, the rumbling earth cracked open behind her, cutting Ivy loose from the mayhem behind and forcing her feet toward the mountain ridges to the west.

Run. Run. Run.

Within minutes she had reached the first rocks. Ahead of her, crumbling granite pelted down from the ridge. Ivy dodged as the ground shifted underfoot, sucking gaping holes at her feet. She spun, dripping with cold sweat. A savage chasm now ran the length of the ridge, all the way south to the ocean. In the distance, the stegodon herd were stampeding back the way they had come. The Karathah were scattered, leaving more corpses than running men.

Ivy realised with panic that there was no way back to Xiou, Guntah and Gihn. No way of even knowing if they were alive. The chasm between them was uncrossable. She brought shaking fingers to her lips, too scared to collapse in case the rattling earth gave way underneath her. Ivy squeezed her eyes shut. *You're on your own.* The thought made her nauseous. *And there's no going back.*

For a few minutes, Ivy crouched, her fingers too tight around the razor-sharp rocks. *Breathe. Breathe. Just breathe.* The sun beat mercilessly. The only way was forward –v to continue the path between the chasm and mountain ridges toward the south, and hope that the ocean might reunite her with the others at the end. *Will they find me? Will I find them?* Ivy couldn't imagine navigating the island without her guides. Without her friends. Without her spear. Without food or water.

But there was no choice. Ivy pulled a sharpened stone knife from her travelling skirt, one of the few belongings that remained, and scratched a series of dots onto a rock that had fallen. Five holes, in the shape of the constellation of stars of the Southern Cross. Five points, identical to the ones scratched into the back of her amulet. *I'll leave signs for them to follow,* she decided, *if they come this way.* She knew the hobbits would recognise the symbol from her amulet. The constellation represented her as much as anything else could. The Southern Cross, the lobed points of an ivy leaf. *Hiranah.*

Finally, resolutely, Ivy took a terrified breath and pushed up off the rock. She took a step forward. Then another.

I'm alone now. Nothing else has changed. I still need to get to the Savu Sea caves. I need to search for more hobbits. That's what Gihn would want me to do, with or without him. Then try to get back to Kelimutu. Ivy glanced across the rift between where she stood now and where she had lost her friends. *They'll find me.* She tried to convince herself. *I know they will.*

As the sun beat down and the earth settled, Ivy's steps led her south toward the sea.

Six hours of walking and climbing alone, brought the sunset with it. There was no food in the folds of her hide skirt, only a stone knife, her empty water bladder and the flint rocks and tuft of oleos-soaked bamboo she carried for starting a fire. There was little vegetation that she recognised on the ridges, and none of it looked edible. Ivy pushed on, heading south, knowing that the coastline of the Savu Sea should greet her if she just kept going. The tough soles of her feet burned. She held foliage above her head to shade the blistering sun. Her skin shocked with new freckles, drawn out by the UV rays. But night fell too soon, without food or water. Ivy wedged herself into a cradle-shaped ridge mid-mountainside to sleep, feeling safe from the low-dwelling Komodos, but exposed to the many snakes she knew were partial to the warm stone.

And she'd slept.

"No! Oh, my!" Ivy sat bolt upright, heart hammering as two beady eyes stared at her from only inches away. The bird's head was cocked to the side as if considering what kind of animal she might be. Ivy suspected it hoped she was a dead one. "I'm still alive! I'm alive!" The enormous vulture shuffled back, but seemed unperturbed by the woman it clearly considered no threat. It opened a sharp, curved pink beak and unfurled wings over two meters wide, shaking them out. With a contemptuous look, the vulture gave a raspy, drawn-out hissing sound. Ivy scrambled to her feet. "Sorry! No, no, no! I'm definitely not the breakfast you're looking for."

The bird was enormous, at least a meter long. It had a pale bald head and gangly neck ruffled in white feathers, its body hunched and draped in dark brown plumage. Black wings and tail feathers contrasted against white legs with gaunt boney talons, giving the austere impression of a gothic priest. It eyeballed Ivy, bobbing its long neck with a grunting noise that sounded like a hungry pig.

"Still alive," Ivy reassured the bird, her palms out. She looked around. There was no point trying to climb further up the ridge, it was too steep. "I'm going to have to get past you, aren't I?" She pushed up from the rock and took a step forward, risking a similar advance by the vulture. It stepped sideways instead. "I'm still not carrion," Ivy assured it. "Sorry about that." The vulture turned slightly, looking unimpressed and took a few flat-footed steps away from her. Though Ivy knew giant vultures were endemic to prehistoric Flores, she had never seen one up close. The bizarre, gangly-necked creature would be extinct by her own time, along with so many other species from the island. Ivy was intrigued by it, but the sharp beak and talons, strong enough to tear the hide off a stegodon, kept her at bay. "Sorry to disappoint you," Ivy murmured, sidestepping the bird in a cautious arc. It studied her as she moved. "You never know though," she dead panned, "give me a few days and I might be worth circling."

With one last grunt and bob, the giant vulture spread its wings and took off, leaving her alone on the rocky ridge. Ivy desperately hoped she didn't see it again. The bird felt like a bad omen.

Loneliness prickled her neck, and Ivy couldn't help but throw glances over her shoulder as she walked. Another full day had passed under the sweltering sun as she continued south along the spine of the monstrous divide. A scatter of rocks underfoot sent her stumbling for what seemed like the hundredth time. "Damn it!" Ivy collapsed onto a boulder. Her skin was glowing red from the combined effort of UV rays and endless exertion. She squeezed her eyes tight and let oxygen fill her slowly, tempering the anger rising in her chest. "What the bloody hell am I doing?" She said aloud. Her words drifted off on the breeze. "Honestly Ivy, what *is* the point of this? You're completely alone in the middle of *God-knows-where* and you have no idea where you're going." It wasn't true of course; she felt the defensive hackles rise in her shoulders. *I kind-of know where I'm going,* her indignation replied. Ivy dropped her head into her hands. "And now I'm arguing with myself." Her overactive mind had always been both worst enemy and best friend, dragging her between vivid night-mares and spiralling worst-case scenarios, before lifting her to the heights of inspiration and self-belief with a thrumming moti-vation that her body could barely contain. "Well, I can't see where I'm going." Ivy looked up at the rising moon. "No point tripping over myself for another hour. I may as well set up camp." She gave up for the night, settling down in another rocky outcrop. After a long while staring at the stars, she slept fitfully until the sun rose again.

Just breathe, Ivy reminded herself as she set off again at dawn. *You can do this.* She squinted at the rising sun. *Just keep walking. And find some water.* The sparse tree cover thickened up ahead, and Ivy fervently hoped she'd discover a creek. Each morning, she had sucked the condensation from any rocky crevice it had been caught in, but her dry throat complained. Each time she rested Ivy scratched the constellation into a rock before forcing herself back to her feet. Over a dozen engravings of the Southern Cross trailed the ridge so far. She hoped the others found them. The ridges behind her were still empty though, with no sign of human life, of either species since she'd become separated from them. Ivy's feet found a rhythm. She pushed on.

Two hours later, her reward was crystal clear water. A sparkling pool had been captured in the crags of limestone and pumice tuff, surrounded by bushes. Ivy satiated her thirst to the point of bursting. She pulled the empty water bladder from her travelling hide and refilled it, tying the vessel end closed tightly with a thin vine, the way Shahn had taught her. A chatter of birds flitted through the copse above. Ivy counted at least a half-dozen species within arm's length of where she sat and couldn't help but marvel at the diversity of the island. Ivy closed her eyes, listening to bird calls and the soft whooshing of the breeze. Beneath it all, the meditative roll of ocean waves whispered. Ivy smiled. Without the mortal threats of interspecies genocide, volcanic eruptions, and earthquakes - Flores really was an island paradise.

And I must be close to the Savu Sea, Ivy realised. A faint taste of salt spray was in the air. A quickening of the breeze tempted her southward.

"Well, I prefer your company to that vulture," she yawned to a couple of plovers perched an arm's length away. The birds plumped and preened themselves, ignoring her. "You're lucky Kora isn't here, you know. I'm pretty sure you're her favourite dinner." Ivy stretched and stood up, feeling refreshed.

She set off again, quite sure she'd find the glittering edge of the ocean beyond the tree line. After trekking a further ten minutes, she pushed her way through. To Ivy's surprise, her path had ended. But instead of a gradual decline downward toward the ocean, she was faced with a vertical wall. The mountain ridge rose ahead of her in both directions, blocking her view of the sea entirely.

"Great," she muttered. She followed the western side of it for a short way, but quickly realised it was too steep to climb. Ivy turned back to follow the wall eastward instead, figuring that at least she was still heading in the right direction. Her toes hit the end of the path to find nothing at all – the mountain fell away in a hanging cliff. From her vantage point on the edge, at least fifty meters below, the blue ocean glittered up at her. A sandy coastline trailed away toward the east, disappearing around forested mountain ranges as far as she could see. Somewhere in those mountains, the caves she sought were hidden away like precious jewels. With any luck, hobbit tribes might be tucked safely within them.

"How the hell do I get down there?" Ivy wondered aloud. She walked a short way back along the eastern edge, then inward again to the forested copse she had rested in. She traced her steps toward the wall again, followed it west until she hit the vertical wall, then back again to the eastern edge. There was no way down.

"Seriously?" Ivy fumed, swatting away mosquitoes. "I've come all this way and there's no way down. You have got to be kidding!" She retraced her steps for a third time, pushing aside branches and pondering how likely it was that she could climb a vertical wall without plummeting to her death. Finally, with tears threatening to wash the sweat from her face, Ivy harrumphed, and plonked herself at the base of the wall.

Her foot slipped beneath a bush and dropped. She pulled it back. Ivy leaned forward and tugged on the bush itself. It was growing outward on an angle, leaving a dark space beneath its spread branches. She jumped to her feet, pulling them back as far as she could. Within the shadows beneath, the rocky floor disappeared into a dark, narrow tunnel. It was perhaps half a meter wide, but she couldn't see the bottom of it. She grabbed a small rock from the dirt at her feet and dropped it into the hole, listening closely for the soft clatter of its landing. The rock seemed to hit something, roll a little, and then continue to fall.

"Oh no." Ivy looked around desperately. She got to her feet. "Please don't tell me this is the only way?!" She paced back and forth at the tunnel entrance, wondering how crazy she would have to be to get into it. "It's the only way," she muttered. "No, it can't be." Her voice shook over the chatter of birdsong. Her heart raced. Two days walking had brought her here. She was cut off from her friends by the earthquake's chasm. Glancing back the way she came, Ivy realised there was no other option. She could either take the tunnel and hope for the best, or return to where she'd come from, then continue further north to the beginning the great chasm separated her from the east. She'd lose at least a week. "This is it," Ivy finally decided. "It's the only way. If I can get down this cliff through the tunnel, I can follow the beach as far east as Kelimutu." She stared down into the darkness at her feet. "*If* I can make it through." Ivy lay on her belly and let her head drop into the open hole. She thought she could hear the whoosh of air passing through it. Above that, a high-pitched clicking noise was growing louder.

Suddenly, a rush of feathers ricocheted off her face. Ivy screeched and sprang back, rolling sideways as a handful of tiny birds gushed from the tunnel entrance in twittering hysterics.

She rubbed her cheek where the soft little bodies had collided with her. "You nearly gave me a heart attack," Ivy chided them. She took a deep breath, willing her racing heart to slow. "Actually, now that I think about it, you're probably a good sign." She eyed the birds as they took off into the trees, then peered carefully back into the darkness of the tunnel. "Because if you live in there, that means it might open up down at the sea somewhere."

There had been various species of cave-dwelling birds in fossils dug out of Floresian archaeological sites, particularly in coastal caves, where they nested. Ivy recognised these little furies as swiftlets. Slender bodies with narrow wings kept the birds in flight all day catching insects, while their short legs allowed them to cling to vertical cave walls to build nests. In modern times, the opaque nests, made exclusively of solidified saliva, had become a Chinese delicacy, and the main ingredient of bird's nest soup.

"You can see down there in the dark, can you?" Ivy asked the birds riding the wind. She shot a doubtful look back into the tunnel entrance. "More likely, you can *hear* where you are." She leaned back as another handful of birds shot out of the tunnel in a flurry of feathers. "That must be what that clicking sound is," she surmised. Ivy leant over again, her ear to the tunnel. Sure enough, a chorus of sharp clicking noises greeted her again.

To roost and breed on the vertical walls of dark caves, the swiftlets used echolocation to navigate through the chasms and shafts. "I bet it's pitch black down there," Ivy sighed. It was a long shot, but considering her bleak options, Ivy decided there was no point procrastinating any longer. She got to her feet, tightened the knots of her hide skirt and pulled her hair back into a flatter ponytail. "Well, I'll need some sort of light." She rummaged around in the folds of her skirt. There wasn't much on offer. Ivy patted the flint rocks she carried to make sure they were still safe, then scoured the surrounding bushes for dry kindling and vines. She found a thick solid stick and set to work wrapping up her oleos-soaked bamboo fuzz close to one end. She added a layer of kindling on top, then strapped it together with dry vines. Shahn had given her the oil-soaked bamboo before she'd left Liang Bua cave and this was the last of it. Ivy hated to see it go. Fires were far more difficult to start without it. "Right. It's time to dive in then," she said aloud, hoping her own voice carried enough conviction to boost her confidence. "For better or worse. I just hope these birds can help me find the way through."

Ivy scratched one last symbol on the rock wall above the tunnel, and pulled the bush clear away, exposing the entrance for anyone that might come after her. Carefully, she lowered herself into the ground. Her toes slipped and scraped the edge of the rock, grasping for purchase. When she found it, Ivy carefully began to drop. The tunnel was dim. A watery ray from the opening illuminated a slight decline, then it continued downward into the dark. With a final, desperate look back toward the sun, Ivy squatted, then flattened herself out and crawled headfirst into the tunnel.

Each inch forward brought a fresh wave of fear. The clicking and screeching of birds grew louder as she progressed. Ivy slid, as often as not, as rubble found its way underneath to quicken her descent. She cursed. Held her breath. Hoped against all hope that the tunnel would not disappear beneath her. *Don't think about it,* she willed herself. Ivy grit her teeth, trying not to imagine falling to her death inside the cliff. The tunnel felt like a tomb. She knew well enough that it could easily become one.

Swiftlets pushed past her to escape the tunnel. Others hit her back and returned outside, waiting for a clear path to reclaim their nests.

About ten meters down, the tunnel narrowed. Ivy sucked in her breath and shoulders. The still-unlit oleos torch was held ahead of her, gripped tight while her other hand scraped sharp edges away. Elbows and knees in the dirt. She felt herself descending, and wondered how far down the cliff she already was. A quarter of the way, perhaps. It was impossible to tell in the dark. Ivy inched forward. The clatter and chatter of birds ahead grew louder. A few more body lengths finally opened up into an airy chamber.

Ivy's head emerged, gratefully, only a couple of meters above the floor of a wide cave. Turning on her hands and knees, she grasped the edge of the tunnel, and dropped. *Hmph.* Her lungs compressed as Ivy's feet hit the dirt. Pulling herself straight, stale air drew fast into her lungs.

"Like a noisy mausoleum," Ivy breathed, looking around in awe. The cave was, perhaps, three meters wide by four, and unevenly surfaced. It felt cloistered, as if the walls had been waiting thousands of years for new eyes to find them. Finger-width poke-holes of light broke through from the opposite wall, illuminating the cave with enough brightness for her eyes to comfortably adjust. Ivy guessed the other side of that wall must be the outer cliff that overlooked the Savu Sea. But it was the noise that Ivy found most astonishing. Hundreds of swiftlets clung to the vertical walls, tucked inside opaque nests glued to the limestone. Dozens flit from one side of the cave to the other all at once. The roof of the cave was alive with raucous activity. Ivy took a step, watching for a reaction from the tiny birds. There was none. She picked her way across the floor to the far side, bending down to look through one of the holes in the wall. The rock was thick, at least a meter, so all she could see was bright blue sky.

"At least I know where I am." Ivy's voice, though quiet, amplified in the acoustics of the cave, send a fresh wave of twittering through its residents. "Now, how on earth do I get out?" Gingerly stepping across the floor, Ivy traced the inner edges of the cave. "Guano." She wrinkled her nose in distaste at the cemented floor of excrement. "That's not though." Ivy crouched down. Pale bones were resting in the corner, layered in part by bird droppings. "A perfect mandible," Ivy murmured. She gently turned it over in her hands. She held the fossil under the light of a poke-hole, studying the familiar primitive features of a hobbit jawbone.

It had the classic sweep of the v-shaped lower jaw, typical of *Homo* species but holding premolar roots that suggest a far older ancestor, like *Homo Habilis* from Africa. The bony point of a modern human chin was missing, instead offering a bony shelf at the front of the lower jaw – a primitive feature not consistent with *Homo Erectus* as an anatomic predecessor. The little jaw was an evolutionary puzzle – but in the perfect composite of an ancestor to Gihn's species. Ivy sifted gently through the pile at her feet. Tiny wrist bones looked almost indistinguishable from an African ape. But there was nothing about the small skull she found that suggested the owner was ape-like. It was a curious skull. *Complex.* Illuminating a strange combination of features not seen in any other hominin species. Ivy brushed her fingers gently inside the braincase. The Broadmann area 10 was enlarged – *higher level cognitive abilities*. A long and low cranial shape – more familiar in *Homo erectus* than modern humans. Narrow nose. Flat face. Delicate, individual brow ridges. This was no brute caveman. This was a tiny, intelligent species of human.

The bones looked old – far older than any she had seen before. Remains, perhaps, of an ancestor to the friends she had made here, perhaps even one of the earliest to colonise the island. *Homo floresiensis* had been living on Flores for at least 700,000 years. A precursor to the current population might have displayed these slightly different features.

Time changes all things, Ivy thought, *even bones.* She looked around, marvelling at the irony. She'd studied human bones her entire adult life. But these weren't just fossils. They were the ancestors of the people she was trying to save. Gihn's ancestors. Shahn's ancestors. Her new family. Ivy's breath was reverent as she spoke to the bones in the dark.

"How many thousands of years have you been waiting in this cave for someone to find you?"

She gently placed the skull back on top of the neat pile. Ivy drew up to her feet, ducking, as a fresh flutter of wings brushed past her head.

"I'm afraid you're going to have to keep waiting though," she said. "Maybe one day, if I ever make it home, I'll come back for you."

From the furthest wall of the cave, a new arrival of swiftlets led Ivy to a hole in the floor. It was a continuation of the tunnel, narrower and without the light of the poke holes she had come to rely on.

"If you can get in through here, I hope I can get out," she sighed, stuffing the oleos-torch down the side of her skirt. "I'm a lot bigger than you birds though." Ivy lowered herself inside, head-first. Every fibre of her being told her this was a terrible idea. The lack of options kept her moving. Elbows dug into the rock floor. Legs dragged behind. The twittering pandemonium of the swiftlets faded away and silence suffocated the air like black smoke. Gravity helped her along – perhaps a forty-five-degree angle sloped downward for what felt like miles. There was no way she could back up to return to the cave. If she hit a dead-end, Ivy knew she was dead. *Just keep moving,* she chanted, breath shallow and fast as she battled her failing nerves. *Keep moving.* Ivy pressed onward. Another half hour that felt like years passed in aching limbs. *Keep moving. Keep moving.*

Something soft and hairy scuttled across her hand. Ivy sucked in a breath. *A spider.* Bigger than any spider should rightly feel. She flicked her wrist, hearing a soft *flump* as the creature hit a wall.

"Okay, that's it." Ivy was panting. Sweat and dust caked her face. She blinked hard to clear her eyes. Reaching back, Ivy twisted and fumbled, desperately pulling the oleos torch from her waistband, and inching it forward underneath her body until it was ahead of her. Her fingers grappled for the flint chips she knew were buried somewhere in the folds of her skirt. Her own grunts echoed up the tunnel ahead. "I just need light for a second, that's all," she grumbled. It was risky, lighting the torch in such a confined space. Ivy's gut wrenched at the thought of it. *Too much smoke. Not enough oxygen.* "But if I could see where I'm going, just for a moment–" Desperation made her fingers slippery. The flint was hard to catch. Finally, she caught the sharp edges in her fingers and twisted her arm carefully back up toward her face. She flopped onto her chest, taking a moment to breathe before setting to the task of snapping the flint rocks together. The tiny clatter produced nothing but broken silence until at last, a red spark broke free. "Yes!" She huffed, dragging the kindling end of the torch closer. She tried again. And again. "This was easier when I could move my arms," she growled. Her bottom lip was shaking. The stillness was oppressive. Ivy stretched her neck, arched her back as far as she could to relieve a growing cramp, and tried again. "Come on!" She begged. "Just one more little–" her eyes lit up in the pitch "–spark!" The whisper of red landed squarely on a soft tuft of dried grass. It curled, bright and eager across its bed and began to crackle and hiss. It was the best thing Ivy had ever seen. With an enormous grin, Ivy picked up the end of the torch as the oleos oil began to fuel its head. She held it out triumphantly ahead of her. The tunnel walls lit up like beacons.

They were moving.

"No–" It took Ivy a moment for her brain to make sense of the shifting rock. "Oh no–"

The walls were *not* moving. *Legs* were. Thousands of them. Legs attached to flat, hairy bodies the size of dinner plates.

The tunnel was writhing in spiders.

"*Oh-my-god, oh-my-god, oh-my-god*–" Ivy squeezed her eyes shut, willing her heart to slow. Tremors shook her fingers, jolting the torchlight around the tunnel like a strobe. Hot breath licked the cold sweat on her face and lifted hair on the nape of her neck and arms. Ivy's face was stark white. Muscles pulled tight, as if making her body as small as possible might save it from being seen.

"I don't hate spiders," Ivy breathed, trying to calm herself. "I love *all* animals. I really do," she tried to convince herself. "I just – I just need to – try not to–" She took a firm breath, blinked furiously, and carefully slid her fist down toward her skirt, tucking the flint fire-starters back into a fold in the leather. She made a tiny move forward. It seemed to have no effect on the arachnids swarming over one another ahead of her. "Try not to touch them–" she inched forward again, forcing herself into the tangle of crawlers, "–just don't touch them." The spiders scuttled away from the flame. Ivy lifted it, gently sweeping above the wall beside her. An army of bodies raced to cling to the roof above instead. A few fell, landing squarely on her head and Ivy couldn't stifle the screech that escaped. "You're just – you're just huntsman's, I think, that's all. You can't hurt me. I hope." There was no conviction in the words. The flattened shape and soft brown bodies were a familiar sight – a few had even shared her space in the tiny apartment she rented near the university. Huntsman spiders were swift and aggressive if provoked, but individually no more venomous than a bee sting. Still, Ivy didn't like her chances against the thousands that swarmed around her. She lowered the torch, coughing as smoke filled the tunnel. She needed to douse the flame. But the flame seemed the only thing that might shift the mass of spiders. She pushed forward a few more inches, clearing the way with the blazing torch and back of her forearm. "This –is – fine–" Ivy coughed. She felt a little unhinged, as if her mind and body were separating as she moved. "I'm-fine-and-you're-all-just-living-happily-in-this-dark-hellscape-of-a-tunnel-that-I'm-crawling-through-and-it's-my-own-fault-that-I'm-here–" she broke into another ravage of coughing. "If-I-can-just-get-through-a-little-faster." Ivy sped up, pushing spiders ahead of her as she shuffled the torch along the floor. The tunnel seemed to be clearing. Spiders swept along the roof and walls either side of her body. A shadow of movement escaped over her head and down her back, retreating to the tunnel behind. The walls swam. Ivy's vision blurred. She felt lightheaded.

The smoke. She pulled the torch toward her and smacked it hard against the dirt floor. Sparks flew up and singed her face. *Burnt hair smell.* Ivy rolled the torch against the rocky floor ahead of her, gathering handfuls of dirt to sweep and smother it.

"What-the-hell-was-I-thinking?!" She was furious now, with her own poor judgement and the terror of being asphyxiated within a tunnel inside a cliff. Ivy clawed at the dirt, scraping it up and piling it onto the oleos torch, rolling and pressing the flames against the rock. Spiders were moving as one, rushing forward now, in a wave of legs and plump bodies, descending further into the bowels of the tunnel to escape the smoke. The air must be clearer ahead. *They're clever,* Ivy realised, *far cleverer than me.*

Finally, the torch stuttered and hissed. The tunnel went black.

Ivy coughed and heaved as she scraped her way forward again, pushing the now-impotent torch ahead of her. Spiders were still moving *en masse*, so she followed them, carefully sweeping her forearms ahead in the dark, trying to lift them away from the rock, rather than crush them against it. Bites came hard and fast – at least a dozen, as the unfortunates got caught beneath her and fought back. *"Just keep moving,"* she chanted, her throat hoarse and jaw clamped shut. *Keep moving. Keep moving.* Everything hurt.

There was sharp dip in the tunnel and Ivy landed on her collarbones, head snapping back with the jolt. Her eyes began to stream. She rubbed them with filthy fingers.

Light was ahead. *Natural light.* Thousands of spiders moved around her, racing toward it. *An opening to the outside,* Ivy realised. *I must be getting close.* She straightened up and shuffled faster. A trail of blood streamed from her elbows and knees as she went. *I'm getting close.* Hope was suddenly oxygen to her starved lungs. The tunnel widened. It was levelling out.

As the swarm of hairy bodies escaped the tunnel mouth onto the walls of a cool, damp cave at the base of the mountain, Ivy fell in behind them.

She hit the ground with a hard thud.

Relief was so overwhelming, it wasn't until Ivy had pulled herself shakily to her feet, that a heavy rasping sound penetrated her brain.

A deep throated rattle was shuddering through the cave. Behind it, the rushing sound of water. Ivy's feet stumbled under crumbling rocks. Her shoulder blades backed up against the tunnel entrance.

The sweet, fresh air petrified in her lungs.

She had fallen straight into a Komodo nest.

CHAPTER 18

NEIL

"*N*ee-el! Nee-el!" Atasi came bursting from the trees, her arm held out. Instantly, Charat grabbed her wrist, swinging the woman to a halt, mid-step. Neil jumped to his feet and jogged toward them. Atasi was speaking quickly, pointing back into the trees with dirty fingers. Her collecting basket was still strapped to her back, half full of greenery.

Charat gestured for Neil to hurry. His lips pouted. His eyes turned greedy as he took something from Atasi's outstretched hand, studied it for a moment and then pushed her behind him. Charat held up a black stone as Neil drew close. Neil took it. His fingers trembled as he turned it over gently. *This is it.* The stone was pitch black, dull, and unimpressive. Except for its shape, which was squarish and a bit rough on one side, it looked identical to the rock Ivy carried around her wrist. *Jesus Christ.* It was nothing but a filthy rock, but he was spellbound. *Home. Benjamin. Home.* Neil squeezed it tight, tearing his eyes away to find Atasi peering out from behind Charat.

"Thank you." He whispered, overcome. Atasi smiled. Charat clapped her shoulder roughly, as if in praise, and then gave her some new instruction. She shrank back at his touch, nodded obediently, dropping her eyes to the ground. Charat signaled for the watching hunters to join him. There were only two, as he had sent the others off on some mission hours ago. As the remaining two hunters sprang to their feet, Atasi hurried away in the direction she had come. A moment before she disappeared though, she hesitated, glancing back over her shoulder to Neil.

For a moment of paused time, their eyes met.

It was as if everything and nothing was spoken at once. The silence spilled between them in a thousand commiserations for the miserable existence they both found themselves in. Neil's heart stuttered. His skin prickled and the jabbering of men around him fell on deaf ears. *She knows. Maybe not all of it, but enough to understand. My desperation. My loneliness.* Neil was stunned at the empathy he found in her eyes. He barely knew her, really. He couldn't even speak to her. But it was there.

Creeping humiliation burned up his chest. Neil was gutted. Wracked with guilt. Because as wretched as her own life was, there had been hope in the look Atasi offered him, hope that he, at least, could escape. Gratitude surged within him like a shockwave, bleeding to the tips of his fingers where he clutched the black stone. Gratitude and something else. Something he'd never felt before. Something deep and warm and not entirely uncomfortable. Neil swallowed hard as the woman turned away again, disappearing between the trees.

"Nee-el," growled Charat. As if stumbling out of a dream, Neil found his focus. The hunters were gathered around the hearth beside him, standing tall and looking expectantly. "Ebu gogo." Charat slapped the knife on his belt, with clear intention then pointed back to the stone in Neil's fist. "Ebu gogo *watki atinu-carrapu...*" The others laughed at his undoubtedly crude reference to killing hobbits.

Neil nodded tiredly. *Of course.* Now that he had the stone they had come searching for, they wanted it to prove its use. It was meant to kill hobbits. *Shit.* Charat stepped forward, crowding his space. "Ebu gogo," he said again eagerly, tapping the sheathed blade. Charat looked upward, searching for the sun between the treetops. Neil followed his gaze and found the sun. It was only an hour or two past midday. Charat grinned and pointed upward, speaking again in native tongue. The hunters shouted and slapped their weapons gleefully. *They want to do it today. Shit. Shit. Shit.*

"I need a moment," said Neil, waving them back. "Just, just – wait." He strode back to the battery cell line, feeling the back of his neck prick with cold. *Shit.* His plan all along was to find a stone and use it to get the hell out of here. He didn't think he'd be around long enough to actually have to prove its falsified power to them. He'd only said it would help them kill hobbits, in order to get the entourage of protection and guides he needed to locate it. *Shit. Shit.* Neil sat abruptly in the dirt with his back to the waiting men. He opened his palm and studied the stone. *I can't give them what they want. I don't know where the hell any hobbits are. They'll kill me when they realise that I've been lying all along.* His breath stuttered and Neil stiffened his muscles to keep from betraying his emotion to the men watching from behind. *Whatever mercy is out there,* he thought, *help me now.* He squeezed his eyes and hand shut, clamping his fist to his chest. *Take me home,* he begged. *I need to get home. My son needs me.* Neil waited for the pain or a rush of air or some other sign that his plea had worked. *Nothing.* He tried again and again, whispering, too desperate to feel ridiculous as tears pricked his eyes. *There's no place like home. There's no place like home.*

It was cruel, this morsel of hope. It was torture to hold the muted power he knew the stone had but refused to release. *Please. Please. I beg you. God, Satan, whoever the hell is out there – pity me, please!* Neil's shoulders sagged and he fell forward, shaking. *Nothing.*

He took a deep breath, then another. He righted himself, gritting his jaw. The others would be watching. *Think. Think!* It was the same type of stone; Neil was sure of it. But he knew he hadn't done enough. His copper lightning rod lay in the dirt beside him. There was just something wrong, he convinced himself. Something he was missing or had forgotten. He needed to buy some time to figure out what.

Neil rubbed his leg in agitation and pulled the polished lighter from his pocket. He spun it slowly through his fingers as he considered. *They want hobbits to kill, and they think this stone can provide that. I need to figure out how the damn stone works and keep them off my back while I do it.* His eyes raked the scattered belongings on the ground in front of him. His mobile phone was fully charged. *Compass will work again, so I've got navigation. I could go it alone.* Neil reached forward, tugging Ivy's journal from the hide carry bag he'd been given. He flicked through the pages slowly; searching for something he wasn't quite sure would help. A worn copy of a photograph fell out. It was a rock wall, strangely banded with something uneven and glittering between grey rock. *Maybe...* Within the page of scribbled notes that had enveloped it, he recognised the hand-drawn map, one of many he'd scanned over the past week. This one was sketchy, probably used as a quick reference for something the redhead already knew, but it was usable. Hidden within the stratigraphic notes, dates and latitudes were the magic words that would save his neck.

Kelimutu - future excavation site?

Dig site is south/south-east, cave, near base of mountain. Stone tools found, also bones - vertebrae + scapula, partial jaw. Tiny size!

Preliminary date of 50K yrs BP

Potential H. floresiensis!

Neil almost laughed in relief. *Gotcha.*

"We should leave," Neil said. His fingers detailed a line in the dirt – a rude diagram of where he wanted to lead them. He stabbed the ground with an index finger. "Time to go. *Ebu gogo here.*" Charat shook his head. Apparently, despite his insistence for action, he was determined to wait.

"Agung," he said. "Churik." Charat wouldn't leave until his two missing hunters returned. Neil would have happily left them behind. Charat returned to sharpening his knife with a sly grin. A shiver ran up Neil's spine. He didn't want to know what Charat was scheming. Soon enough though, it became clear. As dusk fell, Charat's missing hunters returned. They were not alone.

"Agung!" Charat cheered his friend, who walked ahead of another two dozen men. They moved through the forest as a wave, spilling into the spaces between trees until Neil was surrounded. These hunters were ornamented differently to Charat's tribe. Neil didn't recognise any of them. Agung, the sycophant that hung on every word barked from Charat's lips, looked like the cat who had got the cream. Whatever mission his master had sent him on, he'd returned victorious.

One of the new men stepped forward, eyeing Neil suspiciously. Every new face reflected his shock at finding a pale-skinned man amongst themselves. A man that looked so different to anything they'd seen before. Neil knew – to be *different* was never a good thing. He rose to his feet. Heart thumping. Neck tingling. *Was this an ambush?* But before Neil could speak, Charat intercepted. He launched into a rapid-fire welcome, hands moving emphatically. Every so often Neil caught the word *Ebu Gogo* fly about, and it became clear that Charat was regaling the newcomers with their journey so far. Neil's own name was thrown at them. *Berap*, Volcano. *Mutu*. Coloured lakes. An adventure woven with embellishments and built on Neil's own foundation of lies. Whatever Charat wanted from these men, it seemed to warrant his greatest performance yet.

The new hunters listened with tense shoulders. Every few words, they would hold up a hand, and Charat would repeat himself. Words lost in translation. Apparently, their language was similar enough to understand, but different enough to cause stumbling blocks. Charat upped his game. Spoke louder, clearer. Hands and spittle flying in equal measure. But whatever the red-beaded hunter was trying to sell wasn't sticking. One man, who Neil took to be their leader, stepped forward. He was bullish and broad, with sharp eyes. He asked questions. A web of glances between the two groups. An undercurrent of hostility. Charat drew up to his full height, twisting his spearpoint into the dirt as he spoke. A subtle threat. He was questioned further. Tense shoulders froze, spears clutched a little tighter, eyes narrowed all around.

At the end of his pitch, Charat drew on his showstopper.

"Nee-el!" The man's tone left no room for refusal. Charat bent down, sweeping up in front of Neil in an elaborate display. "Nee-el!" The name was meant to imply a state of wonder. Of terror. Under Charat's direction, his remaining sycophants took up the chant. *"Nee-el!"* A title worthy of the false God.

All eyes on him, Neil had no choice but to comply. *I'm a dancing monkey,* he thought, easing into the role with practiced theatrics. He hated it.

The silver lighter became a demonstration of Neil's omnipotence. Flames flicked into life within his hands.

His phone screen shone like a demon in the dusk. Each new photo Neil held up wove a story of the arcane. Faces frozen in time. Souls captured within stone. Fingertips flicking through the images like a deck of cards in the hand of a magician.

Neil recited his old threats and prophesies, knowing the men couldn't understand a word of it. Knowing that it didn't matter. Charat was playing his part, shouting and whispering in turn to emphasize the parts of his scheme that warranted it. Extortions of the truth. Believable enough to rile his audience into action. Neil knew the story Charat spun. He had, himself, come up with it.

Ebu Gogo were being blamed for the earthquakes. Framed for the death of Charat's men. Charged with the destruction of his cave.

The diatribe reached a crescendo. Nostrils flared. Feet stamped against the forest floor. Jeers and curses leapt from tongues.

Neil stepped back a little, shrinking away from the riot he'd fuelled. The new hunters were incensed, their eyes now opened to the bigger picture that Charat had laid out for them so clearly. Before, the Ebu gogo had been but a nuisance. A pest to be rid of.

But now... now, it was clear that they had underestimated the little people. The Ebu gogo were capable of greed, murder, and thievery beyond expectation. They needed to be dealt with, before the situation got out of hand. Charat's warning might save his audience the same fate as his own tribe. The leader of the new tribe stepped forward. He nodded, clasped Charat's hand in his own, crossing the other fist over his heart. Head bowed in respect; he swivelled toward Neil. He opened his arms.

"Datang!" He declared, with open arms. He gestured for them all to follow. *"Nee-el. Charat. Datang."*

Charat began barking orders. They had been invited to move, Neil realised. He rushed to gather up his belongings. *Bowls, Sulphur. Copper rods. Journal. Knife. Phone. Cable.*

Atasi fell into line behind Neil as the string of hunters began a winding descent down the mountain. They were heading south. Neil struggled to recall Ivy's maps in the journal, flicking pages as he trekked. *Toward the sea?* The shells adorning some of the hunters suggested it likely. He threw a look back over his shoulder. Atasi's eyes were fearful. Any words of comfort he might have offered dried up in his mouth as he watched the back of the men in front of him. He knew he was Charat's pawn. Nothing more, nothing less. And still no closer to saving himself. Let alone anyone else.

The following morning, Charat and his band of hunters were travelling again. There were even more of them now – nearly fifty – recruited around the embers of the evening fire. Charat had again regaled his new friends with the depravity of the Ebu gogo. The ruthlessness of their attacks. Greed for possessing the best caves. Their idolatry of the sinister pale woman with hair like flames, and the wild black beast that did her bidding.

By the time he had finished, the men were itching for a fight.

This morning, their destination was close. The party traveled briefly east and then followed a vein of the mountain south, immersing themselves in ancient roots. The base of the volcano was jungled and buttressed, and twice, they transected steep rifts to save negotiating narrow valleys.

At Charat's insistence, Neil was leading. He had his mobile compass in his pocket and checked it regularly, keeping them on the most direct route to the potential hobbit cave Ivy had mapped out in her journal. In his left hand, held up high for greater effect, he held the black stone that Atasi had found. A show of power, as ludicrous as it was. His authority had taken a battering in the last week and Neil knew it. Charat's sycophants needed a reminder of why he was *God*. The new tribe needed to see him in action. Every so often Neil stopped the procession, held the black stone to his forehead dramatically as if hearing its intention, and then continued the hunt with renewed conviction. *I just hope the bloody little apes are actually here.* Neil had no back up plan this time. If he got the chance though, he was going to run. He clutched his copper rods in one hand. Slung over his shoulder in the hide bag, Neil also carried the black stone she had found him, along with Ivy's journal, his cell phone and battery pack. Today was the day. He had run out of time. Today Neil was giving Charat what he had promised weeks ago – an opportunity to kill more of the hobbit creatures. He didn't want to do it. But he sure as hell wasn't going to die for them. Neil was playing his part – the black stone was leading the hunters toward their despised *Ebu gogo*. Neil would fulfil his part of the bargain, then wait it out alone until he could get the stone to work.

This hunting trip was the perfect decoy to escape. With the confusion and chaos of a fight happening around him, no one would notice until he was gone until it was too late.

"Stop!" Neil said. Charat appeared by his side, pushing ahead from the back of the line. "Charat. Come with me." Neil waved him forward, holding a hand up to keep the hunters and women in their place behind. The two of them continued alone for a few minutes, then crouched as Neil scanned the valley walls for signs of life. His compass told him a hobbit cave should be here.

For a few tense minutes, they saw nothing. Then the red-beaded hunter let out a grunt of satisfaction and nodded toward the valley wall. *Of course.* About thirty meters away, a dark band of black between grey slices of rock could just be seen. It was identical to the photograph from Ivy's journal. Slightly further along, nn overhanging foothold of rock shadowed a cave in the wall. It was barely visible, but for the movement at its mouth. One of the little creatures was sitting there – *two, no, three of them* – Neil thought. They were whittling spear points with stone knives. There must be more inside. With an unexpected chatter of noise, a handful of tiny ones came running from the cave. *Kids. No,* Neil reminded himself. *Animals.* They chattered to each other as they skittered around the carvers, then trailed down a path into the forest. The smallest of them were holding hands.

Bloody hell. Neil felt inexplicably angry. He pursed his lips shut and rubbed the silver lighter through the fabric of his pocket. *Benjamin. Home. Benjamin.* He looked across at Charat. The hunter was focused intently on the cave mouth and its unsuspecting occupants. Finally, he turned to Neil with a grin and slapped him hard on the back. The bastard was so fucking pleased.

The hunters were eager. The attack was fast. Neil fell back as the other men ran forward and launched their spears and burning firesticks to the air. At the cave mouth, the first hobbit was dead before the others could even scramble to attention. Shrill screams erupted and the creatures spilled out. They grabbed whatever weapons they could reach and launched themselves over the rocky lip and into the valley, slinging rocks and spears, fuelled by adrenaline. Their lips and eyes were wide with terror. Charats' were wide with the thrill. Within seconds it was clear there were more hobbits than Charat had anticipated. They continued to spill from the cave, males and females both. The sapiens were far outnumbered. But the element of surprise made a difference. So did the size of the men that attacked. A dozen hobbit bodies lay slain within minutes. Hidden in the deep cave came A tangle of cries came from the depths of the cave. It was anarchy.

Shit. Through a haze of panic, Neil grasped his chance. With lead in his gut and bile in his throat, he turned and ran. A sharp jab in his side forced the wind from him. Stumbling, he lost his copper rods to the bushes. *No air* – he choked. It was as if all oxygen had all been sucked from his lungs with the impact. He stared down at his own belly, shocked as a spray of deep red began to seep through his filthy shirt on the left-hand side. *No.* Shaking his head to snap sense into it, Neil grabbed a fistful of the fabric and squeezed his wound tight. *Keep running. Just get away.* He scrambled to pick up his treasured copper rods. Within a few seconds he was running again. *Escaping.*

"Nee-el!" He froze and skidded to a stop. Spun back.

"Move!" Neil heard himself shout; his mouth unable to articulate what his mind was racing ahead to see. But it was too late. Although the women had been warned to stay hidden, Atasi was in plain view, trembling on her knees, a sharp stone knife beneath her chin. The creature had her glossy hair in his grip, crushing the beautiful blue feathers as he exposed her neck to the blade. Neil had seen what those snapped blades were capable of. He'd felt it.

"God, no!" For all his desperation to escape, Neil found himself running back into the fray. He stumbled, releasing his wound to grab a chunk of fallen limestone from his path. He threw it, hard. As the knife pierced Atasi's skin, Neil's stone found the hobbit's temple. The creature fell away. Neil skidded as it began to rise again. He grabbed another rock, heavier this time, and smashed it into the hobbit's head. Atasi's attacker fell at her feet. Neil froze, terrifyingly close to the woman he'd saved, breathing hard and swaying. In that single moment, all the love he'd ever had, all the women, all the sex, his entire marriage, paled into insignificance.

He couldn't bear to see her dead, for no reason other than that he realised he loved her. Not as a wife, nor as a lover. Not even a daughter. Simply as the only person who truly *saw* him. Saw through the intimidation to his desperation underneath. They were both trapped. Both lonely. And despite her own abuse, Atasi still offered Neil the tiny sparks of kindness that brought him hope.

Neil felt the crushing weight of responsibility inside him. *It was Benjamin all over again.* Violence filled every space of the forest around them. The young woman was terrified, vulnerable. She needed protection. The image of his own son flashed before his eyes. Curled in a hospital bed in the arms of his ex-wife while Neil watched, devastated and impotent from behind glass doors. Fury burned in his gut.

Not this time. This time, I won't look away.

He knew what he had to do. Neil grabbed Atasi's wrist.

"Go! Go! Run with me!" He dragged at her arm, screaming over the war cries. In an instant, her legs began to move.

Running. Escaping. Together.

CHAPTER 19

ORRIN

*S*even more days had passed. Seven days of bone-aching frustration scrolling through newsfeeds and research. Geological surveys. Astronomical data. Environmental decay.

Seven days of failure.

It was two in the morning when he was woken by a loud knock. Orrin sat bolt upright, too fast, nearly slipping from the couch that he had fallen asleep on as he stared into the glassy bay below, scotch in hand. Disoriented, he clutched the edge of the lounge as he stood, sidestepping the empty glass on the floor. Again, there was a knock at the door, this time louder, more insistent, and Orrin scratched his fingers through his hair to wake himself up as he shuffled toward it. His heart leapt as he unchecked the latch and it pushed open from inside.

"Christ O, you look like shit." Dimi stepped into the room, looking around. He let out a low whistle at the dishevelled state of the apartment he had arrived in.

Exhaustion and relief escaped Orrin's mouth in half choked sob and his knees nearly buckled. He staggered backwards against the wall. There were just over one week left until the next full moon. "You bastard. Why the hell didn't you call?" The admonition was tarnished by a lopsided smile and a look that seemed to shed pounds of worry from Orrin's shoulders.

Dimi studied Orrin's face critically under the entrance lights, then quickly stepped forward and stuck his head out of the door. "You coming?" He turned back to face his friend with a grin. "You didn't give up on me, did you?"

"Nearly."

"Well, that's your problem then isn't it, O. You lack faith." Dimi invited himself through the tiled hallway and into the loungeroom, still talking. "Cassandra's been watching me; I barely get a moment to myself. I couldn't contact you any earlier than this because she's got me recreating your experiments on the thirteenth floor in anticipation of the next electromagnetic surge. Not that it will do her any good. But either way, it's taken Eli and I up until now to figure out what the hell is in that amulet anyway." Dimi noticed the bottle on the table and poured himself a large drink, sitting down with it. He took a swig and grimaced. "Ouch, that's hard stuff, man."

"Eli?" Orrin's brain raced with his pulse as he struggled to keep up with Dimi's train of thought. Beyond all others, sheer relief broke the strongest against his disorientation.

"Sure," Dimi turned and nodded toward the front door. Dr. Elijah Nnamani strode through it, his face awash with a smile that seemed too bright for the midnight hour.

"Hello again," he said, offering his hand as he grew close. Orrin took it, as astonished grin on his face.

"Dr. Nnamani–"

"Eli, please–"

"Eli, then." Orrin shook his hand and stared at the geologist that had suddenly appeared in his lounge room. "I've never been happier to see someone in all my life."

"Hey!" Dimi said, in mock offence.

"Both of you." Orrin laughed. He stood back, eyes almost as glassy as the floor-length window behind him as he willed the night's alcohol from his system. Scouring his thoughts, Orrin managed to find his manners. "Please take a seat."

Dimi looked dubiously at the couch, then began to shift papers to make a space. "You might want a coffee for this conversation, mate," he said. "You look half dead."

"Well, it *is* two o'clock in the morning," Eli countered kindly. "Do you mind?" The geologist was already making his way behind the kitchen bench to reach for the kettle. "I've got a long day ahead of me."

Bemused, Orrin looked between his friend and the geologist. Though they could not have known each other for more than week, they seemed entirely at ease with one another.

"Eli has been working nights with me to analyse your amulet," Dimi said. "It's the only time I can get away, and then only for a few hours. He's been doing long shifts behind a microscope. You *owe* him one man, *seriously*. I couldn't have managed the past week without him." The two other men exchanged a look, and Orrin was sure he caught a glimpse of something pass between them. Despite the dire situation, he had never seen his best friend look so happy.

Orrin raised an eyebrow and grinned. "That so?" He finally noticed the dark rings under Dimi's eyes and the slightly manic shine to them. "It looks like I owe you one too."

"You do. But my current state of exhaustion is as much Cassandra's fault as it is yours."

Orrin's mind finally caught up with Dimi's inference. "Hang on, when you said it won't do her any good – I mean Cassandra recreating my experiments–"

"Yep, I mean it. She'll be in for one hell of a show of course, but I can't see her being able to store or manipulate this energy."

"Why not?" Orrin's heart was pumping so fast he could hear the swoosh of blood against his ear drums.

Dimi took a deep breath. "Well firstly because I plan to alter the coordinates on the receiver right before the surge. They'll miss the capture."

"Jaysus, man! You'll lose your job! They'll burn you so hard for that, as soon as they figure out what you did – which they will! You could go to jail for subversion."

"Well, yeah. I will. But we have have a week before that happens so we need to make the most of it. There's a lot to do before then." Dimi looked resolutely at Orrin, his stare suddenly intense and discriminating. "I'll lose my job. I'll face jail time – there's no doubt of that. But what's happening to the world outside of that really makes my plight pale in significance. Still, I'm hoping to hell you can fix that for me by reversing the time shift. Whatever happens to me in this reality will no longer exist if you get Ivy back and sort this crazy shit out."

"Wait? You believe me?" Orrin was shocked. "How?"

Dimi answered by reaching into his pocket. Bending down he placed a small object onto the glass coffee table between them with a metallic clatter. "This."

All at once, Orrin knew he had been right. The amulet *was* the catalyst for the time shift. A tidal wave of vindication swelled within him. "So, what is it – the black intrusion?"

Dimi grinned, suddenly looking like a child who held a desperately coveted secret. He looked over to Eli in the kitchen, who was pouring three strong black coffees into mugs. Dimi sat on the couch, leaning forward with elbows on his knees as Orrin took the warm black stone from the cold table. "Are you ready for this, O?" Dimi's eyes sparkled with excitement as Eli placed a steaming coffee on the table in front of him. Dimi sat back, gesturing to Eli to speak instead. The geologist took a few steps back to the bench, returned with the remaining coffees and took a seat next to Dimi on the couch. He looked at Orrin seriously, then spoke.

"I identified the black ribbon material within the crystalline magnetite. It's *moscovium*."

"*Moscovium?*" Orrin repeated the word, willing it to make sense.

"Moscovium." Dimi said. "And I know what you're gonna say because I said it too–"

"It just can't be," Orrin argued. "It's solid. And stable! It just can't be, there must be a mistake." Although Orrin was familiar with the superheavy element 115, he knew it had never been detected in a solid form on Earth. The addition to the periodic table in fact had only ever been synthetically created within a laboratory, and only about 100 atoms of the element at that. The compound nuclei had been created by hot fusion reactions and at best had a half-life of only 0.65 seconds. To find a stable isotope of the element was impossible. Orrin heart sank a little. "I'm sorry. You've got it wrong, guys. A stable form of element 115? Just can't be."

"Look Orrin, I'm not telling you what's possible, I'm telling you what I found," Eli said gently.

"I had to get some equipment moved from the physics lab for the analysis," Dimi added. "I paid one of the night janitors to help me relocate it. Turns out you made quite an impact on some of the staff with your hobbit stunt. They're sympathetic to your cause."

Eli continued. "We scattered high energy radiation over the crystals within that amulet to examine the arrangement of atoms. We tried both x-rays and electrons, and we got a stunning and distinct spectra both times. The composition of the element *is* moscovium."

"God knows where it came from," Dimi cut in, "and god knows how it ended up in this rock, but believe me, this is unequivocal, O. It's *Element 115.* Not only that, but I observed its omission spectra under electron paramagnetic resonance. You've got to trust me on this one man, it's *moscovium.* I have no doubt. Solid, stable, and – given it has never been found on earth in this state before, quite possibly, extra-terrestrial in origin. Geez man, you know the theories." Dimi sat back; his face still flushed. He waited for Orrin to respond.

For a moment Orrin could only stare at them. He was dumbfounded. The implications of this discovery were almost more overwhelming than its potential to help him reverse the time shift. Stable moscovium. There were stories of course. But he'd dismissed them, as any other decent scientist did, as folklore of the SciFi junkies and alien obsessed.

Physicists had already succeeded in creating Element 115 within a particle accelerator by bombarding a more stable isotope with atomic particles, effectively forcing the isotopic nucleus to accept more protons and neutrons than it could normally possess, transmuting it into the heavier element. But the result was unstable, and the element decayed within milliseconds. The experiment itself had been regaled as a success, of sorts. But no stable version of the element had existed. *Until now.*

Atomic theory held that a stable version of this super-heavy element 115 – *moscovium* – should have enough neutrons and protons within its nucleus to create an additional gravity wave that could conceivably extend beyond the perimeter of its own atomic structure. This gravity wave was just like any other wave in the electromagnetic spectrum. It could be accessed. Its wavelength, frequency and amplitude would be tangible properties allowing it to be amplified and focused past its atomic walls and into the surrounding matter. The only other phenomenon known to humankind that could feasibly accomplish such a feat, was a black hole. And a black hole had the ability to do just that – amplify the gravity waves it created to cause a space-time distortion across the universe. *Time travel.* As insane as it seemed, as utterly *inconceivable* as Orrin considered it, it also made perfect sense.

If the amulet contained a condensed, stable version of element 115, it would have a resonant frequency associated with it. A frequency that, when amplified, could push its natural gravity field past the boundaries of its crystalline structure. Past the boundaries of the amulet itself, encapsulating the physical matter – *the person* – connected to it. *Ivy.*

Dimi watched Orrin's face carefully, reading his expressions. It seemed he'd already arrived at this conclusion and was merely waiting for Orrin to catch up. Suddenly, there were more questions again than answers.

"So – if I suspend disbelief–" Orrin began, "If I believe what you're telling me and accept that this stone has moscovium imbedded in the crystalline magnetite – tell me this–" Orrin took a deep breath and closed his eyes. The words came slowly, as he gathered his thoughts. He had to make it make sense. "What is the resonant frequency of this element in its stable form?" He looked between the two scientists before him. Both were highly esteemed, heavily published and knew their stuff. If anyone could help him now, it would be them.

"Clearly something amplified the gravitational wave of the moscovium in that laboratory..." Orrin felt himself pulling threads of logic together, weaving a scenario in his mind that could accommodate this blend of insanity and logic. "So, if its gravitational field was amplified, it could have caused a microscopic singularity within the amulet that expanded and expanded – distorting the space time continuum and taking Ivy along for the ride! But what? What caused the amplification of the wave? What was the frequency that reached it? Was it from my equipment? Or something else? Any why there? Why Flores of all the places in on this earth?"

This time though, Dimi had no answers. "We haven't figured that part out yet."

"God damn it!" Orrin was pacing now, pushing his thumb and forefinger under his glasses in frustration. "I need my lab! How the hell am I supposed to work this out without my lab and equipment? Only one more week and then it's all over. I need to get back in there!"

"That I can help you with." Dimi reached into his back pocket and flipped a swipe card and key onto the coffee table. He exchanged a conspiratorial look with Eli. "Phil swiped the card from one of the cleaners. The key was a spare. I'm working upstairs now and as far as Cassandra's concerned, your lab has been gutted. The place is useless so there's no need for anyone to be using this anymore. It's yours."

"Thanks mate, but what's the good of having access to a laboratory that's gutted of my equipment – not to mention the high likelihood I'll be arrested the minute I step foot on university grounds."

"For that we have a plan." Dimi took a deep breath and a drink.

Orrin's head shot out of his hands. "What plan?"

Eli answered for him. "Cassandra is holding a press conference tomorrow afternoon in the penthouse lab. After that, she and some government officials are flying to Canberra for a Heads of State meeting for the night. So, we have an eight-hour window overnight to get someone back into the lab without being seen. After that, we have one week until the next full moon. That means one week to figure out this mess. We'll smuggle food in when we can. There's a security guard change every night at 8pm and again at 6am. So whoever is in the lab will have to work at night, quiet as a mouse."

Orrin mulled it over, hope threatening to rise. "I'll need equipment." With a sudden flash of recognition, he stared at Dimi. "You know where my equipment is, don't you? Phil was arrested–"

Dimi shifted uncomfortably. "I'll admit it was my idea to steal the equipment back piece by piece. I knew you'd need it, and I hoped if we sourced it from multiple labs they'd take longer to notice."

"So, this plan of yours has already had Phil arrested? He's just a kid, Dimi. *Jaysus,* man."

"He's an adult, and I didn't say it was perfect, mate. I couldn't do it on my own and Phil knows the department. He also knew the risks. He understood that if we succeeded with this, then his arrest would no longer matter in the scheme of things. In the correct version of reality, none of this will have happened. In that reality, he *wasn't* arrested so his record is clean. He's counting on you to make that right again too." Dimi surveyed Orrin from beneath his eyebrows. "No pressure, of course."

"Yeah right." Orrin rubbed his palm across his face, wiping the sweat that had pricked on his skin. He stood and pushed open a window, letting cool air spill into the stuffy room. "So where is it? My equipment?" He turned to find both men grinning at him.

"Well, that's my stroke of genius, if I do say so myself. I put it in the only place they aren't looking for it. The one room in the entire physics department that has been gutted and cleaned and locked up until further notice. They have no use for it anymore you see. It's a bloody brilliant move."

"It really is," Eli chuckled.

"Where, Dimi?"

"It's all back in your lab." Grinning like a Cheshire cat, Dimi stretched back, inordinately pleased with himself. Eli grinned and clapped him on the knee, laughing.

"You're so cocky when you think you've won, you know that."

"Check mate to the lot of them, Eli. You don't know how long I've wanted to pull a stunt like this under Cassandra's nose."

"My own lab in the physics department? *My actual laboratory?"* Orrin was astounded.

"The very one, O. It's all locked up in your back office. Of course, that's all I've stashed in there, you've got no chairs, tables or anything else. Whoever's in there will have to make do. And we'll need to *borrow* another audio spectrum analyser from some-where. That's the one thing they recovered from Phil when he was caught." Dimi frowned.

"Anyway, we'll cover for you whenever we can mate, but the

place is crawling with security right now. It's not going to be easy. And as far as the lab work goes, I can't help you at all, I need to be upstairs to play my part."

"But my data – you took all my data."

Dimi grinned, a spark of mischief again breaking his intensity. "You might find old Tek is still worth a surprise, mate."

Orrin's nerves felt shot with electricity. It was going to be frustrating to wait until tomorrow night to break into the laboratory to get answers. But still, there was a lot of planning to do before then. He looked at his oldest friend, grateful for how little he had changed even across realities. "Thank you, Dimi." There didn't seem to be enough words.

Dimi just smiled. "I understand, O. This woman must be sure something. Screwing the world up so badly for one thing," he laughed, "but more so, for screwing your heart up so badly."

"She is." Orrin smiled weakly. "You have no idea."

"You know what," Dimi chanced a look at Eli, and the other man took his hand. "I actually think I might finally have an idea myself."

Orrin beamed. "Finally, hey?"

"Finally," Dimi grinned.

"Pretty bad timing though," Eli shook his head.

Orrin smiled sadly. "Terrible timing." He looked out of the window at the black water far below. Above the water, hazy ribbons of Aurora australis bled bright green and pink in the night sky. A stunning reminder of the dystopian magnetosphere that existed beyond the glass panes.

He drained his coffee in silence and stood perfectly still for a moment. "Well, I'd better get her back then. For all our sakes."

Dimi got up from the couch and walked over to the window. For a moment they both stood, just staring at the southern lights. Finally, Dimi spoke, almost to himself. "It's beautiful down there in the water. So dark and compelling. Reminds me of the night sky the way it used to be. Before all of this–" He gestured to the hazy colours that lit the night, then turned and placed his empty mug on the coffee table. "You know O, if this works, if you can change this screwed up reality back to what it's apparently meant to be, Eli and I won't remember that any of this even happened. We won't even remember each other."

Orrin saw a shimmer of fear in his best friends' eyes.

"No, you won't Dimi," he said. "But I will."

The three men looked at one another. There was risk involved for all of them.

"So, the first thing we need to do, is get that amulet back into the lab tomorrow night," Eli said, bringing his hands together and getting to his feet. "And get someone to start working on isolating the resonant frequency that triggers it."

"Why do you both keep saying *someone?*" Orrin exclaimed. "It's my lab, right? I need to sort this out. Why on earth wouldn't it be me in the lab?"

Eli took a deep breath and exchanged a look with Dimi.

"What?" Orrin demanded.

"The thing is," Eli said, stepping toward them. "There might be a better opportunity for you right now."

Orrin narrowed his eyes sceptically. "I can't imagine what could possibly be more important–"

"Do you remember when you brought that rock to my geology lab a couple of weeks ago?" Eli nodded to the amulet in Orrin's hand.

"Of course."

"Well, I think I mentioned at the time that I've been doing some work for a big mining conglomerate in the Indonesian Archipelago. In any case, they're flying me back over there for a new geological survey. It turns out this one is in Flores. Near Kelimutu, in fact. I'm flying out tomorrow." Eli gave a little shrug. "If you think it would help you figure this mess out, I could wrangle a *research assistant* position. You could jump onboard."

Orrin's whole body tensed. "You're going to Kelimutu?"

"That's right."

"Tomorrow?"

"First thing. Five days there and back. I'll sort out the paperwork for you, all you need is your passport."

Despite his best efforts to remain calm, Orrin's voice was torn. "But what about the experiments? I can't afford losing that sort of time in the lab–"

"We've got that covered, O," Dimi spoke up. "Phil made bail a couple of days ago. He's got another week until the hearing. Until then he's off the hook."

"Phil's out of jail?" Orrin hadn't heard from Jayne since he'd seen her at Ivy's old apartment.

"Yeah," Dimi continued, "and he put up his hand for the job. I can smuggle him into the lab tomorrow night. He'll start the frequency experiments while you're gone. But you'll have to leave the amulet."

"Leave it?" Orrin reeled. He clutched the amulet, suddenly faced with the prospect of being in Flores within 24 hours. Of standing where she stood. Of looking for clues, signs, *anything*, that might help him bring Ivy home. Still, he was reluctant to leave Ivy's amulet. It had been his constant companion since Jayne had let him keep it. He looked down at the stone in his hand. "You're right though, if I take this out of the country and it got lost, or confiscated–" With reluctance, he handed it back to Dimi.

"Phil will take care of it," Dimi said.

"You'll explain about the intrusion? Element 115."

"Trust me, O."

Orrin took a deep breath. Of course, he did. Dimi was risking everything just to be here. In just one hour, Orrin's life had tipped sideways again.

"I'll pack a bag."

EXTINCT

CHAPTER 20

IVY

*I*vy clung to the back wall of the dark cave. Limestone sang with the rush of water. The heavy rasping sound was terrifyingly close.

With toes still poised on the lip of the tunnel entrance behind her, Ivy knew there was no way back. Her breath petrified in her lungs. Her legs trembled, barely able to hold her body straight.

Ivy dropped her eyes down to her bare feet. In the space between them and the dragon, a nest chamber had been clawed deep into the dirt. Over two dozen leathery white eggs, each the size of a grapefruit, were piled inside, scattered with dirt and detritus for their nine-month incubation. It was no longer the winter breeding season, Ivy knew that much, which meant the reptilian mother had already been fiercely defending her nest for months, refusing to leave it unprotected. As the weeks passed, the Komodo's appetite would have grown as her body weight dropped. By now, she would be starving.

Behind the dragon, a wide pool of water blocked Ivy's entrance to the mouth of the cave. Another ten meters of dirt and rock lay beyond it, stretching to the cave mouth which yawned wide and high. A thick sheet of water fell across it. *A waterfall.*

Darkness beyond. *It's dusk already,* Ivy realised with a jolt. She'd been in the tunnel all day. The Komodo flicked its tongue.

I've got no chance. Cold sweat pricked anew.

The sudden purge of hundreds of giant huntsman spiders onto the cave walls surrounding the tunnel entrance had piqued the Komodo dragons' interest. But it was the fleshy animal that smelled of blood that drew her attention now. Black eyes stared at Ivy, unblinking, as a yellow forked tongue tasted Ivy's wound in the air. Her reptilian reflex was instant. Toxic saliva began to drip from the venom gland at the base of her curved teeth. It fell in long gelatinous strings to the dirt floor.

The Komodo inched forward. A potential predator had fallen into her territory, setting her defences alight. She was born ready to fight. But this, potential prey, was far more interesting.

The yellow tongue flicked again. The deep-throated rattle, like knives sawing through ice, chilled Ivy to the bone. She pushed her foot slowly back into the tunnel. Moving, even breathing, seemed too high a risk.

I've got no chance. Her heart was hammering now. She was sure the reptile could hear it. The Komodo could move faster over short distances. It could swim better than she. It turned its head ever so slightly. Ivy caught the glint in the Komodo's eye. *It's watching me. Oh-God-what-do-I-do? I have nothing. No weapon. All I have is –* A flicker of hope teased her heart – *fire. I have fire!* With a trembling hand, Ivy slowly felt the folds of her skirt to locate the two chunks of flint. The oleos-oiled torch was still in one white-knuckled fist but looking terribly worse for wear. The vines and kindling on the end had been smothered with dirt and smashed against the floor of the tunnel to douse the previous flame. The head of it was barely in one piece. The Komodo took a step toward her. There was perhaps, only six meters between them, including an eight-foot drop into the egg-laden nest first.

Ivy fumbled with the torch. *I can't do it. I need two hands.* There was no way to hold the torch while snapping the flint rocks together. *I need to put it down.* The Komodo took another step. Ivy desperately scanned the cave. The obvious place to go, was back into the tunnel. But even then, the lizards' long, muscular body might follow. Once in, if she could start a fire, there was nowhere near enough room to turn around and come back out head – and fire – first.

To the right of her, thick ledges punctuated the wall, rising almost to the roof. They were shallow, some barely a foot's width, the result of ground water wearing rock away over millennia. Without giving herself time to think, she made up her mind. *And bolted.* One foot edged the nest. The next step splashed water. The Komodo moved like lightning, racing behind. Ivy's fingers clutched at the rocky wall. Stretched arms, clinging, grasping for purchase against the vertical rock face to hoist herself up.

A thump of dust as reptilian claws scraped the floor. It heaved its body down into the pit of eggs. Clawed back up the other side, sending a cloud of dust over the water behind.

Ivy's unlit torch caught a snag and she grappled for it. It slipped through her fingers. She barely snatched the end, gripped it tighter. Her foot hit a second wedge. *Higher. But nowhere near high enough.*

The Komodo belched, heaving up onto hind legs. A slap of saliva hit Ivy's ankle before she whipped it up higher. *Another ledge.* Scrambling. Wings on her feet and terror in her gut. Faster than she'd ever moved in her life.

The ball of Ivy's foot slipped, raining a shower of dirt on the Komodo behind. Her heel hit its crown. It was climbing too. *It lunged.* Missed. Hot, fetid breath carried a furious growl as her foot whipped higher. Ivy's calf stung as the skin scraped off, leaving a trail of blood up the rocky wall. *Higher. Up. Another ledge. Higher.* The Komodo was underneath her now, clawing up the wall. Six foot tall on its hind legs, Ivy was scarcely above.

Higher or I'm dead. Her foot slipped again the dark. *Higher, higher.* Scrambling for her life.

Perched on a precarious outcrop, barely wide enough to stand, Ivy finally froze. She was halfway up the cave wall. *Panting. Terrified.* The Komodo dragon was directly beneath her, two feet clear and straining to reach, stretched from tail to jaw. *I'm high enough.* With one trembling hand clutching the bamboo torch, Ivy pushed her back against the rock wall and slid the other into the fold of her skirt, carefully pulling the two flint rocks from their hiding place. She crouched as low she dared, clamping the battered oleos-torch between her knees, trying desperately not to fall forward. *Please. Please. Please.*

Ivy clapped the rocks together. Sweat stung her eyes. A tiny spark hit the filthy torch-head and fizzled out. *Please.* She tried again and again. There was too much dirt, the soft puff of kindling inside almost burnt away. Nothing left for the spark to cling onto. *Please.* Tears of desperation washed away sweat as Ivy doggedly snapped the flint together. The low rumble of the Komodo below was more encouragement than she needed. *Please.* Behind the reptile, the shadow of water looked deep. Beyond it, the monotonous shatter of the waterfall beat against rocks. Time was frozen, waiting for Ivy's fingers to slip. To drop the flint. To fail. *Please.* Ivy buffed the top of the oleos torch with her hand. It was still burning hot. A puff of dirt floated away. *Please.* Her skin blistered. *Please.*

It felt like the hundredth time. Ivy's eyes streamed with the effort. A tiny spark flew, and by pure chance, caught the remnants of oil inside. The oleos began to curl and smoke.

"Ha!" Relief sounded like exhaustion and despair. Ivy's thighs ached beyond belief from being perched awkwardly on the thin, rocky shelf, three meters up the cave wall. As a tiny flame licked its way through the kindling and took hold, she stood up, stretching her muscles in an agonising roar.

From her vantage point on the wall, Ivy could see the inside of the cave. A small path wound its way around the edge of the lake. Midway, the path disappeared into water, until it sloped back up, a few meters on, to become dirt once more. It wasn't far, perhaps twenty meters around the perimeter, then another ten in a clear run to reach the waterfall. *Calm. Calm.* Ivy counted her breath. *Focus.* There were few ledges to her right, continuing across the wall. To return left, back toward the nest, was suicide. Ivy's heart threatened to explode. Her stomach churned like the falling water. *You can do this.* She steadied her breath and gathered her resolve. The flames grew and black smoke curled. *You have to do this.* There was only one option. *I'm gonna run for it.*

"I have fire," Ivy shouted down at the Komodo. Her bravado bounced off the walls. She leant forward as far as she dared, sweeping the flames across the reptile's muzzle. It dropped back, tongue darting out to taste the offence. "That's right," Ivy growled. "I'm coming down with *fire*." Gingerly, Ivy stepped across to the closest ledge. The rocky outcrop cracked under her sudden weight and crumbled to the ground below as Ivy staggered forward to the next. She was getting lower again, and it was not lost on the predator waiting for her. Ivy assaulted the Komodo again with her torch. Wary, it held back as she descended.

Serrated teeth glistened as the reptile opened its jaws, flicking a forked tongue compulsively. The blood of injured prey incited a ravenous rush of adrenaline. Ivy's scent was familiar now. It could have tracked her down from seven miles away. Ivy shouted another warning and waved the fames above its head as she moved.

"Don't make me hurt you!" She screamed, not believing for a single moment that she'd ever have the upper hand. Her threats were less to scare the predator, as to distract herself from the terror of descending. The Komodo dragon's venomous teeth were angled backward. A one-way trap. Laceration and blood loss would kill her quickly, but not quickly enough. If it got a hold of her, Ivy knew she'd still be alive when the reptile started shearing her apart. Even the possibility of escape with only one bite was tantamount to a death sentence. Komodo venom itself was toxic. A plummet of blood pressure, hypothermia and dizziness would render her too weak to escape. Ivy knew that if she made it out injured, another day would see her dead. Weakened, she'd never get far enough that the starving mother couldn't hunt her down and finish her off before the venom did its work.

Ivy was as low as she dared. One more leap would take her to the ground.

"Argh!" Her torch swept erratically above the Komodo. The reptile stayed in place, wary of the flames. *Now or never,* Ivy decided, hating the moment. *Or stay here and die.*

Drawing every scrap of resolve within her, Ivy leapt from the final ledge and threw her feet to the ground. Rocks underfoot, she flew, her body half-twisted, waving the flame behind her in one fist. A heroic battle cry did as much to fuel Ivy's adrenaline as vocalise her terror. *One step. Another.* Feet pounding in great leaps away from the safety of the rock wall, and toward the black water ahead.

Ivy felt, rather than saw, the Komodo give chase. Her foot hit the pool as the reptile left the wall, its enormity propelled by bloodlust. Ivy spun around as she fell waist deep, thrashing toward the far edge, desperately keeping her flame above water. Without fire, she was lost. Meters from the far edge, the water whooshed, like a tidal wave drawing through. She submerged and resurfaced, coughing water as a huge head drew close.

"No!" Ivy screamed, thrashing the fire against its wet skin in a violent hiss. She beat it again and again, struggling to stay afloat as the Komodo whirled about her, snapping at flailing limbs. Screams reverberated through the cavern, as Ivy propelled herself backward, flame outstretched until she felt her heels hit the rocky bottom of the lake. The flames thrashed, seared, burned at the open jaws. Heaving one leg, then the other up the bank, Ivy forced herself backward until her legs were out of the water. Another dozen meters of dirt edged the small lake until it curved around, leaving a clear run toward the waterfall at the front.

Brandishing her only advantage, Ivy swept the flame in wide arcs, backing away from the Komodo as quickly as she dared. With no light behind her, and only the shadows to guide her steps, she stumbled and bumped her way along the inner wall. Tufts of dried grass clung to the edges, left over from a time sunlight had filtered in far enough to give life to it. Ivy clawed at it, grabbing tufts of dried grass from the rocky wall. She threw them on the ground at her feet as she stepped backward, leaving a trail between them. Fierce growls spewed from Ivy's chest, more bestial than the rasping rattle of the reptile. Adrenaline coursed through her veins and pounded in her ears. The echo of her own panic magnified, until there was no distinction between the rushing blood, her own clamour and the Komodo's ravenous fury.

It wasn't until the wall grating at her elbow tapered away, that Ivy realised she had reached the far end of the lake. Only ten meters of empty ground separated her from the waterfall that offered an escape. Beyond its glassy sheet was an unknown path. There was no time to wonder.

Ivy chanced a low sweep of the flame. It took, sending an artery of fire from her feet along the trail of dried grass. It cracked and smoked against the rebellion of wet dirt underneath. The Komodo twisted away as its path was broken, but only for a moment.

A moment was long enough.

Ivy spun and raced for the waterfall. Her feet wanted to make a straight path, but her brain, through its adrenaline fog, forced them to zig and zag. The Komodo burst through the small fire in its way, and pursued her faster than its enormity should allow. It shot through the dark at twice Ivy's speed. Her only advantage was agility. The Komodo's turns were laborious and wide, its body incapable of twisting. Ivy raced this way, then that, pivoting diagonally toward the entrance, each manoeuvre adding precious steps between the predators' lunge and her burning calves.

With the greatest leap of faith in her life, Ivy burst through the pounding sheet of water that guarded the dragon's lair and disappeared into the black night beyond.

She fell.

One meter. Two meters.

A churning ocean slapped the air out of her lungs. Seawater filled her nose and mouth. The sudden pain of water in her sinus cavities burned as she rolled beneath the waves. Ivy felt her back hit the sand underneath and twisted, kicked up, and burst through the surface just as her lungs felt as if they might burst. She hocked and wretched up salty water, struggling to keep her head above it. When her eyes had ceased streaming enough to see, Ivy realised she was only a few meters beyond the waterfall. On the ledge above, the crescendo of the cascade continued. Ivy spun around treading water, trying to get her bearings. It was surprisingly bright. The waning gibbous moon glowed above like an enormous hourglass – a terrifying reminder of how little time she had left. A week before the next fell moon; perhaps a few days more. Moonlight spread glitter across the ocean, which stretched as far as Ivy could see. *The Savu Sea.* She coughed it from her lungs. *I guess I found it.*

She turned and swam toward the eastern shore, giving the base of the waterfall a wide berth. The rocky base of cliff met sand. Ivy dragged herself from the water, falling to her hands and knees on the shore. Her face was aching with the intrusion of water into every orifice, and she coughed so violently her lungs ached. After a few minutes, her instincts resurfaced. Ivy scrambled to her feet, keen to put as much distance between herself and the Komodo as she could. She shivered and looked around. Every night call and crackle seemed to come from behind her shoulder. Every whoosh of waves tried to sweep her off her feet.

A wide ledge trailed from the side of the cave mouth down to the sandy beach, bypassing the waterfall overhanging it. Obscured by darkness and desperation, Ivy had not seen the hidden exit and instead had leapt straight out into the sea beyond. Ivy realised now that the Komodo though, could enter her cave via a gentle slope from the beach without ever getting wet. It was a perfect nesting site, hidden from predators and safe from the elements. But there was no sign of it. The reptiles' cold blood preferred night sleeping to regulate its body temperature and conserve heat. With that in mind, Ivy walked briskly along the shore, heading eastward, hoping that any other dragons on the beach were curled up in their burrows until sunrise.

No more damn caves, Ivy promised herself as she left footprints in the sand. Her mood soured. Her stomach ached with hunger. Despite the limitless sea water, she was desperate for a drink. Ivy patted down the folds of her hide skirt as she walked, slipping her fingers inside with relief to find she still had her two flint stones and knife. They were wet, of course, and her oleos-oil torch had been lost to the sea. Her water-bladder was still secure, but empty. Finding fresh water became Ivy's priority. She had had her last drink in the tunnel hours ago.

Ivy walked toward the rising moon. By the time it arced above and began to fall over her shoulder to the west, her feet dragged with exhaustion and the monotonous sand had become a blur. At the first rays of light hit the beach, Ivy turned toward the forest that tangled the rocky skyline off the beach. High boughs of an enormous tree cocooned her. Ivy slept deeply. It was not until the ache in her stomach and thirst in her throat surpassed her exhaustion and forced her awake, that she cautiously descended, only a few hours before the sun was due to set again.

Fresh water was surprisingly easy to find. As she'd walked along the beach, Ivy had not realised a river ran parallel to the sea, only a few hundred meters inland from where she'd slept. It was clear and cool. A lifesaver. Keeping a sharp eye out for Komodos, Ivy drank until she was full, then scrubbed the past days travel grime from her skin. She filled her water bladder and lay it on the riverbank then set about looking for food. A telling swarm of bees led her another twenty meters into the forest. There, Ivy found a rambutan tree dripping with clusters of fruit. She tore away a mass of drupes, waving off the haze of insects, and returned to the riverbank to eat them. Swishing her feet in the cool water, Ivy peeled red leathery skin from the small fruit. Her stone knife pushed away soft spines as Shahn had taught her. The translucent flesh inside was slightly acidic and refreshing. Ivy ate her fill, then wrapped the leftover fruit in a large leaf, determined to carry it for later.

"Well, hello there," she exclaimed, as something bumped her toes in the water. Brown nostrils appeared on the surface, followed by a glossy green shell. Tiny eyes blinked up at her, then disappeared again beneath the water. Ivy swirled her hand gently over the rippling surface, finding her friend again in its depths. The little turtle was only as big as her palm. It nipped curiously at Ivy's pink fingers, and she heard her own laugh out loud. It felt like a lifetime since her shoulders had relaxed and the worry lines melted away for more than a minute. "What do you think, little one?" Ivy asked, breathing in the suddenly sweet air. "Do I camp here again tonight, or keep walking?" Her gaze found the sun through the canopy. There was only an hour or two remaining until dark. "I've still got a long way to go." The turtle circled around her fingers, apparently unconcerned by any potential predation on her part. "I nearly got eaten by a Komodo, you know," she said to the turtle. "I've never run so fast in my life." After three days alone, it felt good to be heard. "You're so small it wouldn't have bothered with you." Ivy looked around. "You haven't got a care in the world, have you little guy?" she gave a wistful smile. "You just swim around in your river and eat what-ever you can find." The forest was idyllic. Cascading water over rocky falls lent a meditative mood to the air. Insects buzzed and chirruped in chorus. Flashes of iridescent blue and copper lit the mirrored water as kingfishers dove headfirst to pick out tiny fish beneath. Shrill chirps announced their victories, watched over by sharp-eyed snipes with their metronome of jarring *jick* calls across the way.

"You're right," Ivy murmured, her mind mulling over the journey ahead. "I could still get a few good hours of walking in before it gets dark. I've spent long enough lazing around today." Despite her words, tired muscles were reluctant to move. Since she had begun the search with Xiou, Gihn and the other hunters, there'd been scarcely a moment when she wasn't on her feet. "Besides," she continued, still trying to force motivation into her limbs, "I'm on my own now. If I don't push on, how will I make it to Kelimutu by the full moon?" Her voice dropped almost to a whisper. "And back home." It was a relief to acknowledge her intentions out loud. She wanted to go home. Not just *help* her friends at Kelimutu but *leave* them there. Ultimately, Ivy knew the time would come to say goodbye. Or at least, she *hoped* the time would come. And it would hurt.

Her intention to leave was still unspoken. Ivy knew Gihn was aware of it, though he said nothing to the others. Xiou was no fool though, his intuition was only matched by that of his mate, Shahn. The two of them had offered Ivy a home at their hearth. They saw her suffer and knew what she had sacrificed to be pulled into their lives and thrown out of her own. *They'll understand*, she hoped. *If I ever make it that far.* Orrin's grin flashed into her mind and Ivy's heart fluttered. *He's trying to find me on the other side.* Steely resolution returned to her chest. *We'll figure it out. I'll get home.*

Ivy lent forward and scratched the tiny turtle's shell with her fingers. "I guess this is goodbye." She sighed. "Good luck, little one. Thanks for the chat." She pulled herself to her feet, turned and picked her way along the river for a while, then hiked back toward the beach. The filtered sun had made short work of her wet clothes. Soon Ivy was pacing the sand again, soaking up the warmth of the sun on her back. The sand was powder white, and the water, crystal clear. The sea itself was breathtaking, and Ivy imagined she'd never see another beach so incredibly untouched.

She travelled eastward, keeping her eyes to the north, where the sand abruptly gave way to a border of thick forest, as if someone had drawn a line to separate the two. The great mountain peak of Iya lay ahead, undulating in valleys and peaks, some reaching into clouds. The volcano jutted into the sea, creating a vast loop of beach that Ivy had to circle before reaching the far side of the bay. From there, Mount Sukaria set its foot into the earth, ringed by a halo of dark smoke.

Cliffs cradled shadows of vegetation underneath, teasing Ivy that they might hide the caves she was searching for. The forest itself looked as impenetrable as the rest of the island, but after spending so long with hunters that knew how to navigate the suffusion of greenery, Ivy knew better. Her sharp eye monitored the tapering valleys as she walked, searching for recognisable landmarks that might indicate where the caves of her past archaeological research might be hiding. There were three that she knew of, and many others she suspected.

The first glimpse she got of Pulau Koa told her she was close. A thrill shot through her veins. Pulau Koa was a tiny island, like a head bobbing out of the Savu Sea off the coast of what would one day become Ende Regency. To the north-east, ridges of forest fanned upward to Mount Sukaria. Somewhere in those folds, overlooking the ocean, a cave was waiting. The cave had been the subject of an archaeological dig that bore little more than stone tools and the remains of cooked animal bones. But the radio-carbon dating done on them had brought it within the realm of possibility that *Homo floresiensis* might have been responsible for putting them there. That was enough for Ivy to seek it out.

It was on the sand of Nanganesa beach that Ivy's questions were settled. A large shell midden, the archaeological equivalent of a prehistoric rubbish bin, was sitting quite plainly in her way. The remnants of a family eating, cooking, and discarding their waste by the seashore. Shellfish and mollusc shells and small animal bones were left in a pile. Ivy picked through it, curiously, as an investigator might sort through a suspect's trash. Discarded flaked stones had been tossed onto it as well, dull and chipped and no longer useful. The domed carapace of a large sea turtle had been butchered out, leaving nothing but a hollow shell. Vines of seaweed and fishbones and other organic detritus heaped on top.

There are humans living nearby, Ivy surmised. *But which species?* The stone tools were too broken and non-specific to tell whether they belonged to sapiens or hobbits. She earnestly hoped the latter.

It was too late to begin searching for forest caves, so Ivy collected driftwood as the sun went down. She had detoured around a half dozen Komodo's sunning themselves along the beach, but thankfully had moved unnoticed. Still, a roaring fire should keep them at bay until morning. Ivy's legs were far too tired to continue. She settled in a small alcove on the beach where the dry sand was sheltered from the wind by two rocky ridges either side. She was higher than the shore, so wouldn't be submerged with the incoming tide, but still had a decent view of the beach below. Ivy arranged her driftwood over the fuzz of dry kindling she had collected and settled in. She was sure a cave site was nearby and determined to set off again at first light.

Sparks flew and a tiny whisper of smoke curled from the kindling. Pleased with herself, Ivy blew it to life. Then just as suddenly, she grabbed handful of sand and smothered it. The flame disappeared. Her heart raced. She could hear something – *voices.* Human voices. It was such an unnatural sound after four days alone that Ivy's shoulders cringed. She ducked low.

A rabble of Karathah were spilling from the forest and onto the beach. There were forty or fifty of them, loud and cheeringly happy. They were descending as if returning from some great event, full of twilight fervour and energy. She'd never seen so many people, so many *Homo sapiens* – at one time since she'd arrived in Flores. There had been perhaps twenty hunters at the stegodon hunt where the hobbits had been ambushed, but this was different. There were women and children in this group too, as well as many men. They carried weapons and hide bags. Some had armfuls of kindling and boughs. At the head of the group, two men carried flaming torches for light. Many of the adults seemed a little unruly, as if they might be drunk. She recalled Leihna telling her the elders often made a fermented drink called tuak from dalunut palm. There was no reason that the Karathah wouldn't have an equivalent intoxication. Perhaps this tribe were celebrating something?

Though she had no intention of letting them see her, Ivy was beguiled by their sudden appearance. These people were the living ancestors of modern Flores' population. Fifty thousand years in the future, Ivy had studied these long-lost lives through their whispers left on stone tools and butchered bones. But here they were, a vibrant living community of Stone Age humans, travelling, celebrating, and socialising together. If she hadn't been so terrified of being seen, Ivy might have laughed aloud in wonder.

But Ivy's wonderment didn't last. As the group moved up the

beach, her eyes fell on a single man. Terror gripped her gut and every nerve in her neck froze up like ice. The red-beaded hunter was toward the front of the group, carrying something. Dusk was falling and Ivy's eyes were failing in the light. For a moment, she stared, flat on her belly in the crevice, unable to pick out the odd shape thrown over his shoulder. *Why is he here? He's so far from home, this can't be his tribe.* The raw scar on her thigh tingled. It was barely three weeks since the red-beaded hunter had sunk his knife into her flesh and driven her to the brink of death with its infection. *Is he following me? How could he even know I am here?* Ivy thought back to the Karathah hunters that had dogged their footsteps as they crossed through the Soa Basin. There were only two of them then, she was sure of it, and neither had been the red-beaded hunter. *Were they lookouts from another tribe, as Xiou had suggested? Had they told the others about her travels with Kyah and the hobbits?*

Ivy studied the group as they made their way along the beach, searching for other faces she might recognise. In the fading light, it was hard to tell. A couple of the men looked familiar, but she'd never seen the any of them long enough to commit their faces to memory. *Unless perhaps...* Women were easier to pick out from the large group. Ivy scanned faces, searching for the young woman with the blue feathers in her hair. None of them looked like her. She forced her eyes back to the red-beaded hunter. *Did he follow me here?* With no hope for answers, she focused on what the man was carrying instead. It was hoisted over his shoulder and flopped heavily against his back as he walked. *A rope – with four coconuts attached. No.* The bile rose in Ivy's throat. *Not coconuts.* The four spheres dangling from his shoulder were draped in something shaggy and long. *Hair. Human hair.* The red-beaded hunter was carrying four decapitated heads, slung over his shoulder as if they were nothing but a sack. Ivy squeezed her eyes shut and ducked her head down until her forehead was pressing into the cold sand. Tears stung her eyes and the chill that swept her body brought a nausea that threatened to expel itself. Those were hobbit heads. The size and distinctive shape were recognisable, even in the orange light of the rising moon. Her heart jolted as she realised it could be Xiou, Guntah and Gihn that the red-beaded man had murdered and carried so callously – or worse – Kora, Setian and their charge of orphans.

Oh no, no, no, no. A fist of grief squeezed Ivy's chest. She could barely breathe. *Had Xiou been searching for her? Had he been discovered by the Karathah instead?* The Karathah hunter's face loomed behind her eyes. Memories flashed, taunting her. He had grinned such a cruel and single-minded determination to ruin her at the Karathah hunt. Fanatical violence had fuelled his attack as he'd tried to steal the amulet from her wrist. Ivy had cracked his ribs and broken his nose, slammed his abdomen and smashed her forehead against his throat. She'd fought like a lion to escape the man and barely came away with her life. *Was he after retribution? Ivy had foiled his goal of poisoning the Liang Bua hobbits at the waterhole. Why was this man so hell-bent on destroying them? What could possibly drive him to such horror?* There was no question in her mind that whoever he was, and whatever his motivation, the red-beaded hunter would not rest until he had annihilated the *Homo floresiensis* tribes. There would be no safety or peace for them while he lived.

It was a half hour before the beach was quiet again and Ivy dared to move. The Karathah tribe had continued up the beach and disappeared. Their torches blinked into darkness beyond the bay, but Ivy had been too scared to move. *I can't sleep, not now.* Her mind whirled with unanswered questions. Her nerves fired with restless energy. *I need to keep moving.*

So, she did.

Ivy turned toward the forest. She slipped and stumbled in the dark. Her bare soles were tough, and her determination became impenetrable. The rifted foot of the Mount Sukaria soon disappeared into long trenches of rocks and trees. Somewhere, in one of them, would be a cave hidden in the rocky folds. The growing dread in Ivy's gut told her she was too late.

By the time the sun hit, Ivy knew she was lost.

Still, she searched. Scrambling over boulders and crawling through masses of liana. She scratched the stinging swathes of mosquitos from her arms and face and rubbed saliva into the wounds.

Another hour passed. Ankle-deep in a brackish river, Ivy refilled her water bladder and picked off a dozen fat leeches. Tiny potholes of blood washed down her calves as she kept walking.

And another. She gave up scratching the Southern Cross onto boughs and rocks. Even hobbits, with their sharp tracking skills, could never have found her through the tangled web of vegetation. Visions of Xiou swam beneath the sweat in her eyes. His head hanging over the red-beaded hunter's shoulder. His eyes staring empty at the sand. Ivy suffocated her fear with determination. *You don't know who it was. Just keep searching,* she insisted. *This is what Gihn wants. This is the only way to save them all.*

Another hour. *I know you're here;* she begged the hidden tribe in her thoughts. *And I know why you're hiding. But it's time to be found.*

Another hour of stumbling. The chorus of birds and insects grew louder as the morning wore on. Ivy fell into, rather than found, a hollow where ripe durian fruit littered the ground. She heard the tell-tale rustle of disturbed animals as she gathered some. She ate as she searched, wiping sticky hands on her hide skirt. There was no time to wash.

It was the band of glittering obsidian that Ivy first recognized. It was thin, a line of it sandwiched between limestone shelves, just like in the photographs that had been pressed between the pages of her lost journal. The geology was unimpressive in and of itself, but priceless for what it meant. *The first hidden cave.* Pressed beneath an overhanging pass, its wide, dark opening was almost lost in trees. *Almost.* She took a step forward, the forest carpet cracking underneath her feet. She froze.

They're here.

Ivy's heart raced. Every contour sharpened. Her ears pricked at the flutter of a single leaf falling to the ground. Every instinct she could lay claim to, screamed for attention.

They're watching me.

Ivy could feel hunters in the shadows her eyes weren't trained to see. It suddenly dawned on her. *They've been following me.*

Slowly, she lifted her palms to the sky. She folded, collapsing her legs gently beneath her to halve her height. Somehow, Ivy knew every invisible spear was aimed at her heart.

She waited.

Nothing.

Finally, Ivy drew in a tremulous breath. She spoke aloud. Not in her own language. Not through the amulet. For the first time, Ivy spoke purely in their own words. The language that Gihn had been teaching her. The language of the *Homo floresiensis* people.

"My name is Hiranah." She took a deep breath. "I know you are watching me. Please – show yourselves."

CHAPTER 21

"Christ, that hurts." Neil sucked the humidity between closed teeth, reeling a little as Atasi pulled the fabric of his shirt away from his wound. Dried blood had caused the filthy business shirt to stick solidly to the gash in his side, and as she pried it away, a good portion of newly scabbed skin came away with it. The blood began anew. Groaning, Neil removed the remainder of his shirt.

"I'll need to wash it," he said, making a rubbing motion with his hands as he gestured to the river. "To get the blood and dirt off." Neil began to pull at the seam of one arm, tearing the fabric at the shoulder. It took all the energy he had left. Seeing him struggle with the second, Atasi took it, and finished the job. He took them back from her, holding them up. "If I tie them together, they'll go right around me. Like a bandage. Keep that stuff you've made from falling off when I walk." Atasi had prepared a poultice of some astringent-scented leaves, mashed up in one of his battery bowls. Neil tied a knot between the shoulder seams, then winced as he stood. "You know a month ago, these sleeves wouldn't have made it round my guts. I guess I've lost weight." He grinned at her, then swayed a little on the spot as a wave of light-headedness overtook him. Atasi shushed him, jumping to her feet, leaving her bowl of mashed leaves on the ground. "No, no, I've gotta wash it, to keep the germs off," he said. Neil lay a gentle hand on her shoulder in a show of appreciation, then took the few final steps down to the river. They'd spent the first harrowing day running from Charat, then the night and second day following a small river they'd discovered until their exhaustion had become too much. Neil had lost a lot of blood, and his thoughts were becoming unclear. He needed rest.

Neil squatted at the riverbank and began to scrub the sleeves clean. White sparks danced before his eyes, and he fell backward with a thump. His breath came fast, his skin suddenly cold and clammy. Atasi gently took the sleeve bandage from his hands and swished it in the water. Throwing him a concerned glance, she quickly washed and wrung the joined sleeves, then collected the remainder of his shirt and repeated the action. In a few minutes, Neil's Armani business shirt – once pure white, now grey, tattered and stained with blood, but clean – was strung along the low branch of a tree to dry. While she worked, Neil had splashed some clean water on the side of his belly. The wound was deep. Too deep. Only a couple of inches long, but jagged, with white fatty edges that curled around a dark red centre. It was bleeding far too much.

When the wound was as clean as he could get it, he pinched the sides together and made his way back to the rock where Atasi sat waiting. He collapsed next to her, feeling far older than he had done only days before.

"I need to start a fire. This cut here," he gestured to his side, which again had begun a stream of red down his pale belly, "this isn't going to heal fast enough. I need to get a fire going so I can heat up my knife. *Fire.*" He pulled the silver lighter from his pocket and held it up. Recognising what he needed, Atasi began to gather kindling. Before long, a small crackling fire was smoking near the river's edge on a slab of rock. Neil sat beside it. He pulled his copper knife from his bag and wrapped the handle with a hide strip. He held it as close to the base of the flames as he could without burning his fingers. "This is going to hurt," he muttered, shooting a glance at Atasi. She was watching with interest, unsure of his next move but clearly wanting to help. Neil felt around the leaf litter beside him, coming up with a stick as thick as a finger. He shoved it horizontally across his mouth, biting down on the hard wood. He couldn't afford to scream. Not with Charat out there looking for him.

Heart stammering, Neil pulled his copper knife from the fire. It was glowing a dull red. *Just get it done.* One hand to stretch the wound apart, exposing the deep red centre that bubbled with blood. *Breathe. Just breathe.* A fortifying rush of air, then Neil flattened the burning blade against his own flesh, first inside one edge, then inside the other, poking the knife as hard and flat as he possibly could. Every instinct screamed at him to tear it away. His eyes streamed with the agony. Strangled cries broke around the stick between his teeth, sending a shattering of squawking birds from the canopy. *Keep it on. A bit longer. Push harder.* White flecks danced before his eyes. The noise of the forest was growing dimmer, further away. His vision blurred. Blackened around the edges. Neil felt himself falling into unconsciousness.

Flesh sizzled, cauterising his wound, and stemming the constant flow of blood. The fat and tissue denatured; blood coagulated. The bleeding stopped. *It's done.* As Neil's hand fell away with the knife, his eyes rolled, and he thumped backward against the forest floor.

"I've put you in terrible danger," Neil choked out. His breathing was laboured. The pain indescribable. The young woman didn't reply to his admission. He knew she didn't understand a word of it. But it felt so good to talk to her, he persisted anyway. "If Charat finds us, he'll punish you for this. And he'll probably kill me straight up. I think we both know that." Atasi gave him a smile, and replied with something he couldn't understand. Neil nodded back and took a deep breath.

"You remind me of my son." Neil hadn't meant to say that aloud. He looked away. "You know I haven't said his name for so long it feels like I shouldn't. His name doesn't belong in this wretched place." He forced himself to look up at her. Atasi followed his movements with concerned eyes. When he had come around, she had been singing to him. Sitting beside his head, a wet hand gently patting down his face. Nursing him out of the state he'd forced on himself. Neil couldn't have been more grateful. The woman was an angel.

"*Benjamin,* that's his name. He's my boy. He's ten." Neil held his hand off the ground, as if measuring an invisible child. "About that tall. I got him a telescope, you know. For the hospital bed. Every so often he'd get out of the bed and use it to look at the stars. I thought it might make it a bit easier for him, you now. Being in there so long. Better than staring at four walls, anyway."

Atasi shuffled. She picked up the bowl of poultice she had made and began prodding the concoction with her index finger. She watched him closely, listening.

"My ex-wife takes care of him. And her new husband. He's fine. The kid's fine." Before he could stop himself, Neil's shoulders sagged. He fell forward in a strangled cry. "*He's not fine.* He's sick. And I wasn't there for him." Wracking sobs overtook Neil's body. Sharp elbows dug into the softness above his knees as he buried his burning face in his hands. It had been years – decades even since he'd shed a tear. But once they'd begun, the tears wouldn't stop. "I couldn't bear to see him like that you know, with all the bloody machines everywhere and tubes in his little body. He never did a single thing wrong, and he's had to suffer."

His foot stamped into the dirt beneath it, sending a shot of pain into his side. "And I'm his father and I can't do a damn thing about it!" Neil could barely see for tears. "That was my job, wasn't it? I mean if I can't even–" A long minute passed as the guilt poured from Neil's eyes into his hands. As the sobs subsided, his shoulders shuddered.

"They said maybe five years." Neil's skin grew blotchy. His fist tightened. "He went into remission, and it was looking good, you know. But then about a year ago, it all started up again. He's not taking the new chemo well." He looked up at Atasi through bleary eyes. "The strongest medicine they've got, and it's not working." Atasi didn't reply. Couldn't reply. Instead, she offered her hand, listening to the man ramble as he broke down.

"That's why I've got to get out of this bloody jungle, see? I have to save him. I need to get back to him." Neil felt around in his hide bag and pulled out the black stone Atasi had found, squeezing it tight. "This stone is my way out. Whatever's in *this* can do it. I just have to set up my copper rod to harness the lightning and channel it into this stone. If I figure this all out, I can recreate the conditions that brought me here. If I can get that stone to work, I could get back there to Benjamin. I mean, I could even use the stone to travel forward in time – to find a cure for his Leukaemia." Neil's eyes were all desperation. His voice hoarse with emotion. "I could *save him*, Atasi."

"Saya akan bantu, Nee-el," she shushed him. "Ben-ja-min."

Neil squeezed her hand but didn't reply. He was bone tired. The cauterised wound in his side was aching beyond belief and he felt as if a chill was settling in his spine. He closed his eyes as Atasi gently shushed him. She pushed him back a little, straightening him up, then applied the poultice she had made. She wrapped the damp sleeve-bandage around his middle, securing the medicinal lump to keep it from slipping off. Holding out her hand, the young woman led Neil back down to the small riverbank, and settled him on the bed of warm, flat stones near the fire.

"Hush-ane-lune." Soft words brushed over him like a breeze. *"Hush-ane-lune, Nee-el."* Neil closed his eyes. Atasi's voice floated further away. Lulling his torment into peace. *"Hush-ane-lune."* Within a minute, deep sleep had overtaken him.

"When we get to the top of Kelimutu, we'll have to stay hidden somehow," Neil said, as he walked. "It's exposed up there. I can't remember exactly what the eastern side of the top is like – I came down the west, but if Charat's men are anywhere nearby, they'll see us. We'll need to be careful."

A snap in the leaf litter nearby made them both freeze. Paranoia flicked Neil's nerves. His shoulders were stone. Charat's hunters were all expert trackers. After his attack on the hobbits was complete, Neil knew the red-beaded hunter would direct his aggression to their betrayal instead.

"Charat?" Atasi whispered. Her face was ashen, eyes sharp. The copper feather that Neil had shaped her, glittered amongst the crushed blue in her hair.

"It's alright," Neil murmured, his eyes scouring the shadows. "Just an animal or something." He lay a gentle hand on her shoulder. "I won't let him hurt you. Not again." He nodded at the way ahead and gestured with his hand. "Go."

"Go?" Atasi repeated, trying the word.

"That's right," Neil stepped forward, smiling, "Let's go. *Go.*"

They were travelling again, albeit much slower than Neil would have liked. The wound in his side was swollen and weeping. Neil did his best to keep it clean, but there was no way around the fact that he was in a filthy jungle, sweating, and constantly on the move. Cortisol and fitful sleep had become his new bedfellows. If it wasn't for Atasi's ability to find food, he might not have had the energy to proceed with his new plan. Neil walked with his copper knife in one hand, and his lightning rod in the other. The rod had become a walking stick to support his slow progress.

"Damn it." Neil fell to his hands and knees in the scrub. It wasn't the first time he'd tripped.

"Kamu lunishan anoktora varneth," Atasi said, offering a hand to help him up. She gestured to a fallen trunk. "Kamu istarin boja."

At her insistence, Neil sat. He met Atasi's concerned eyes with the uncomfortable warmth of humility. "Thank you." Atasi took a sip from her water bladder, then passed it to Neil. He took it gratefully. Throwing his head back to sip, even just a little bit, brought a new wave of light-headedness. Atasi noticed and grabbed his shoulder. After a few deep breaths, Neil felt better.

"I've just got to make it a few more days," he said. "When I get to the other side, I can get to a hospital. Get myself some antibiotics for this infection. The wonders of modern medicine, you know." Neil gave a wry chuckle. "The world where I come from would set your head spinning, Atasi. Fifty thousand years of science. Cars. Houses. Aeroplanes in the sky." The young woman stood up and smiled. She began to pick through the undergrowth. Atasi was used to Neil's stream of conversation now. Neither of them required the other to feign understanding. It was simply enough to have someone listen. Neil watched as she retrieved her knife to scrape fungi off a tree trunk. Sunlight broke through the canopy above and caught her hair like spiderwebs of spun gold on the dark, spilling down her naked back. Neil watched, a frown deepening on his face. The woman was nature incarnate. As much a part of this forest as the blue feathers in her hair.

What am I doing? Neil thought. *Could she even survive out of the forest? Why would she want to?* A nagging doubt crept over him. *I'm saving her,* he tried to convince himself. *Aren't I?*

"I was hoping when we escaped that night," Neil's voice was gruff, "that you'd want to come back home with me." Neil was grateful for once that Atasi couldn't understand him. "Not as my wife or anything like that. Just – so I could keep you safe from Charat." He took a deep breath, willing the words away as he spoke them. "But I'm not sure now that you'd actually want to go, if you knew where I was from. I mean – *modern life, modern education, modern medicine,*" malcontent settled in his gut, "it's still not enough to save Benjamin, is it? I'd take care of you, of course. But you'd have no family. No one to talk to." He looked away. The truth was bitterly disappointing. "And you were happy here before Charat had the power to – I mean, before I gave him the *opportunity* to–" Neil's jaw tightened. "Before I came here, he was just another snivelling hunter chasing your heels, wasn't he? I did this. I gave him the power that he has. It's my fault the bastard was ever given the authority in your tribe to be able to hurt you." Neil sat for a while, staring out into the suffocation of green. Guilt was crushing him. "There's nothing for you if you come with me, Atasi. I'm only saving you away from a terror I created myself." Atasi walked back over to him. She had a full basket of trimmed mushrooms, tiny black berries, and green shoots. "So that means – I don't know how to save you."

Atasi sat beside him, laying the basket at her feet. The crushed turquoise blue feathers brushed her shoulders. She began speaking in an earnest, gentle, conversational tone that spoke to Neil of nothing but her trust in him. She understood he was trying to get the stone to do something. She knew he was searching for a way to get home. Beyond that, she had followed him in blind faith because he promised an escape from Charat's abuse. Neil couldn't stand it. If there was one thing he hated most, it was indecision.

"Right, then," Neil said, getting to his feet and swaying a little as the blood rushed from his head. The wound in his side amplified from a dull resting ache into sharp throbs. He squeezed his eyes shut then blinked hard a few times, carefully bending to gather his belongings.

"Time to go."

"Go?" Atasi repeated, gathering her things.

"That's right. Let's go. The longer we stay, the more likely he'll catch up to us. If Charat finds us–" Neil turned to Atasi, a sudden shot of clarity breaking through his pain "–*when* he finds us, we need to be ready to deal with him. It was me that gave the bastard the avalanche of power he has. Somehow, *I'm* going to have to take it away."

CHAPTER 22

ORRIN

"*I* should probably ask who I'm supposedly working for," Orrin said, passing Eli his backpack. The geologist stowed it in the overhead locker, then took his seat beside Orrin on the Boeing 737. The flight to Denpasar was nearly empty. Few holiday makers were willing to risk air-travel to return home, and international flights had been restricted to urgent business only.

If it weren't dire circumstances, Orrin was not convinced he would have boarded the plane himself. He looked out the porthole window and suppressed a shudder.

"You look as nervous as I feel," Eli said.

Orrin nodded toward the window. Outside, ribbons of aurora australis still lit the sky, despite the dawn sun breaking over the horizon. "The geomagnetic storms are getting worse."

Eli nodded gravely. "It's risky to fly. If I didn't think you needed to do this so urgently, I might have cancelled the trip and gone by ship instead."

"Thanks for sticking with it. I appreciate this more than you know."

Eli nodded, his expression grim but clearly trying to keep his tone light. "The pilots don't rely on their instrumentation anymore, you know. Navigation and global positioning systems cut out whenever we get a solar flare big enough to disrupt them. Which is constantly, of course. A few of the satellites are already dead in the sky." He gestured out of the tiny porthole-sized window, then clipped his lapsash tight across his waist as the alarm started to sound.

"I know," Orrin replied. "And it will get worse fast. It's only a matter of time before a full-scale state of emergency in every country. The International Space Station has been abandoned. Power grids are failing everywhere under the massive current surges. There are already millions of people without electricity in some cities and God knows how long it will take to repair them."

"Loss of life is inevitable." Eli pushed his shoulders back as the plane began to roll forward along the runway.

"But big business is still booming, hey?" Orrin said with chagrin. "So tell me about this job of yours."

"Preliminary geological surveys," Eli replied. "For a multi-national mining conglomerate called IPM – *International Pulp and Mining*. They want someone on the ground, as it were, to give them an idea of where to focus their efforts."

"And you're that someone?"

"I have specialist knowledge in their particular mining interests."

"Fair play to you, then. Which interests are they?"

"Intrusions into elemental rocks, as it happens. Copper. Hematite. Magnetite. Gold. A few others. There are sparse high yield opportunities for them left though, even given the archipelago is a melting pot of volcanic geomorphology. It's already been strip mined to buggery, so they're branching out – looking for new opportunities."

"And you've been sent to Flores before?"

"Plenty of times. IPM have been sending me from one island to the next over the past twelve months. They have their own people of course, but they want an expert opinion to sign off before they start digging. Mining isn't cheap."

"I'll bet." Orrin shook his head. There was something bothering him – an uneasy thought that had found home in his worries and couldn't be explained away. He rubbed his eyes under his glasses as the wheels of the plane lifted from the tarmac. The rush of acceleration forced him back into his seat. The last time he had flown was his final voyage from Ireland to Melbourne. It seemed like a lifetime ago. "Listen, how do you know that this mining isn't somehow triggering the environmental destruction we're seeing around us?"

"Because people have been mining the earth for decades. Why do you think Flores is any different?"

"I don't know." Orrin looked at his new friend. "It's just this niggling feeling I have. Like something about this situation, and those hobbits isn't right. There was this guy I meant a few weeks back. *Alex Someone-or-other.* He worked for the Animal Research Regulation Department and came to uni to check on a hobbit that was being used for experiments in the anatomy labs. It turns out he was the whistle-blower on that Cosmitech shite that was all over the papers not long ago."

"Nasty stuff."

"Terrible," agreed Orrin. "But the thing is, Alex told me they found magnetite in the hobbit brains. That *that discovery* is what set off the mining companies to investigate Flores in the first place. That's what got them digging."

"That's true." Eli nodded thoughtfully. "Though I don't see how it makes a difference. We never found enough magnetite under Flores to cause this level of impact on the magnetosphere by exposing it, if that's where you're going with this. Magnetite affects the hobbit's inner navigation, for sure. The mineral deposits underground lead them around like a homing pigeon. It's an incredible evolutionary adaptation."

"Well, that's just my point," Orrin said. He leaned forward, frustrated by his inability to articulate his thoughts. "Sorry, shite, I'm just not making sense, am I?" He took a deep breath. "Okay – before the time shift happened, in *my* version of the earth, I'd detected a change in the magnetosphere. It was weakening over time. Something sinister was happening but I couldn't put my finger on what was causing it. But what was happening then, was this! Whatever *this is, right now* that's affecting us on *your version* of the earth – only back then, for me, it was happening on a much smaller scale. Then, when I was shot into your version of the earth, it's like I'm seeing the same phenomenon but amplified a-thousand-fold – as if the repercussions of what was just begin-ning *for me* is already here in full-blown intensity *for you*."

"Okay." Eli looked confused. "What do you think that means?"

"Ah!" Orrin threw his head back against the seat in agitation. "I don't exactly *know* what I mean. But what I do know is this–" he lowered his voice and met Eli's eyes with a critical look. "In my version of earth, there were no hobbits – they were extinct – but we did have mining in Flores, though nowhere near the scale you're dealing with on your earth. So I'm wondering if the hobbits somehow set off this chain of events. Just by, you know, *existing?*" Orrin shrugged. It was too abstract a connection to pinpoint exactly what he meant.

Eli looked thoughtful. "You might be on to something, I suppose. I mean, the guts of those islands are exposed more and more every day. But until we can find evidence of what exactly is causing the weakness in our magnetosphere, there's no stopping it."

"You're right." Orrin settled back into his chair with a sigh. "We need to find evidence."

They had a six-hour flight ahead of them to reach Denpasar International airport in Bali, then another hour flying east to Komodo Airport on the western-most tip of Flores Island. Orrin decided he had plenty of time to dwell on the problem. And planned to do just that. He slipped his earphones in and flicked through his phone to find the music he so desperately needed to hear. *Le Cygne. Ivy's cello.* The fact that the song, recorded before the time shift and stolen clandestinely from the audio recorder in the room she had practiced, was still saved on his phone despite her lack of existence, brought him a heady mix of comfort and desperation.

Leaning back, Orrin closed his eyes, but minutes later, exhaustion finally took him. He woke up as the airplane was coming in to land.

The stopover in Bali at Denpasar Airport was a heart-stopping race from one gate to another. Travelling without luggage was a blessing, and Orrin ducked along corridors with his backpack, determined not to let the late arrival miss their connecting flight. Eli, for his part, was clearly a seasoned traveller. His familiarity with the airport led them straight to the Airbus A330 that was issuing a final boarding call.

Just over one hour later, Orrin's feet hit the tarmac of Komodo Airport in Labuan Bajo. A wall of humidity hit his face.

Flores.

"I've booked us a hotel for the night," Eli said, leading him through the airport and out through the sliding front doors. The airport was unexpectedly sleek and modern, with a stretched oval face of glass that glittered under the floodlights. Enormous window decals of Komodo dragons stretched three stories up to greet tourists with a tantalising promise of the island's star attraction. "It's too dark to begin our journey across the island tonight," Eli explained, "and I don't know about you, but I'm absolutely starved."

"I could eat a horse," Orrin agreed.

"Can't help you there," Eli laughed. "But how about a lobster?

There's a little restaurant in the cliffs with the most amazing sweet and spicy lime sauce."

"Agh," Orrin replied, "that sounds grand. If you keep on like this, Dimi's going to lose top spot in my books."

Eli grinned as he hailed a taxi and gave the driver instructions. An hour later, and they were finishing the most sumptuous meal Orrin could remember.

"I don't think I've even eaten in the past couple of months," he explained, scooping up the last of his rice as Eli watched his enthusiasm in amusement. "I mean, I suppose I have, but honestly, I don't even remember what. Since Ivy went missing, it's like – every part of my life has tipped arseways. I swear I thought I was losing my mind, man." He paused, shaking his head. "It's like she just suddenly didn't exist anymore. No one knew her. Her house was empty, all her published research was gone. The people she spent every day with before had never even heard of her." Orrin put down his fork, picked up his Guinness, and stared into it for a moment. "I can't sleep, I can't eat." He took a sip, wondering how much of his plight Dimi had already passed on to Eli over the past week. "I've done nothing but try to get Ivy back and figure out what went wrong in my lab that night." Orrin looked up at the man sitting opposite him. "You can't imagine how terrifying this whole situation has been, I mean I thought *I broke the world* that night Ivy disappeared. And maybe I did because now the whole world feels like it's falling apart around me. I've lost my job, of course. My whole career is down the jacks, and still–" Orrin paused, an odd smile coming to his lips, "when I think about her face, those green eyes, and that mad red hair like, like, *fire* – I get this rush of energy inside, like I've got to just keep going and going until I find her. Like I can't let anything stop me." He let out a deep breath. "I sound crazy, right?"

"Crazy in love, maybe," Eli replied. "Not usually my department, but I think I get it. Listen Orrin, I'll do whatever I can to help you. When Dimi brought that amulet back in to me to analyse and I finally figured out that the intrusion in the magnetite was element 115 – well, I knew we were dealing with some next level business. I'm as worried as anyone else about this damn *environmental implosion* going on around us, but I guess I just figured it was something we had to live with. For as long as I remember it's been getting worse. Every major institution from the local college all the way up to NASA have been throwing their best people at this for years. We've all been acclimatised to accept we just have to adapt to the new threats and cut our losses as we go. Big losses, you know, even loss of life. But it's the way our world works. I can see that maybe we've all become a bit," he shrugged, "*apathetic,* about it." And now you just waltz in and tell me it doesn't have to be that way? That something specific caused this breakdown. Something we've done and that you're trying to figure out what it is."

Eli sat forward. His shoulders were tense, his eyes a little overwhelmed. "Look, I really don't know how we can figure this all out either. All my life I've been a pretty pragmatic guy. I like rocks because they're *real*, you know. I can see them; I can hold them. I know they're *there.* My research is solid and what I do makes sense to me. What you're talking about, that you *broke the world* by sending a woman back in time by accident, well, none of that makes sense. But then I look around and see where we're heading, and I know this is not sustainable. We're crashing. This whole world is crashing, and no one knows how to keep it together. There's something seriously wrong with what we've come to accept as our *new normal.* And suddenly some crazy guy who's in love with a woman who doesn't exist is actually the most sensible thing out there right now. So, I'm throwing my hat in the ring – because if it means saving the world, then to hell with it all – *I'm on board.*"

Orrin sat for a moment. After weeks of hellish despair, the sudden validation was almost too much for him. Then he threw his head back in glee. He lifted his drink and held it aloft it to Eli, who clinked his beer glass in salute.

"To saving the world, yeah?" Orrin laughed.

"Someone's gotta do it." Eli joined in and soon they were gasping for breath at the dinner table as they considered the absurdity of their conversation. It was Orrin who finally spoke, brushing off the burden they both carried with the darkest humour he had left in him.

"You're an absolute champion, boyo, you know that?"

"Cheers."

They sat in comfortable silence for a few moments.

"So, you and Dimi have really hit it off, hey?" Orrin said. "I haven't seen him so chuffed since we won the three-legged race in the beer tent at orientation."

"Ha," Eli's smile lit the room. "Yeah, well, I wasn't expecting that either, I can tell you. Relationships have always taken a back seat to my research. But when he came into my lab last week, well, something hit me like a tonne of bricks." Eli looked into his beer. A blush was creeping up his neck.

"Well, I'm happy for you both," Orrin said earnestly. "Dimi is a good guy, the best, and he's been alone way too long. Now there's a man who lives for his work." Orrin took another sip of Guinness. "All I can tell you, is that he's the best friend I've ever had. Dimi's one of the quiet ones. He's an artist with a telescope, absolutely feckin' brilliant at what he does. And you won't find a more loyal person on the planet. I feel so stupid for ever doubting him," Orrin admitted. "He's risking so much to help me. And I was so terrified of – well, losing everything I've ever had, to be honest. I'd already lost my old life and my sanity with it, but it seems that no matter what reality I'm living in, Dimi's the same guy he always was. You can't know how relieved I am about that."

Eli took that insight on board, nodding into his drink with a quiet smile.

"He plays the piano, did he tell you that?" Orrin added.

"He did not."

"He's grand at it, too. I never appreciated it until now, but anyway, the cat's out of the bag, as they say. So make sure he shows you before all this–" Orrin's fingers, held aloft in the air, hesitated and fell.

"Before it all ends?"

Orrin's gut twisted. "Yeah, I guess so." If he did manage to correct the timeline and return the earth to way it was before he'd messed it up, only he and Ivy would remember any of this had ever happened. These two men who had finally found one another, and were so integral to his ability to succeed, could pass in the street and not recognise the other. "Geez, I've really made a right haymes of things for you two, haven't I?"

Eli gave a small shrug. "As they say, you can't have it all." He took a deep breath and offered a conciliatory smile. "This situation is bigger than any of us. Besides, sometimes things are best left to fate."

"Fate." Orrin took a final swig of his beer. "Maybe you're right," he said, not believing a word of it.

"What do you say we head back to the hotel?" Eli said, draining his drink to stand. "We've got an early start tomorrow. Six hours on the road to reach Kelimutu, and that's if the weather holds."

"Right." Orrin got to his feet as well. A sudden thrill shot through him. He was in Flores. He was about to embark on a journey through the jungle that Ivy herself was living in. Nothing but fifty thousand years separated them.

And God-damn-it, I'm gonna figure out how to make this right.

They had been travelling for nearly two hours. The dawn sun was glued firmly above the horizon. Eli had called on a driver he was already familiar with to take them across the island over the coming days. The man had a wild white brush of beard, high cheekbones, and an enormous smile. He had greeted Eli like an old friend.

"Terrible luck, Orrin," Eli had said, as he introduced the two men, "Arif is one of very few drivers in Flores who speaks fluent English. Which means we'll suffer his awful jokes as we travel."

"You love my jokes!" Arif had roared laughing, shuffling the two men into his taxi. Orrin grinned as he slid into the back seat of the sleek silver four-wheel-drive. It was clear that Eli and Arif had a long-standing friendship, and the jibes were taken in good humour. Arif's mood was contagious. "I've been saving the good ones for you, Eli – here now, what type of music does a volcano listen to?"

"Here we go," Eli grinned. "Tell me."

"Rock!" Arif declared. "Your favourite kind!"

"I love it," Eli said, gently clapping him on the back. "It's so *en pointe*."

"I thought so too," Arif slipped into the driver's seat. Eli slid into the front passenger seat beside him. "Tell me, my new friend," Arif looked back at Orrin through the mirror, "why should you never do math in the jungle?" He was already chuckling.

"I don't know, why?"

"Because if you add four and four, you might get ate!" Arif hit the ignition and the engine roared to life as Orrin chuckled along with him. It was impossible not to like the man.

"Have you been doing this for a long time, Arif?" Orrin asked. "The guided tours, I mean."

"Oh, yes," Arif said, jovially. "I've been up and down these mountains like a goat since I was a boy. Only now I get to do it in the comfort of air-conditioning. You want to see anything special while you're here? The Nada villages and spider-web rice fields are something great to see, or Koka beach, now there's a pretty view – crystal clear water. You brought your swimming clothes?"

"I'm afraid we won't have time for stops," Eli interjected. "We've got a flight booked out of Labuan Bajo in four days time. Orrin needs to get back to his lab in Melbourne rather urgently. A flight out of Ende would have been far quicker, but with the electrical storms over Kelimutu getting worse every day, all the flights are grounded."

"Suits me," Arif said. "More time on the road, more easy money."

"Right," smiled Eli. "Only we've got to get to Kelimutu for the survey and then it's *whoosh*–" he flew his palm in front of his face, simulating a plane taking off.

"All work, no play again, hey?"

"I'm afraid so."

"You're missing out, boy. I've told you this before."

"I know, I know. But Orrin has never been to Flores, so it's all new to him. You can give him the full tourist spiel as we drive."

"Ah, you'll love it," Arif said, smiling back at Orrin through the rear-vision mirror as he pulled out of the hotel carpark. "Most spectacular place on Earth. I'll point out our beauties as we speed by."

And *speed by* he had. It was clear immediately that Arif knew the roads better than Orrin knew his own mind.

The ocean cliffs of Labuan Bajo had been swiftly left behind them as they disappeared into the jungled mountains to the south-east. The road twisted and turned through a suffusion of green trees, occasionally dotted by small village houses, shops and places of worship. The road hugged the low-lying routes wherever possible, but when Arif ascended ancient volcanic ridges like an eagle soaring on a thermal breeze, Orrin felt his knuckles tighten around his phone.

To distract himself from the dizzying ride, Orrin pulled his phone from his pocket and thumbed through his playlist. <*Unti-*

tled>. He sucked in a breath and felt the familiar chill that raced his spine.

"What is that you're listening to?" Eli turned around in his seat and raised an eyebrow. "I should have downloaded something new before the trip. I'm sick of listening to the same old stuff. It's my go-to playlist for travelling, though I feel like it's a bit *been-there, done-that*. I need something new."

Orrin plucked an earphone from his ear and passed it forward. "It's Ivy," he replied. "Or at least, it's Ivy playing the cello."

Eli took the earpiece. His eyebrow raised as he listened. "Classical music?"

"*Le Cygne*, by Camille Saint-Saëns," Orrin answered. "I'd never heard of it before I met her. Now I know every note. I've listened to it so many times it's a wonder my phone still works."

"How did you get this?" Eli asked. "I thought everything she'd ever done had disappeared?"

"Pure luck," Orrin explained. "Ivy used to practise her cello in one of the tutorial rooms in the archaeology department. There's an audio recording facility in each room so students can download lectures after the fact to help with revision, rather than just scribbling down notes while we're talking."

"And let them catch some *zzz*'s in the lecture theatres – the geology department has them too."

"So does physics," Orrin nodded. "So anyway, Ivy would record herself practicing the cello using the internal equipment, so that she could listen to it later and pick up any mistakes she made. I caught her at it one day, and I decided to download the music after I got home. So I could listen again."

"Creepy," Eli said, a smirk on his lips.

"Probably," Orrin admitted, "well, yeah definitely. Not my finest moment. But I'm bloody glad I did. My phone was with me in my office when the time shift was triggered. It was a lead-lined room, used to be used for radiation testing. Nothing in my office was affected by Ivy's accident so the recording survived, though I didn't realise until later. It's the only thing that stopped me going off the deep end, you know. The fact that I have proof that she was alive. Finding this recording saved my sanity."

"It's nice," Eli said. His eyes closed as he absorbed the music. "She's good."

"She is, yeah."

"You in love, young man?" Arif called back to him from the driver's seat. "Nothing is better, you know."

"Are you married?" Orrin asked him in reply.

"Oh, yes, yes, yes. Got five children all grown up now. I am surrounded by grandbabies most of the time. I love it."

"That's fantastic," Orrin said. "You're a lucky man." It was hard to imagine himself in a future so content. Or any future at all.

"I know it," the driver winked back at him in the mirror. "Lucky Arif! They never tire of my jokes either." Orrin grinned.

"Where are we?" Eli asked, passing Orrin his earpiece, and turning back to face the front.

"About 20 minutes from Ruteng."

"Right, thanks."

"Are you sure you have no time for sight-seeing?" Arif asked. "We'll be heading straight past Liang Bua cave. *Home of the Hobbits*, they call it. Not that anyone lives there now, but still, the archaeologists ran a dig there not long ago. It's worth a look."

"Did you say Liang Bua cave?" Orrin sat forward. A shot of adrenaline hit his veins.

"Sure, the *Cool Cave*, it's called around here. It's about twenty minutes north of Ruteng, so if you want to take a detour–"

"We don't really have time–" Eli began, as Orrin cut in "Yes!"

"Which is it boys?" Arif asked, looking between them. Eli looked at his watch. He glanced at Orrin, noting the sudden change in his mood.

"We're making good time," he conceded. "Go on then."

Cool Cave, Arif had told him as they arrived, is what the name *Liang Bua* meant in the Manggarai language of East Nusa Tenggara. As they trailed up the dirt path toward the cave mouth, Orrin pushed ahead. He couldn't shake the illogical hope he might find Ivy standing there, waiting for him.

A few tourists dribbled past, back down to the road where their bus was waiting for them. They looked disappointed. He soon found out why.

Any sign that the cave had been excavated by an archaeological team – *a salvage dig*, is what Jayne had called it, was gone. Jayne had told him that the archaeologists had been hired to get in and out as quickly as possible. To recover whatever they could before the mining corporation moved in. Apparently, they had surveyed, excavated, and left already. The mining surveyors had taken their place.

The cave mouth was now stretched wide with ugly metal railings, enclosing it like a jail within. *Keep Out* and *Danger* signs had been concreted into the rock. The great limestone cavern, yawning fifty meters back into the mountainside behind the fence, was an uneven mosaic of deep, scaffolded pits and teetering piles of removed earth. Soon enough, Orrin knew the face of it would change again when the diggers came in.

Arif gave a low whistle. "Sorry boys. This is new,'" he said, shaking his head sadly. "Another tourist spot about to be turned into a big hole in the ground. Not gonna be anything left to show anyone soon." He clucked, disappointed, and turned away to wait back down the path at the car.

"Not much left to see, apparently," Eli said quietly, coming to stand beside him. "I knew IPM had the cave in their sites as a potential magnetite mine, but I didn't realise they were going to move on it so fast. I'm sorry."

"Is this where they found it then?" Eli said. "The amulet?"

"Yeah," Orrin replied. "It ended up back with Jayne in the archaeology lab for residues testing. They dug it out of a pit over a meter underground. Somewhere over there, I imagine." He pointed to the wall of the cave, where most of the digging seemed to have been done. "Mapped and photographed it, labelled, and sent it off to Jayne for analysis. Had to work fast. Apparently a salvage dig is a bit like a grab and run for archaeological sites that are about to be bulldozed."

"Yeah," Eli said. "I'm familiar with the process. "Money tends to be a polarising factor when it comes to timelines."

Orrin nodded. "So the amulet was still covered in dirt when Jayne got it. Archaeologists didn't brush it off for risk of losing any blood residue or adding site contaminants, no time to be too careful – that's why they never saw Ivy's initials engraved in the stone until it got back to the lab. I did though. There it was. *I.C.* Written plain as day on the front face of it."

"And so you think she's stuck here, fifty thousand years ago."

"I know she is."

"It's a helluva story, Orrin."

"Yeah." An overwhelming frustration filled him. For a moment, it caught Orrin's breath and gripped him tight, as if it might not let him ever breathe again. With a growl, he grabbed hold of the metal fence, and launched himself up and over the top of it.

Eli watched, concerned, but made no move to follow. "That's a hard hat area, mate," was all he offered. "Be careful. Could be unstable."

Orrin granted him a small nod, then stepped up the incline to the lip of the cave. Shadow blanketed him in cool air as he stepped beyond it. It was like stepping into another world.

He moved between piles of broken earth and offcuts of scaffolding timber. Long stalactites dripped like ancient candles from the limestone ceiling which arched twenty- five meters above his head. Monstrous speleothems of dissolved minerals jutted out of the limestone floor. Low walls of leftover sandbags and stone partitions jigsawed the floor into a maze. Against the western wall, deep rectangular pits framed inside by timber scaffolding, dropped away into darkness at his feet. Jayne had told him that they were close to eleven meters deep. Orrin stepped back, away from the edge. He was suddenly angry that the place had been neglected and discarded by people who should had have fallen to their knees and worshipped it.

He looked up. Let his eyes linger on the empty space. Far beyond him, where the cavern closed in on itself inside the belly of the mountain, the floor rose up in layers and terraces, inching closer to the ceiling. They touched in a sweep of limestone beyond a rear chamber. Enormous boulders littered the balcony slope, like sentinels in the dark.

The place was overwhelming. Orrin turned slowly, trying to take it all in at once. The cave felt like a cathedral. *So much has happened in here*, Orrin thought to himself. *Two hundred thousand years of human lives. People being born, eating, dying on this dirt floor.* He stared into the shadows, willing his eyes to find ghosts of the past. *Ivy was here.* He could almost feel her in the walls. Orrin closed his fist tight, wishing Ivy's amulet was still in his pocket and not thousands of miles across the ocean. He needed to feel its peculiar warmth in his palm. Wanted to know if it would recognise this place. If some connection existed between the stone and its burial ground.

It was uncanny. Something in the damp cave air felt so familiar. Rough, cold limestone found his fingertips as Orrin traced the wall back to the entrance of the cave. He stopped suddenly. Not less than a meter away, another excavation pit fell into blackness at Orrin's feet. With his palm flattened against the wall of the cave, he knew with a certainty that seemed to come from nowhere, that Ivy had slept there. He pressed his palm into the rough wall like a pilgrim at a shrine. Spread his fingers across it. Closed his eyes.

The limestone pressed back, her hand touching his.

Fifty thousand years. Not long enough to erase her.

"Orrin?" Eli's voice was gentle but cut through the cool cave like a knife. "We've got to get back on the road. IPM are expecting me in Moni tonight. I'm sorry."

"It's okay." Orrin found his voice. "I'm coming."

CHAPTER 23

IVY

othing.

"Please," Ivy said to the shadows. "I have no weapon. I cannot hurt you." The forest was unnaturally still. Even the trees held their breath. No one stepped forward. Not a single pair of eyes could be seen amongst the leaves. But even with no proof, Ivy's heart leapt in joy at small mercies. *I found them.* "I promise – I am not here to hurt you." Her voice was gentle and cajoling. "I am not Karathah. I am from a different place – a land far away from here." Her heart panged with the sudden reminder of her own dislocation. She pushed the pain away. "Please – for just a moment, trust me."

There was no response, but Ivy felt a shift in the air. She could almost feel them, judging and assessing her intrusion, deciding whether to kill her immediately or let her speak. The sight of a tall, white-skinned sapien was no doubt terrifying to the reclusive tribe. And Ivy suspected they had more than enough reason to be afraid.

"The Karathah attacked you last night." Ivy's resolve almost faltered. She hoped, even the tiniest bit, that she was wrong, and that the tribe had been hidden well enough to remain unscathed from last nights' butchery. But the alternative, that it had been her own friends that were killed and strung so callously over the red-beaded hunter's shoulder, was even worse to imagine. Ivy looked around, straining to catch a glimpse of movement in the air. There had been death here, Ivy was certain of it. Grief hung on the vines like spectres in dappled sunlight. "I saw the Karathah pass by near the sea. One hunter, with strings of red beads through his hair, was among them. He is a violent man and did unspeakable things." A moment's pause. *Nothing.* "I know you are grieving today."

A twitch in the leaves. A whisper came from the shadows. A woman. Words spat, as if they were bitter.

"We grieve for more than those murdered last night."

"I know you do," Ivy said. "And your anger is justified. The Karathah are spreading closer to your Home Cave every day. There are many of them – far more than your own tribe. Their hunting trails are expanding from the sea up into your mountains. They take too many probech, and the forests are growing empty of food for your people." Ivy had seen the archaeological evidence to prove it. *Homo sapiens* had only been in Flores for five thousand years, but their exponential population growth had already disrupted the delicate balance of predator and prey. Extinction, for more species than the ancient hobbits, was coming soon.

"You know this because you are Karathah yourself."

Ivy couldn't bring herself to deny it. Her humanity was devastatingly defined. "Perhaps in body. But I am family with your own people too."

"Never!"

"It's true! I have lived with others like you in the forest over the mountains. Their tribe carries the same burden as yours. They have been attacked and poisoned by the Karathah. Their cave was set on fire. I have fought against the Karathah beside them. I am helping them to survive by teaching them what I know about the Karathah. I can teach you to survive as well. This is your land, your home, *Shirahn-tah*! This is the forest of your ancestors. There are more tribes of your people out there, fighting to survive. I want to help you, but you can only survive if you all come together."

"Even together we cannot survive." The woman's voice cracked with grief. The words she used were truncated and slightly different to those spoken by the Liang Bua tribe. Generations of incremental change had left a mark on their language, but it was close enough to understand. Ivy felt a tiny thrill at how much she had learned from Shahn at the cave. "Our women no longer bear children," the weary voice said. "And our babies do not thrive."

"There are simply too few of you left to build families here," Ivy tried to explain. She had already struggled against the ethical quandary of whether to explain genetic inbreeding to Gihn. When he had described the *Slow Death* that impacted his tribe more each generation, Ivy felt sure of the cause. According to their oral history, the hobbit tribes had separated thousands of years ago, splintering across the island with no contact thereafter. With only a hundred or so individuals left together in any one place, inbreeding within the tribe became a necessity. As blood-relative mating partners have similar DNA, the chances of them carrying the same recessive gene was greatly increased. The rate of prenatal and childhood death grew as the odds stacked against babies being born without genetic mutations. Over time, individual reproductive fitness declined; the population of each tribe dropped. Extinction was terrifyingly close. The only way to reverse the damage, Ivy realised, was to *outbreed*. The *Homo floresiensis* tribes needed to unite to save themselves. Young people needed the opportunity to find new mates and expand the genetic pool. Only by doing so, could they revive the variation in genes that had been lost and give themselves a fighting chance for survival. That is, if the Karathah didn't kill them first.

"Your babies are born too early, or die too soon," Ivy agreed. "Your women can't carry children well anymore; they won't grow inside. There are deformities when they are born. You grieve for your lost children. I know you do." Ivy closed her eyes and the memory of Emiri's face found her there. The tiny hobbit woman had lived beneath a shroud of grief. Five children had been lost to her, all born too soon or passed not long after birth. Leihna had told her that after dusk song every night, Emiri walked through the forest calling for them. It was the only sound she made. The woman had been broken by sadness. Then killed by the Karathah.

"Your family is your heart," Ivy said. "I understand. There is still time to save yourselves if you can trust me to help you."

"Why should we trust a Karathah?" The bitterness had returned.

Ivy sighed. She felt she was losing both the battle and the war. "Because I want to help you. I will fight for you."

"Help us?" The woman growled. "We have tried fighting. They only kill us faster. Do you think this is the first time we have been attacked?" The woman's voice fell silent. When it returned, her words were shrouded in defeat. "They want our Home Cave. They want our hunting trails. They have already killed too many, and our children are too few to carry on alone. We are nothing now but living death. Leave us, Karathah."

"I won't leave until you listen!" Ivy insisted. "You have tried fighting with your spears, yes. But there are other ways to fight! You can survive this with your cleverness. Find it in your heart to keep fighting."

"Our hearts died long ago." The woman's voice was a whisper. "We are already gone."

Ivy squeezed her eyes closed, willing hot tears away. Gihn and his family had been willing to fight, even if it took the last breath in them. But these people were already ghosts. They had given up.

"I will not accept that!" Ivy shouted into the shadows. "You are not gone until your last child is gone! Will you be the one to deny them life when you can still fight for them? They live and breathe now, you all do! The Karathah should not get to decide who lives and who dies in this forest. You decide! You have a choice!" Ivy's breath was fast, her hands shaking. "I say you deserve to live!" Ivy searched the shadows, wide eyed, challenging the woman's defeat.

Silence. Ivy's shoulders fell.

A snapped twig. A rustle of leaves. An elderly woman stepped from shadow into light, like shape defined from watercolour. Her face was heavily lined. Her body worn out. She had scars all over.

"You are not welcome here, Karathah. You cannot help us."

"But I am here to fight for you. To teach you to fight for yourselves!"

"There is nothing left for us to fight for, as we have already lost. We once filled the valleys below. Strong hands. So many voices. Now, there are only seven families remaining. We want to live quietly, as we did once before. Even if we don't live long, we will be at peace," the hobbit said. She turned away, as if to slip back into shadow.

"At peace?" Ivy cried. "With the Karathah hunting you and claiming your land? With your children dying?"

"There are too many of them to fight."

"So, you just sit and wait to die!? I can't let you do that!"

"And why should you care, Karathah!?" The woman growled through gritted teeth.

"Because I choose to care!" Defiance burned in Ivy's chest. "And because I love the people I am trying to save. They are just like you, and they are family to me. I'm here because I know they are worth saving. And I thought you were too. But perhaps I was wrong. Perhaps the story they tell is wrong too." Ivy placed her hand behind her and pulled herself up from the ground. She towered over the woman in front of her, who held her ground, and spear, tight.

"What story?" Beneath the anger, a flash of curiosity weakened the old woman's grip.

"The story of the Life Stone," Ivy said. "The stone that your ancestors found at the Sister Lakes. It was said to carry the life of the earth, *aneirlah*, within it and that when you, the forest people, become lost, the Life Stone would send you someone to show you the way."

"We know the story. The stone was lost long ago. That story means nothing now."

Ivy continued, ignoring her. "The stone showed the ancestors a vision – a tall woman with eyes that were green like the trees. White skin like the moon and hair red like fire."

"I've heard enough." She began to back away. "This is a trick. Leave now, Karathah."

"No." Ivy held out her hand, dangling the amulet from her wrist for all the hidden eyes of the forest to see.

A shadow of fear passed over the tiny woman's face. "We don't want you here," she hissed.

"Then you have already condemned your family." Ivy's glare pierced the shadows, inviting others to defy their leader. "Don't let her fear stop you from living. I can't promise to save you, but I will promise to give my life trying! *This is the Life Stone.* It is mine to carry. I answered that call for help. Because I *chose* to. Now *you* need to make a choice. Fight for your lives or accept death in fear."

Whispers.

It was as if the leaves themselves began to speak. From the crags and shadows and boughs above her, hidden figures appeared. Dozens of them, with open wounds and bloody skin. Spears were aimed at her, but there was no malice behind their eyes. Only *hope.*

"Why should they believe you?" growled the elder. "Life Stone or not, you are no saviour for our people. You are Karathah, you said so yourself!" She hit her own chest, grief overflowing into words. "My children were killed by the Karathah last night. They fought back and died for it. Should we not kill you the same way?!"

Ivy stepped forward, pulling the woman's spear tip to her own chest, and holding it there. "Kill me right now if you think it will bring back your children," she said, her voice steady. "Choose to learn nothing and we will all die here together."

Ivy waited, offering every spear a chance to claim her. "You are right. I am no saviour. I'm just one person, like you. One *human* like you. But I'm willing to fight to save you from the Karathah and from yourselves. If you will not do the same, then your people are already lost."

Nobody moved.

Then one man stepped forward.

Then another. A third.

One by one, the remaining tribe pushed past the old woman in their way.

"I will hear you," a woman called out.

"Tell us what you know," called another. Questions flew at Ivy thick and fast. She held up her hands, asking for one at a time.

"Who are you?" A young hunter called above the others.

Ivy smiled. "They call me *Hiranah*," she said. "Fire-hair."

It was another two hours before Ivy left the tribe. She left alone.

They had asked many questions. Most of the hunters had seemed roused by the thought that there were more people of their own kind. They argued that meeting them, and joining forces, was their only means to survive. But the leader, whose name Ivy learned was Tica, remained steadfastly against her tribe's involvement. No amount of pleading could convince her otherwise.

"You are luring us into a trap," Tica had insisted. "How foolish would we be to follow a Karathah away from our Home? The others will be waiting with spears to greet us." Ivy had turned to the younger members of the tribe instead.

"Other Shirahn-tah are gathering at the Sister Lakes," she urged. "We have been travelling from far away, searching for more of your family. Everyone must come together before the next full moon and decide then on the future of your tribe. United, you have a chance to survive."

A rumble of urgency moved through the family.

"But that is less than seven days from now!"

"If we leave our Home Cave the Karathah will claim it – there will be no home to return to if we fail."

Ivy counted the desperate faces. Sixty had survived the Karathah's latest attack. Not enough to survive more than a few more generations.

"I have seen your future," Ivy implored. "And you must believe me, that there isn't one at all unless you take this chance!" She had taken Tica's hand then, forcing the amulet between them, and spilled a devastation of memories into the old woman's mind.

A skull on the laboratory shelf. Bones in the dust. *EXTINCT.*

"Can you see it?" Ivy begged her. The images fell in sorrow from her own mind. It broke Ivy's heart to share them with somebody already so overcome with loss. "Do you see now why I am here, Tica? I am not here as Karathah, but as a friend. I'm offering you a chance to fight for your future!"

Tica had no reply. Wilting in desolation, she had turned and disappeared back into the shadows. Her command needed no words. One by one, her family followed her, eyes regretful, heads bowing in sadness as they left.

As Ivy picked her way back through the forest, her jaw was tight, her nerves frayed. *There are more caves,* she repeated to herself, as every step felt like a failure. *There are more tribes hidden in these forests. I'll find them. I have to find them.* Sweat ran down her neck. Leeches sucked her ankles as walked. *I will find them.*

Hunger gnawed inside. Ivy paused to drain the last of her water bladder. *I need to eat.* Through the dappled sunlight above the canopy, the sun trailed from east to west. Ivy turned her back to it, traversing over the mountain ridges that led back down toward the sea. She searched the cavities of foothills, her heart lifting at any shadow. But she found no sign of life. Veering back up into the mountain, Ivy slipped and slid down muddy banks as she crawled into the tangled briars, searching for any indication that she may not be alone.

"Are you there?" She called out loud, as her thoughts turned hazy with hunger. "Please show yourselves, I only want to help–" But only birds answered her calls.

A stirring melody took to her brain like an earwig and repeated itself until she was humming out loud. *Le Cygne.* The rich bass of her cello. As Ivy walked, her fingers tingled, imagining them gliding along the strings. *I miss my life. I want it all back.* Visions of everything she had lost, taunted her mercilessly. *What have I done? I had so much time with them, and I squandered it alone. I should have called dad more and gone to see the kids.* After cancer had taken her mother eight years earlier, Ivy's father had remarried. His chaotic new brood had moved him away from the solitary life Ivy chose. Her isolation went unnoticed, punctuated only by the bonobo that had captured her heart. Until Orrin had broken through. *All that time. I was so alone.* Ivy saw herself as she had been, hunched over a microscope, scribbling notes as she worked. Drowning in the solitary bliss of books and research papers. Human connection became as dismembered as the bones she studied. Work became a sanctuary. *A safe, dependable prison.*

Until Gihn had forced her hand.

With each step, regret tore Ivy apart. Grief sent her reeling. Lost faces come back to haunt. Green eyes and a maternal smile. The carefree laugh of her first love, lost before childhood had faded. Their memories had been safely looked away, but this new battle had torn the wound open again. *I miss them, how I miss them.* Old Tom, with his daisies and kindness. Liam's fire and steadfast loyalty. Jayne's easy conversation through long nights of micro-scopes and chocolate. And then there was Orrin. Ivy's heart flipped. *How did he dig his way so deeply inside?* Ivy rubbed filthy fingers into her eyes, brushing away tears. *And what kind of insanity was I under to resist it for so long? What I wouldn't give for one more moment. A single night together – unafraid of tomorrow.*

With grief came piercing clarity. *I was so scared of losing them, I stole them away from myself.* Ivy stumbled over a fallen branch; her path lost to the memories swirling in her head. *Now I'd take a moment of their love and lose it forever, than live a lifetime without it.* The potential for more loss loomed over her and brought desper-ation to her stride. The terror of falling in love with Gihn's family, person by person, soul by soul, grew, until the thought of losing them too, was almost too much to bear.

I was too scared to love, Ivy realised. She straightened her shoul-ders. *But not now.* Her resolution was absolute. *Now, I'm going to save the ones I love. Then save myself.*

She channelled her heartache into each step, as if to fuel the mechanisms of survival with her own pain. Hunger was clouding Ivy's thoughts. An animal screeched and she jerked her head toward the sky, sure that Kyah was following in the tree tops. But the branches were empty. Her own steps were still alone. As the trees thinned and the loamy soil turned sandy, Ivy found herself by the ocean again. The monotony of footfall replaced whirring memories. The orange glow fell behind her shoulders. Ivy continued for hours, circling the ring of beach that led back past the tiny island of Pulau Koa, and past it, along the southern shore of what would one day become the Ende Regency.

A scream broke her trance.

Ivy's eyes drew a long gaze, refocusing as spine-tingling fear gripped her bones. Where ocean met the forest ahead, a hunt was playing out. The prey was being buffeted between the sharp beaks of two enormous storks. Towering over six feet tall, the carnivorous birds threatened to tear their captive to shreds. Their prey was a boy. A hobbit boy, barely reaching their underbelly in height.

Ivy's heart stopped, then burst to life again as her feet began pounding the sand. Where the *Homo sapiens* had driven her to hide, this time, instinct forced her out into the open. She dropped low as she ran, grappling for a branch that had fallen into bush at her feet. Ahead of her, the storks ducked and jabbed their sharp beaks, wings unfurled and flapping in aggression. Feathers were ruffled out, and their tails fanned from side to side as the birds circled the hobbit boy with pinning pupils. They were angry, and it was soon clear why.

The hobbit boy was holding an enormous egg in his arms. He could not have been more than a young teen, barely old enough to hunt, but he shouted and raged at the birds that loomed above him, twice his height. The beaks clattered as they eyeballed their quarry. At the boy's feet, a second egg the size of a football was shattered into a slime of yolk and albumin in the leaf litter. A flutter of leaves was raining from the tree above. It seemed that the hobbit boy had dared to steal an egg from their nest and had been caught in the act. A bow was strung across his shoulder, but there were no arrows to be seen. *A lone hunter,* Ivy guessed. *He must have been desperate to go after this nest unarmed.*

"Here!" Ivy screeched, waving the branch wildly as she threw herself into the fray. She was a head shorter than the two storks, but far taller than the boy. All three creatures shrieked in surprise at the sight of her. The storks descended, jousting their clattering beaks. The foot-long edges were deadly sharp. Ivy had seen animals eviscerated within seconds by beaks like those. She had no desire to be eaten alive. She belted the stork's head away with her branch, sending it scuttling backward as the other took a lunge. Both storks had turned toward Ivy now, and the hobbit boy stood petrified behind them.

"I'm trying to help you!" Ivy shouted at him in Gihn's language, hoping he understood enough of it to do as he was told. He stepped backward. "Take the egg and run!" Apparently, he didn't need to be told twice. The hobbit boy turned tail and ran along the beach, clutching his prize. A bald head swung at the movement. One of the storks lurched after him. Ivy threw herself toward it, overbalancing the branch as she beat its back. Irritated, the stork lunged. Ivy's stegodon hide skirt ripped up one side. It lunged again and earned a solid *whack!* to the side of its head.

"Get away you nightmares!" Ivy screeched, letting fly with another blow as the second stork swiped at her from behind. She felt a shot of pain and burst of warm blood down her arm. The laceration wasn't deep, but the blood was inviting enough to incite a new wave of determination by the carnivorous birds. *And others.* With a jolt of terror, a familiar shape caught the edge of Ivy's vision. She was swinging the bough wildly, backing her way from the tree toward the forest as the storks parried and stabbed back at her. *A slip of steel grey scales* – a whip of forked tongue, tasting the enticement of fresh blood and egg yolk on the air. Before the storks had time to register their new intruder, Ivy leapt through the middle of the pair, dragging her branch behind her and raced down toward the beach. She didn't look back as the clatters turned to chaos.

First one way, then another, Ivy dragged the branch in her wake, too scared to lose it in case the Komodo had followed her. She swerved back around, dashing parallel to the storks further up the beach. As she turned, she saw the dragon had one bird by its gangly neck. Already, the bald head was covered in blood, but not its own. The Komodo had been punctured, a chunk torn from the back of its neck by the bird's mate who was viciously fighting to free it. Deathly rattles and clattering squarks rose in violent symphony. The sight was so gruesome that Ivy almost missed the streak that emerged from the tree line beyond them. A second Komodo bypassed the clash and ran full bolt toward her, strings of pink saliva flinging in its wake. Ivy screamed. Her legs flew toward the forest. Sparse trees were not enough to impede it. She dove further in, hoping the thicker vegetation might slow it down. But the Komodo was relentless. It was larger than the first, and hungry for blood carried on the air. It sped through the undergrowth.

I can't outrun it here, Ivy realised with horror. The same trees she'd hoped would slow it were impeding her far more. Long legs were a disadvantage to swoop underneath branches. Human thighs carried a fraction of the power of reptilian muscle. In a fit of desperation, Ivy leapt for a tree, hauling herself up into its lower branches. The Komodo reared instantly onto hind legs, easily reaching the six feet she was scrambling upward to gain. Saliva draped her foot and Ivy stomped, thumping her bare heel into the crown of its head. She wrenched her foot up again, teeth scraping skin. Her arms were strong, far more than they had been only weeks ago, and Ivy felt a rush of exhilaration as each grasp lifted her higher.

Thunk! Thunk. Thunk!

An arrow whizzed by her ankle. *Thunk!* The Komodo fell back, pierced through its thick hide as a second arrow hit, bounced off and disappeared into the bushes.

Thunk! Ivy dared to look away from the dragon for just a moment, but there was no one standing in the direction the arrow had been cast.

Thunk! Another arrow. She had seen no other people nearby –

only the hobbit boy that had stolen the egg. Could it be him, returned to save her?

"Thank you!" Ivy shouted. "Please don't stop! If you can just keep it away for long enough, I will run again!" But her hidden saviour did not reply. In quick succession, a half dozen more arrows pierced the Komodo's almost impenetrable hide. The creature fell back, writhing under the tree. It turned, attempting to flee, but staggered. The injuries were too much. Ivy waited a moment, her breath caught in her throat, wide eyes searching for a sign that she should run. But no more arrows came to claim the Komodo. "Wait!" Ivy called toward the forest, "don't leave now – please don't let it suffer. The shirakan is hurt badly, you must kill it!" No response came back to her. Shrieking and squawking still clamoured from the fighting stork and its own attacking Komodo. The dragon was crushing one stork carcass with its forelegs while tearing chunks of flesh from its plump body. The bird's head was missing, yet its mate still fought furiously.

"Please," Ivy implored again, her eyes filled with terrified tears, "don't leave without killing this shirakan. I have no weapon. Grant it a swift death!"

Thunk! Her plea was granted. One arrow, a shot so sure and true between its eyes that the writhing Komodo collapsed in merciful death.

"I'm so sorry," Ivy's voice tremored as she picked her way down the tree, shooting furtive glances at the other Komodo and stork. "I didn't want you to die any more than those awful birds." She stepped around the dead Komodo and stared into the greenery, searching for the invisible hunter. She saw nothing. She ducked further into shadow.

"Thank you for saving my life," she called to the undergrowth. There was no reply. Ivy kept walking. "I know that I look like a strange Karathah," she called out. "You don't trust me – I understand why." If the hobbit boy didn't want to be seen, Ivy knew she had no chance of spotting him. Xiou and his hunters could disappear into the undergrowth like ghosts. They had tracked her for a full day when she'd Fallen, and she had only realised she was being followed when they wanted her to know about it. "If you were going to kill me, I'd be dead already," Ivy said. "I know that too. You saved my life, so I am not afraid of you. Please do not be afraid of me." *Snap.* A broken twig behind her. The hair on Ivy's neck rose as she turned around, but only the tangle of vines and leaves were there. She breathed out slowly. "I have been searching for you," she continued, walking slowly again. "I have travelled from a Home Cave to the west where I lived with others like you. I learned their language. They are traveling with me, just north of here. We are searching for more of your people. The ones descended from the ancient Shirahn-tah. The Forest People, who have lived here long before the Karathah came."

Ivy paused as she reached a small glade. "I must speak to your tribe. We are trying to save your family from a thing we call the Slow Death. There are many reasons to come together and talk with the other tribes. They want to join you. They want to be your family!" The silence was deafening. Ivy stopped. She collapsed onto a fallen branch. *"Please."*

It was a long minute before her saviour stepped out of the shadows. Or rather, dropped. The hobbit boy who had stolen the egg, fell to the ground in front of her from the branches above her head, landing lightly on his feet and giving Ivy such a start that she fell back in surprise. He was not alone. Another boy dropped to her right. A third to her left.

"No wonder there was so many arrows," Ivy laughed nervously as she stood. With a sharp intake of breath, the boys stepped back. Ivy quickly sat back down on the branch. "I am too tall, I know," she said, holding her hands up. "Sometimes I forget." She looked critically at the three hunters surrounding her. None of them were older than Kari or Rinap. A sharp pain pierced her memory of the sparkling girl, barely past womanhood, who had died too young at the hands of the red-beaded hunter. "You are very young," Ivy said, trying to keep the tremor from her voice. The three young men looked at each other but gave no response. "Thank you for saving me from the shirakan," she said.

"You first saved me," said one of the boys. He looked to be the youngest, perhaps twelve. He was still holding the stolen stork egg. Ivy nodded at it.

"It was brave of you to steal it. Those birds are vicious." The boy simply looked at her. "You're hungry," Ivy said. "Are you hunting for your tribe? Where are they? Can you take me to them?" Before the words had left her mouth, Ivy knew she had pushed too far. The three shot frightened glances to one another, then stepped away.

"Please!" Ivy pleaded. "Please don't leave! I'm sorry, let me explain myself to you. Honestly, I mean no harm at all." She sighed with relief as the eldest boy paused to look back at her. "I am right though, aren't I? About the Karathah invading your territory? And the babies – women have trouble bringing new babies to the world?"

"We have had only one child born since the rainy season before last," the oldest boy replied, his eyes narrowing. "My own brother." The third boy, who had not yet spoken, hushed him. His shoulders were tense, and he looked skittish, as if he might disappear if Ivy blinked. "One that has survived, I mean," the oldest continued. "What do you know of it, Karathath? And why should we trust you?"

"I am not Karathah," Ivy insisted. "At least, not the type you know. I come from far away, and I've been staying with a tribe of your people, far to the east of here. I know you. I know how you live, and what is important to you. I also know how you are suffering as the Karathah spread so quickly across this land."

"There is no point fighting them," the youngest boy said, clutching his egg. "The Karathah have spread quickly through the forest. There are too many now. So we hunt further, even if it means stealing eggs from a vicious nest or being eaten by a shirakan. Our tribe needs food." His little face was lifted, as if in defiance of a rebuke for taking such a risk. But Ivy could not blame him. Her own pangs of starvation were getting harder to ignore.

"Of course you need to eat," Ivy placated him. "You must feed your family." She took a moment to think. There seemed no way to soften the distrust these boys carried. If she'd had anything to offer, she would have given it willingly. "Wait," she said, realising she still had, in fact, the only thing that might reach them. "Do you know the story of the Life Stone? It is from the Beginning Time, when your tribes lived together at the Falling Place – the Three Sister lakes to the north of here."

"We know the Sister Lakes," the youngest boy said.

"But the story of the Life Stone – do you know it?"

"Of course. The Elders tell it to children," replied the oldest, as if a year or so earlier, he was not one of the children that might have listened.

"Alright," Ivy said, trying to keep her voice light. "Can you tell it to me? Please?"

The eldest frowned, his eyes suspicious. "It is the story of our ancestors. The Stone appeared to them at the Falling Place. They say it carried the life of the earth within it. It speaks to our people and calls us home when we are lost."

"Right," Ivy said. "But how did your people find the stone? Do you remember the story?"

"Blue lightning." The boy looked away; his mouth twisted as he searched his memory. "The stone fell from the sky. An elder picked it up. One of the ancient ones."

"And the Life Stone spoke to the woman in her mind, didn't it?" Ivy prodded. "Do you know what she saw?"

"A vision." The boy shuffled uncomfortably. "A tall woman with–"

Ivy got to her feet. She towered above the hobbit boys, each no more than three feet fall.

"Green eyes like the trees?" Ivy smiled. "Skin as white as the moon? Hair like fire?"

With each description, the boys shrank back. *Disbelief. Fear. And the tiniest glint of hope.*

"It was *me* she saw," Ivy said. Her heart was racing. "The Life Stone brought her a vision of the woman who could help you survive. One day – when your tribes were so lost that it felt like there was no hope left." Ivy lifted her hand, allowing the amulet to hang from her wrist. Their eyes widened. Their mouths dropped open. "This Life Stone has brought me to you," Ivy said. "Let me help you to save yourselves."

CHAPTER 24

ORRIN

*E*ight hours sped by on the roads between Ruteng and Kelimutu. The spider-web rice fields of Ruteng soon gave way to miles and miles of palm oil plantations. *International Pulp and Mining* had left far more than a fingerprint on the land, and as they travelled west to east toward Kelimutu volcano – the site of IPM's latest geological survey – it was clear that the island of Flores was no longer the jungled oasis it once was. Orrin was astounded. He'd never seen anything like it.

"They're a conglomerate with almost unparalleled resources," Eli explained. "Most of Indonesia has been mined now. Malaysia too. They found it by following the magnetoreception trails. The hobbits tipped us off about the magnetite underground with their uncanny ability to sense the Earth's magnetic field and use it for their own navigation."

"Unwittingly, I'm sure."

"Of course. Scientists picked their brains – *literally* – for years. Once it was confirmed, IPM got in first to mine the magnetite. They bought massive tracks of land across South-East Asia. More than you could possibly imagine."

"And the local people and government?"

"Initially they needed the money offered to survive – now they need the jobs IPM brought with their contracts. There are massive deposits of rare earth metals underground which they've been systematically ripping out for the last fifty years. Here in Flores, they started on the continental shelf first and have been moving slowly inland. It's speeding up now. The mining, the need for more resources, the urgency to get it done. There have been rumours about litigation against them for environmental damage for years, plenty have taken a crack at it, but finally some are starting to get traction. As it happens, the mineral deposits are running out anyway. I think IPM are trying to take what they can before it all comes crashing down."

"Another grab and run, then." Orrin said, dourly. "And no environmental restoration after the mining?"

"Yes, and no. Let's just say, it's *selective*."

"What are all these plantations?" Orrin asked, his curiosity finally getting the better of him. Hour after hour, a monotonous sea of leafy green trees had filled the landscape.

"Palm oil," Eli said, looking out the window. "Once the mining is done, a subsidiary comes in to backfill the land with palm oil Plantations. On one hand it looks like environmental restoration, sure – on the other, it's a financial double dip. Palm oil is a sixty-six-billion-dollar industry, and it's only getting bigger."

"So, a win-win for IPM."

"That's it."

Orrin thought back on what seemed an age ago, but was less than two months. He shook his head. *Could it have only been a couple of months?* The memory was jarring in its intensity and a wave of emotion rushed over him. Ivy had stood in the Great Court of the university at a podium as the keynote speaker of a rally organised by Liam Kent, Kyah's keeper in the behavioural research lab. Orrin had been shocked to see Ivy step up, and then stunned when she shed the reclusive shield she usually wore so protectively, to address the buzzing crowd. Her words had been riveting and powerful, inciting rebellion against the loss of Indonesian rainforest to palm oil plantations. Hundreds of students had taken up her chant, piled onto busses and taken their voices and petitions into the city.

It seemed the environmental devastation Ivy had been fore-warning them of that day, had long-since gripped this new, dystopian version of reality with devastating consequences.

"And all these lawsuits in the news" Orrin asked, "biodiversity loss and bleaching coral reefs and the rest? What of them?"

Eli shot him a meaningful look. "It's a noble fight for sure, but the financial stronghold this industry already has is overwhelm-ing. The environmentalists can fight all they want, but they can't win."

"You work for these bastards, Eli," Orrin shook his head, confounded. "How can you reconcile this – this *dismal* view of what they do, with your own conscience as a scientist?"

Eli shrugged sadly. "I can't do the science I love without a job, can I? I'm a researcher, Orrin. An academic. International Pulp and Mining financially support the research of countless geolog-ical institutions across the world. My own department at the university is no different. My expertise is considered part of their arrangement. They're not interested in my conscience, or my opinions. Just what I know about rocks."

"Politics," Orrin frowned.

"Isn't it always?"

"So, they're lobbying the government by buying out education."

"Nothing's free these days, mate. Especially education."

It was after dark when Arif finally pulled into the driveway of a guest house in the village of Moni. The little village was the closest to Kelimutu and sat about forty-five minutes from the eastern base of the volcano. From his hotel room window, Orrin stared out at the first quarter moon. A perfect slice of white, as if it had been nailed to the pitch-black sky like a painting on a wall. Every few minutes, spits and flashes of lightning threw the volcano's silhouette into sharp relief.

Orrin set his backpack on a single bed and pulled out his phone charger and toiletries. It was a clean room with white-washed timber and modern facilities. Balmy curtains sucked and billowed against the mosquito screens at the window. Eli had taken the room next door to his own. It was identical in every way except for the colour of the curtains. The geologist had dumped his backpack when they'd arrived, then set out immediately to contact the survey supervisor, encouraging Orrin to have a shower and rest.

"It's an early start tomorrow," he had said, "and a steep climb."

A steaming bowl of Nasi Ayam had been delivered to Orrin's room soon after arrival. He had gulped it down gratefully. The shower felt good. Orrin closed his eyes and let hot water cascade over his face. He scrubbed his hair and shoulders, washing frustration away. *I'm here. In Flores. At Kelimutu.* He couldn't help the smile that found his lips. It had been a whirlwind journey, and a harrowing few weeks. The worst in his life. But now, as Orrin stepped out of the shower, towel wrapped and singularly focussed on the looming shadow of the volcano beyond his curtains, he felt closer to Ivy than ever before. Somewhere out there, was the key to unravelling her disappearance.

I can do this. I can figure this out, he assured himself.

I'm going to get her back.

EXTINCT

Before sunrise, they set off. International Pulp and Mining had sent a jeep to collect Eli and Orrin at the guesthouse in Moni and deliver them to the base of Kelimutu. Two representatives of the survey were already buckled in to join them. They'd been informed the night before that the road was treacherous in places due to recent landslides, so Arif's more luxury vehicle wasn't appropriate.

As his services weren't required for the day, Arif could have spent the day relaxing at the motel. He was being paid handsomely by IPM regardless. However, the Floresian driver had cheerfully offered to escort a group of American tourists back to Labuan Bajo for their flight home instead. It was a ten-hour journey. Arif declared that if he timed it right, he could bring a carful of new arrivals back to Moni the following morning and still make it back in time for their return drive the day after.

More money, happy company and my favourite roads, he had declared cheerfully as he gathered up the tourists like a mother hen.

Though it was still dark, the motel was already milling with staff and guests. Early risers were common, as the tri-coloured volcanic lakes looked to their best advantage at sunrise.

"Steven Dawes." One of the men waiting in the jeep leaned forward to shake Orrin's hand as he climbed in. Overhead, thin peels of lightning snapped across the sky.

"Steve's the head mining engineer in this region," Eli added as he climbed in behind Orrin. "And this is Dr. Ken Stringer, hydrogeologist. Ken makes sure we don't mess with those crater lakes or hit a subsurface water formation in the pit." The hydrogeologist gave a tired smile to Orrin from the front passenger seat, then turned back to his phone.

"We'll head to the lakes first," the man named Dawes said to Orrin, as they set off. "Dr. Nnamani said you wanted to see them before we move on. Then I'll take you down the western side to our working pit. I'm not sure how much you already know about our operation here, Dr. James?"

"Not too much," Orrin smiled.

Dawes nodded. "Eli said you're working with him?"

"That's right," Orrin said. He wasn't sure how much he could divulge without getting Eli in trouble. "I'm a physicist. Some of my recent experimental work involves magnetite, so Eli thought I might be of some use to this project, and vice versa."

"Sounds intriguing."

"Nothing ground-breaking," Orrin lied and decided he'd better redirect the conversation. "But Flores seems to be the hub of innovation in mining these days. I'm in awe of the work IPM are doing here. We passed numerous mines on the drive from Labuan Bajo." He allowed the false compliment to sit for a moment.

"Biggest mining operation in the archipelago," Dawes grinned, his chest puffing out as if he'd dug every mine on the island with his own shovel. "Kelimutu's our Crown Jewel though. This area's been fanning the magnetite flame for decades. There's so much ore down there it's like printing your own money."

"Fantastic," Orrin replied. The enthusiasm in his voice didn't reach his eyes. "No sign of slowing down then?"

"Interesting you'd ask." Dawes gave him a funny look. "If you'd come a couple of months ago, I'd have said we were about ready to pack up. Kelimutu has been a high-yield magnetite mine for years now. Multi-billion tonne load and haul operation. But it's getting difficult. Electrical storms have been plaguing us for months. It interferes with our schedule and to be honest – the unpredictability is becoming a right pain in the arse. The place becomes an OH&S nightmare. We've got to get our guys off their excavators and drills, pull out all the blasters, and shut things down. Sometimes for days at a time."

"Why the increase in electrical storms?" Orrin was intrigued. "Is that a seasonal thing?"

It was the hydrogeologist that answered, swinging his head around from the front passenger seat. "It's the volcano," he said. His expression was grave. "Volcanic activity has been increasing. You can see it in the craters. There's movement underground."

Dawes gave a soft laugh and indulgent smile. "Ken's our resident doomsday-ist. He thinks Kelimutu is about to blow."

Dr. Stringer turned back to the front, looking irritated. Apparently, this was a conversation they'd had before. "I'm telling you, Steve," he continued, staring out at the road ahead, "the volume of fine ash and gas clouds from the crater lakes are increasing every day. More static charge created in the atmosphere means more lightning above the volcano. There's something going on down there. It's not going to get any better." He looked back to his phone, apparently finished with his droll warning.

Dawes looked slightly embarrassed by his colleague. "Well, in any case, until recently, the Kelimutu mine has been a success, no question. But with the electrical storms ramping up and slowing things down onsite, and then this new issue – well, let's just say there are other opportunities in this area we could turn our attention to. Bigger, easier fish to fry, if you know what I mean. So we were ready to decommission this open pit and close her up." He turned to Eli. "Or so we thought, anyway."

"So you thought?" Eli said. "What do you mean?"

"This is confidential information, you understand." Dawes fixed the two men with a stern look.

"Of course."

"Alright. We've recently found an – *anomaly* in the bed. I'd like your opinion on it before we bring in the reclamation team."

Orrin tried to keep his face neutral. *Reclamation.* Eli had already explained that IPM's reclamation of the land was more about palm oil profit than restoration of the ruined ecosystem for the good of the local people.

"I'm happy to help any way I can." Eli smiled at Dawes. "What sort of anomaly are we talking about?"

"Hard to say," Dawes looked concerned. "An intrusion of some kind. We don't have the equipment here to analyse its molecular structure, so I need you to take a sample back to your lab. Run some tests."

Eli caught Orrin's eye. "An intrusion?" He was clearly trying to keep his voice light.

"That's right," Dawes said. "Ribbons of black mineral in the crystalline magnetite under the SEM. That's the best equipment I've got out here in the field. I need more definitive tests done; with someone we can trust."

"Why not send it out to Gadjah Mada?" Eli asked. "They've got a well-equipped Geology department and we've collaborated with them before."

"Aren't they the biggest university in Indonesia?" Orrin asked.

"That's right." Dawes shot a critical look at Orrin.

"He's with us," Eli assured him. "I trust Dr. James implicitly."

"Right. Well, *politics*," Dawes frowned at Eli. "I've been told to keep this one under our hat for now. Whatever this is, there's lots of it down there. This new resource could turn out to be a considerable financial boon for IPM. As in, worth negotiating another ten-year extension on our current contract. But we'll be in a stronger position if we negotiate a continuation of our existing Production Operation IUP's with the Indonesian Government *before* we let them know what we've found. If they think it's just more magnetite."

"I thought IPM were looking to get out of Flores? All the lawsuits and red tape…"

"They were. This site discovery has changed their minds. If this intrusion turns out to be something big – something worthwhile, then it's worth the trouble. Big money is always worth the trouble."

"And you're worried the Indonesian government won't approve the extension if they know about it?"

"We can't risk GM sharing their findings with the Ministry of Energy and Mineral Resources before we're ready. If this intrusion is anything special, then it will be worth turning us down and mining it in-house. We'll lose our extension. Lose the windfall that follows."

Eli caught Orrin's eye with a silent warning. Orrin bit his tongue so hard he tasted blood. IPM didn't know it yet, but he was sure they'd found deposits of Moscovium. *Stable Element 115.* And they were looking to mine it out from under the nose of the local communities that owned it and short-change them for the privilege.

The jeep pulled up at the base of Kelimutu mountain. Small buses and private charter jeeps were already there, a small throng of tourists readying themselves to hike the trail.

"Fair enough," Eli said, placidly. "Let's go have a look at what you've got, then."

Orrin watched Eli's back as he climbed out of the jeep, astounded his new friend could be so calm in the face of such blatant moral corruption. He wrestled down his Irish temper that wanted nothing more than to take Dawes on. They left the jeep driver at the base of Kelimutu and began to hike on foot. The wide path leading up to the coloured lakes was roughly paved.

"Got your walking boots on?" Dawes said good-naturedly to Orrin as they began the hike. "It gets steep up ahead."

"I'm looking forward to it," Orrin replied. The past weeks of madness and isolation had seen him abandon his morning swim in the university pool. The petrichor of mountain air felt like a tonic.

"It's a fascinating part of the world," Dawes continued. "Glad we can show you around." He inclined his head to include Ken Stringer, the hydrogeologist, who was trailing behind, still studying his phone.

The path began snaking up the hillside at a breath-catching incline. The men fell into silence as they climbed higher and higher above sea level. There were better uses for oxygen here than talking.

Though he was dubious about the ethics of IPM, Orrin was desperate to see the tri-coloured lakes. It was the place Ivy had found herself after the Time Shift. After she'd fallen fifty thousand years through time. Orrin could still remember her words, breathless and scrambling, as she tried to describe what had happened to her on the night they'd made contact.

"That's what I did – I Fell," she had said. Her voice had been trembling. *"On a volcano, nearly five days walk from this cave, Kelimutu – they saw me Fall from the sky as they sang. Like a streak of lightning to the earth."*

At the top of Kelimutu volcano, the crater lakes sat together like three ancient sisters. Orrin longed to be there already, to stand where Ivy stood, and see what she saw. He picked up his pace.

The first lake came into view on Orrin's right as they left the tree cover. The path traversed the ridge of a sandy rock face, which fell dramatically down into a deep lake. *Tiwu Ata Polo*, a sign read. The first of the sister lakes. The walls of the mountain dipped around it, cradling the water in a rocky bowl. Orrin couldn't tell what colour the lake was, the night sky still cast it in shadow. A heavy shroud of gas hung over its inky surface. On its northern wall, the bowl dipped back down again to form a second bowl on the other side – a second lake. This sister was equally dark and vast. *Tiwu Nuwa Muri Koo Fai*, a sign said.

Only a shared wall of rock was between them. The sisters seemed like two halves of a whole. *Twins*, Orrin thought. *But where is the third?* Orrin followed the trail of tourists. His feet scuffed occasionally as they itched to leave the path and explore alone. It was a quarter to six in the morning. Within minutes, sunrise would come. A halo of light in the East was already threatening to break the dark sky.

"Keep up, Dr. James," Dawes called back, as Orrin paused again to look at the dark lakes. "You'll want to reach the summit by sunrise. Trust me, it's worth the view."

Less than half an hour from when they'd set out, the concreted and fenced viewing platform came into sight. It was a flat, cobbled area perched on the summit of the volcano, and surrounded by a ring of steel fencing. In the centre, a little monument was built into climbing steps, like a tiny Mayan temple. Tourists were already sitting on it and circling the guard rails, waiting for sunrise with cameras at the ready.

Puncak Kelimutu, a sign read.

The Peak.

The viewing platform was situated on the ridge line almost equidistant between the two lakes they had already passed, and a third lake resting below them to the west. Orrin leaned over the guard rail, trying to make out her shape in the dark. The third sister was sunk further into the mountainside. Where the other two were surrounded by bare rock, this one, *Tiwu Ata Mbupu,* according to the sign on the rail, was nestled in a hollow of forest. She was slightly smaller, almost perfectly round, and looked cold and uninviting in the dark. Like the others, a heavy cloud of gas ghosted her surface.

"It's about to hit," one of the tourists called. A dozen or so cameras aligned east, ready to capture the rising sun. Orrin followed their gaze. He climbed the monument to its highest step. His heart was pounding.

A haze of gold.

A thin band of blinding white.

Then the sun split across the horizon.

Brightness crept behind the silhouette of volcanic mountains to the east, and slowly flooded toward him. Soupy darkness crystallised the landscape into vivid colour. Orrin stared, spellbound.

The first crater lake, *Tiwu Ata Polo,* was touched by sunlight, and revealed deep green water. Within a minute, its twin, *Tiwu Nuwa Muri Koo Fai,* glowed an almost translucent pale blue. They were exquisite. Above both, a swirl of soft ash and volcanic gases hung in the air. A pencil line of electrical charge split the sky above, following charged particles through the air. Instinctively, Orrin wanted to duck and cover. But instead, he lifted his face to the lightning, studying it with keen eyes.

Sunlight crept along the cobblestones. It hit the viewing platform. Orrin followed the light to the west side of the ridge, leaving the monument. He leaned against the outer steel fence and caught his breath as the morning rays lit up the third crater lake. *Tiwu Ata Mbupu.* Unlike the others, it wasn't an arresting shade of watery green or cool blue. This lake was deep red. A sunken, bloody eye in the mountain side. Hisses and spits of lightning sizzled from the volcanic gas draped above its surface. White flashes snapped down from the sky above.

Three lakes, all so different. All equally captivating. Orrin slowly walked the perimeter of the fence, taking in each beauty. One icy blue in colour, like a glacial melt; the next, a vibrant emerald reflection of its jungle home; and the last, deep red, like blood poured from stone.

They were mesmerising.

By the time Orrin had come full circle, back to the western rail, the land beyond the red lake was also lit bright enough to see. At the base of the mountain, and for miles toward the east, the jungle had been transformed into a wasteland. Exposed grey rock in sunken oblong steppes descended into an enormous open pit mine. A scatter of heavy machinery was already crawling along the gargantuan ramps of road, hauling rock up from the depths of the amphitheatre.

The bowels of Kelimutu were being mined for magnetite. Though Orrin had already known it, until now, the prospect had seemed academic. But staring at the pit from the peak of the ancient volcano, the juxtaposition of such an ugly wound against the natural beauty of the lakes was more than jarring. It felt heinous.

"They change colours, you know," came a voice beside him.

Orrin looked up to find Dr. Stringer, the other occupant of their jeep, looking out from the railing. *The hydrogeologist*, he recalled. Until now, the man hadn't spoken since his doomsday predictions in the jeep. He'd been distracted during their drive, tapping away on his phone. Now that Orrin observed him properly, he could see that the man had a nervous energy about him, despite his obvious tiredness. Even watching the sunrise, Dr. Stringer's fingers were tapping the steel guard rail beneath them.

"I'm sorry?"

"The lakes – they change colour frequently." The hydrogeologist looked down at the deep red water below them. He clearly assumed that Orrin's thoughts had been on the lakes, rather than the magnetite mine beyond them. "This one, *Tiwu Ata Mbupu* is usually blue. And the most eastern lake, *Tiwu Ata Polo*, is usually red. Milky white, green, black, blue, red, brown – they all change colour, take turns. It's the only place on earth it happens, you know."

"Really?" Orrin was surprised. "What causes the change?"

"Same thing I think is causing the volcanic lightning," Stringer said. "Gas." He stepped back away from the guard rail. "Fumaroles release gasses into the water from underneath. See all this here?" He started back toward the eastern rail. Orrin followed him. Heavy clouds of steam hung over the water's surface, along with a plume of fine grey ash that swirled within it, like potion being gently mixed. "Down there you've got toxic concentrations of sulfur dioxide in the water. Also zinc, lead. All coming up from volcanic vents underneath the lake."

"So, no swimming then," grinned Orrin. He liked this man's no-nonsense approach to conversation.

"God, no." Stringer almost cracked a smile. "If the minerals don't kill you – which they will – the churning undercurrents will. There's bubbling magma under those crater lakes if you go down far enough. Lots of internal movement. It'll suck you down and keep you there."

"Terrifying." Orrin took a small step back. Suddenly the guard rail didn't seem quite solid enough.

"Yes, it is a bit, isn't it." Stringer squinted, thoughtfully. "Makes you feel a little *mortal*. See those offerings?" He pointed to a small pile of flowers at the rim of the closest lake. Orrin hadn't noticed them before. "These lakes are sacred to the local people. They believe that when a person dies, their spirit enters one of the three. This one closest to us, *Tiwu Nuwa Muri Koo Fai*, is called the *Lake of Young Men and Maidens*. If a young person dies before their time, their spirit comes here. Behind us over there, the dark red. *Tiwu Ata Mbupu*." Orrin looked back to where Stringer pointed on the western side of the mountain. "*The Lake of Old People*. Best to end up there, I think. It means you've lived a long and good life."

"I'll say," Orrin agreed. Though the thought of his soul ending up in any volcanic lake for all eternity seemed an unpleasant prospect. "And what about the third lake?" He looked back across to the stunning deep aquamarine twin he had hiked past first on his way up the trail.

"*Tiwu Ata Polo*," Stringer said. "She's glorious, isn't she?"

"Incredible," Orrin agreed.

"*The Bewitched Lake*." Stringer gave an odd smile. "They say that only the souls of those who have committed wickedness and evil end up in that one."

"Yikes."

"Better keep it off your bucket list."

"I'll do my best."

The two men stood for a moment admiring the view. It was clear that Dr. Ken Stringer was wholly devoted to this place, not just his work at the mine itself, but the landscape and people within it. Orrin felt a strange affinity for him. Unlike Dawes, he didn't seem to be selling something.

"So, the minerals drive the change in water colour?" Orrin clarified. "And that's normal, is it?"

"That's right." Stringer smiled, though it looked a little strained. "As the concentrations of minerals change, the colour changes too. More oxygen released into the water, and it turns bright red or even black. Less oxygen, you get these lighter green and blue waters."

Orrin nodded, looking out to twin lakes. He'd never heard of such a bizarre phenomenon. Then again, he'd never seen such a bizarre display of lakes.

"They changed colour six times last year," Stringer continued. "At the moment though, it's a new colour every week." The man was rubbing his hands together, though the morning air had lost its chill. His brow furrowed.

"And is that – normal too?" Orrin pressed. "For them to change so frequently?" He wasn't sure whether the man was still just making small talk, or if there was something else beneath his words.

"Sure," Stringer said, looking around. He spied Dawes on the trail talking to Eli. "Actually, no. Possibly not. Much too frequent. It's the same issue as we're seeing with the volcanic lightning I think." He ran his hand over his mouth, staring out at the ice blue lake intently. As if on cue, thin roots of lightning split over *Tiwu Nuwa Muri Koo Fai*, and laced the sky above. For a moment he seemed to forget that Orrin was there. When he looked back, he found concern on Orrin's face. "I'm looking into it." His lips became a thin line.

"Do you think the mine has something to do with it?" Orrin was probing now. He couldn't help it. There was something in Stringer's manner that seemed edgy.

Stringer walked back across to the west guard rail and looked down at the mine.

"It's possible. Like I said, I'm looking into it." The hydrogeologist gave a grim smile. "Shall we?"

Reluctantly, Orrin followed him back to the paved trail to meet Eli and Dawes. He didn't want to leave. Kelimutu's eerie dawn felt like a siren call. Up here, his senses were heightened. His mind was still. A warm breeze wrapped around each tiny hair on his body, leaving them tingling like the lightning overhead.

Orrin could almost feel Ivy here. Every muscle pulled him back toward the lakes. To Kelimutu's peak, where Ivy had Fallen through time, forsaken on the ridge between the three coloured lakes. He desperately wanted to stay, to explore a little. To hold on to that closeness a little longer.

With a sigh, Orrin picked up his pace. He was obliged to leave. The men, and the mine, were waiting.

CHAPTER 25

IVY

"The elders will punish us for bringing you."

"Even if I can help?" Ivy trailed the three boys along the coastline, following them to their Home Cave. An almost full moon above illuminated the surface of the ocean. The oldest boy, Ko, who could not have been more than fourteen, shot a sceptical look at her.

"You look like a Karathah and they have plenty of reason to fear that," he said. "More of us are dead than alive since they came into our territory. They forced us out of our cave. They hunt all the animals in our forest. We are left to survive on fish and stolen eggs." Before they had begun walking, the boys had cooked the huge stork egg over a fire pit and shared it with Ivy. The taste was odd, more meaty than a chicken egg, a taste Ivy had long forgotten. But the enormity of the egg had meant all their stomachs were finally filled. She was grateful.

"They forced you out of your cave?"

"We fought for it," Ko said. "And we lost." His expression suggested they'd lost far more than the cave in that fight. "The Karathah forced us out," he scowled. "The elders said they used to trade with us, but not anymore. There are so many of them now. I suppose they think it is easier to simply get rid of us and take what they need themselves."

"I believe you are right," Ivy frowned. "More people require more food and space. If they thought your cave was better than theirs…" Ivy trailed off, looking ahead. They were approaching a curve in the beach, where a cliff cut into the sand to overlook the sea, breaking their path. "Where do you live now then?"

The egg-stealer, whose name was Hiron, looked up at the cliff looming ahead of them. With a sly smile he nodded to the sheer face of it. "Up there."

Ivy's chin lifted. Her mouth fell open. The rock wall was almost vertical and utterly unscalable. "But," she stuttered, "but how do you get up?"

"We climb." Throwing a smirk at her, Hiron set a foot against the rock wall and began to hoist himself up. Ivy watched, heart pounding. The boys' curved fingers and slightly-too-long arms were as well evolved for an arboreal lifestyle as his legs were for bipedalism. Hers, on the other hand, were not.

"I forgot you could do that," Ivy said, with chagrin. She screwed up her nose. A foul smell was wafting in the air. "But it's so high! I suppose that's one way to stop the Karathah from stealing your new cave."

"Exactly," said the second boy, called Tinud. "Though there is another entrance, but only from above. Are you coming?" He began to climb. "I thought you were desperate to speak to our elders."

"I am," Ivy frowned at the cliff lit by the silver moon. "I guess I have no choice then." Still, she couldn't bring herself to step any closer. She wasn't afraid of heights exactly, but this seemed like an invitation to fall. "Maybe I should wait until dawn. So I can see better."

"I wouldn't," Ko said, as he jammed his toes into a ridge of rock, "by then, this beach is crawling with shirakan. They make nests in those hills of sand." With a brush of panic, Ivy's feet followed him. He paused just above her, clinging to the rock like a limpet. "Do you see that?" Ko pointed to a pile on the dark sand that Ivy had side-stepped, not noticing what it was. "That's what happens if the shirakan catch you here at dawn." Ivy stepped back. Looked closer. In the moonlight, she could just make out a tangle of tusks, hair and feathers that resembled some hideous creature, or more likely, a few, that had been eaten and since regurgitated. The mass was covered in a malodorous mucus, Ivy imagined it was to ease the passage of undigestible body parts as they were brought back up. Ko began to climb. "Another thing to keep the Karathah away from us."

"Yeah, I bet." Ivy felt the rock wall, searching for a crevice to grip onto. "Can you at least help me?" Hiron and Tinud were already so far ahead she was losing sight of them in the dark. With a sigh, Ko looked back at her. "Just keep your eyes up and put your hands and feet where I do. And don't expect the elders to greet you well."

Ivy's fingers slipped as she clutched the cliff. Her toes grated against the rock leaving scuffs of blood as she climbed. Within a few minutes, her shoulders and arms ached. Her abdominal muscles shook with the desperate strength required to keep from falling backward. More than once, Ivy's toes lost hold and her knees scraped the wall, sending her heart into a frenzy of adrenaline. There was no time to think of what might be waiting above. Every ounce of concentration kept her clinging to the wall. Inching her way upward. Slowly. Meticulously. Her nails ripped and shredded back to the bed. She was too terrified to release even a finger to wipe the sweat from her eyes.

Despite it, Ivy's welcome to the cliff tribe came soon enough. Ko was right. By the time she climbed her way to the top of the cliff, Hiron and Tinud had already warned the others she was coming. As she grappled for purchase and hauled herself over the lip of the cave entrance, panting, three spears greeted her chest. The desperate haul of oxygen into her lungs was enough to raise them close enough to feel the prick of obsidian points through the thin singlet she wore.

"Please," Ivy puffed, her startled fingers spread in surrender. "I just want to talk to you." Her hands were trembling with the effort of clutching rock. "I have no weapon. I saved Hiron from the giant birds. The boys saved me from the shirakan. I am – a *friend*." Ivy's voice rose, despite her best efforts to remain calm. "I mean no harm to any of you. I promise."

The spears relented only enough to allow space for Ivy to sit up. "Please," she implored again. They pulled back a little further. Shakily, she pulled up to her feet, standing far too tall to be innocent. The spears rose again. Behind her, thirty feet dropped to the beach in certain death.

"The promise of Karathah has come to mean nothing," a voice said. "What do you want?" In the dark, it was hard to make out faces.

"My name is Hiranah," Ivy said. "I have already explained myself to these young men. They will have told you my story by now. They are faster climbers than I am."

A man, older than Gihn, stepped forward. The moon lit his expression, which was impassive. Still, he made no move to call down the spears others still held at her chest. "They say you claim to have the Life Stone."

"I saw it with my own eyes," Hiron interjected. "She spoke to me through the stone." The elder dismissed him with a wave of his hand.

"Will you let me show you?" Ivy held up the amulet attached to her wrist. There was an intake of breath as sharp eyes caught it. Ivy lifted it into her palm, holding her hand out to the elder. With a shudder, she prepared her mind to to be pulled apart again as the memories of Gihn's people, and her own fated knowledge of what was to come were exposed to him. The man shook as he saw her memories, his own palm sweaty. When he pulled away, unable to take any more, Ivy felt his devastation in her core.

"I'm so sorry," she whispered. The old man did not answer. He dragged his eyes from the ground to look at his people, then, apparently unable to stomach what he knew would happen to them, looked away again. "I really am sorry," Ivy said again. "I only want to help you. I want to save your people. I believe there is a way."

The other bodies shifted uncomfortably. Ivy looked around, her eyes adjusting to the dim light. There were at least thirty people here, Ivy estimated. The cave was barely that – it was more of a recess at the top of the cliff, shallow enough that the moonlight found the back of it. The roof projected about three-quarters of its width and continued climbing above, leaving the front ledge where she stood, exposed to the elements. Wind and tropical storms would certainly reach inside, making it a poor choice of shelter. Ivy knew not much choice was involved. She took a deep breath.

"I've come to beseech you to join others of your kind," Ivy said, this time addressing the group at large. "I have been staying with a tribe of your people, *Shirantah people*, from far west of here. They are being tormented by the Karathah, forced from their Home Cave, their hunting territory has been infiltrated and their hunters poisoned. They have suffered the loss of many members of their tribe and family. They have had enough. They want to survive and fight back against the Karathah."

"We did fight back," the elder said. "Which is why there are so few of us left. All we can do to survive now, is hide."

Ivy considered this. He was closer to the truth of it than any others had been. She filed the thought away for a later time.

"You are right," she conceded. "Hiding will keep you safe for a while. But it won't allow your people to survive. By the time your youngest are grown, there may not be enough left of them to carry on. Hiding alone, is simply a slower way to die."

"I will not subject my family to more fighting!" The old man's voice coloured with anger. "Our best hunters fought bravely, but still died quickly. Those left of us are very old, or very young – we have no chance against the Karathah."

"But I do not mean for you to fight with weapons," Ivy said. "It is knowledge you need, and a united front. Your people have been splintered across this land for thousands of years. It is easy for the Karathah to defeat a people who are already so broken apart. But together, you have a chance to survive."

"I do not see it." The elder's voice was calm again, his face unreadable.

"Other Shirahn-tah are gathering at the Sister Lakes," Ivy said. "We have been travelling across the forests, from far away, searching for more of your family. We will meet before the next full moon to discuss the future of your tribe. If you join with them, you can find a way to survive together."

"We will not be leaving," the elder said, with an air of finality. "Karathah hunters patrol our territory now. It isn't safe for us out there."

"But surely it is better than staying here in a cave that is not your home? A cave of wind and rain that sits above nests of shirakan that would make a meal of you? Your children have no future here. What will happen when your elders die and leave these young ones alone? They need the strength of a tribe to protect them, a tribe of your own people! Please, just consider what I say," Ivy implored him. "Come and join the others at the Sister Lakes."

"I will – consider what you are saying." The elder turned away. "You may stay here tonight. Then leave us be."

Long before the sun rose, Ivy left. She stepped over the sleeping bodies huddled by the glowing hearth stones, and climbed the final few feet of cliff face, eyes staunchly ahead. At the top of the cliff, she stood up to find Ko beside her. He pointed north.

"The Sister Lakes are beyond those mountains. North-east of here."

"Thank you."

"I should tell you, there were other tribes of our people in those mountains," he said, staring into the distant dark, "though we never see them. They hide, as we do. But old stories tell us they were there."

"I'll try to find them Ko," Ivy said. "Just – please do whatever you can to convince your tribe to join us at the Sister Lakes."

"The elders won't listen to me," Ko frowned. "I am only just made a hunter, and only because the others were killed." There was a landslide of emotion behind his words. Ivy guessed his own parents were among the dead.

"Make them listen," Ivy said. "You're brave, Ko. You were clever enough to listen to me. One day the elders will be gone, maybe sooner than they would like, and you'll be a leader for your tribe. Perhaps now is the time to show them what you are capable of."

"I can't promise they will listen, Hiranah." A radiant smile broke across Ivy's face. Until now, he had never acknowledged the name Gihn's tribe had given her. Ko looked away; his own face twisted into a frown. "But I will try."

"That is all I ask."

The glittering Savu Sea stretched for eternity behind her. Ivy stood on a ridge that continued far into the distance, rolling down on the right into the ancient caldera of Mount Sukaria.

The volcano had once erupted, then collapsed inward as the rock above the magma chamber gave way, forming a great sinkhole, eight kilometres across. Now, teeming with life, the basin rose up like the edges of a cauldron. To reach the Sister Lakes at Kelimutu, Ivy knew her path lay through the middle of the old volcanic field, and then beyond it to the north-east.

Once again, Ivy left alone, shoulders slumped, and feeling defeated. One foot in front of the other, she walked away from Ko. She began her descent from the ridge down to the basin. Another labyrinth of jungle lay ahead. Another chance to find lost tribes. Or to lose herself in the effort.

"They could all die anyway," Ivy muttered to herself, as she scrambled through Mount Sukaria's jungled roots. The lack of conversation ached. The day had crawled as she picked her way through caves along the inner-western ridges of the mountain. She'd found signs of Karathah. But no hobbits. Now, with failure clawing at her bones, hearing her own voice aloud felt somehow less lonely. "They have no immunity to modern human diseases," she continued, flicking away a hanging vine. "Even the common cold could kill them all, just like *that*." She slapped a mosquito. "That's another risk." Ivy's conscience had been gnawing at her for hours. The slog, and effort to push through dense bush was wearing her down.

"There are so many risks though." She grumbled aloud. "I can't fight them all. I must be *selective* about what I tell them." She hadn't dared voice her concerns to Gihn. He already carried the weight of saving his entire species. She could not add another burden by explaining the risks of communicable diseases and immunology. It was too far beyond his understanding of the natural world. Ivy had resolved only to tell the hobbits what they needed to know to survive this extinction. To survive the Karathah, as they were, *here, now.* "Surely that's the right thing to do? But is it enough?" She pondered, slipping in mud as she tried to slap away another handful of insects. "It might get them through this extinction event. But how much further? How many years? A few generations more? One thousand years? Two? Am I delaying the inevitable?" Ivy argued with herself as she stumbled along.

"But they deserve to fight for their survival," she said aloud. Her indignant tone served only to goad her conscience further. "They're intelligent people. Surely this is their choice to make. I give them knowledge. They choose how to use it." Her filthy palm wiped a brow.

"I'm playing God." Guilt was set so solidly in her gut that it slowed her feet. "Well, maybe I am, but there's no God here. At least, not yet." It would be tens of thousands of years before Abrahamic and Indian religions crossed through the archipelago. Ivy looked up at the glorious green canopy. Wild with life. Breathtaking. It was as overwhelming as any domed cathedral. "No. In these forests there are only humans doing what we do best. Creating war. Dividing to conquer. Committing genocide for the sake of land and resources. The hobbits are being murdered, whichever way you look at it." She scuffed a log before stepping over it. "You already know where this ends for the hobbits anyway. In blood. Then fossils." Ivy walked for a few minutes, contemplating her oscillating views.

"What would I do? Tell Gihn to accept defeat and lay down to die?" Her shoulders sunk lower. "No. They need my strength. Gihn already knows their odds of survival. They want to fight for it – at least some of them do. So, it's their choice to make," she decided. "All I'm doing is giving them that choice. They can build their future together, all of them." Ivy's failure in recruiting any other tribes cast doubt over her plan. "Create enough genetic variation to keep the mutations at bay." Ivy grazed her palms on fallen tree trunks as she clambered over them. Her feet turned uphill again, eyes scouring for a shadow in the ravine ahead that could indicate a cave. This species, these *humans*, were so much a part of their landscape that they could hide in plain sight. "I won't give up on them now."

Ivy's own demons couldn't help but torment her. "But where will they live? Destruction of their habitat is inevitable too. *Eventually.*" She couldn't imagine these people dislocated from the forest. Colonialism was an eventuality that would bring more loss than any war. "This forest will shrink. They'll be thrown out of the jungle into the arms of … what? Slavery? Consumerism? Treated as what? Pets? Experiments? Food?" Her voice cracked beneath the devastating possibility. *"Equals?"* Ivy squeezed her eyes shut, willing her thoughts to slow down. "Oh, when have we ever considered another species our *equals*? Even our beloved pets have no real rights. Nothing to save them if humans see a profit for their use." The orange shirts of her palm oil rally flashed in Ivy's mind, like memories from another life. "Some people are willing to fight though. Maybe not many, but hopefully – enough." Her steps were dogged. Her skin flushed and sweaty in the tropical heat. Ivy's hands flicked like flies, constantly shooing away a barrage of mosquitos as she walked. "If only there was some other solution. Another way to survive the Karathah–" Every part of her felt too insignificant to face the challenge ahead. But no solutions appeared. Ivy fortified her resolve. "This is it, then. The only chance they have." Hours passed as she hiked the undulating skirt of Mount Sukaria, burrowing into each ridge in search of the lost tribes. *No stone left unturned,* Ivy repeated to herself as she climbed. *No stone left unturned.*

Two more tribes discovered. Two more sparks of hope.

Ivy's efforts across Mount Sukaria had not been wasted, and though she had again walked away from the caves alone, there was a growing lightness beneath her feet. The first tribe had been hostile, as expected. But eventually, they'd listened enough to consider her offer to meet Gihn's family at the Sister Lakes. The second tribe was barely a tribe at all. Only seven people remained of it; a mother and her two young children, an elderly man and three adolescents. They were the remains of another coastal tribe, fled to the mountains after the Karathah had forced them out. Ivy followed them into the recesses of their cave with a pounding heart, waiting for a spear to find silence it. But the family were terrified and weaponless. After witnessing Gihn's tribe through the amulet, they seemed only too willing to share the burden of survival with others. First, they had to survive the Karathah attacks and unpredictable volcanic activity of the island. So many factors were already working against their survival.

Those seven will join us. Ivy paused to pick a handful of edible leaves, then continued, chewing thoughtfully. *Plus, the sixteen orphans we found in the Soa Basin.* She frowned. *Still less than one hundred people.* It was nowhere near enough to combat the inbreeding issue. Even with the additional hobbits Ivy had found, not all of the new tribe were likely to reproduce. Women past reproductive age could not make babies, nor men or women who suffered reduced fertility due to the low genetic diversity that already negatively affected their genes. Ivy had heard Phren's many stories of stillborn children and women unable to carry pregnancies to full-term. The impact and heartache it brought amplified with each generation. Welcoming new members into the tribe was the only way to combat inbred genetics. Two hundred, maybe more, could provide enough genetic variety to maintain a dozen more generations. But Ivy had a much more expansive end-goal in mind.

Inbreeding was only the first part of the problem, she knew. Such a meagre population would still be under the pressure of extinction by genetic drift. If the tribe was too small and too isolated to recover, a single random mutation could be enough to wipe the species out. If an essential genetic trait was somehow lost, the entire tribe itself would soon follow. Ivy estimated, that to guard against genetic drift, the tribe needed a minimum viable population of at least five hundred individuals to survive. The burden of that failure narrowed her focus and made Ivy all the more determined to give them what they so desperately wanted. That chance to survive.

No stone left unturned, she chanted again to herself as she travelled. *Find them all. Give them the courage to fight.*

She turned north-east. It was time to leave the western ridges behind to search the basin. The Sister Lakes were still two days' walk, allowing for time to search. Time was running short. A clear, bubbling stream found her ankles and Ivy waded upstream for a while, checking the area was clear of decaying animals before she dared a drink. Fresh, cool water filled her stomach and Ivy washed her face and hands, revelling in the opportunity for cleanliness. She filled her water bladder and dug some fresh shoots from the riverbank, tucking them into a fold in her hide skirt to chew on later. A fresh breeze filtered through the green fingers of the valley. Bare feet sank into the muddy edge and Ivy smiled at the cool squelch between her toes. The forest felt alive. Energy pulsed around her, as if the soil and sky were singing the same song. Bird calls floated above, and a gentle breeze brushed the fine hair of her wet skin. Ivy ducked out of the stream and back into the forest. Humility rode on her shoulders. The sublime majesty of nature ruled around her. The forest was a body with a million moving parts, and Ivy knew she was simply one of them. Hours passed. There was no ego in this world of flowers and claws and vines and sweat. Only acceptance of nature's dominion and her own attempt to survive within it. Take only what you need. Give everything you have.

Ivy walked. Scrambled. Slid. Scoured. The sun fell behind her. She was lost in thought when a sharp crack came from above. The forest noise ruptured and adrenaline hit. She froze, wide-eyed, as a body dropped to its feet right in front of her.

"Hiranah!"

Ivy's impulse to strike out was only barely suppressed by her cry of utter relief.

"Xiou!" She fell to her knees. Xiou's enormous grin stretched even further as he lay his hands on Ivy's shoulders, then brought his forehead in to rest against hers, laying his palm against the amulet on her wrist. Ivy accepted his affection. She'd never been so happy to see someone in all of her life. After a moment, she pulled away, concerned.

"I found you at last," Xiou said. "Your legs are too long to keep up with." Ivy gently pulled his hand off the amulet. She wanted to speak to him using his own words, not the ones that filtered through her thoughts.

"I see the Karathah tried their hardest to kill you again," Ivy observed. The latticework of scars on Xiou's face had a few raw additions. Thin lines of dried blood were edged with swollen pink skin.

"Tried – but they did not succeed," he said. "They will have to try harder next time."

"Urgh," Ivy said, getting to her feet. She continued walking, her friend falling in beside her. "Don't say that. You know they *will* try."

"And I will fight," the hunter said. "As always." He smiled at her. "Your language has improved. You do not need to speak through the Life Stone anymore."

"I've had a lot of practice since I lost you." Ivy straightened her shoulders. "The other tribes would not let me get close enough to speak through the amulet. In fact, I had to beg them to listen to me at all."

"But you did speak to them."

"For what it was worth." Ivy looked around. "Where are Guntah and Gihn? I was worried you might never find me."

"We separated after the Karathah fight," Xiou said. "I asked Guntah to continue with my father so I could follow you alone. It took me two days walking to reach the north end of the broken earth before I could begin following you south toward the Savu Sea. You did well, Hiranah. I found the trail marks you left." Cold sweat gripped Ivy's neck.

"Oh no! The Komodo nest! I led you straight into the cave down at the beach!" The thought of her friend popping out of that dark tunnel only to be faced by a giant Komodo sent a tidal wave of guilt down her chest. "When I started leaving the symbols, I didn't know what I was leading you toward–"

"I have managed worse," Xiou said, holding up his hand to belay the outpouring of apologies.

"That's true," Ivy sighed. "And you still managed to track me down through all of this jungle."

"Tracking you was the easy part," Xiou chuckled. "You leave a distinctive trail – it is like following a herd of probech."

Ivy looked behind her, slightly offended. She thought she'd done a pretty good job of getting through the jungle without leaving too much damage.

"Well, I did my best."

"And here you are. *Surviving.* I told you that you were stronger than you think."

"You did," Ivy remembered fondly. "Though I'll admit that I am sick of eating these river shoots. Maybe you can help me find something else."

"Happily," Xiou said. "But we will need to travel faster. Guntah was going to search the western face of these ridges and meet us at the northern end of the centre. I told him I'd have you there by tomorrow morning, assuming you had survived."

"I appreciate your optimism," Ivy laughed. "Lead on, then." As they walked, Ivy filled Xiou in on the hobbit tribes she had come across, and the many sightings of Karathah she'd had since they'd separated.

"Was it the probech hunters, that carried the severed heads of the sea tribe with them?" Xiou asked, his expression grim.

"I don't know, but I don't think so. I think it was a different tribe." She took a deep breath. "And the red-beaded hunter was amongst them."

Xiou stopped still, turning to look up at her. "He was with them?"

"Yes," Ivy said. "I think he is travelling between the Karathah tribes now, stirring up trouble." Xiou didn't respond to this. It was clear that the red-beaded hunter wanted them dead, though his motives were still unclear.

"But they will come, will they?" Xiou asked. "This sea tribe you found? I saw no sign of them in my own travels."

"I'm not sure," Ivy replied. "Their leader was suspicious of me, being a Karathah myself. I tried my best to convince her but she wouldn't listen. It might have been different if you or Gihn were with me."

"You have the Life Stone," Xiou said, as if their mistrust could only have been a temporary thing. "Perhaps they have already left for the Sister Lakes?"

Ivy gave him a wry look. "Or perhaps I scared them from their new cave and they are now homeless again."

"We will see, Hiranah." Xiou looked forward, confidently. "You are more convincing than you think."

The two friends trudged together through the belly of Sukaria. The sky darkened as a heavy cloud of smoke and ash billowed from somewhere north-east, raining onto the canopy.

"I almost forgot," Ivy said, brushing the soot from her skin. "The earth has been quiet, just for a day or two."

Xiou looked at the oppressive sky. "She is never quiet for long, these days." As if to consolidate this thought, a low rumble wove its way through the earth below their feet. From north to south, the caldera shook. The crack of trees snapped Ivy's focus from one trunk to the next, watching for falling branches. By the time the earth settled, Ivy and Xiou were already walking again.

"Gihn!" Ivy had been relieved to reunite with Xiou, but what she felt as she pressed her forehead to the elder could only be described as pure joy. The old man drew his palm down Ivy's face, and his voice trembled as he spoke.

"Once again you give me hope, Hiranah." His eyes were wrinkled in kindness. "I am so thankful for your strength to continue on without us."

"And I am thankful Xiou found me."

"Guntah thought you would be eaten by a shirakan within one day," Xiou said.

Guntah laughed, stepping forward to greet Ivy. "This is not true at all. Hiranah has enough fire in her heart to beat any shirakan. It was you who worried me, Xiou. I thought you may starve to death without my help. You are a terrible hunter." The familiar jest was accompanied by a twinkle in Guntah's eye. Their false competition masked a deep affection between the two.

"You are both terrible hunters," Ivy said. "Which is why you are lucky to have me back. I have enough water roots for all of us." She tossed a green shoot to Guntah, who caught it.

"I hope you didn't eat these, Hiranah," he said, dolefully. "This plant will kill you." For a moment, Ivy reeled in panic, then caught the tease in Guntah's expression.

"I nearly believed you!" The men burst into laughter. "Trust me," Ivy sighed, "there are already so many things trying to kill me, my dinner will have to wait its turn."

"This is true," Guntah said, his expression darkening. "We passed more Karathah in the mountains."

"There were many south of here too," Ivy said.

Gihn gave the sky a critical sweep. "The ash cloud had brought night on us earlier tonight. We will have to camp early."

"But the Sister Lakes are so close," Ivy frowned. "Only one day's walk, surely?"

"This is unstable ground," Gihn said. "It is better to arrive in one piece, than not at all." Ivy knew he was right, of course. The caldera had already proven difficult to navigate. The southern wall had jagged ground and a fumarolic field in the western flanks was littered with vents and boiling water columns that shot up like geysers at irregular intervals. They'd lost time in circumnavigating the most dangerous areas. But a single foot wrong could mean death.

"We'll need to make up some time in the morning then," Ivy said, scouring the hillside for a good place to camp. "Get an early start."

"How you have changed," Xiou laughed. "I remember when you arrived here you hated to see the sun rise."

Ivy smiled. "I didn't know what I was missing."

Their hearth was small that evening, but the warmth of her friends filled Ivy's heart. She curled her legs beneath her and listened as Gihn, Guntah and Xiou sang their Dusk Song in low harmonies, a lonely fraction of the full tribes' vocal orchestra. It was still hauntingly beautiful, but the notes seemed to disappear too quickly in the night air, as if the song knew it was splintered, and didn't have the heart to stay. The rest of the evening passed in quiet camaraderie and the sharing of stories of the days they had been separated from each other. Gihn and Guntah had seen many Karathah moving across the land, and Ivy told them her suspicion that the red-beaded hunter was behind it. Guntah had no doubt; he'd had another run-in with the man on the northern hills of the plains, and swore the hunter with the red beads in his hair had been searching him out. The night's shadows allowed Guntah to escape with his life. The Karathah's motive for stirring up unrest within the sapien tribes remained a mystery. Ivy suspected a man like him barely needed one. Ruthlessness, and an overwhelming desire for power was more than enough.

As Ivy lay awake that night, her thoughts tumbled and twisted over the danger she was putting her friends in by forcing their travel. They were walking targets. *Am I exposing them too much?* she worried. *No other tribes have committed to join them at the Sister Lakes. My plan is failing, and every step now is placing them in more danger. After I get to Kelimutu,* she decided, *I'll search the final caves alone.*

By mid-afternoon the following day, the base of Kelimutu was finally in sight. To its north and south, the ancient cones of Kelido and Eklibara flanked the dormant volcano. Ivy shuddered at the disquiet growing steadily inside her. On the southern slopes of this monstrosity, she prayed to find one more cave that might harbour more of this beautiful, wretched species. If the final cave gave her nothing but dust and bones, the hobbits' lives were all but lost. Their small party had arrived from the south-west, and Ivy guessed it would take at least another hour to climb to the cratered lakes on the very top. It was steep and difficult, but the fastest way. Every minute counted.

Ahead of them, a dead expanse of rock led to the base of the volcano. Dozens of tiny fissures in the surface let out a continuous stream of steam and hot gas that curled into the sky. Ivy worried her bottom lip between her teeth. She took a deep breath.

"I don't like this place," said Guntah, falling in beside her. "It feels unsafe."

"I agree," Ivy replied. The fumarole field was at least two kilometres across. Ivy spotted several bubbling mud-pools sunk into the ground bed.

"Guntah is right, Hiranah," Xiou said, rubbing the sweat from his neck. "We should travel around this place. The ground is unstable."

Ivy tucked her hair behind her ears and scanned the expanse before them. Gihn, who had been falling further behind as they walked, finally caught up to them. He looked exhausted.

"I don't like it either," Ivy said, "but traveling around this could cost us hours. Night will fall soon. We can't rest until we get to the Sister Lakes." She frowned. "This is the fastest way across."

"My father needs to rest," Xiou argued. "He won't make it up the mountain."

"I can carry you Gihn," Ivy offered. She knew his pride would never allow it, but there was still far to go, and little sunlight left. It wasn't just the urgency of their mission that pushed her, but the Falling Place itself. Ivy was desperate to see it again. She felt its pull as strongly as the hobbits felt the Sister Lakes as their ancestral home.

"I will walk myself," Gihn said. "I may be slower than the rest of you, but my legs still carry me." He brushed away his son's concern. "We need to get to the Sister Lakes before nightfall; I feel it calling me. You must feel it too." The two younger hunters couldn't deny it. Whatever was drawing them to Kelimutu became more insistent with each step. "Hiranah is right," Gihn continued, "This is the fastest way, so we must take it." He walked ahead of them into the field. The others followed single file.

Bright yellow sulphur was pasted to the ground around the fissures. Everywhere else, a white coating borne of sulphuric acid, smothered the rocks.

It was past halfway across that Guntah suddenly stopped in front of her. Xiou was almost to the other side, and Gihn had fallen far behind again. Ivy took a few more steps and then paused, to save bumping into him. She turned to Guntah, surprised. His eyes were wide with fear. For a moment, time froze as Ivy realized their mistake. Too late.

A tremendous shudder beneath their feet threw them all sideways. The earth groaned and began to crack.

Guntah lunged at Ivy from behind. Their bodies fell hard across the rocks, propelled by his brute strength. They rolled and skidded in a tangle of bruised arms and scraped legs. Ivy forced her eyes open.

Where she had stood only seconds before, a great geyser of boiling mud now shot ten meters into the air, raining steam and liquid earth upon the ground.

"Run!" Ivy screamed. She scrambled up, pushing Guntah ahead of her. She had never seen him move so fast. In every direction, tiny fissures were punching through the baked earth in violent hisses of steam. The stench of sulphur dioxide choked the air.

"Nnnggaahhh!" A strangled cry caught Ivy from behind, gripping her like a nightmare in the dark. She skidded and spun back around. Beneath the pooling mud she had left, a movement caught her eye. Her heart lurched. Bile rose. *No!* She raced back. With each step, her blood in her veins seemed to thicken. She couldn't move fast enough. Her feet were too clumsy. Her mind too senseless. *Please, no. Not this! Not now!*

"Gihn!" Ivy launched herself toward the exploding mud. "Please, Gihn! No!" She grabbed the old man's legs and dragged him from the mud pool, across the cracked earth, immune to the burns raining upon her skin. There was no pain but for the screaming of her heart. With a wretched heave, Ivy lifted the old man's body into her arms, clutched him burning to her chest, and ran for all her life was worth.

Steam geysers shot indiscriminately as she bolted across the wasteland. There was no time to duck or weave. A blast caught the back of her legs and Ivy stumbled. Gihn screamed as her hands slipped around his burning skin.

"I'm so sorry," she cried, almost blinded with tears. She kept running. Xiou was running back toward her, his shouts lost in her haze of fear.

They met, she stumbled and clutched Gihn tighter as Xiou dragged her by the arm toward the base of Kelimutu, where the desert of steam and boiling mud ended. When the rock finally gave way to grass and small shrubs held tight to the earth, Ivy fell, exhausted, to her knees. She uncurled her trembling arms and rolled Gihn away from her chest. As gently as she could, she lay him on the ground. Through blinding tears, Ivy finally saw what she was carrying.

Gihn's face was swollen and barely recognizable. His arms and chest were covered in mud. Underneath, Ivy had no doubt that his skin was burnt and sloughing off with the drying mud. His legs were clean of filth, but where his skin had been, Gihn was red raw and charred and with great swathes of blistering. He took sharp, shallow breaths, his tiny ribcage rising and falling with each one.

"I did this. Oh my, *oh no*, this is all my fault." Ivy fingers brushed gently at Gihn's hair, desperate to hold and to help but knowing her touch was agony. "I'm so sorry. I'm so, so sorry." The amulet swung softly against his hair from her wrist. Sobbing, Ivy held it to his temple, the only place that seemed untouched by burns. "I'm so sorry," she sobbed. "Please don't die – I need to save you. *I will–*" She looked frantically around her, but there was nothing to heal him. Guntah knelt beside her. Xiou was staring, grim faced at his father. The hunters' eyes were unfathomable.

With what seemed like colossal effort, Gihn's swollen eyes opened to slits. He took a few shallow breaths then spoke in a whisper.

"Xiou?"

"I'm here." Xiou shifted, leaning forward so his father's gaze could find him.

"Help her – but don't let–"

"I know, father."

"–not until the end."

"Yes." Xiou looked to Ivy, then back to his father. "At the end."

Gihn blinked, slowly. Painfully. "Keep them safe," he murmured. His lips barely moved.

"I will." Xiou's eyes were shining with unshed tears.

"You are a good leader." Xiou buried his face in his father's mud caked hand, nodding slowly as Gihn spoke.

With a shallow breathe, Gihn's gaze fell to Ivy.

"Find the others. Make them understand–"

"I am trying," Ivy spluttered. With a fierce wipe, she cleared her face of tears. "I am trying but they won't listen! I am Karathah – an enemy, a stranger to them."

"No." Gihn's breath hitched. He began to cough, a sickening gurgle of blood. Ivy stroked his hair, tears falling unheeded. "You are family, Hiranah," Gihn said. "You were always meant to be here." His voice grew stronger. "You chose us. Remember that – *you chose to save us.*"

Ivy nodded, her mouth set, swallowing back tears. *But I've killed you instead.*

Gihn's eyes twitched at her blame. The amulet hung gently against his forehead as she stroked his hair. He spoke directly to her thoughts instead. *There is always death where there is life, Hiranah. I have done what I could. I brought you here. The Karathah are changing the earth around us. This fight belongs to the young ones who can learn to change with it. You said so yourself.*

But they need you, Gihn.

No, Hiranah. Gihn's eyes fluttered closed. *They need you.*

Gihn's chest slowly sank. The enormity of his leadership slipped away. In death, his body was child-like. So tiny. So mortal. *So human.*

But the burden and responsibility he had carried on his shoulders was immense.

And Ivy had just inherited it.

CHAPTER 26

NEIL

"*I* just need a minute," Neil said. "Just one minute."

A decaying log had never looked so appealing. Neil held out one hand, bracing himself as he lowered onto it. Despite his efforts, a shot of pain still seared through his middle. A glossy sheen covered every pore. Neil knew it wasn't the oppressing humidity that wrung sweat from his skin. It was infection. The wound was swollen, each day a little bigger. More painful. Though he'd been successful in staunching the blood loss by cauterising his wound, the risk of infection had multiplied. Burned flesh was a perfect petrie-dish for bacterial growth. Delirium had threatened to overtake his senses on more than one occasion and Neil guessed the infection was now coursing through his blood. *Nothing that a decent course of antibiotics won't fix when I'm home,* he tried to convince himself. Neil took the water bladder that Atasi handed him and drank from it gratefully.

Atasi spoke for a minute, her voice lilting with the inflections of whatever she was telling him. Neil caught the odd word but hadn't managed to pick up enough to follow her conversation.

He shook his head. They were in the same world, but worlds away.

"I think–" Neil forced his eyes closed for a minute. *Pull it together.* "I think we're nearly close enough to wait it out. Four days now until the full moon. The lunar energy field should be getting back to its peak." Panic ghosted him. Neil's grip tightened on the bundled copper rods leaning against his knee.

"I'm worried I might not make it out of here, Atasi." Neil gave his head a sharp shake. The fog lifted a little. "So, I've gotta make some plans, just in case. I need someone to know where I am. What's happened to me. Someone to tell Benjamin that–" The rest of that sentence was too hard. *That I'm sorry.*

"Here, give me a hand with this?" Neil slid from the log onto the ground below, beckoning. He pulled the array of pottery from his hide bag and poured a measure of yellow sulphur into the largest bowl. He held out his silver lighter, running his thumb reflexively over the nautical helm engraved on the front. *Benjamin.* Neil flicked the spark wheel. The tiny spark died as instantly it appeared. Neil's hand tremored. He tried again, holding his wrist still with the other hand. *Fail.* Weakness in his thumb. The tiny metal wheel couldn't turn fast enough to catch a light.

"Ashimani, Nee-el," Atasi's hand curled over his shaking one. She gently pried the silver lighter from his grip, then copied the move she had seen him do so many times. A tiny spark flicked into life. Carefully, she lowered the flame over the bowl of powdered sulphur, eliciting a sudden blaze of iridescent blue flames. Her eyes danced on the flames nervously. She quickly handed the silver lighter back.

"You're very brave," Neil said. "Even Charat was scared of this thing."

"Ma-jeek." Atasi said, nodding at the lighter.

"No, love. That's just what I told him," Neil smiled, shaking his head. "It's not magic. It's science. It's all science." He took a deep breath. "Let get the rags done before I run out of steam again." Neil shuffled in his bag, pulling out the four hide strips he carried. He pushed them into an empty bowl and covered them with water, prodding them down with his fingers to give them a good soak. Atasi stepped a few feet away and broke a couple of finger-width sticks off a tree branch. She seen Neil repeat his routine many times now and anticipated his next move. She passed Neil the sticks and he used them to hold each dripping strip aloft over the blue flames in turn. Once the rags had soaked enough sulphur dioxide gas from the fire, he stuffed each one into adjacent segments of his battery bowl. Atasi quickly took over, laying the alternate copper and zinc alloy between the electrolytic cells. He took his stripped USB lead and connected to either end, plugging it into his phone. No matter how many times Neil had done it, he still got a thrill of relief when the charging signal flashed on.

This time though, it was imperative that the phone had enough battery to last. This time, he was sending a message home.

"My name is Dr. Neil Crawford." Neil's voice cracked with unexpected emotion. "And I'm the Director of the Division for Astronomy and Space at the CSIRO. I'm usually based in Sydney, Australia. But right now, I'm in some other place. *And some other time.*" Neil looked away, wiped the sweat from his brow and then looked resolutely back to the screen of his mobile phone. His own face stared back at him. Haggard, bearded. He looked so much older than he remembered. "I'm 58 years old," he said. "The last couple of months – well, for the last two months I've been living in the past. I know this is going to sound insane. If I wasn't here right now, if I hadn't been through this – *shit-show* myself, I wouldn't believe me either. But I have travelled back through time, about 50,000 years give or take, and I've landed myself on the island of Flores, in Indonesia."

He squeezed his eyes shut, feeling the sting of sweat in them and shot a look at the young woman watching him from behind a tree. He let her hide. She didn't need to be part of this story. With a deep breath, Neil continued.

"The purpose of this video recording is two-fold: Firstly, I don't know what my chances are of getting out of here, but they're not looking good. I've got an open wound. Infected. If I don't make it back home, then I need to tell someone what happened to me. All of it. I need you to understand that time-travel *is* possible, and I'm gonna help you out by giving you the knowledge you need to recreate it. There are various elements at play here – straight physics, which means if we get it all right, this Time Shift could happen again. That's what I'm counting on. So, I'm giving you my brain, my knowledge."

"The second reason I'm recording my story, is because I have a son. Benjamin Crawford, ten years old. He lives in Bondi, Sydney, with his mother Francine and her husband Stephen Wiltshire. If I don't get out of here, you've got to find them for me. I need Benjamin to know why I didn't come home – that I love him – and that I tried my best to save him." Neil's shoulders fell forward in a shudder. He jabbed his index finger and thumb into his eyes, wiping them clear. Determination forced him to keep talking. The battery wouldn't last long in video-mode.

"I'm going to start at the beginning. Tell you everything I know. Coordinates, times, events. The whole bit. And when I'm finished, you're going to take this information, and figure out what the fuck happened to me in that lab at the University of Melbourne. And then you're gonna use that knowledge, *that power*, that I've given you, to travel forward in time, to get the medicine my boy needs to stay alive. Then you're gonna get it back to him." Neil's mouth was a hard, thin line. His eyes unrelenting. He challenged his accomplice to dare disobey. "You hear me? I'm giving you the knowledge that will bring you more success and power than you've ever dreamed of. *And in return, you're going to use it to save Benjamin Crawford's life.*"

Neil took a breath. Gathered his thoughts. Beyond the camera, out of view, Atasi watched Neil as he spoke feverishly to the mobile phone. Her young face betrayed a deep and constant worry.

"Right," Neil said. "Okay. Right. Listen up. I've taken photos of everything I've got here – maps and stuff written in the journal. Anything important. Check the image roll on this device. Notes are in dictation. Take it all. Now I'm going to tell you what happened. I'll begin at the beginning." Neil twisted his fingers together underneath his chin. "It all started with the redhead…"

CHAPTER 27

IVY

*I*t began to rain. Every step Ivy climbed was penance to her guilt. She shifted Gihn's body in her arms, glad for each painful burn on her own skin, every ache and slide and stumble. *If I hadn't insisted... If I'd taken the long way around... If I gave them more time... didn't put myself first...*

It tore at her, that fine line between self-loathing and a promise to herself she couldn't quite regret. No matter how hard she had tried to circumvent it, the cruel humanity she carried within herself – the drive for self-preservation, the carelessness, the ruthlessness – had won again. She held her face up to the drizzling rain, inviting more punishment. *That's two. I've killed two men now.* But there was no self defense to justify this second murder. The moisture clung to her eyelashes and skin. It was a hot rain, humid and oppressive, and Ivy breathed the weight of it inside.

She despised herself but clung to flecks of justification. Gihn had also used her to save his own family; he had kidnapped and manipulated Ivy to keep her here. They were all as devastatingly flawed as one another. *They were all human.*

But if it wasn't for me – her feet stumbled. She clutched his body tighter. Could not look at his face. *I did this.*

Ivy reached the summit of Kelimutu, drenched, and filthy, barely aware of the others that watched from afar and came running to greet her. Their welcoming calls fell into silent shock as she continued past them. Ivy kept her eyes to the ground, not ready to face their grief. Instead, she climbed the transverse ridge as far as its slope would allow, finally collapsing to her knees on a thin layer of mud. *I'm so sorry, Gihn. I'll save them, I promise I will.* With her back curled in sorrow, she brushed his grey hair back from his forehead and gently touched her own to his. No memories came from his mind to hers through the amulet that fell onto his cheek. But Ivy's own memories swirled inside her head. Gihn had listened to her grief. Reasoned with her stubbornness. Ultimately, he'd forced her to show the strength he knew she had inside. He had believed in her ability to save his people so interminably, he'd given his life for it.

"Thank you," Ivy whispered. She felt someone kneel beside her. She looked across. Tears were dripping from the end of Xiou's nose to mix with the soft, fat raindrops on his fathers' body.

"He made it home," Xiou said, quietly. "This place has been calling us. We all feel it."

We. Ivy stood up, her mind finding a window in the grief long enough to identify the faces crowding around them.

Gihn's tribe had surrounded her. Phren, Shahn, Leihna and the elders. All the women and children. All that had travelled from Liang Bua together to meet her here. Kora and Setian stood to the back of the group, where the orphaned children from the Soa Basin gathered timidly around Kyah. *Kyah.* Ivy's heart jolted as her eyes met those of her best friend. The rush of relief nearly floored her again. The bonobo's eyes were wide with concern, her soft hoots meant to soothe as she scooted toward Ivy and leapt into her friend's body in a hug that knocked the air from

EXTINCT

Ivy's lungs. They swayed, Ivy forcing herself not to stumble or fall under the extra weight, desperate to hold her close.

"How I've missed you," Ivy whispered into Kyah's black hair. "It's okay, Ky. I'm alright."

There was a gentle touch on Ivy's wrist as someone took hold of the amulet. She looked down. Shahn was standing beside Xiou's bent shoulders, her eyes sad, but her expression as serene as always.

"We are here together, Hiranah," she said. "Do you see it?"

Shahn's question took a moment to sink in. Ivy looked up past the faces to see for the first time what she knew must be there. Nothing could have prepared her for it. Breath caught in her throat and fresh tears sprang to her eyes. The three coloured lakes were overwhelmingly beautiful, even water-marked by grey drizzle. No drawing, no photograph or description in a research paper, had ever done them justice. At the bottom of the vertical ridge beside her, a blood-red lake had collected deep inside the dormant crater. It looked as though the very stone itself were bleeding. To her north, two great sister lakes sat side by side. One was icy blue like a glacial melt and the other was a vibrant emerald reflection of the jungle that lay far below. A thin layer of mist shrouded them all, ribboning crags and softening sharp ridges. Kelimutu was breathtaking.

"Hiranah," Leihna smiled, coming up to stand beside Shahn. "We missed you." Ivy placed Kyah back onto her feet as the young woman put her hands either side of Ivy's face and pressed their foreheads together in greeting.

"Welcome home, Hiranah," Phren said, stepping forward to do the same. Phren led her through the group, each family member greeting Ivy with gentle warmth. Grief tripped her up again and each loving pair of hands was an aching reminder of how close Gihn had come to returning to them. But not all were there. Ivy looked anxiously for the faces of Kari, Shia and Boru. They had each led a group of travellers from Liang Bua in different directions to search for the hidden tribes.

"Has no one else arrived?" She asked.

"No," Shahn replied. "But they will." She gave Ivy a bolstering smile. "We still have four days until the full moon."

Only four days. Such a tiny slip of time to achieve the insurmountable task that still lay ahead of her.

As the first light of dawn, the entire tribe gathered near the summit of Kelimutu. An overcast, murky sky muted the orange glow. The air felt alive with electricity, as if a storm was waiting in the wings. Gihn's body had been brought down to their temporary camp in the tree line, and Ivy had spent most of the night in vigil beside it, before finally falling into an exhausted sleep. Only hours later she'd been gently woken by Shahn. It was time to say goodbye.

Ivy knelt, feeling Xiou's shoulder cave ever so slightly under her touch. The hunter was well accustomed to death, but clearly the grief of it never lessened.

"The people that live in this place in my time believe that the souls of the dead come to these lakes to rest," said Ivy.

"Souls?" The heavy lines under Xiou's eyes seemed to have aged him overnight. Ivy hesitated, considering how to word the concept of an afterlife to a man whose own life was infinitely organic and mortal.

"Some people believe that a part of life goes on living after the body is left behind. Their *soul.*" She leaned forward, smoothing Gihn's hair away from his face. The mud had been washed from it, and his burned face was painted with pigment. "They would say that after Gihn's death," she continued, "a part of him continues to live here at these lakes, as well as in your own memories of him."

"What part of him remains?"

"I suppose – the best part of him," Ivy mused. "His energy, like Aneirlah, but instead of the energy of the land, it's just his own energy, by itself. The life he carried within his own heart and mind."

Xiou looked at the thundering sky. "An energy separate to the earth?" He offered her a small smile. "That doesn't make sense, Hiranah. His mind and heart came from this earth. Now the earth has taken it back." A moment passed. Xiou looked across to the lakes. "It was the earth that called him home. He felt the pull of it as I do, here–" he reached out, touching Gihn gently between his closed eyes then skimming his index finger down his father's chest "–and here. And so, he returns to the earth." A tear fell. Xiou sat back on his heels. One by one, Shahn, Kora, Setian and the others of the tribe joined them, forming a ring around the elder's body. "It is time to let him go." As Setian began the low, mournful note of their Dusk Song, Xiou added softly, "But still, if the Karathah of your time are right, then perhaps he really is home now – body, and *soul*."

Each of the tribe took their turn adding a harmonic note to the song that Ivy was now so familiar with. The sound engulfed her. Each person breathed rhythmically, their notes long and gently controlled with no beginning nor end. Without the acoustics of the cave to mull and amplify the sound, the song seemed to float, disappearing into the empty sky around the huddled bodies.

Ivy stood up. Stepped back. The mountaintop felt too sad to dwell in. And she felt too tall and too lonely to be a part of it. She pulled her damp hair over her shoulder, wringing it out. A few yards away, Ivy listened to their mournful lament, then kept walking. Kyah was sitting a little further on with some children, drawing in the mud. Ivy walked over to her, combing fingers through the bonobo's fine hair. She was filthy as well but seemed to have done a better job at grooming herself than any of the humans.

Kyah moved a little away from the children, then drew new symbols in the mud. Her preoccupation was clear. *Old man. Dead.* She peered up at Ivy with concern. Ivy nodded tightly. The weight of guilt stretched the surface of her control. She squeezed her eyes shut, biting her lip and took a deep breath.

The bonobo hooted softly and stood up. Bringing her finger to Ivy's cheek, Kyah drew it downwards, tracing the path a tear would make. *Cry.*

Ivy leaned into the leathery fingers as tears threatened to fall. She nodded. *Yes. Sad.* Although Kyah couldn't cry herself, Ivy knew she understood.

They stood together, enveloped in the Dusk Song for a few minutes. The mountaintop grew warmer and the dawn sun brighter until the children began to fuss, wanting Kyah to re-join them. She had become their constant companion and guard. They could never have found a more devoted one.

"Go on, go play with them," Ivy encouraged her. "I'm okay." She smiled, brushing the bonobo's shoulder with her fingers. "I'm not going far." Kyah made a soft noise and rejoined the tiny artists, wiping the muddy slate clear to start again.

Ivy climbed a little higher onto the crag that seemed equidistant from all three lakes. Turquoise and ice blue water glittered under the fingers of the wind. The lower crater of blood red shone like oil. The air felt thin but warm in her lungs and smelt acrid with sulphur. Dark rain clouds were settled ominously above, trapping the humidity beneath. They flashed with lightning. It felt appropriate, that the morning sky echoed her state of mind.

Behind her, the singing grew louder.

"Ouch!" Ivy jolted her hand up and rubbed her wrist. "What?!" The edges of the amulet were diffused with an electric blue glow.

She caught the stone on her palm, flattening her hand to decrease the surface area touching her skin. The amulet was burning hot. Ivy froze, terrified. Her mind seemed to stall. *What is – No! It's happening. It's happening again!* Panic twisted inside. *But I'm not ready to leave –* "Kyah!"

Crack! Lightning split the sky above her. Ivy quaked, petrified, hand still extended in front. A splinter of blue light shot upward from the glowing stone on her palm, meeting an electrostatic discharge coursing down from the sky. They connected. Ivy felt the impact, rather than heard it. It was as if all sound on earth went suddenly mute, an anti-thunder. The vibration of the collision reached into her veins instead, dragging the noise down through her body like a metal instrument. It coursed through the adrenaline in Ivy's blood, tracing her nerves until it hit the ground beneath, then radiated out, up and over her in a great dome. Ivy wheezed in a breath. She spun, horrified. In every direction, the air sizzled and moved like a wave of heat around her. The dome was like a living thing, a wall of space, thick and opaque, rather than the nothing it should have been. The shoulders of Kelimutu shimmered beyond it in a haze.

Crack! Another bolt of lightning. This time, Ivy dropped to the ground, coiled like a spring, ready to run. Pale skin drained to grey. Pupils shocked wide and fine hairs stood on end. Her heart was bursting.

But no shredding pain touched her. Everything went still. The opaque dome simply shivered above Ivy's head and around her body, encasing her entirely.

I'm trapped.

Ivy clenched her jaw tight and reached a shaking hand toward the wall of molten nothing. Her fingertips tingled with anticipation. But it was the amulet on her wrist that touched the wall first. It swung out gently with the movement.

Snap!

The dome shattered. It became clear, air like glass, but broken into shards all around. The shards domed upward as the opaque version had, but each shard was unique, throwing light in every direction. Carefully, Ivy stood up. *"Oh my–"* She turned, slowly, on the spot. There were dozens of pieces. Large, tiny, long. All splintered. The world around her had become a shattered window. Each shard was discernible from the next by a thin hazy line like smoke; lines of that opaque, thick air she had been surrounded with only moments before. But inside the shards themselves, there was nothing. Just a clear, curved window looking out toward Kelimutu's crown. Just as it was before.

No, not as it was. Parts of it were different.

Ivy turned east, staring down the slope of the mountain. It was a prism of chaos.

Through a single shard of landscape far below, a collection of creatures grazed on lush volcanic grassland. Creatures like none she'd ever seen in her life. *What the hell?* They were giant rodents of some kind, shaggy and humped.

A glint caught her eye. Above where she stood, an aircraft crossed the sky through a shard. It was close, skimming the top of the mountain. Ivy's heart raced, and she couldn't stop her arms from flinging up, waving above her head. But the jet was sleek and fast, disappearing at the smoky edge of its shard almost immediately. Ivy's hopes plummeted, she was gutted and confused all at once. *What am I doing? I need to stay.* Automatically Ivy's eyes followed the aircraft's trajectory, but the connecting shard was empty sky, a little darker than the first. The jet had disappeared into nothing. The next connecting piece of sky remained empty as well. Ivy let out a puff of surprise, as the aircraft appeared once more in another splinter of the sky, still heading on its original course. Before she could wave, it had disappeared beyond that shard's edge. This time, it stayed gone.

Desperate eyes raked the mosaic. The more Ivy looked, the more she saw. Several shards showed a blackened, smoking earth with rivulets of red lava oozing down their crevices. *Kelimutu was a volcano. Of course.* Ivy flashed a look at her own feet, but there was nothing but mud beneath them. She stared into a different splinter. Inside, a creature was descending into a heavily jungled landscape. *"A human,"* she muttered. *"No... that's not human."*

It was huge, even from the distance where Ivy stood. *"What the hell?"* In roughly human form, but monstrous in muscle, she guessed at least three times heavier than a silverback gorilla. The primate walked on all fours using its knuckles to support the massive weight of its body. It was awkward and ungainly with dirty brown hair covering it entirely, blackened in places by soot. If she hadn't known better, Ivy would have guessed it was an orangutan, but *no*. The creature stopped knuckle-walking, pulling its body up tall to look around. *"Oh my goodness. Oh my–"* Ivy froze, in shock and awe. It stood at least nine feet tall, with heavily bowed legs. Hands the size of Ivy's entire torso stretched out, one reaching back to scratch its own neck. The other hand dangled by its side, then casually tore a pole of bamboo from the ground by its side. Ivy knew what this creature was. The biggest extinct species of primate ever to exist, by fossil record at least. *Gigantopithecus blacki.* By rights, it should have seen her, but the round black eyes buried in its face scanned the top of the mountain where Ivy stood with no recognition at all. It seemed to see right through her. Relief flooded every cell. This gentle giant likely preferred bamboo over flesh, but still, Ivy didn't want to test that theory.

"How are you here?" Ivy whispered. Fossils for *blacki* had never been discovered further south than Vietnam. And at this point in primate evolution, even fifty thousand years before her own time, it shouldn't exist. *Blacki* was a slice of past with no rationale. An animal displaced. The presence of that one creature could represent any time from nine million years to one hundred thousand ago. It belonged in a different time and a different place. A different world.

Ivy searched another window. The rainforest far below was

now gone altogether, replaced by a patchwork of rice fields stitched into neat rows. Ivy's pulse raced – in yet another shard the landscape bore a shining city, stretching tall and glinting toward the sun with silver roots dug tight into the rifted valleys. Zipping lights like pinpricks appeared and disappeared in the morning sky above it. This was not the modern world as she knew it. *"What is it then?* When *is it?"*

Ivy looked up to find herself under a wide prism of water, lapping at a non-existent skylight that kept her separated from it. She shrunk back. Within the depths of blue, a great shadow was passing overhead. Open jaws of serrated teeth preceded a reptilian head over a meter long. A beady black eye stared out as it moved. *Tylosaurus. "Oh no, no, no. I'm going to die."* Ivy squeezed her eyes shut, dropping low to the ground. *"It isn't real. It can't be here."* The prehistoric beast went extinct eighty million years before Ivy stood there, leaving nothing but bone in the rocks. *"Please be extinct."* She squinted one eye open, peering up. A mass of body followed for what seemed like minutes of trying to slow her breathing and tame her wild imagination. This was all too real. Ivy caught a glimpse of an enormous paddled fin before the reptile sped up, leaving its arrow-tipped tail to flick at the pane's surface, spraying Ivy with cool water and a fresh wave of terror. The skylight wobbled and bulged with the force of movement but held tight. Then the beast was gone, leaving only ocean above.

Ivy forced her knees straight, wincing as they cracked. The seascape above her was impossibly higher than the sea level of this world. Bile burned her throat as Ivy stared up at it. She looked back down at her feet for support. They gave little. A meter past them, where the shards connected to the earth on which she stood, a large piece of solid ground fell away instead to nothing. Vertigo hit. This slice of reality was terrifying in its own way – the Indonesian archipelago had not even formed. A flock of pterosaurs, each with a wingspan over fifteen feet, were circling an ocean far below.

Elongated snouts glinted with serrated teeth. Bright red crests bejewelled their upper and lower jaws, tempting Ivy with a long-forgotten name from her university lectures. *Lieeo, Liano - Liaoningopterus! Oh my goodness, 130 million years gone. Is that what I'm looking at? Is this – the past? Or is it right now – but with a different version of evolution at play?* For a split, crazy moment, Ivy desperately wanted to reach forward, immersing her body and soul into a world she had obsessed over as a child. Pterosaurs had always been her favourite. The precious link between dinosaurs and birds. Ivy buried her face in her hands, squealing with panicked delight. *I could almost touch them.* They swooped low in a mesmerising ballet across thermal currents, scooping fish out the water into claws and beaks. *They'd eat me alive.*

Ivy tore her gaze away. Every window seemed to hold a different version of what she should have rightly seen. In one, a strange web-like connection of wires hovered over the surface of Kelimutu. *Electricity?* Ivy wondered. *Or a conduit for some other source of energy?* In that shard, no greenery blanketed the mountain and there were no other signs of life. In an adjoining shard, a dozen Karathah were hunting stegodon in a grassland far below. Ivy's impulse to hide almost overtook her. So far, she had seen no sign of her beloved *Homo floresiensis* tribes in any shard – no version of the earth where they existed alongside the one she was in.

Until she did.

An irregular shard, no bigger than her hand seemed at first to be a moving blur of figures. But as Ivy focussed in on it, the figures took form. Hobbits were walking past where she stood, faces hallowed and starved, dragging one after the other in a line chained at the ankles. *Prisoners.* Ivy watched as one fell and was dragged back onto his feet but a rough hand. A sapien hand. A *modern* sapien hand. The hand belonged to a man in a grey uniform with pale skin and a sun hat. His eyes were not cruel, but impassive. He was simply doing his job. Another uniform stood ten feet away, directing bodies up a ramp into a troop carrier. A third stood by, overseeing the operation with a grim expression.

"Please, no. Leave them here," Ivy cried, oblivious to the tears falling onto her chest. *"They can't survive without their land; they're connected to it!"* She felt the impending dislocation like an open wound. But Ivy's words fell on deaf ears as the engine of the truck roared. Though the hobbits were compliant, this was no relocation out of concern or safety. The chains said it all. The grey uniforms had riot batons tucked into their belts but there was no use for them here. Their prisoners were child-sized and already defeated. Dull eyes reflected no hope for their own free-dom. This was a people being stolen. Ivy's fingers trembled, as she lifted her hand closer to the shard. Injustice raged inside her heart. There were children amongst the prisoners. Elders and…
Shahn. Ivy's fingers froze in front of her face. The most serene and gentle of all her new family, Shahn was climbing up the ramp with difficulty, burdened by the ankle chains and a tiny baby in her arms.

"Shahn!" Ivy cried out. But her voice did not carry beyond the translucent wall. *"Shahn!"* Ivy screamed again. But the hobbit woman's eyes turned only to meet her captors with sudden terror. A woman in grey uniform was stepping forward. She took the baby from Shahn's arms and turned away. Shahn collapsed at the top of the ramp, begging for her child back. In horror, Ivy's followed the woman's path to see a second truck. Small children and babies with wide, fearful eyes, stood within the open back doors, held back by a half dozen grey uniforms. All were crying out for their parents. A scuffle and a shout rose as a man fought against his chains to reach them. The baton came out. From the back of the troop carrier, tiny Trahg saw his father fall.

"Xiou! No!" Ivy cried out. But her words never left the dome. *"Where are you taking them?"* She shouted into the void around

her, ears ringing against her own assault. Ivy's heart raced. Vision blurred. *"Don't take them!"* Vomit threatened to fill her mouth. Each child crying set off another, until all were wailing at the terror of being kept from their mothers' arms. Ivy couldn't think of a reason where such cruelty could be justified.

Until she did.

The annals of human history bore too many devastating examples for her to ignore. Stolen generations of indigenous children across the world had been put through hell in the name of forced assimilation. Decades of unwed mothers had had newborns pried from their arms by religious orders, only for their babies to be raised in loveless institutions rife with abuse. Almost all malnourished and abused, with the most pitiable suffering through medical trials and a mortality rate twice that of children in loving homes. Ivy knew that every country could lay claim to a history of dark secrets. The Catholic mother's homes in Ireland that hid generations of child theft and mistreatment. Threats and beatings against Chinese mothers who violated the one-child policy by falling pregnant until they succumbed to abortion or forced adoption. Abused and impoverished Swiss children used for farm labour, while their government turned a blind eye for over a century. English babies stolen from their mothers who believed them dead, then shipped to institution-alised abuse in Australia. The German Stasi had torn families apart for years to ensure parents could not flee the communist regime they were forced to live under. In Spain, babies were stolen and trafficked, sanctioned by the church and doctors. Australia's stolen generations, and New Zealand's forced removals to state care; all still affected the psyche of the popula-tion half a century on. Babies stripped of identity, starved of love and affection, buried in unmarked plots and septic tanks. Chil-dren left to endure violence and imprisonment alone.

There had been generation upon generation of stolen children.

I should have expected this, Ivy realised. *It's what humans have always done, in one form or another.*

She watched the scene before her unfold with streaming, desperate eyes. *Why did I think these children would be treated any differently?* If anything, the *Homo floresiensis* people were easier to disregard. They looked different. Thought different. They were an entirely different species of human.

They were 'other'.

And it was always the *others*, who suffered most.

"What was I thinking?" Ivy's voice was cracked, the words breaking as they fell from her mouth. "They aren't even *seen* as human." The chain of adults were dragged toward the back of the troop carrier. Wherever they were being taken, there was clearly no promise of a happy life ahead. In the eyes of the grey suits that corralled them, they were animals, like any other. And the way humans treated other animals, was notorious. Mothers of animal species were routinely stripped of their babies. For food. Milk. Entertainment. Pets. Bred deliberately for impending loss. Cries fell on deaf ears. Heartbreak brought no sympathy.

Deep in the broken shard, a truck roared to life. It rolled carefully away, taking its cargo of human life with it. Imprisoned within a metal belly, Ivy's tribe were removed from Kelimutu. Ivy tore her eyes away, searching for some other end to the story she was seeing. But no window showed the hobbits' fate. *I can't save them,* Ivy realised. *Because I'm only saving them for a future like this. They'll be taken from their land, in one way or another. Broken apart. By saving them now, I'm only forcing them to die later.*

A crushing realisation forced the breath from her lungs. *I'm going to lose them all.* Her fingers found the dirt under her knees. The weight of grief dragged her down. *Loss.* Years of loss had already left their mark so cruelly on her soul. Rebellion reared up. *Not again. I have to think! Think! What if they find another way out?* Ivy's eyes scoured the shards around her. *There must be a place*

– a version of the world where they can be safe? If these shards show the possibilities of our world – surely one of them could save these people?

But no storybook ending was illuminated. In one shard the ground was torn and gaping. Great black machines drilled and dug into it, exposing the deep underbelly of rock and raping its value. Sluggish trucks moved across the landscape, flattening tiers of roads behind them, filled to the brim with black shiny metal. Her gut churned at the sight. As she turned away, a lone figure began his ascent of Kelimutu in the distance.

In the next prism, Ivy was shocked to recognise row upon row of palm oil plantations. The convex edges of the shard reflected a peripheral world of mass production within bleached and dying soil. *"No, not here."* Ivy covered her mouth with shaking fingers. It was almost worse than the prisoners. Ivy knew all too well what the future held for the hobbits of those forests. *Anywhere but here.*

Interspersed with dozens of strange landscapes were shards of reality that showed only what she expected. Kelimutu as it had been for her only minutes ago, drizzly grey and muddy, with its breathtaking coloured lakes and the fall of washed-out greenery that sloped into the horizon. *Were those safe worlds?* Ivy wondered. *Did hobbits exist safely in any of those?* There was no way of knowing. The shards gave little hint at what alternate reality or time lay beyond the mirage of everyday that they showed.

Of those that did, Ivy's mind was too overwhelmed to take in their clues.

She didn't notice the flash of bright green eyes in a shard behind her. Nor the pale outstretched hand in another, paused in deliberation, before it tucked fiery hair under a hood and raced away. Nor did Ivy see the silhouette of a young woman facing away, with her shoulders strong and resolute against the dawn that curled around her.

Ivy didn't see because she was suddenly distracted. By voices.

"Come on, Sean, we're nearly at the top."

"Yeah, well you're not the one carrying the equipment." A groan.

"Ha ha! A bet's a bet and you lost. Besides, you could do with the exercise." A woman laughed.

"It wasn't a fair bet!"

"I never said it was going to be fair."

"Yeah well, you owe me a massage after this, Dee. I'm not as young as I used to be."

A man and woman appeared on top of a ridge not far from where Ivy stood. They were in their early sixties, dressed in modern clothes, well worn, with backpacks and sunglasses and aluminium flasks in their hands. The man had an expensive camera case draped around his neck and a folded tripod in one hand that he used as a walking stick. An Indonesian man followed a few meters behind, also in modern clothes but empty handed and smiling. He had an old water bottle tied to his waist. *A guide,* Ivy guessed. *They're sightseeing.* Her heart stuttered. *Oh my god. They're just like me. That window must be my world.*

"Oh, you'll get a massage alright," the woman called Dee grinned at her male companion, raising an eyebrow. She leaned forward, taking the tripod from his hand to set it up. She stood tall, taking in the view. As her eyes passed Ivy, they didn't pause. She simply looked straight through, as if the dome and woman inside it, weren't there at all.

"Really?" Sean looked hopeful. His eyes flicked reflexively over the woman's body.

"Absolutely, darling." Dee gave him a good-natured pat on the back. "Makarius was just saying his brother-in-law gives a mean *pijit.* We saw him at the dock, remember, six-foot tall, nice big hands – hey!" Dee finished in a peal of laughter as Sean hit his shoulder into hers, knocking her off balance. Makarius, whom Ivy guessed was the local guide, chuckled behind them.

"And here I was imagining you had some hopelessly romantic evening planned," Sean winked, shaking his head. "I'd cross worlds for you, and this is what I get." The woman called Dee laughed and pulled him in for a kiss, then set back to work on the tripod. The man began to fix his camera to it, continuing their banter.

It was as if the world stopped. Ivy's bare toes stuck to the earth, her chest pounding and mouth dry.

These are people. My people. There were no hobbits behind them, no Karathah. No death, nor fighting. No grief or fear or children being taken from their mothers. It was, simply as it should have been. *My people. The place I came from. Free. So easy. Oh my god. This is home.*

Ivy didn't notice the anomalies in their world. Didn't see that Sean's camera was of a technology too far removed from her own. She couldn't see that underneath her sunglasses, Dee's eyes were a shade too light to be considered blue. That Makarius wore a wristband of shells never found in Ivy's world. Or that curled around the tripod, Dee's fingers counted six.

Ivy reached out her hand. The temptation was shocking. A sudden desperation to connect. Logic disappeared – as Ivy realised that she *needed* to be part of that world again.

She felt the cool slide of air upon air through the prismatic pane as her fingers slipped through, then her hand. The dangling amulet stretched toward the shard wall, dragging her wrist like a magnet to its opposite.

Until the pain.

A bone-aching wrench pulled her toward the shard. Tearing through her veins. Ivy threw her head back and screamed. The power of it dragged her forward. Her body felt as if it was being ripped to pieces, limb by limb. The shard expanded. From a jagged, tiny window it bubbled and stretched as she was pulled inward. More and more of the world that was encasing her body grew around her.

This was a mistake.

"No!" She screamed. Gasps of astonishment from the other-world visitors, and a flash of recognition in Sean's eyes barely registered before Ivy was wrenched backward again by strong hands. She was crashing. A strange noise like suction filled her head as Ivy tore away. A soft, crushing weight fell upon her body on the rocky ground.

Breathe. Breathe. Eyes closed. The bone-deep ache haunted her limbs. *Breathe.* As the pain subsided, Ivy opened her eyes. Terrified. *Breathe.*

The dome was gone. Beside her, Xiou was panting with exertion. His scarred face was the most furious Ivy had ever seen it. It was Xiou's arms that had dragged her out. They were still shaking. The hunter's eyes were wet. His breath came fast and hard. Beside him, Kyah was rocking back and forth, picking at her chest, reopening a scar that had long since healed.

Xiou got to his feet. His hard glare said it all. Any trust he had once had in her, was gone. Ivy felt her own heart shatter.

"Xiou, please–"

"Not until the end," he growled. Xiou turned away.

"I'm so sorry."

A tremored hoot from beside her. A mournful cry. Ivy pulled Kyah's hand from her bleeding chest and buried her own tears there instead.

"Ky, I'm so sorry."

CHAPTER 28

ORRIN

*B*y the time they had descended the trail and taken the jeep around the west side of the mountain to the magnetite mine, routine daily operations were in full swing. Dawes stood proudly outside a demountable office block that sat upon the upper lip of the chasm. His arm stretched out, gesturing down to the dizzying excavation below. In the far distance, mountainous piles of waste rock storage were overflowing.

"Biggest drill-and-blast, load-and-haul operation in the archipelago," Dawes was crowing. "With some of the most sophisticated mining equipment in the world." A promotional flyer had already informed Orrin that the gargantuan oblong-shaped pit was five-and-a-half kilometres in length and more than two kilometres wide, and already dug nearly six hundred meters deep into the earth. "We've got a crew on the ground loading new drill holes with explosives. I've got ore loading and hauling to stockpiles for processing, but I can't risk sending it into the grinding mills. Too many unknowns, too risky. This bloody intrusion in the magnetite is causing me serious headaches. I need to know what it is, and whether it's going to affect the quality of our ore. I can't delay grinding and shipment much longer."

"You haven't shipped any out yet?" Eli looked surprised.

"I want your word on it first, Dr Nnamani," Dawes said. He put his hand in his pocket and pulled out a palm-sized black rock. He turned it over in his hand, a scowl on his face, then passed it over to Eli. "One of the samples I ran through the SEM." He nodded toward the rock. "If it's something bad, I'll call the board and get the placed finished up. The mine was almost ready for reparation, so we'll close up shop and start again somewhere else. But if that black stuff is something good, then plans can be made to capitalise on what we have here before we sell it. I'll take either option, but right now, I'm in the dark." A sharp crack split the air. All three men instinctively tensed. Orrin turned to see lightning split the sky above Kelimutu. White fingers raked the atmosphere as the current connected above. Dawes took a deep breath and walked to the very edge of the pit. "I'm not a man who likes surprises," he finished. Only a steel guard rail kept him from falling into his own creation. "There's just too much of this stuff to ignore now. We can't get through it to find clean ore."

"You mean the entire base floor is carrying this intrusion?" Eli's usually passive face was etched with concern.

"Everything we've dug in the last past couple of months, from what I can see. I've had probe holes drilled across the entire working area. I've analysed the samples myself. Whatever it is, it's everywhere."

Orrin felt his heart race. Eli caught his eye. He knew they were both thinking the same thing.

"This, *ah*–" Eli paused, pretending to draw on his memory for something he was already far too familiar with, "*unidentified black ribbon*, is that what you've observed in the crystalline magnetite under the Scanning Electron Microscope? That's the sample contaminant that you're finding across the base floor?"

"Exactly."

"I see." Eli looked out across the landscape ahead of them. His calm persona was slipping badly. Panic filled his eyes.

The problem was not just an isolated sample, Orrin thought as he followed his friend's gaze, *it was in every direction, trailing for miles across the upturned earth in the exposed footprint of a volcano.*

When he had boarded the plane from Melbourne to Flores, Orrin had hoped he would get lucky and identify where Ivy's mysterious amulet had come from. But this new reality was horrific.

It was everywhere.

Element 115. Moscovium.

An unpredictable heavy metal, never before seen in stable form. Twisted and entwined with the most magnetic mineral on earth, right down to its crystalline bonds. This unpredictable, *unknowable,* substance, was no longer buried far beneath earth's surface, dampened, and tempered by the mass of rock above it.

No. Now, thousands of tonnes of Moscovium were exposed across the base surface of the pit. Orrin's mind stumbled over the potential surface area, like slippery feet over wet rocks. The pit was more than five kilometres long; two kilometres wide. He did a quick calculation in his head. *That's more than eight and a half million square meters of exposed Moscovium.* He felt the blood drain from his face.

"Eli," said Orrin, quietly. "If I could have a private word?" The two men stepped aside, away from the curious ears of Dawes. Below them, the magnetite mine yawned at their feet, like a monstrous mouth, threatening to engulf them.

It all makes sense, Orrin realised. *The natural disasters. Extreme global warming. Wildly fluctuating magnetosphere. Dead satellites in the sky. Flooding. Droughts.* The world seemed to shift beneath his feet. *It. All. Makes. Sense.*

"Boyo," Orrin breathed. He tried to keep his voice from shaking. "I think we've just found the reason the world is falling apart."

The following morning, Orrin was back in the jeep. But this time, he was alone. Eli had taken the trip to IPM's Kelimutu mine at daybreak, once again with Dawes, this time to take his own samples from the base pit of the mine. Both he and Orrin already knew what they would find.

Orrin had begged Eli not to tell Dawes what they knew yet, and Eli had not taken much convincing.

"If IPM know they have a new discovery of this magnitude," Orrin had argued, "–a stable form of element 115 – something so new, something *unknown* and with possible commercial potential – lord knows what they'll try to make of it. They'll step up their operations, extend their production licence and launch a full-scale resurgence."

"We're better to say the intrusion is something malicious then," Eli said. He held the sample of magnetite that Dawes had drilled from the pit and given him to test. Eli turned the rock over in his palm, thoughtfully. "Render their current stockpiles unusable and prompt them to start backfilling the pit. Cover the stuff up."

"Sure. But that's not going to happen overnight in any case. It'll take years to backfill a mine that deep. Years to reverse the damage. And they could decide to just begin reparations on the current base floor level and leave it exposed. Fill it with topsoil and palm oil plantations and walk away, not realising the implications of what they've done."

"Alright, what if we release the information directly to the Indonesian government? Tell them what's in there and what it's doing to the magnetosphere?"

"First up, you'll lose your job with IPM and lose our chance to study it any further," Orrin warned. "And I'll lose any hope I have of figuring out its connection to Ivy's disappearance. Once we raise the alarm on this place, every university in the world will turn its attention to Flores, to IPM, and to what the CSIRO are doing at Melbourne University. The entire campus is already swarming with security and government officials. I won't be able to get in the carpark, let alone my lab."

"There is no easy solution here." Eli shook his head. He was hunched on the end of his bed, carrying the weight of the world on his shoulders.

"Give me until the full moon," Orrin had pleaded. "Four more days. We'll fly out of here early – leave tomorrow night. I'll get your new samples back in my lab and then you can let loose if you have to – but *after* I try to recreate the time shift. Ring some alarm bells. Academic papers. Prime-time news releases. We'll get the university involved – whatever you've gotta do to make sure the right people know what's going on over here."

"And what if the time shift doesn't happen, Orrin?" Eli's tone was gentle. "What if you can't get Ivy back?"

Orrin looked at the geologist, steeling himself. His eyes pricked with tears. He took a deep breath. The thought that he might fail was terrifying. Of losing Ivy, after all they'd been through. But the thought of staying here, trapped in this cataclysmic version of reality was even more so. This earth was slowly falling apart. But the truth was undeniable. If he failed, this *was* his new Earth. His new existence. Orrin's entire life from this point forward, and his own eventual death, belonged to the new reality he had somehow created. There was no escaping it.

"If I can't get Ivy back," Orrin said quietly, "Then that means I'll have to live without her." The words felt bitter in his mouth. "I'll be as much a part of this broken world as you are, boyo. So, I'll do everything in my power to help you save it." He took a deep breath. "With or without Ivy." His voice trailed off.

Eli dropped his head. "I don't want you to fail, mate."

"I know you don't. But we both know I could." He offered Eli a weak smile. "Just give me four days before I have to accept that's the way it's gonna be."

"Four days," Eli had conceded. He passed the sample of magnetite over to Orrin. "But if Dawes puts pressure on me to give them information–"

"Then you do what you've got to do."

*

Orrin thanked the driver and left the jeep at the base of the Kelimutu trail. The sample chunk of magnetite that Eli had given him was safely stowed in the front pocket of his shorts. It was quieter today. The sunrise tourists had come and gone already, leaving him alone with his thoughts.

It was a sweaty, oppressive morning, with dank grey clouds that almost swallowed the top of the volcano. Dawes had warned him that electrical storms were no longer forecast around the mine – they were expected. Whenever lightning descended, tours up the mountain were cancelled and heavy machinery at the mine stood down. Orrin had thanked Dawes for the warning. And gone anyway. He refused to lose his final opportunity to see the lakes, despite the risk.

The paved path grew steeper. One foot doggedly followed the other. There was no breeze today to lick the humidity off his face. Sulphur, an acrid rotten stench, hung in the air. Somewhere, deep within the lakes, the bowels of Kelimutu were churning. Orrin's footfall slowed.

Just like the day before, he realised that Ivy felt inexplicably *close*. Fifty thousand years separated her being in this place from his own visit, but *still*. She felt *close*.

It is all in my head? Orrin wondered, as he grew closer to the peak. *Of course it is.* On a whim, he pulled out his phone as he walked, and scrolled though his music playlist. *<Untitled>*. The haunting timbre of Ivy's cello sang through the speaker on his phone. *Le Cygne.* A familiar chill raced his spine. Orrin hit repeat, allowing the song to play on a continuous loop as he walked. He pushed his mobile into his back pocket, the soft melody filling the quietude of heavy mountain air. One foot in front of the other. The song played again and again.

Orrin reached the top of the trail and followed the path toward the west, across the crest of the volcano. The three spectacular lakes greeted him once more.

Vibrant emerald, like its jungle home. Pale icy blue, like a glacial melt. Deep red, like blood from stone.

The deceptively deadly beauty of the coloured water called to him like a siren as he passed. He imagined how tempting it might have been for those poor souls that had been decided to swim its waters and never came out. Orrin shivered, despite the exercise that put sweat in his pores. There was an odd ambience about the place. An *other-worldliness. No wonder the locals imagined it brimming with souls of the dead,* he thought.

He made his way across the sharp ridge that separated the crater lakes. Stepped up onto the concrete monument built on the peak where *Tiwu Ata Mbupu*, the deep red, and *Tiwu Nuwa Muri Koo Fai*, the icy blue, shared a thick expanse of rocky wall. The majesty of Kelimutu seemed to shrink the world below it, as if ancient secrets were all that mattered in the world. From 1600 meters above sea level, Orrin felt as if he was standing on the top of the world.

For a long moment, he simply stood and took it all in. From his back pocket, the deep, rich voice of Ivy's cello continued to sing into the air around him.

A sharp *crack* broke Orrin from his reverie. "Jaysus!" He scanned the sky. Tendrils of electricity were etching paths within the clouds that touched the lakes. It seemed the threat of a storm had finally hit home.

"Ouch!" Something stung Orrin's thigh. He looked down,

expecting to find an insect on his leg. "What nasty little –?" But there was nothing there. As he lifted his gaze back to the lake, it happened again. A sharp sting. Same place. *"Shite!"* Orrin almost jumped this time. He brushed his hands down the shorts, determined to rid himself of the little biter. As they brushed the chunk of magnetite in his front pocket, a third sting hit him. *It's my pocket. The rock.* He reached in and pulled out the palm-sized black chunk of magnetite. It was burning hot. And a little – *blue?*

"What the hell?" Orrin dribbled it from one palm to the next. A moment too long, and his skin burned underneath. The magnetite *was* glowing blue. He froze, hand outstretched in astonishment. If Orrin had known what would happen mere milliseconds later, he might have dropped the burning stone to the ground. But it all came too fast.

A sharp *crack* broke the sky above. A whisp of iridescent blue shot upward. It connected with a blazing trail of negative electrostatic discharge coursing toward it from above. As the channels of lightning collided, the chunk of magnetite on Orrin's outstretched palm seemed to bulge, and *snap.*

From a moment, there was no sound. Orrin's eardrums begged for noise against the terrifying void, until it was suddenly granted. A rolling wave of vibration that left his ears ringing with pain and his body trembling, crashing to him down to his knees. The wave of energy passed through each muscle, each tendon, hair and nerve cell until it hit the concrete underneath. Then the energy recoiled, spreading out around his body and upward toward its origin, converging at an apex above his head. Inside a wall of thick shimmering air, Orrin trembled, knees hard to the concrete, petrified, trapped like a prisoner in a cage.

Breathe. He told himself. *Just bloody breathe.* There was no helping his heart, which was racing so fast he felt death must be inescapable. Rounded above him, left. Right. All around him, a haze of slightly opaque air held Orrin captive. *I'm trapped*, he thought, struggling to keep bile from reaching his mouth. It was as if someone had brought a glass down over his head, and he was caught inside, like a lilliputian on the table of a giant.

What the hell? Sudden light-headedness insisted he was in danger of hyperventilating. He shoved his one hand over his mouth and nose, forcing himself to breath slowly. *Focus,* a tiny part of his brain insisted. *Figure this out. Nothing can't be figured out.*

Leaving his hand to his mouth as if it might hold his body together, Orrin got shakily to his feet. As he drew up, the dome above him rose too. He took a tremulous step forward. His knees nearly buckled. The dome swayed. *What the hell is it?* With a trembling fist, Orrin stretched out his free hand. The magnetite was clutched inside it so tight that the sharp edges were in danger of cutting his palm. Pain didn't register. Only cold fear and morbid curiosity.

I need to touch it. The oily haze of air around him pulsed and shifted. Despite his dread, Orrin needed to know how thick it was. Whether there was something solid on the other side of it. Or whether, perhaps, he could walk right through, and leave the nightmare behind him. The magnetite encased in his palm felt as if it was pulling his hand toward the surface of the dome, desperate to make connection.

Until it did.

Snap!

The air became crystal clear. Orrin spun, his first thought that the dome had disappeared. He swung his head one way, then the other. He looked upward to a sky that should have been stormy.

But no – patches above him were clear blue, others were dark. *Some were red?* He looked closer. They were not the muddied patches of a landscape painting, but rather, sharply outlined sections of sky with crisp, clean edges. Sharp triangular pieces, slivers of broken, shattered shapes. *What the hell?*

One shape – *no, a slice*, of sky, was in fact deep red and bubbling as it rolled over top like thick sludge about to drip.

Orrin stared. *It looks like – like – lava,* he realised. Orrin ducked, his heart racing as it anticipated the burning hell that was about to descend onto his head. But it didn't fall. Thin lines of opaque air seemed to form the edges of the slice above. The lava rolled and belched – then simply disappeared into the smokey line surrounding the shape, leaving the clear blue sky that filled its neighbour untouched.

"Holy Mary and babby Jesus," he choked out. Orrin pushed back up to his feet. The dome encasing him was no longer the thick shimming wall of air, but instead, had become a cage of crystal-clear shards, like a glass dome shattered into a hundred shapes and sizes, all held precariously in place by the pressure of each upon the other. A crawl tightened his skin. He was barely aware of the music that still sung from his back pocket. Ivy's cello. *Le Cygne.* The notes made a chilling soundtrack to the aberration in front of his eyes.

Heart drumming, breath too fast, Orrin stepped forward to study them closer. Inside each shard, the world beyond was slightly different. Life in mosaic form. Kelimutu was still visible from the exact same vantage point in all directions. In some windows, the view was as magnificent as it should have been. But in others, an unexplainable sense of something *not quite right* made Orrin's spine tingle. He turned slowly. In other shards, the landscape was desperately, wretchedly wrong.

What have I done? Orrin's breath was jagged in his throat. An avalanche of fear was rising from his gut. Far below the path he had walked up to reach the summit, a view beyond the southern Kelimutu slopes were dominated but a sea of grey. The slow crawl of enormous machinery terraformed bare earth through a polluted lens. Behind them, megalithic columns of steel stamped in rows upon rows to the horizon beyond, suffocating every inch of land. Horrified, Orrin turned westward toward the magnetite mine he had visited only yesterday. The space it should have been was broken into multiple shards. In only one, he saw what he expected to see. It was the mine, a terraced and gaping chasm into the roots of Kelimutu. On each stepped bench that sunk lower into its belly, escalators and loaders tracked along like steel ants. Though the site was unpleasant, it was, at least, familiar. A shimmering border cut across the image diagonally. In its neighbouring shard, the scene couldn't have more different. A grassy plain, rich and luscious with vegetation. Across the land, a tightly packed herd of elephants lumbered along. *No – not elephants.* A prickle caught the back of Orrin's neck. These were like no elephants Orrin had ever seen. The beasts were massive. No less than thirteen foot high at the shoulder, and twenty-six long, sporting at least another ten feet of thick, straight tusks that jutted out like warrior spears ahead of them. Sharply sloping backs fell away from high shoulders topped by a crown of bulbous domed heads. They were not the animals Orrin had seen many times in zoos or on the Discovery channel. They looked – strangely – *prehistoric.*

With a start, Orrin realised he could also see people. In the shard adjacent to the *not*-elephants, a dozen or so humans were striding across the grassy landscape. He almost called out to them, before realising what a futile thing it would be to do. They were much too far away to hear and as he stared, he realised that they, like the not-elephants, also looked a little *wrong.* They were tall and straight backed, but naked. Tan-skinned with slightly misshapen skulls. Even at such a distance, Orrin could see they were not entirely human. They seemed to be carrying something, and as the groups approached the place where the prehistoric *not-elephants* were travelling toward them, Orrin fully expected an altercation. But no, each group simply disappeared into the hazy edges of the shard it occupied. Neither group emerged from the other shard, and after a moment, both shards were empty.

What does that mean? Orrin pushed through his fear, searching for answers.

"It's a different earth," he whispered to himself. "Every one of these is different." His brain struggled to make sense of what he was seeing. *Those creatures looked prehistoric. That ruined earth looked human made.* He swung back to the terraforming dystopia to the south. Twisted again, finding the lava above his head. It was still rolling, deep red and seething within the confines of its invisible walls. But no single drop of it violated the edges. It's another earth. One where Kelimutu has erupted. He swung back to the empty field where the *not-elephants* had never emerged to meet the *not-humans. Are these realities where modern humans didn't exist? A Kelimutu that was still occupied by the prehistoric creatures that had evolved there hundreds of thousands of years before? What am I seeing?* Orrin considered Ivy's Time Shift. He *knew* she had been thrown back 50,000 years in time. He *knew* that she had fundamentally changed their shared earth by doing so.

The earth had become something it never was. Or perhaps, life on earth had become something it *could have been*, if the strings of evolution had been pulled differently.

A new thought came unbidden to Orrin's mind. Is this simply – life *as it is?* Different versions of the same earth, each affected by different evolutionary pressures over the course of time? Had each version subjected to tiny variations in its foundations and environment that snowballed into fundamental transformations over time for the landscape and animals that inhabited it?

Is each one of these versions of earth coexisting right now? Orrin wondered. *A multi-verse, as it were?* He couldn't deny it was possible. Not after all that had happened since Ivy had disappeared. As Ivy had changed the past, Orrin's own future had been thrown into a new and terrifying dystopia. Was he, in fact, simply living now, in a different version of the earth, flicked over by Ivy's interference, like a radio channel switched to a different song? Or were these windows into Kelimutu showing him different times in prehistory? *The future of the volcano?* he wondered. *The past?* Or do I see only Kelimutu at this very moment, each version warped under the mutations and events that *might have been.*

Orrin looked around. There were too many windows to see through at once. Too many variations to process.

Beside him, the icy blue lake of *Tiwu Nuwa Muri Koo Fai* filled a dozen shards. In some, the water rippled with secrets beneath the pale surface. In others, it flatlined bloody red. Still others swirled deep marine green. In all shards, a haze of volcanic gas hung above the water. Different versions of the same place.

Orrin lifted his gaze to a prism of faultless blue sky that hung above his head in sharp angles. It was stunning – but not empty. Tiny balls of silver zipped across one of the shards, sunlight reflecting in blinding white spots. In the shard beside it, there was no sky at all. Instead – it was liquid. The weight of an ocean seemed to be held in check by the thin floor of its triangular shard. A groan came from inside of it. Shadow fell upon Orrin's face as the water turned dark. A monstrous creature was moving through, inch by inch. Orrin instinctively ducked again, but there was nowhere to hide. The beast drifted past in an endless bulk and Orrin's eyes grew painfully dry as he stared transfixed. Rows of razor-sharp teeth were encased in a primordial crocodilian head. A gargantuan body followed, too long, too terrifying to find a name for. Tiny scales glittered like black diamonds. Orrin cowered as the creature passed above him, propelled by slow paddled fins, each the length of a man. Then it disappeared, *vanished*, into the thin hazy line that separated one shard from the next, leaving the adjoining ocean empty, a clear sky beside that, and Orrin's heart pounding in his mouth.

The ocean is above me. Orrin looked through a different shard. Within it, as with most of them, Kelimutu still stood strong and ancient, 1600 meters above sea level. He turned back to the groaning ocean above him. *Perhaps, in that version of the earth, the sea level kept rising? That prehistoric* whatever-the-hell-it-was *could be the dominant form of life?* The thought that there could be more of them, or other equally horrifying reptiles in the ocean above him, sent a chill through his spine. *Not a version of Earth I ever want to be in,* he decided. *How the hell do I get out of this?*

He turned slowly. *Le Cygne* turned with him. The haunting notes of Ivy's cello began to stutter. The failing music though, didn't register in his mind.

Orrin's eyes scoured the mosaic ahead. Several shards showed a blackened, smoking earth with rivulets of red lava oozing down their crevices. Kelimutu was burning. Others were smothered in dense jungle. Another flashed with midday lightning storms. In the distance, the coastline of the Savu Sea was visible through some of the lower shards – at a far closer distance than Orrin knew it should touch.

I have to find a way out.

A movement in his peripheral vision caught Orrin's attention. He turned slowly. A shard behind him – so small he hadn't noticed it, was staring back at him. *No, not the window itself, but a pair of eyes within it.* Orrin stepped closer, transfixed by the eyes. Deep brown eyes, framed by a petite black face with long, fine hair neatly parted down the middle of her head. He knew those eyes.

"Kyah!" A strangled cry of joy caught in his throat. "Is that you?" He strained to see past the eyes into the remainder of the shard, but the bonobo was too close, blocking the view with her body. "It's me, Orrin!" The bonobo hooted softly, narrowing her eyes as if trying to understand where the man had suddenly appeared from. He imagined that from her perspective, he was partially obscured in some way. Kyah shuffled back a little, and brought her hands together, one on top of the other near her chest, moving them up and down twice. Orrin recognised the gesture. Ivy had begun teaching him a few signs over coffee, in anticipation of his seeing Kyah again. "That's right!" He cried out. Orrin's heart felt like it might burst with excitement. *"Friend!"* He repeated the gesture back at her, thrilled she still knew him. "I'm Ivy's friend, remember!" He tried to see past her again with no luck. "Is she there?" Orrin begged. "Is she with you?" His voice cracked in desperation. Could it simply be as easy as reaching in and pulling Ivy out of there? Was that even possible? Could he drag her back into his own world from the other side? With a surge of adrenaline, Orrin reached out his hand, closer to Kyah's face. He paused mid-reach. The thrum of rushing blood inside his ears gave him pause. *Is it dangerous? Will it hurt?* Until now, Orrin hadn't touched the inside surface of his prison. He took a deep breath, trying not to think of the repercussions. Kyah's head shifted slightly, and Orrin realised that Ivy's cello was still singing from his back pocket. The melody was stuttering more frequently now. For an infinitesimal moment, Orrin was aware of it – the battery on his mobile was running out, he realised. He wondered if Kyah could hear the music too, beyond the veil of alternate worlds. *Is that what had caught her attention? The music?* But his errant thought was lost as a spoken word stole his attention.

"Kyah?" a soft voice called. Before Orrin could touch the shard, Kyah turned away. Something was tugging her back, and as she followed, knuckle-walking across the dirt, more of her world within the shard became visible. She was right there, on the top of Kelimutu, just as he was. But there was no concrete monument on her side. No tourist signs or steel fencing. Just rock and dirt, shrubbery and – *hobbits.* Orrin froze. He'd almost forgotten where Kyah really was. What world she was living in. It was a child who was tugging Kyah by the hand, a tiny hobbit boy. Barely two feet tall, infantile in size, but Orrin had seen his face as he turned away. He had self-awareness and intelligence. If the boy saw Orrin in the fissure of exposed shard, he didn't acknowledge it, but instead gently tugged Kyah away. Behind her, a small group of children played, oblivious to Kyah's distraction. The hobbit children were dragging their fingers through loose dirt to leave shapes and symbols in the dust. *She's teaching them,* Orrin realised. Kyah settled the tiny boy back with his friends, crouching beside him. She gently brushed his hair from his face, then lifted her wrist and presented the back of her long hand to the little boy's lips. The boy said something to her, and Kyah hooted softly then stood up.

An uneasy feeling settled inside him. Orrin's elation at finding Kyah drained away. *I can't go in there,* Orrin realised. *I'll find Ivy, I know it. But then I'll be stuck in there with her. I'll be stuck 50,000 years in the past with no hope of helping either of us get home. Home –* the very thought of it made Orrin's stomach churn. *And this isn't her home either.* Orrin cast his eyes over the shimmering threads that intersected the web of different worlds. Was one of these worlds home? Their real home? There was no way of knowing. He thought of Eli, working down at the magnetite mine that had gored a raw wound in the earth. Of Phil, arrested at Melbourne University for stealing laboratory equipment to reverse the Time Shift. Liam facing assault charges for trying to protect Indah and her baby from being taken by Nerov.

His dread was growing. Orrin blanched as he recalled the way hobbits were mistreated in the world he was stuck in. Abused, sold as pets and pharmaceutical test subjects. Their homelands ripped and ruined. Their connection to nature aborted at the hands of the ever-dominant species on planet Earth. *Homo sapiens. If I bring Ivy back to this world as it is, it will break her. She doesn't belong here any more than I do. She doesn't even exist in this version of the world. I can't bring her back here.* Devastation caught Orrin by surprise. His eyes filled with angry tears. *But she's there, she's right there! I know it. And I can't do anything about it.*

Kyah was peering in at him again, her long, graceful arms held up to her chest. With one swift movement, her curled fingers moved from her shoulder toward him, tracing the shape of a hill, her eyebrows raised in a question. *Home?*

Orrin's heart sank. He was drowning.

No. He signed. His fist moved downwards as he shook his head, then copied her sign back to her. *No. Home.*

"Not yet." Orrin pleaded for forgiveness. "I'm so sorry, Kyah. You just have to look after her for me for a bit longer. I can't bring you home yet."

Kyah simply looked at him, an unfathomable expression in her eyes.

"Soon, I promise."

Kyah turned and shifted to the side, glancing behind her to the huddle of hobbit children drawing in the dirt. As the bonobo turned back to Orrin there was a shift in her mood. Her eyes narrowed. *No. Home.* Kyah's voice rose in a shrill bark. Her fists drew up again. The message was clear.

Friend. Go. Her long fingers flicked him away. *Go. Home.* Every sign felt like a punch to the gut. Kyah swung her hand forward again, palm out. *Go.*

With a final bark, she turned her back on him, and loped away.

Orrin's mouth fell open. The weight of her dismissal was crushing. He stared after her, regretting his decision more than any he had ever made in his life.

"Kyah!" He called. The terror that she might not even want to come home made his blood run cold. Would Ivy leave her best friend if the bonobo refused to return? A gnawing doubt crept into his veins. *Surely she would. Wouldn't she? What the hell did I just do? I should have brought them both back straight away. Broken world be damned.* But the truth of how Ivy would break at seeing the fate of these people couldn't be denied. *Ivy could never accept that reality, especially knowing that her own actions led to it. And she'd be stuck here forever.*

"Please, Kyah!" Orrin tried once more, but the thin shard that Kyah had disappeared within was flicking and stuttering. He snapped to his senses. "I'm losing them," he whispered to himself. He stepped back, eyes frantic. The dome around him was losing form, the clear lens into each world had become oily and hazy. The border lines blurred. Orrin grabbed at his back pocket. The

battery of his mobile phone had dropped to one percent. The music stuttered. He tapped it hard as his mind grappled at the causation he had been overlooking. "It's the music!" Orrin panted. He threw his head back and shouted into the air around him. "It's the music!"

But it was too late. As his mobile screen blacked out, Ivy's cello fell silent. The shimmering dome around him disappeared. The sky was once again overcast and damp. Fat drops of rain confirmed his return to reality. Orrin was stood alone on the peak of Kelimutu, his feet solid on the concrete monument, surrounded by steel fencing and tourist signs. The three crater lakes churned within their mesmerising, coloured waters.

And Ivy was still trapped fifty thousand years in the past.

He unrolled his fingers to find a thin line of blood in his palm. The chunk of magnetite that Eli had given him had left a cut. With a heave of emotion, Orrin collapsed to the ground. She had been *so close.*

"I am done with this place!" Orrin threw his phone to the ground, instantly regretting it. He crawled forward to pick it up, cursing as his fingers traced the cracked screen. He slumped back against the monument letting the rain wash him away. Hopelessness devoured him. Orrin clawed at the edges of it, fighting back against its gravity.

"No!" He shook his head violently, eyes squeezed shut as he tried to force logic into the misery within his mind. He began to babble, the words a rush of comfort to fill the void inside. "I just need – I need her amulet. That's all. I need to get myself home. Back to the lab. I can do this properly – I'll – I'll recreate the parameters of the original experiment in the lab, so that they're identical to the ones she left under. Yes! That's what I have to do! I'll use the music – she said the hobbits were singing when she Fell, so there's something about music that's causing the Time Shift. Something that reacts with the moscovium in the magnetite." Tiny pieces of puzzle fell into place inside his mind, filling the empty space. "This is what happened the night I heard her in my lab – her song was playing then! And again now – the music triggered it somehow. I can figure this out. I can. *I can.*" The weight of his convictions lifted Orrin to his feet. He looked around. Not a soul was in sight. "Just me," he scoffed, breath heavy and a wry smile creeping back to his face, "a madman arguing with himself on the top of a mountain." Orrin gripped his cracked mobile in one hand, the palm-sized black chunk of magnetite in the other. "I need to get her back to *our* time! God-damn-it! I have to do this!"

With one last look at the empty space where Kyah sat in another world, Orrin turned his back and began to race down the trail toward the road.

It was a ten-hour drive back to Labuan Bajo. Another hour in the air from Komodo Airport to Denpasar International in Bali, then a six-hour flight home to Melbourne, Australia.

There was no time to lose.

PART III
SURVIVAL

CHAPTER 29

IVY

"*I* do not know what came over me." Ivy picked at the bowl of boiled roots in front of her. She licked her fingers, but her appetite was gone. Placing the bowl on the ground, she buried her face in her hands. "I felt him out there, Shahn." Ivy found the eyes of her friend. Though she didn't deserve a sympathetic ear from Xiou's mate, as always, she found one. Shahn listened quietly, one hand rubbing her pregnant belly, the other nudging Ivy's bowl gently toward her again, encouraging her to eat. "It felt as if Orrin was so close to me, I might have reached out to touch him."

"He is worlds away, Hiranah," Shahn said. "And I'm sorry for it."

"I know." Ivy picked out a morsel for Shahn's sake and ate it. The other woman gave a small nod. Ever since Ivy had returned, Shahn had been trying to feed her up. "Xiou does not trust me anymore," Ivy said. "As soon as I began to fall into that – whatever it was – I tried to fight it, I really did. I knew I had made a mistake. Xiou didn't let me explain–" After he had pulled Ivy out of the vortex the night before, Xiou had disappeared into the forest. Though she assured Ivy that Xiou would return when he had time to calm down, Shahn's anxious glances toward the west forest were telling. She was worried for him.

"He will listen when he is ready," Shahn reassured them both. She shifted, and winced. Her baby was overdue. "He carries a great burden, as our new leader. Xiou needs some time to mourn the loss of his father."

"Also my fault," Ivy added. "I have betrayed him twice within days."

"You brought us home," Shahn said. "And gave us hope."

Hope. Ivy sighed. Hope wasn't good enough. These people needed more than hope. They needed protection. They needed a future. Xiou's tribe and the orphans had arrived at Kelimutu, but no others had returned. It felt a hopeless case. If she wanted to secure their survival before the full moon, Ivy knew she needed more people. She refused to leave until she had exhausted every option she had left to save them.

I only have two days left. I need to use every minute.

Ivy got to her feet. "When Xiou returns, tell him I'm sorry but that I'm not giving up yet. I'll be back before the full moon. He knows what to do." She took a few steps to retrieve the new spear Kora had made for her. It was strong and sharp and perfectly balanced to her height. A surge of confidence swept Ivy as she held it.

"You can not go out searching again alone!" Shahn pushed to her feet with a groan. "There are Karathah hunters in the forests below. Guntah and Kora have seen them."

Ivy turned and gave a soft hoot call. Kyah looked up from where she was playing with the children in the dirt.

Come with me? Ivy signed to the bonobo. *To the forest.*

Kyah turned back to the little boy who had become her shadow. She pulled him in for a hug, then gently brushed Trahg's hair back from his face. Kyah lifted her wrist and presented the back of her long hand to the little boy's lips. Trahg kissed it, then enthusiastically rubbed his forehead against that of his bonobo friend. No two creatures could have been closer.

"She is devoted to him," Shahn observed. "And as good a mother as I am."

"Kyah?" Ivy called again, her stomach tightening. *You stay here,* she signed. *I'll be back soon.*

Looking between Ivy and Trahg, Kyah gave a soft hoot, then turned and knuckle-walked to Ivy.

Come, Kyah signed. *Trees.*

The knot in Ivy's stomach lessened. She wouldn't have to go alone, after all. She tried to ignore the twinge of guilt.

"Alright." Ivy held out her arms. Kyah climbed into them. "We're going to find more of your people, Shahn." She announced decisively. "We only have two days before the full moon. I know there are more tribes out there. I intend to find them – no matter what."

"You cannot go alone, Hiranah," Shahn pleaded. "Wait for Xiou, he will be back soon, I am sure of it. Or take Kora or Setian with you."

"No." Ivy straightened her back. "I have risked too many lives already. This is something I must do myself."

Ivy stared up at the night sky. She sat on a sharp outcrop at the southern foot of Kelimutu. Hours had passed searching ridge over valley until her feet were cut and bleeding, and Kyah had insisted on nesting for the night. The bonobo had built a soft bed in the trees above her, but despite exhaustion, Ivy couldn't sleep. The undercurrent of new danger was too strong to ignore. Mother Earth had grumbled and shifted beneath her feet all day. To the north, the belching cracks and roll of an erupting volcano were unmistakable. Another heavy cloud of ash arrived, darkening the sky for hours so that it felt like night. Earlier, Ivy and Kyah had paused on an outcrop to watch a herd of stegodon cross the plains below. Their sensitive footpads had felt the threat underfoot long before it sounded. The herd had tried to outrun the ash, but fine powder had coated their long rust-coloured hair into black shadow before Ivy had lost sight of them. Flores was about to erupt.

Fifty thousand years.

Ivy knew a geological guillotine was about to drop on the island. Every species that had evolved here was living on the knife-edge of this major extinction event. She had seen it written in the stratigraphy. The inevitability of what would come was terrifying. Ivy had dusted this volcanic ash off ancient bones in her laboratory. She stared, long after the stegodon herd had disappeared from view. They were not going to survive. And neither should the species she was determined to save.

Eventually, a strong south-easterly wind had ushered the smoke and ash away, opening a tiny window to the stars.

"I feel you," Ivy whispered toward the pinpricks of light far above. "I feel you, Orrin. Up there in the stars." The pull of him made her bones ache. "A satellite, circling me from a world away." Ivy closed her eyes, filling up with memories. "I'm coming home soon. I promise."

CHAPTER 30

ORRIN

*O*rrin rubbed his eyes under his glasses as the cab zipped across the Melbourne overpass, leaving the airport behind. Eli was dozing in the back seat, his head rolling gently with each turn of the car.

He glanced at his watch. *11pm.*

"Busy night?" Orrin asked the driver. Polite habit bid him speak, but the answer didn't matter. His thoughts were firmly on the obstacles still ahead of him.

"Just the usual," the driver said, eyeing Eli through the rear-vision mirror. "Long flight?"

"It's been a long few days," Orrin sighed.

After he had returned from the peak of Kelimutu, Orrin had thrown every ounce of energy into getting home. A massive electrical storm had thrown every bolt of lightning into preventing it. For another 24 hours they waited it out while Eli rescheduled their flights, frustration burning a trail in the carpet under Orrin's feet. Finally, they jumped into Arif's four-wheel-drive, and made the ten-hour drive back to Labuan Bajo in eight and a half. After a restless night in East Nusa Tengarra, they flew from

Komodo airport to Denpasar, and began the six-hour flight back to Melbourne.

Flight delays had cost them more hours, and now as the clock sped toward midnight, Orrin carried the weight of his looming deadline like a grenade in his pocket.

In twenty-five hours, the full moon would peak, and his opportunity to bring Ivy back would disappear.

"Where in Port Melbourne are you heading?" The taxi driver asked. Orrin shot a look back at Eli. He hadn't thought to get his address. *Never mind. After everything I've put him through, the least I can offer is my spare room for the night.*

"25 Beach Street," Orrin replied.

"Sure thing," the cab driver said as he punched the address into his map. "Nice night, anyhow," he added noncommittally, then settled into this seat, eyes fixed firmly on the road.

"Yeah." Orrin looked out the window as headlights streamed past. Against the dark, a brilliant *aurora australis* shimmered across the sky. Its misplaced beauty sent a shiver down his spine.

*

"Take the couch for now," Orrin offered, rattling his keys into the door of his apartment. "I've got a spare room, but I'll need a few minutes to dump all the laundry off to find the bed underneath though." He pushed through the door of his apartment, flicking on lights as he went. It felt like he'd been gone a year, not less than a week. Behind him, Eli murmured something that sounded like thanks.

"Urgh," a familiar voice groaned, "someone turned on the ugly lights!"

"What on earth are you doing here?" Orrin dropped his backpack, astonished to see Phil's face staring blearily up at him from his own couch.

"Well, that's a fine thank you for all my hard work," Phil grunted back. "I'm here to save your arse, of course."

"We all are," a woman's voice added. Jayne appeared in the doorway at the other end of the lounge room. "I made up your spare bed."

"And didn't invite me into it," Phil pouted.

"I picked the lesser of three evils," Jayne rolled her eyes. Dimi appeared beside her wearing flannelette pyjamas.

"Borrowed your pj's mate," he grinned. "Hope you don't mind." He stepped past Jayne toward Eli, wrapping his arms around him. "I think that was the longest six days of my life."

"You don't know the half of it," Eli said, returning his hug. Orrin and Eli had decided not to forewarn the others of what they had discovered in the open-pit mines of Kelimutu. Sending the information via message was too risky and Orrin wasn't convinced his mobile phone hadn't been tapped by Cassandra. Radio silence had left his friends in the dark about when exactly they would return.

"Cutting it fine, O," Dimi said, glancing up at the clock.

"What's going on?" A man with a huge mop of curly hair appeared behind Jayne. "Oh damn, I guess you'll want your bedroom back then?"

"Liam?" Orrin wasn't sure whether he was dreaming. "The last time I saw you, you were getting dragged out of the behavioural research lab by Nerov's security guards."

"Bastards," Liam muttered. "Worth it though."

"And a week before that you nearly broke my nose."

"We got off to a bad start, I'll admit–"

"And now you're sleeping in my bed?"

"Far more comfortable than a jail cell."

"I can vouch for that," Phil added.

"Nice apartment you've got here by the way," Liam said, giving an appreciative whistle. "*Fancy.* Clearly I'm in the wrong department."

"None of us are in any department anymore are we," Phil sighed. "Sacked. Except for Jayne here, keeping her nose clean."

"Someone's got to keep bailing you all out of jail," Jayne said. "And I have been kicked out of my lab, *unofficially*. Besides, my nose won't be clean for much longer, will it?"

"True enough," Phil said.

"Right," Orrin looked from one unexpected house guest to another. "Okay. Well, as much as I appreciate your company – I still don't know why you've taken over my house."

Dimi dropped Eli's hand and moved to the kitchen, flicking on the kettle. "I'm making coffee," he said. "We've got a lot to figure out. It's going to be a long night."

The loudest groan came from Phil, who flopped back down onto the couch.

*

"You're sure it's *all* Moscovium?" Dimi's face was ashen.

"Positive." Eli put down his coffee cup and squeezed Dimi's hand.

"I just don't understand," Jayne said, running her hands through her short blonde hair. "How is this *Mosco-what-ee-um* making such a dramatic impact on the environment? What's in it? Is it radioactive or something?"

"Worse," Phil replied. "It's a complete wild card. Moscovium has never been discovered in a stable form before now. It's been created in a lab as an unstable element a few times, but it always decayed within milliseconds. The fact that we've got so much of this, dug up and exposed on the surface explains why the Earth's magnetic fields have gone to the dogs. They've dug up Pandora's Box over there."

"Quit the theatrics," Jayne growled at him. "And just tell me why this stuff is so bad."

"It's bad because of its ability to distort gravitational waves,"

Dimi cut in. "We only ever guessed at what it could do, but what we're seeing seems to justify our hypothesis. Theoretically, there are enough neutrons and protons within its nucleus to create an additional gravity wave that could extend beyond the perimeter of its own atomic structure. To put it simply – the properties of this wave, can push past its own atomic walls and amplify into anything outside of it. For example, past the amulet into the hand that holds it. If you got it in quantities large enough – then beyond the earth surface into the magnetosphere above."

"Which explains all the fluctuations and solar flares we're seeing," Jayne nodded.

"Right," Orrin said. "But when you're dealing with a localised amount contained in a tightly bound crystalline structure like the magnetite in Ivy's amulet, the amplification can be triggered by the resonant frequency of the crystals that bind it. So with Ivy's amulet–" Orrin paused looking around. Phil reached in his pocket and tossed the black stone to Orrin, who caught it one hand, "the gravity wave amplified to create a space-time distortion. A tiny black hole, if you will. Enough to drag any matter that's attached to it, like *Ivy*, inside."

"Which explains the time-travel," Jayne nodded, her mind mulling over the science. She cast a dubious look at the stone in Orrin's hand. "So why isn't it reacting right now?"

"Because the resonant frequency of the crystals need to be triggered to begin the amplification of the gravitational waves it produces." Phil cut in.

Jayne raised an eyebrow. "And again in English?"

"It was triggered by music," Orrin said. The others all looked to him, surprised. "But not just any music." Orrin looked at Phil. "While you've been testing in the lab, did you come up with any specific frequencies that react strongly to the stone?"

"Yeah," Phil said. "At least a dozen. All in the range between 100 Hertz and 17 KiloHertz. But the trouble is that none of them vibrate strongly enough to drive the reaction. There's still something missing."

"Did you try them all together?" Orrin bounced on his toes. "When I was at the peak of Kelimutu, right between the three volcanic lakes, the most incredible thing happened." He looked to Eli, who nodded in encouragement. Orrin filled the others in on his experience in the dome of shards, and the multi-faceted versions of reality he had seen. They all listened, transfixed, as he described his encounter with Kyah, and how he was sure that Ivy had been somewhere in that world.

"Could you have stepped into another time, do you think?" Phil asked, his demeanour unusually subdued.

"I think I could have. But then I'd never have been able to fix the world we're currently in. Or get Ivy out of hers."

"What about the bonobo?" Liam asked. "You said she was originally from the uni lab right, one of our observation animals that Ivy had with her when she disappeared? Well, Flores isn't the native habitat for her species. What sort of shape was she in? Why didn't you pull her out?"

Orrin held up his hands. "She looked fine, Liam. And she refused to come. In fact, she told me to get lost in no uncertain terms. When she found out I wasn't going to take her and Ivy home right then, she signed for me to go home. Besides, this reality isn't the one she belongs in, any more than where she is right now. What would they do to her back in Nerov's lab?"

Liam scowled. "Fair call."

Orrin stood up and began to pace. He needed to keep his body moving if his brain was going to stay sharp. "My point is, I had Ivy's cello music playing on my phone as this all happened. You know the one, Le Cygne–" He reached for the phone in his pocket and was met with a chorus of hands in the air.

"We know it–"

"Not again–"

"If you play that song again I'll shut your head in a door," Phil warned.

"Alright," Orrin tried to stifle his laugh. He shoved the mobile back in his pocket. "Well, when Ivy's music stopped playing, that's when the dome collapsed. All the other worlds disappeared, and I was right back where I started. Alone on the top of the mountain."

"So, you're saying the resonant frequency that triggers the Moscovium is in the music?" Dimi asked.

"I'm saying that the *frequencies* that react with the element are in the music. There's more than one. Think of it this way, if you play any of the frequencies on their own, the amulet reacts, but only in a short, unsustained capacity. But by producing multiple frequencies at once you can create a sustained and increasing charge in the amulet, giving it the opportunity to amplify."

"You've lost me," Liam frowned. "Not a physicist."

"Okay," Orrin thought for a moment. "Think of it like a combination lock. There are thousands of potential numbers, but only a few of them, in a very specific combination, are going to open the door, right? So, to set off our reaction, every frequency needs to be be sustained individually for long enough and in the right combination that the reaction reaches critical mass and can sustain itself. This essentially builds up the amplification that has the potential to set off the time shift. Then lightning from the Telsa Coil in my lab hit the amulet and excited the electrons in the oxygen around it into an ionised state to multiply the reaction further, and – *BAM! Amulet unlocked.*"

"Right. So, we just play that thing some music and pop it near a Tesla coil, and it sucks us back to the Stone Age?" Jayne asked.

"Not quite," Orrin said, "the resonant frequencies are just the final step. We need the lightning, and we need those energy fields at full strength for this to work. That's midnight tomorrow. Dimi has already identified that the electromagnetic fields over the university are starting to peak again."

Dimi got to his feet. "And not just over the uni, either. Tomorrow night, electromagnetic fields around the world will hit an all-time high. We've got hot spots of reversed polarity in all sorts of weird co-ordinates, and we still can't find a common link between them."

"Dale did," Jayne cut in.

"Dale did what?" Dimi asked. "Dale as in–" he shot an awkward look at Orrin, "the guy that sold you out to Cassandra?"

"That's the one," Orrin said. The memory left a sour taste in his mouth. It had been weeks since he'd last seen his lab tech after their altercation at the university. Guilt sat heavy in his gut over the way things had ended between them.

"Dale found a common link between all of the hot spots of reversed polarity, remember?" Jayne pushed. "They're all archae-ological sites."

"That's right!" Phil said. "So, he wasn't just a backstabbing piece of crap after all." Orrin shot Phil a dirty look. "Someone had to say it–" Phil shrugged.

"They were all sites where some important aspect of human evolution took place," Jayne continued. She looked thoughtful. "You know, maybe if the conditions were right, someone might use these locations to travel through time and influence human prehistory?" She looked around. "Maybe someone already has?"

"Ivy has." Phil rolled his eyes, "and look at the mess we're in now."

"I mean someone else, obviously," Jayne rolled her eyes. "*In the past*, you twit. I mean, how do we know someone hasn't done this before? Influenced human evolution in ways we don't realise by going into these specific locations and precipitating a major change in the development of our civilisation at pivotal moments in human history – *creating* these sites of archaeological signifi-cance that we then uncover thousands of years later – you know what I mean?"

For a few long moments, there was silence. They all stared at her.

Then Phil spat out a laugh. "Bloody hell. As if we don't have enough to worry about!"

Jayne scowled and tried to swipe him across the lounge.

"Right. Well... fair point, Jayne." Dimi stepped in between them. "But for now, should we focus on one problem at a time? The electro-magnetic fields at all of these points are about to hit an all-time high, but the strongest of them are at the uni and above Kelimutu volcano in Flores. The exposed magnetite on the ground would account for that. But just as strong, are the fields drawing down toward us from the Clavious crater on the moon. As the full moon passes over those co-ordinates, those surges of energy – from the Earth and the moon – are reaching for each other like, like – like a pair of star-crossed lovers. Massive, elongated energy fields reaching through space toward each other. Honestly, I've never seen anything like it."

"What did you say?" Eli looked up, his voice uncharacteristically sharp.

"I said I've never seen anything like it," Dimi said, surprised.

"No, the other thing – about the lovers." Eli's brow was furrowed in a way that suggested his mind was working overtime. "You said the electromagnetic fields on the earth in Kelimutu and Melbourne and then the ones coming from the Clavious crater on the moon are reaching for each other – *like lovers.*"

"Well, it's just an analogy–"

"But you're absolutely right," Eli mumbled. "They *are* lovers, or at least – very, very old friends. I think I know where the Moscovium came from." He got to his feet, placing his empty coffee cup on the bench. He gave Dimi a significant look. "Theia."

"You think?" Dimi said. Everyone's attention turned to Eli.

"How else? It's embedded in the mantle. Both bodies–"

Dimi's mouth fell open. "You know what? I think you're right–"

"Excuse me?" Liam raised an eyebrow. "Anyone else not following this?"

"Who's Theia?" Jayne asked.

"Not who, *what*," Eli said, turning to her. Liam perched on the edge of Jayne's chair, listening closely. "Theia is only the most incredible story you've never heard. She's the reason I became a geologist."

"Another stone unturned," Dimi smiled. "Damn, I love learning new things about you."

Eli grinned, brushing him off. "You'll love this story, Jayne. Okay, imagine this." Dimi turned to face the group sitting around the lounge room. Behind him, a wall of glass windows overlooked the inky water of Port Phillip Bay. Shimmering ribbons of an aurora danced through the night sky above. "Four and a half billion years ago," Eli began, "out of the vast nothing, a comet is spinning slowly on an invisible axis as it hurtles through space. Its celestial body is all grainy silicones and blackest carbon – a primordial collection of the unused elements of the Solar System. And maybe," he shot a look at Dimi, "hidden in its core, is an alien metal, in hibernation. *Moscovium*."

Eli took a breath, watching their intrigued faces as he continued. "So, this comet spins for millennia, round and round it goes, never slowing down. As it passes the blistering heat of the sun, frozen gases below its surface explode like nuclear missiles, throwing off chunks of dust and gas. Crusted ice clings to its back and it leaves a trail of frozen debris in its wake." Eli's voice rose and fell hypnotically. "Solar ultraviolet light tear apart the gas molecules, charging and mutating them as it flies." His arms stretched out. "And millions of kilometres behind the comet, the ion tail grows longer and longer, fluorescing like a glittering trail between worlds."

"Wow," Jayne breathed. Her eyes were trained on Eli's face as he spoke. Every word captivated his audience. Dimi couldn't look away.

"So, the comet cycles endlessly through space," Eli said, his voice softening, "growing smaller and smaller as it decays under the sun's radiation until it's nothing but a fragile old rock spinning through the sky. There are new comets now, and new worlds growing around it. On its final orbit, it sails and sails, until – *bang!*" Eli clapped his hand together, and his audience jolted in their seats. "With a shattering crash lost to the voids of space, the ancient comet smashes into an even bigger celestial goddess. *Theia.*"

"Brilliant," Liam whispered. "They collided."

"Exactly," Eli said. "And the alien element that was buried within that old comet is suddenly given a new direction and purpose. For millennia the new larger comet, Theia, keeps consuming as she glides through space, growing stronger, mightier, expanding with each new conquest of iron and elemental rock. She grows. *Enormous.* Gravity smoothes and rounds her and she sails supreme." Eli held up his hands in surrender. "But she gets greedy. Theia passes too close to a larger planet and loses stability. Its gravitational field is irresistible. In silent devastation, the goddess collides – *smash!* – and is consumed by infant Earth."

"Earth?" Liam repeated, blinking. "Theia collided with *our* Earth?"

"Theia not only collided with Earth," Eli corrected him, "Theia *created* the Earth as we know it."

"And?" Jayne prodded.

"And their bodies shatter together in a *monumental* fusion of metal and gas." Eli threw out his arms. "The Earth's new mantle is thrown out into space as dust. Slivers of Moscovium rain across the planet, seeded by the ancient comet. They fuse wherever they fall, clawing deep into the rocks. And their magnetic energy is absorbed into the neighbouring metals, creating small pockets of reversed polarity – this is what we're seeing now! All of these anomalies that tie into those archaeological sites." Eli's eyes glittered like the glass window behind him. "Theia – as she once was – has been torn apart, her iron heart sucked into our Earth's core, her rocky flesh consumed. And now – Planet Earth emerges whole and massive in a sea of molten lava."

"But what about–" Liam began, but Eli held up a finger.

"The moon?" He anticipated. "The collision with Theia is how our moon was created as well. All that space dust – the catastrophic cloud of debris sent orbiting far above Earth during the collision – well, it spins and coalesces over millions of years to form a bright new moon that orbits the Earth. Molten energy fuses through it creating an ocean of magma. The elemental Moscovium spreads deep into its face. Nine hundred million years pass by. The magma moon finally crystallises into what we see in the night sky above us. *Our moon.*"

Eli paused, his dark eyes seeing something no-one else in the room could see as he turned away to stare out at the near-full moon through the wall of glass behind him. "And there she is, filled with the same alien metal that Theia brought to the earth four and a half billion years ago. The same electromagnetic potential. All bound up so tightly in crystalline magnetite that it stayed stable. Until now."

"So, what changed?" Jayne asked breathlessly. "Why is it unstable now?"

"Because before now," Eli explained, "the massive pool of Moscovium beneath Kelimutu was covered by the flesh of magnetic rare earth after the volcano erupted, eons ago. But now we've torn the cover away and left it exposed. Our magnetosphere is breaking down. The fragile shield between the earth and sun is being stripped. Solar flares are passing through, the likes of which we've never had to deal with before. Massive fluctuations in magnetic radiation. And when the resonant frequency of that crystalline structure was hit, and the electricity of the Tesla Coil touched the amulet and ionised the surrounding oxygen in the lab – then *bam!* The gravitational waves of the element pushed past its own atomic boundaries into the matter around it, and dragged Ivy, and anyone close to her inside." His breath was sharp with excitement. He grinned at them all. *"Singularity."* Eli finished, hitting his hand theatrically on the coffee table with a slap. "And she's gone."

"Geez, man," Liam said, finding his voice. "They need to put you on the Discovery channel."

Eli looked abashed, surprised to find himself the centre of attention. He shrugged. "I just – I really love rocks."

"Dude!" Phil stared at him, apparently too impressed for once to speak.

"I think I want to be a geologist," Jayne whispered.

Dimi had no words. His eyes sparkled and his smile couldn't have been wider. With a look on his face as if he'd just touched the moon with his own bare hands, he launched forward and planted a passionate kiss on Eli's lips.

Around them, the others hooted and catcalled in delighted applause.

"Remember, you've got a window of about three minutes to get in," Phil warned. At six o'clock, the night guard will go down to the front entrance to meet the day guard for their change-over. They'll chat for a minute while the day guard makes a coffee, then he's back doing rounds and watching the camera. You need to get in the back entrance and take the fire stairs up to the lab." Phil passed Orrin a security card and key. "I swiped the card from one of the cleaners. The key's a spare I didn't tell Chandi I had when she confiscated mine. Payback for getting me arrested."

"You were caught stealing tens of thousands of dollars of equipment," Orrin reminded him.

"*Relocating*," Phil said. "And in two days when I go to court, I'll tell them where it all is – if I remember any of this. I'm really hoping you'll put the world to rights and none of this will ever have happened though. I'm already on thin ice – I'm pretty sure my dad will pull my trust fund when he finds out what I'm about to do."

"I'll do my best," Orrin said. He lay a hand on Phil's shoulder. "Thanks boyo. I never thought I'd force you into larceny and breaking and entering for my sake. For what it's worth, I feel terrible about it."

"Well, you can save your guilt and focus on fixing this mess, because if you don't, there'll be more than stealing office equipment on my court order." Phil looked around and caught Jayne's eye. Behind them, Liam was pulling on his boots. All three of them looked exhausted but shared a nervous energy.

Orrin looked between each of his friends slowly. "What do you mean, more than stealing office equipment on your court order?" A sinking feeling hit him. "What are you all up to?"

"Don't look at me," Eli said, from behind Jayne. He shot a look at Dimi, who shrugged.

"It was Phil's idea, actually," Jayne said. "I was impressed."

"I'm just full of surprises, aren't I?" Phil winked at her.

"I'll admit you have the occasional moment of heroics," Jayne smirked. She turned her attention back to Orrin. "Liam, Phil and I are going on a little excursion today."

"What does that–"

"We're going to break into Cosmitech," Liam cut in. "We're getting Indah and Bala out of there, and any other hobbits in cages we find along the way."

"You're what!!?" Orrin was aghast. "That's kidnapping and stealing and espionage or – I don't even know what it is, but it's really bad!"

"We prefer to think of it as hostage retrieval," Phil said. "You saw the way they took her. A tranquilliser dart straight to the chest, and then stole a crying baby from her arms. It's a bloody disgrace," he growled. "It's inhumane!"

"What if you get caught?" Dimi asked. His eyes flared with concern. Eli shook his head.

"Well," Liam said, stepping forward. "Phil and I are already on the chopping block."

"And I'm willing to risk it," Jayne added.

"And to be honest," Phil said, "we're all kind of hoping Orrin will fix everything and we don't go to jail for the rest of our lives." Despite his friend's nonchalant tone, Orrin saw worry behind his eyes. "But none of us can live with the fact that she's in an experimental lab being used for God-knows-what, while we're out here feeling useless. You've got your job to do today – well, this is ours."

Orrin was speechless.

"Maybe it's not the sanest idea," Jayne admitted. "But it's a noble one." She looked at Phil and raised an eyebrow. "He can be astonishingly decent every so often."

"Why thank you," Phil took a small bow. "But honestly, we couldn't pull it off without Liam's expertise. He's got a – um, what should we call it? A *safe house* lined up. And we've blacked up the windows on his van to get there. We're masquerading as cleaning staff. Figured if we're going to be criminals, we should try and look professional about it."

"You're risking too much," Orrin frowned.

"Not as much as you are." Phil stepped forward. "You'll find everything you need stashed in your office at the lab. He handed Orrin a piece of paper scribbled with notes. "The resonant frequencies I isolated in the lab."

"Thank you." The words felt horrifically inadequate.

"It's just missing you now, mate," Phil said, "and that audio spectrum analyser that the buggers stole off me–"

"After you stole it off them–"

"Semantics." Phil shrugged.

"I forgot about that," Dimi murmured.

Phil took a deep breath and gestured to Jayne and Liam. "Come on, you two, let's hit it." He turned to Orrin. "I really hope I don't remember any of this tomorrow, mate."

Orrin's voice caught in his throat as he hugged each of them in turn. "I hope you don't either."

CHAPTER 31

NEIL

*N*eil felt a cool hand on his forehead. He blinked, forcing his eyes open against their will. Atasi was looking down at him, her face drawn and worried. She pushed a water bladder at Neil's mouth, lifting him slightly to cradle his head. He must have dozed off again. It was getting harder to stay awake. The pain was almost unbearable.

"I'm alright," he lied, struggling to sit up. Atasi gave him the strength of her arms. He sat for a moment, panting with the effort. "I don't deserve your help." Neil's skin was flushed and hot. He looked at the beautiful young woman keeping him alive. If it wasn't for her kindness, most of him would be dead. His mind, certainly. His heart might have kept beating, but for no other reason than sheer stubbornness. But not now. Neil knew that now his heartbeat because she gave him hope. Atasi gained nothing from him but friendship. She was doing the hunting. Preparing the food. Finding places to hide during the day when the heat became too much. Slowly, they had made their way to the eastern side of the Kelimutu volcano. If Charat discovered them, Atasi's punishment would be unthinkable. She could never return to her tribe while that man hunted her. And now Neil was slowing her down. Making them both all the easier to find.

Neil shivered. The sweat. The chills. They came in waves.

"All my life, I've been an arsehole, you know that?" The truth of it didn't hurt him. Only the irony stung, that Neil had realised it so late. "I didn't get it. People like you who just – *care* – and ask for nothing in return." He puffed with the effort of speaking. "I never needed anything, so I spent my life thinking it was weak, that kind of selflessness. But look at me now. I was the one who needed help in the end. Imagine that." He winced as a pain shot through his belly. His vision blurred and for a moment all Neil could do was breathe. "I could have done everything better, couldn't I?" He looked up at her. As always, Atasi was watching with quiet concern. "You and Benjamin both deserve better than what I gave you. But at least with you, I can say thank you." He offered a smile that felt more genuine than any he had ever given.

"Ben-jee-men." Atasi repeated softly. She understood that name. She had heard Neil cry it out in his sleep. She rustled through the bag that held his equipment, pulling out his phone. "Talk. Talk." Her fingers opened and closed; the gesture Neil had come up with to describe the act of conversation. "Ben-jee-men." In the past few days, Neil had focussed all his energy on recording his story on the video log of his phone. Every part of it was told now.

The energy fluctuations his team had been tracking out at The Dish in Parkes. His investigations that led to the University of Melbourne Physics Department. Ivy Carter and her chimp. The black amulet she wore. The tattered journal she carried with her. The tiny creatures she was trying to save.

His own misadventures made just as a good as story.

That he'd found himself lost in a prehistoric jungle. Searched for missing satellites. Navigated by the stars. Not all of it was impressive. *Neil had admitted his attempts to kill the red head to save himself. Admitted that he'd manipulated Charat's tribe to stay alive. Taken advantage of their superstitions. Handed Charat power and leadership that he'd never earned, to serve the alliance. Described how the red-beaded hunter had abused his status in the most heinous of ways.*

Neil described his inventions, holding them up to the camera. *The mobile battery charger. The copper lightning rod. His dagger. The clay pots.*

The way he'd run to escape Charat's escalating sociopathy.

How he'd found his own humanity on the brink of death.

There was only one story left to tell.

Neil tapped the screen with his finger. The mobile phone was dead again. "I can't do it," he said. "I'm too tired." His eyes were glassy with infection.

"Talk," Atasi insisted. Neil knew that she was trying to keep him awake. Atasi began to pull out the clay bowls and sulphur. Before Neil could stop her, she had them lined up ready to use. Achingly slowly, together, they forced his mobile screen to light up once more. Neil perched his camera in the knot of a low-lying branch. He sat in front of it. The minutes ticked by. Despite all he'd described and recorded in days past, this story felt too hard to tell. Now, Neil found that no words would come.

"Benjamin," he finally said, looking directly into the camera. He paused, breathing. "I wasn't there when you needed me. But I just – how do I explain to you something you could never under-stand? Because *you're you* and you already *know* these things. You know how to be selfless. *How to love.* Kids just do, until we teach them not to." Neil wiped the sweat and tears from his eyes. *"I didn't know.* I didn't know how to be there for you. I *wasn't* too busy to see you while you were sick. I – I was scared like a baby. I couldn't face it. I couldn't deal with the thought of losing you every time I stepped into that hospital room. And every day you were *so much braver* than I ever was. *And I'm so sorry.*"

CHAPTER 32

IVY

The screech of canopy birds woke her. Ivy found herself curled around the foot of Kyah's tree, sticks in her hair and a thick layer of ash on her pale skin. Kyah had been foraging since dawn, and was now sitting by her side, peeling apart a durian fruit. The bonobo passed one to Ivy and she tore it open with her stone knife releasing the vomit-scented odour to the air. Ivy was so used to it now she didn't think twice. She began to eat.

"There are some shadows on those ridges to the east," Ivy said between mouthfuls. "We'll go there. If I don't find anyone by midday though, we'll have to turn back." She twisted to gaze up at the mountain behind her. "It's at least three hours walk back up to the top of Kelimutu from here, and we can't risk running late. The moon will be fullest tonight, so we need to take our chances." She took her friend's hand and squeezed it with a grin. "We're going home, Kyah. We're going back home to Melbourne tonight." A thrill ran up her spine.

Home. Kyah signed. *Go. Home.*

"Yes. Home."

*

An hour later, a storm began. A sprinkle of rain through the canopy soon became a deluge that clamped Ivy's red hair against her skin like rivulets of blood. Kyah whined, holding oversized leaves over her own head as she knuckle-walked alongside, then gave up to travel faster through the slippery branches instead. Ivy waded knee deep through watery tunnels while Kyah waited diligently at the mouth of every cave they discovered. A nest of giant rats raced squealing from the dark as Ivy tripped over a writhing mass of fur in the recesses of yet another cave.

Ivy called out in the hobbit's own language trying to keep the desperation from her voice.

"Hello?"

"I am a friend, here to help you."

"Please - let me talk to you."

But there was no reply. Another cave empty, another hour lost.

"There's no one here," she called as she trudged back through the mud. "I'm coming out." Ivy's shoulders slumped in failure. She had found no more tribes. Of those that she had searched out on her journey from the west, all had refused to come to Kelimutu. It seemed that despite her best efforts, Xiou's tribe would continue to live, and die alone. There was no hope left. "It's time to go home, Ky." Holding back tears, Ivy looked around for Kyah as stepped out of the darkness into the front of the cave.

The sharp point of a spear bit her chest.

Ivy's legs froze. Her heart faltered. Her mouth fell open - but no words made it through the surge of adrenaline that rushed every inch of her veins.

The red-beaded hunter.

A cruel grin revealed teeth stained with betel juice. He stood a head taller than her, looking down with an air of weighted triumph.

"Kari-ju- gutamenu-jaja-wu." He threw his head back and

laughed. It was the most terrifying sound she had ever heard. Fingers of ice gripped Ivy's spine.

Ivy was certain he was was responsible for the cave fire that had claimed seven innocent lives, including dusty-haired little Turi, only three years old. He had poisoned the hobbit's water-hole with the deadly seeds of the Rosary Pea, inflicting an agonising Swift Death upon Xiou's hunters, as their insides bled out and organs failed.

One month ago, this man had chased Ivy through the jungle with murderous intent. Slaughtered her new family on the stegodon plains. He had plunged a knife into her thigh and torn it open like soft butter. Less than a week past, Ivy had seen him with the severed heads of *Homo floresiensis* people slung over his shoulder, as if they were nothing more than a string of fish caught in the river.

"Ey-vee." The man's hot breath seemed to curl around her name. His eyes danced with glee.

How does he know my name? The insanity of such a thing was too much to comprehend.

"What do you want?" Ivy stammered. But the answer was clear. He wanted her dead. She cursed her own stupidity - she had left her spear at the mouth of the cave with Kyah.

Behind him, four other hunters stood waiting just inside the lip of the cave. One of them held her spear. Behind them, rain fell in a thunderous grey sheet. On the ground to their right, a woven net was lumped on the ground. Within it, Kyah's form lay still.

"What did you do to her!?" Ivy heard her own screams echo in the chambered space. Her vision narrowed in devastation. Fury flared within her chest, burning up the terror that had kept her rooted to the spot. Ivy snapped her forearm upward, dislodging the spear at her chest. She made to run forward. The red-beaded man leapt, grabbed at her wrist instead. He wrapped his fist around her amulet. Discarded his spear. Pulled a copper knife from his belt and sliced it clean through the leather binding. The strap burned her skin as it snapped away.

Ivy's eyes barely registered the knife. Her heart was pounding with each move, her eyes fixed firmly on Kyah's body on the ground. The hunter held his stone prize high in the air, gloating to his men with a hiss of vindication.

None of it mattered. Ivy pushed forward again, her eyes only for Kyah. A fierce blow to her jaw knocked Ivy sprawling backward into the mud. Her ears rung. White sparks flew before her eyes. The sharp point of the hunter's spear forced her back to her feet. She was reeling. Nothing made sense. There wasn't enough air. Beneath the net, Ivy saw Kyah stir at the men's feet. *She's still alive.*

"You have the stone," Ivy shrieked, forcing the terror from her heart. "Keep it! Just let us go!"

The red-beaded hunter turned the amulet over in his hand, studying it with cold curiosity. It was Ivy's escape that he had stolen. The key to her Time Shift. The only way home. And in that instant, Ivy realised that it didn't matter. Nothing mattered as much as saving her best friend, who was injured and bound on the floor. Freedom was only worth having if Kyah was free too.

"Ebu gogo," The man hissed, shaking the amulet. The other men crowed in encouragement. He held it high, as if trying to make it do something. *"Nee-el gamut il ad arivek Ebu Gogo!"* Each syllable amplified the frustration in his voice. He wanted the amulet to do something. It wasn't working.

Ebu gogo? Something stirred in Ivy's memory. A phrase from what seemed like an age ago, in her life before Flores. Ivy had heard it before. *Ebu gogo.* The name given to the little wild creatures in the modern mythology of indigenous Flores. Human-like creatures, but primitive and tiny. Ethnologists had speculated the folklore could even hark back countless generations to a time when *Homo floresiensis* people co-habited the island. It was a superstitious, disparaging concept in modern-day. But a chilling reality for Ivy as she stared into the face of a man hell-bent on killing the people she loved.

Her eyes darted between the red-beaded hunter and his men. They were an impenetrable wall of brute strength and weapons. The only way past was through them. Ivy knew she didn't have a chance.

"Sari-vu-jarrabuntu." The red-beaded hunter spat at her, waving the amulet in her face. He took a step closer.

"I don't understand what you want me to do!" Ivy shouted back. Her right hand slipped to her travelling hide, searching for the stone knife tucked within a fold near her hip. Her fingers curled towards it, hoping the move wasn't noticed. A stone knife could not compete with the man's skill and strength, but only death would stop her trying.

The netted mass of Kyah's body was shifting, rising, as the bonobo recovered from whatever had felled her. The other men hadn't noticed, too intent on watching their leader. Kyah pulled away the net as she drew to her feet. A bloody wound on her forehead told Ivy they had caught her off-guard. Ivy met her friend's eyes. Carefully lifted her hands, leaving the stone knife pocketed so she was free to sign.

Run! Ivy silently warned. *Danger! Run!*

It took only a second for the bonobo to react. Kyah's ever-placid demeanour dissolved. Howling screeches rent the air. Despite her size, the bonobo's innate strength was easily greater than a man.

Before they realised she was up, Kyah pulled the closest man to the ground, pounding him with clubbing blows. Ivy's spear fell from his fist as the others took up their own. But Kyah was faster. She rushed toward the red-beaded hunter, launching, and curling her arms around his neck. Biting his face with a ferocity Ivy had never seen. The other three men were shouting, rushing to help. Ivy dashed for his discarded spear. Barely gripping, she let it fly free again with full force at the entourage. A sickening thud told her it had found a home inside one of them. But Ivy's hands were already back on Kyah, dragging the bonobo away in a screeching caterwaul of aggression. She peeled Kyah off the red-beaded hunter and dragged her to the entrance of the cave, the two able remaining hunters on their heels. With an almighty leap, Kyah landed on Ivy's discarded spear and took it up, swinging it wildly at the closest man. The other held up his own spear and drew back.

"Danuk! Janu kiri-die." Dripping with blood, the red-beaded hunter staggered to his feet. His right ear was torn, his forehead gushing blood. He held up his hands. "Janu kiri-die," he shouted again.

The hunter with the spear lowered it. His comrade pulled him backward. One opened his mouth to argue, but a glare from the leader shut it instantly. The red-beaded hunter turned to Ivy.

"Ey-vee," he said. A chilling smile broke through the blood. His tone was cajoling. His eyes were cold. The red-beaded hunter cocked his head to one side in a question. "Juran-ip-et ka watchu-mura?" He held out his hand. It was empty.

He pointed at Kyah, then down at her hand. The bonobo's delicate black fingers opened to reveal the stone. Her lips pulled back in a grimace of fear as she held it up high for him to see. She had stolen it back.

The man's voice was soft in a babble of unknown words as he stepped closer. His palms out. Ivy caught the tiniest flick of fingers as he moved. To his right, his two offsides began to shift, surreptitiously eyeing the net.

For a moment, the choice seemed so clear. Give him the amulet. He would let them go free. But Ivy knew that would never happen. This man was a murderer many times over. He couldn't be trusted.

Kyah reached up. She took Ivy's hand. Met her eyes with the same soft understanding that had always pierced her very soul.

Ivy felt the warm stone press into her palm. No words passed between them, but Kyah's message was clear.

Run. Home.

Run. Home.

There was no time to think. No time to say goodbye. With a violent shove, Kyah launched Ivy backward through the sheet of rain. Her screeches suffocated under the chaos of teaming rain and incensed shouts as Ivy tumbled and fell down the outside entrance to the cave.

"Ebu gogo!" came the furious shout from inside. Then the shouts were drowned out by the thumping of Ivy's heart. Her body screamed to stay and fight. But Kyah had forbid it. Ivy's elbows and knees slipped against the mud. She pushed up to her feet. Felt them pound the forest floor.

Run. Home. Ivy clutched the amulet like a lifeline. Behind her, men spilled out of the cave entrance, scouring the forest in search of her.

She didn't look back. She couldn't. It was only a matter of time. They were skilled trackers. They would find her and reclaim the amulet they so desperately wanted, killing them both afterward. The only advantage Ivy had now, was the warm stone in her fist as she whipped through the pelting rain.

Ivy's terror spiralled as her tears became more blinding than the deluge upon her. *He knows my name. He wants the amulet. He thinks it can do something but doesn't know how to use it.*

He's been watching us. He knows I'll do anything to save her.

The red-beaded hunter was clearly desperate to have the stone. He had not killed the bonobo, even though he had the chance. He had told his man to lower the spear. When Kyah had stolen the amulet back, he had tried to barter one for the other.

Kyah's life had been his leverage.

The hunter had understood that the only way he was going to get the amulet, was if Ivy offered it in exchange for the life of her friend.

Now, Kyah was his hostage.

As Ivy bolted through the torrent, stumbling and ducking, she resolved to give him exactly what he wanted. The amulet no longer mattered. She would sacrifice it for Kyah. She would sacrifice herself for the sake of her sister.

There was no future if Kyah was not safe.

No freedom worthwhile if Kyah was not free.

Even if I never make it home. I'll fight for her. No matter the cost.

Only eight hours lay between Ivy and the energy peak of the full moon. Her chance to escape. But as fierce rain bit Ivy's skin and branches scraped the fear from her bones, her resolve hardened. Her feet became weightless, hitting the soaked peat as if garnished with wings. The fog of terror lifted. Ivy's mind became clear.

I'll fight.

Even if I lose.

The mountain's roots grew steeper. The summit of Kelimutu grew nearer.

They brought me here to save them.

And maybe I can't save them all.

But I'll die trying to save her.

Repressed grief reared up in determination. Devotion to all those she had lost, and could never give her love, finally reconciled into a shining new purpose.

Grief propelled Ivy's feet.

Love shed the burden of fear.

I need to save her.

But I can't do it alone.

CHAPTER 33

ORRIN

$\mathcal{D}$imi slowed his car to a stop in a residential street. Above, the empty arms of a jacaranda reached for the pre-dawn sky. Summer had passed, and the Christmas carpet of fallen purple flowers had dried up and disappeared. Orrin looked at the building site across the road. The old apartment block where Ivy had lived had been torn down. Darkness hugged the foundations of a sleek new building. Construction was moving fast.

"Are you sure this is the best place?" Dimi asked.

"We can get you closer than this," Eli added, from the back seat.

"No," Orrin insisted. "I'll walk from here. The sun's nearly up and I don't want security to catch you driving me in. There are cameras everywhere. If they think you've been compromised, they'll throw you out of Cassandra's big show and increase security even more. I know the place well enough to sneak in. It's a big campus. Lots of slips and alleys between buildings I can take."

"Be careful," Eli said. He opened his mouth as if to say more but thought better of it. "I wish you luck, Orrin."

"It's been an honour," Orrin said, twisting around from the passenger-side seat to shake his hand. "And an adventure."

"That it has."

Orrin turned back to Dimi. There didn't seem to be enough words to express how grateful he was. With a reassuring grin, Dimi leaned forward to hug him.

"Go get her, mate."

"I will," Orrin said, his voice cracking. "Put on a good show for them, won't you. Keep Cassandra out of my hair."

"I'll do my best." Dimi was risking more than his job today. His plan to alter the coordinates on the receiver right before the energy surge was going to create an instant uproar. Government officials, scientists and press had all been invited along to witness the energy field peak. When Cassandra realised why they missed the capture, she'd know it was sabotage. Dimi was the only one with access. He'd be arrested for subversion. If Orrin failed tonight, Dimi would pay the price with his freedom.

Orrin made to open the car door. He stopped; his fingers frozen on the handle. He turned back around.

"I'm sorry for all this - to both of you. Bringing you two together, only to-"

"Tear us apart?" Dimi shot Eli a sad smile. "Don't be sorry. It's been the best couple of weeks of my life."

"Yeah," Orrin said. "I promise I'll make it right." He opened the door and stepped out. He didn't want to intrude anymore on their own goodbyes.

"I know you will," Dimi said. With one last wave, the car pulled away from the curb, leaving Orrin to make the walk to Melbourne University alone.

*

Within fifteen minutes, the first buildings of the sprawling campus came into view. Dawn rays threatened to split through the branches above him. Orrin quickened his pace. He needed the shadows while they lasted. Soon, the university would be swarming with suits and security. He glanced at his watch. *5:23am.*

The campus was as big as a city suburb, and the physics department sat about halfway down the southern wing. Orrin paced through, hugging corners and avoiding streetlights. He passed the old foundational sandstone buildings with their decorative gargoyles, then crossed beyond into the busy mix of brick lecture theatres and modern multi-stories. The physics department owned an entire block and had become his home away from home in the past months.

As he grew closer, Orrin left the roads to slip through lesser-worn passages where rubbish bins and old equipment waited for collection. His dark hooded jacket was zipped up tight. He'd dressed neatly underneath, in a business shirt and tie with suit pants, hoping at the very least that he might blend into the crowd of reporters if needed. Every so often, a security car rolled by, and he flattened himself against a wall or hid behind bushes. His hands were clammy. Perspiration threatened to ruin his suit shirt. A whirring alarm broke out, and Orrin's pulse hammered as he looked for somewhere to hide. He ducked behind an industrial skip just as a police car went rolling by, the uniforms scanning for intruders.

Cassandra isn't taking any chances. As soon as it had passed, Orrin paced across the road. *5:49am.* If he wasn't in place by 5:55am, he would miss the change of guard. Again, he picked up his pace until he was almost running. The sound of blood whooshing through his ears was only matched by the noise of birds. The campus was full of trees, and Orrin had never been more grateful for the opportunity for concealment they offered.

5:52am. Ahead, the sleek glass and steel building finally appeared. His hopes dropped as he saw a small group of suits standing by the glassy water feature in front of the entrance.

Damn it! I'll have to find a way another way around. He doubled back one street and took a wider route past the mechanical engineering laboratories, finally circling to the back of his own building.

5:58am. Two minutes remained until the night guard knocked off. Orrin watched the back door of the Physics building from the shadows, poised to move. Just as Phil had warned him, a well concealed security camera watched the door. As soon as it struck 6am, Orrin knew he had only three minutes to get in the back door, up the fire stairs and into his laboratory while the camera monitors were unattended. Silently, he thanked Phil again.

One minute left. Orrin felt as if his breath was hissing over a loudspeaker. As if every rustle he made in the bushes was a car crash. He squeezed his eyes closed, ready to dash for the door.

"Orrin?" The voice was loud. "Is that you?" Orrin's heart nearly exploded in panic. He looked up, his glasses tipped askew, adrenaline chasing logic from his mind. All he could do was croak out a reply.

"Yes."

"What are you doing down there? In the bushes?" Dale Brennan was lit by the orange glow of dawn as it broke across the roof of the building above them. His brows were furrowed, his eyes tired and downcast.

Orrin looked toward the door. *Go.* Every part of him felt as if it were spinning out of control. If anyone else had uncovered him, he'd have run, or tried to concoct an elaborate lie. But he was desperate, and out of both luck and time. All he had left in him was the truth.

"I'm breaking in," he said.

"But - you've been sacked," Dale said, shocked. "Cassandra told you if you ever set foot in the building again, she'd-"

"Yeah, " Orrin panted, his eyes darting again to the door. "Yeah, I know."

"Cassandra has everyone on high alert. They're expecting you to try to sabotage this thing. Security are crawling every inch of this place-"

"Yeah, well, I'm making it easy for them then, aren't I? Because as you can see, I'm here and I'm desperate." He looked at the young man he had once considered a friend. "I'm absolutely wretched right now, man. This is my only chance to save Ivy and fix all the shite I've managed to drop on the world. So, I'm breaking in, *right now*. So you can either get me arrested, or get out of my way."

"Arrested?" Panic filled Dale's eyes. "But Orrin, you know I can't let you go in there!"

"Like I said, then try to stop me. Because I'm going in." Orrin's fingers began to twitch. He needed to get to that door. "Why are you even here, Dale?" He growled. "I thought you told Cassandra you didn't want her job."

"I don't want it! Any of it. I'm here because I don't have a choice. Chancellor Thandi called me in for a *meeting* yesterday. She said that supplying all your research data to the CSIRO was in direct violation to the terms of my employment contract with the university. That if I didn't do what she wanted, she'd have the board move to sue me for breach of contract. I'm employed under duress, and only until they get what they want from me."

"She's threatening you? What does she want you to do?"

"She wants me in Cassandra's lab today, pushing buttons and offering whatever secrets I can spill to make sure the uni maintains a legitimate claim on the energy capture. With you and Phil both out of the picture, I'm the only one left that can help set things up the way you did. There's a lot of money on the table for whoever can capture this energy surge. They've got all sorts of crazy equipment up on the penthouse roof. The Department of Natural Resources will be there with the CSIRO and a heap of government officials. Cassandra's team have taken control though. Chancellor Thandi wants to make sure they share the glory and windfall with the uni." Dale looked away. Where his eyes had once been bright with potential, they now were dim with distrust. "I don't have a choice here, Orrin. I have to do it. I'm not like them. I'm not good at playing games. I'm just a research student. I've got no money. I can't risk being sued by some big government bastards."

"I'm sorry, Dale. I get it, you need to save your skin." Orrin frowned. "I don't blame you."

"Yeah, well. I do. Blame me, I mean." Despite his betrayal, Orrin couldn't help but pity the young man in front of him.

"Dale, I know you think I took you for granted," Orrin said, "and I'm sorry I didn't tell you this more. But you've been one of the best things about my life since I came to this country. You've changed universities to stick with me. You've gone from a scrawny little undergrad that barely spoke because you were so shy, to being a legitimate scientist with such a brilliant mind that sometimes I wondered if I'd even have anything left to teach you in a few years. I never considered myself *just* your supervisor or lecturer. I always considered you my friend. I blame myself for what happened between us." Orrin shook his head. "I was so caught up in my own problems, I didn't notice you were suffering as much as I was. I'm sorry."

Dale looked at Orrin, his mouth trembling. "You mean that?"

"You know I do. But here's the thing," Orrin looked again at the door. There was no doubt in his mind that the security guard was heading back to view the cameras. "If I don't get in that lab in the next two minutes, you know what's gonna happen? The security guard is going to see me on camera. I'll be arrested. We'll be stuck in this screwed-up version of the earth forever. Ivy will live and die fifty thousand years before she was born, and Phil, Jayne and Liam are all going to jail for a really long time." Orrin stepped forward. "So Dale, I know this version of the world has worked out better for you than the last one, but it's pretty crap for the rest of us. The planet is falling apart and I'm going to try to fix it." Orrin glanced at the security camera again, barely able to drag his eyes away. He pulled Phil's stolen swipe card from his pocket. "So, what's it gonna be? Are you going to tell them I'm here?" He took a step forward. The two men stared at each other. Dale shrank back but there was no threat in Orrin's stance. He shook his head slightly and took Dale by the shoulder. "You're a good lad, Dale. And you've been the best lab tech I've ever had in my life. But I'm going in there now, whether you like it or not." For a heavy moment, no one moved. Then Dale took a step back.

"I'll delay the guard."

"Really?" Orrin heart skipped a beat.

"Really." Dale gave Orrin a small smile. "I never saw you. Good luck."

Dale pulled his own swipe card from his pocket and let himself through the back door, quickly disappearing down a long corridor toward the front of the building. Orrin took a look in behind him, then dashed up the fire stairs two at a time. The first-floor corridor was still empty. He raced along it, pulling Phil's spare key from his pocket.

Laboratory 179. Dr. Orrin James, Astro-physics.

They still hadn't changed his nameplate.

CHAPTER 34

IVY

"Xiou!" Ivy couldn't hold back the tears streaming down her face. "The Karathah have taken Kyah!"

The final climb of steep forest leading up to Kelimutu's peak sapped the last of her breath, and Ivy stumbled, fingernails grasping soil and rocks as she pushed her way through stabbing pains in her lungs.

"Xiou!" She shouted. "I need your help!"

The glorious crater lakes appeared before her, swathed in hot mist. Blood red, glacial blue and emerald green. Steep and deadly walls of stone separated the Three Sister Lakes from one another upon the vast volcanic crest. This was the resting place of souls, and Ivy had never felt its power as strongly as she did now.

She straightened up, blood pounding in her ears from the climb. Rain obscured her vision. A moment passed before her brain could register what had appeared before her eyes. Ivy's breath left her in a jolt.

Xiou was there. He ran toward her, alerted by her calls for help. All remnants of anger over Ivy's betrayal at the time vortex seemed to have left his face. Only concern remained. But it was not Xiou that took her breath away. Behind him, in numbers far greater than a single tribe, were others. *Homo floresiensis others.* Men and women holding spears and arrows. Children and adolescents that Ivy could not recognise. From within the group, Kari and his band of travellers emerged looking triumphant.

"We have returned, Hiranah!" He called out to her with a grin almost too wide for his face. Ivy's face was ashen as she walked toward them, scanning hundreds of unfamiliar faces.

"We found more tribes," the young bird-hunter Chiri added. Beside him, his sister Sira beamed. "We have brought them to hear you speak." A sea of eyes watched Ivy with fear and curiosity. An undercurrent of whispers began.

Setian stepped forward. "Do not worry, Hiranah," he grinned. "I already warned them that you were very ugly."

Ivy choked out a laugh despite herself. "I can always count on you, Setian." She pulled up short before the crowd, barely able to comprehend their unexpected success. Hands waved at her from the crowd and Ivy greeted each familiar traveller with relieved delight. When she had sent them out on such a dangerous journey, Ivy had worried many might not live to return.

"Shia, Sholon, Buchi! You found people in the north caves!"

"Just as you said we would, Hiranah," Shia called back. "And we have brought them all Home."

"And Boru! You have returned from the west! I was so terrified that the Shirakan might find you before you found your way back."

"They attacked us many times," Boru replied steadily. "But I had Shashi to help me through." He turned and nodded to his friend, who still gripped a spear. "We found people in the Mirror Stone Cave, as you hoped. In Batu Cermin and Rangko Caves as well. There are not as many as we hoped though - all have suffered at the hands of the Karathah." Shouts of anger dotted the crowd. Boru puffed out his chest, proudly. "But no more, friends! We are stronger together."

"We have returned *Home*." An unfamiliar woman called out,

her voice bold and defiant. "Even as we travelled across the forest, the Three Sister Lakes called to us. We all feel it."

"Yes. Our ancestors have called us Home," another man said. There was a rumble of agreement.

"And Ren? Where is she?" Ivy scanned for the kind-hearted hunter who had travelled with Boru to search amongst the Komodo-infested western beaches. Boru simply shook his head. The weight of grief pressed on Ivy's chest once more.

Xiou pushed through the crowd to reach her. The summit of Kelimutu was brimming with hope. The lost tribes of the *Homo floresiensis* species had found one another, reunited after thousands of years apart. From all across the island, Xiou's hunters had unearthed their kin from caves hidden within vast jungles and above deadly cliffs. They had traversed dizzying mountains and braved the ravages of an erupting, untamed earth to bring these people home. As Ivy sought their faces amongst the crowd, she had never been more proud.

"You have done it," she breathed. "Kari, Shia, Boru - her eyes settled on Xiou, who needed no words to share her pride. "Xiou, *they did it.*"

The small valley that sat above the Three Sister Lakes was full to the brim with humanity. No inch of rock was exposed underfoot. Anxious bodies shuffled and backs held tall, watching Ivy's arrival with morbid fascination. Some of them had encountered her before - and turned away from her pleas to come. Others had only heard stories of the pale woman with fire-hair that claimed to be one of an ancient prophesy. But whether curiosity or desperation had led them to Kelimutu, Ivy did not care. They were here, and the sight was overwhelming. Her knees trembled.

"You all came," she heard herself whisper.

For generation upon generation, each tribe had been considered lost in its own isolation. Inbreeding was unavoidable. Genetic mutations inevitable. And so the *Homo floresiensis* species began to die out, just as *Homo sapiens* surged onto their island, strong and proliferate.

But this - Ivy wiped her eyes - *this was hope.* Together, the tribes were nearly one thousand strong.

Will it be enough?

Will they listen?

Can they work together to save themselves?

Perhaps, Ivy thought, *human evolution is about about to change.*

There was a fresh wave of rumbling in the crowd. Ivy lifted her hands and placed them gently aside Xiou's own face. She pulled her forehead in close to his, touching them together. He drew back, scanning her face for clues as to the fear behind her eyes.

"What has happened, Hiranah?" Xiou asked quietly. He looked in the direction that she had come. "Where is Kyah?"

Ivy was desperate to unburden herself, to share her terror of what the red-beaded hunter might do. But not yet. She knew that it was she herself who cast a terrifying figure right now. Before she could seek help from Xiou, she needed to *offer* help to the gathered tribes. They only knew of her what they had been told by Kari and the others. All eyes were on Ivy, waiting to find out if their trust had been a terrible mistake. If she fell apart now, what little trust they had in her would crumble.

From somewhere in the middle of the crowd, a familiar voice called out.

"I did it, Hiranah! I convinced them to come." Ko, the would-be boy leader from the cliff-cave held up a hand. His face was a beacon of pride.

"I knew you would," Ivy smiled. "You have the heart of a leader, Ko, anyone can see that." She recognised his two young friends, Hiron, the egg-stealer, and Tinud, amongst his tribe. At least two dozen had come with them, though nowhere could Ivy see the desolate face of the elder who had banished her from their cave high above the Savu Sea. Apparently, not all were willing to risk the journey.

"You promised us a chance to survive, Karathah," a gruff voice caught Ivy's attention. "What remains of my family will hold you to your word."

"Tica," Ivy caught her breath in disbelief. "You came?"

The leader of the tribe that Ivy had found hiding deep in the forest after a Karathah attack, did not return her smile. The elder's mouth was set in a hard line. Her eyes distrustful. "Since you came to us, there has been talk of nothing else," Tica said. "I may not like it, but my family choose to trust you."

"Then I hope to earn your trust also," Ivy replied.

"We shall see," Tica grunted. "For now, I only lead them where they feel they must be. Apparently, that is here." The woman looked around uncomfortably.

"These are your people, Tica," Ivy smiled.

"It has been generations since these were my people," Tica growled back at her. "I do not know them."

"But we wish to know you." Shahn stepped forward. Her expression was as placid as always, one hand supporting her engorged belly. Behind her, Shahn's younger sister Leihna, offered Tica her friendship with a smile. "We have been searching for you and we welcome your family and the wisdom you bring," Shahn said. "Having you here," she looked up, addressing the entire crowd, "*all of you*, brings us more joy than you can imagine." Tica scowled, shuffling back. "We are all as overwhelmed as you," Shahn continued. "We have grown from one family to so many, all at once. But this is how we will survive! Hiranah has told us this."

Shahn was holding Filhia's hand. The young orphan stared away with vacant sadness, as she had done ever since her older sister Rinap had been murdered by the Karathah. Filhia no longer spoke. Each day, she slipped through life as little more than Shahn's shadow. Ivy waded through the crowd, taking

Filhia's other hand. The girl looked up at her despondently. Ivy gave her hand a gentle squeeze.

"So how will you save us, Hiranah?" Ko stepped forward again, his optimism buoyed by the crowd around him. He seemed to be the only person outside of Xiou's tribe that addressed her without suspicion.

"You will save yourselves," Ivy said. "Just by being here, you have already begun." Ivy lifted her eyes to the group at large, taking in anxious faces as she swept her gaze across. Each expression reflected a beating heart filled with hope that the Slow Death might be behind them.

Ivy took a deep breath, struggling within herself on how to explain the complex problem they were faced with, in a way that they could understand. Each tribe before her had been separated from its peers by millennia. She could already see slight differences in bone structure between families. One group had a slightly narrower nose, another population shared a gene for more pigmentation in their skin. Some were more gracile and shorter than others. The island itself had imposed unique evolutionary pressures. Inbreeding had accentuated them. Over time, each small population had grown unique and beautiful in its isolation. But that isolation was now strangling the life out of them.

As a scientist, Ivy knew that capitalising on that variation within each population now, was the only way to save the species. In each new generation born, genetic drift was stealing their opportunity to survive. Important genes were being lost and detrimental genes increased. Eventually, fewer babies born, combined with negative genetic mutations, had compounded with their increased inability to adapt to the rapidly changing environment imposed by the newcomers to the island, *Homo sapiens.*

A deadly anthropogenic cocktail, modern scientists called it.

Populations fragmented and isolated.

Environments altered by human consumption.

Certain extinction.

The only way to save the species, was to deliberately increase the beneficial variants in their collective genome. In short, they had to unite, and breed.

But to do this, they needed to survive the Karathah first.

"I do not want to give you false hope," Ivy began, gathering her thoughts. "Joining together will stop the Slow Death, but you are still faced with other dangers."

"For a long time now, you have felt the earth shift and groan beneath your feet. Some of you have seen the mountains explode with fire and smoke and great ruptures appear across the land. Every day, the ash clouds grow worse." There was a rumbling of agreement. "Many more eruptions will come, and each will be more dangerous. Soon, a great ash cloud will cover the island, and it will stay for many weeks. To survive it, you will need to work together to protect yourselves. The climate will change – your days will become warmer. Some animals that you hunt for food, like the Probech, will not survive the change. The only way that you can survive yourselves, is to be prepared. Together you are much stronger than apart."

"How do we hunt in the dark with the earth falling apart around us?" a voice cried from within the group.

"There are places that will be safer than others," Ivy explained, "and I have told Xiou where to find them. He will lead you there. I'm afraid your journey for survival is only just beginning."

"We already have a leader," a man shouted from the back. "We do not need another. Why should we follow Xiou when our own hunters are just as skilled?"

Xiou stepped forward, his hands open in conciliation. "I do not wish to lead you alone. There are far too many of us now to follow one person. I invite all leaders to join me equally. I have been given the knowledge we need to survive, but I am willing to share it with you. If we work together, we have a chance."

"How do we know she is telling the truth?" Someone shouted. "Why should we believe this?"

"Because she came from the Falling Place!" Kari growled back. "You know the prophesy, Hidir! Hiranah was sent to save us! Why would she not help us now?"

"Because she is also Karathah!" The other man called back, incensed. "The very ones that are stealing our hunting grounds and killing our people."

"That is true," Xiou stepped in. "Hiranah is a Karathah, but she means no harm. But there are others that *do* mean harm. It is not only a broken earth we must survive. It is the Karathah. We must unite to survive them too."

"I have seen your future as it was before," Ivy said, gathering her thoughts. "Nothing remained of your people but bones in the dust. I can't explain the danger ahead." She looked to Xiou, raising the amulet slightly. He nodded and took her hand, then held his other hand out to Kora. The hunter took it, then offered her other hand to her mate. "But we can show you," Ivy said. "If you are willing to see it. Please, let me share what I have seen."

One by one, hands connected. Ivy felt their apprehension grow with each mind joined. Terror at what they might see, fought with desperation in their hearts. Each mind sought a way out of their endless danger. Hope for their children to survive. As courage grew, and hands joined, the amulet pulsed and burned between Ivy and Xiou's palms. Each day closer to the full moon Ivy had felt it grow warmer, as if the energy within was trying to escape. She caught Xiou's eye. They both knew what it meant. The peak of the full moon was only hours away. It was almost dusk already.

As the last hand joined, Ivy's thoughts were seized by the collective. She could barely breathe. Her mind, no longer her own. Ivy's head fell back. Her back arched, eyes closed as the overwhelming force of knowledge poured from her mind. She was a conduit, of science and nature and love, and the burden of truth. Tears streamed down her face and every muscle tremored as memories poured from within her brain, filling the minds of all those connected. It was their future they had wanted to see. But none existed.

Tiny bones being excavated from an empty cave.
Sifted. Sorted. Assembled with glue.
The dusty shelves of a museum.
A skull in a glass cloche on a shelf.
Small and lonely.
The words EXTINCT written in bold letters underneath.

Ivy's memories travelled to parts of the modern world they could scarcely comprehend. Spectacular feats of architecture. Artistry that soared beyond sublime. The earth in its mechanical glory, demanding the death of its natural heart. Fifty thousand years from now, Earth – *Ivy's earth* – was barely recognisable.

Cars, trains, ships, planes, rockets, satellites.
The brilliance of technology far beyond their understanding.
Simmering wars. Explosions of hate and jealousy.
Battles of such scale they crossed countries and generations.
A vast world full of faces, but none of them familiar.
All of them Karathah.

Cries of despair from within the crowd tore at Ivy's heart. *That is enough,* she begged, *You have seen enough now!* But the collective of the tribe mind needed more. To understand, to reconcile. This world they saw made no sense. Dozens of images flicked through Ivy's mind in a parade of humanity's flaws and failures.

. . .

Robotic jaws that consumed the forest until only patches remained.

Displaced animals emerging from the dust. Homeless. Cut down.

Green gave way to the grey of slip lanes and refugee camps and runways.

Cities swathed beneath curling pyres of smoke.

Ivy's heart felt as if it was splitting open. "There is beauty too," she choked out, but the words caught in her throat. The cost was so high. "Find the small things," she begged. "See the love. The kindness. Each person alone is just like you. We are flawed, just like you–"

But the strength of the tribe united, overpowering Ivy's plea for mercy.

"You began this," their minds cried. "You must show us where it ends."

Innocent lives stolen as men fought over words.

Food production on a scale so massive, blood ran the rivers red.

The Earth consumed, beyond its capacity to renew.

Land burned. Seas poisoned. Rivers choked.

Animals shot. Captives in cages. Lives spent in chains.

Steel and glass reaching for the heavens as souls fell to the ground.

Ivy's knees finally gave way. She collapsed to the dirt, shoulders slumped forward, sobbing in despair.

When did humanity abandon its namesake?

When did we cast aside our desire to be humane?

. . .

"It is enough!" Xiou shouted. He wrenched his hand away from Ivy's, breaking the connection. "You have all seen what Hiranah has seen. Now, the time has come to act. Already, the Karathah are spreading across the earth, in greater numbers than you can imagine. Their hunting territories will expand, and they'll do everything they can to outwit us, out-hunt us, and move into our forests. There is *nothing* we can do about this." A rush of dissension arose. Xiou raised his voice to quell it. "So, tell me then, how will we survive the Karathah?"

"We will hide," one woman called out. "Like Hiranah has told us."

"Yes, we can hide." Xiou frowned, "Perhaps that is the only way. But how long can we stay hidden?"

"I refuse to hide!" called out Hirup. His nostrils flared and dark eyes flashed. "Why should we hide within our own forests! We have been here since the Beginning!"

Cheers of support followed his voice. "How many of us have been attacked by the Karathah? How many of your homes and hunting trails have been invaded, as ours were?"

"They take food within our territory!" Furious cries went out.

"And show no mercy when they steal!"

"Fighting the Karathah is a futile ambition," Xiou growled, trying to placate them. "We cannot win against their size and strength. You all know this." He offered an arm to help Ivy to her feet.

"I admire your courage," Ivy addressed the crowd. "But you already have a difficult journey ahead. Together, you must find a place to survive, far away from the Karathah. Somewhere you can live without the violence they bring. Go together. Hide. Melt into the shadows as you do so beautifully – don't ever let them see you again. So long as you are all together, you will have the strength to survive."

"And what of you, Hiranah? Will you come with us?" Leihna

had stepped forward. Her young face was a picture of optimism. "Will you help us?"

Ivy took a fortifying breath. "Not this time," she said. "I'm sorry, Leihna." She saw Shahn squeeze her little sister's hand. "Your future is with your family, and mine–" she turned her head, looking through the drizzle into the swelling dusk beyond. "I need to go somewhere else."

"Hiranah will leave us tonight," Xiou said, in a clear voice. "She has done all we asked of her. It is time for her to return home."

Ivy shook her head. "No, Xiou," she said. "I had planned to leave; I cannot deny that." Her face burned with shame at the devastation that fell over Leihna's face.

"You were going to leave us, Hiranah?" Beside Leihna, Shahn's eyes held quiet sympathy. Even Filhia looked up from her sorrow. Ivy had never said a word of her intentions to her new family. Only Xiou had uncovered her plan. "I wasn't trying to deceive you, Leihna, I promise. I was simply searching for my way home, as you must find yours."

"We understand, Hiranah." Xiou offered his hand. "And I wasn't ready for you to leave us. I felt betrayed." He held an arm out, gesturing toward the lakes. "But the energy of the Falling Place has been calling you back. We all feel it. You brought us to where you Fell, in the hopes that you might Return home when we had found one another. The prophesy tells us that you must leave. I have always known it, and so did my father. I see now that the time has come."

"I'm not leaving," Ivy said. "But I'm not going home either. Xiou–" But there were no words left. Only fear. As Ivy's amulet brushed the hunter's palm, one final image passed to his mind. This memory, Ivy needed him to see alone.

"The Karathah have Kyah," Xiou said, as her memory filled his thoughts. His expression turned grave.

"The red-beaded hunter has her trapped," Ivy said. She

couldn't help the tears brimming in her eyes. "I don't know why, but he wants my amulet." Ivy held the black stone in an open palm. "And I intend to give it to him to get her back."

"Give the Life Stone to the Karathah?" Xiou whipped back. "You cannot!"

"It's the only way to save her life. I'm going to fight for her," Ivy insisted. "You cannot change my mind."

"Where are they?"

"Near the caves in the southern forest."

Xiou looked southward through the rain. A perfectly full moon had risen while they were gathered. Orange afternoon drizzle had finally dissolved to grey.

"If you go to confront him, you won't make it back before the moon begins to pass over, Hiranah," Xiou frowned. "And without the Life Stone, you will never be able to return home even if you did."

"I know." Ivy squared her shoulders. "But I *will* save Kyah. Her freedom is all that matters to me now. You don't understand Xiou, Kyah has already spent a lifetime in captivity. She has never been truly free. She was taken from her mother as a baby. She was abused by the Karathah in my time. I can't bear the thought of that evil man putting her through it all again. The red-beaded hunter can have the amulet. All I want is Kyah's freedom." Ivy took a deep breath. "I'm willing to die for it."

"This is your choice then, Hiranah? To stay here and fight for her?"

"Yes."

"And never to return to your own time?"

"Yes." Ivy choked back a sob. Through blurred vision, Ivy saw Xiou casting anxious glances to those around him.

"You must understand, Xiou," she began, "this is everything I have ever feared. You, Kyah," she turned and looked across faces lit by startling moonlight. "*All of you.* Every one of you has become part of my heart. Kora, Setian, Guntah, dear Phren – I *love you all. You are my family now.* As much as I wanted to go home, I have also been terrified to lose you. You see, all my life, I've tried to live alone. Be alone. Work alone." The words tumbled from her lips as an epiphany. "Because the people I love, always seem to *leave*." A knot of twisted threads tightened within her heart. Ivy saw her mother's face, a sweetheart's smile, her father's slow estrangement. "Somehow," she continued, *"in some awful way*, people leave me behind. So, I decided that if I just didn't love anyone, it wouldn't matter. That I'd be safe from being hurt again." Tears fell unheeded. "But I just couldn't stop myself from *feeling love*, and I can see how wrong I was to try."

"I thought I was brave by being alone," Ivy continued. "But it takes far more courage *to be loved*. Especially after grief has already torn you apart. I've risked so much, by loving you all. Just being here with you," she smiled to Shahn, blinking her eyes clear, "has taught me that I *need* love," Ivy explained. "And even if I lose the ones I love, like Gihn and Rinap and darling little Turi, I still wouldn't trade a single moment I spent with them for a lifetime without. I *needed* to love Orrin. For my own sake. And I can stay here now knowing that I did love him, and that it was *enough*. I can stand with that loss, I'll embrace the pain of it, because it was mine." Ivy's voice wavered, but she lifted her chin. "I might lose Kyah tonight. I might even die. But I'll do it gladly if it means her freedom." Ivy looked beyond the faces into the dark night ahead. Destiny seemed to be dragging her away again. *"Because I love her the most."*

For a long moment, no one spoke. It was Xiou who stepped forward first.

"You do not have to fight the Karathah alone, Hiranah. I will come."

Ivy squeezed his hand. "You owe me nothing, Xiou. Once I got back here, I couldn't bring myself to ask–"

"You do not need to ask," Xiou stated quietly. "Kyah is family. We protect our family."

"I will go with you," Kora said, stepping forward. Her hand tightened on her spear. Behind her, the orphans watched with wide eyes. "I will not let Kyah suffer in the hands of that man while breath is still in me."

"Nor will I." Setian moved into place beside his mate. "Kyah is one of us."

"Kyah loves us, as we love her," Guntah added. "You should have asked us for help." He stepped forward with his spear. "I will happily fight the red-beaded hunter. The man needs to die."

"I am tired of the Karathah tearing our lives apart," Kari shouted from the crowd. "I will fight them too! The time to hide may come, but it is not tonight!"

"Yes!" A chorus of agreement rallied around him.

Tica pushed her way through the crowd. Revenge burned behind her eyes. "I know the man of which you speak, with the red-beaded hair! He murdered my family, took the heads of my children and left their precious bodies in pieces. He has turned the other Karathah against us and whipped them up with violence. I will gladly kill him," she spat. "These legs may be old, but my arm can still throw a spear."

"He killed my mate!" shouted the man behind her. "I will come!"

"And I!" Within a few moments, roars of agreement shook the surface of the lakes.

Shahn slipped in beside Ivy and squeezed her hand, supporting her pregnant belly with the other. She gave a wince, then grimaced as a pain subsided.

"Are you–?"

"Not yet," Shahn reassured her. "You see? Love is always worth fighting for."

Trahg pushed his way through the crowd, leaving the orphans huddled together behind him.

"I will save Kyah!" He insisted. "I will go too!"

"You are far too young," Shahn shushed him.

Ivy knelt, taking the five-year-old boy by the hands. "I know how much you love Kyah," she said. "And she loves you. That is why she would want you to stay here with your mother. You must stay safe for her, Trahg."

"But I can climb, Hiranah. Kyah and I are the best at climbing!"

"Not this time." Ivy shook her head.

Trahg's little mouth twisted in anger, but he stayed quiet.

The air hummed with anticipation. As strategy crackled through the tribe like wild fire, every able-bodied hunter took up the invitation to fight. Phren and Shahn gathered the children and elders and began to lead them back down to the forest cover of their camp on the western slope of Kelimutu.

"We will not be victims this time, Hiranah," Xiou said, watching them go. "It is time for us to fight back."

"You see?" Setian said, joining her. "You do not have to do everything alone."

"Come, Hiranah," Kora grinned. "Let us go hunting."

CHAPTER 35

ORRIN

*D*imi and Phil had thought of everything. As Orrin dragged the equipment stashed in his office as quietly as he could into the empty laboratory, he wondered how on earth he'd ever managed to get friends as good as the ones he had. Even across realities, they'd proven themselves loyal and selfless; even Dale in the end. He shook his head as he plugged in power leads and cables, trying to clear his thoughts of the emotion that threatened to overwhelm him.

Now, it was all down to him. The final eighteen hours, from 6am to 12 midnight, he needed to remain locked and hidden in his laboratory, recreating the parameters of his experiments as precisely as he'd had it before. If he was going to save Ivy when the energy surge peaked, he couldn't afford to miss the smallest thing.

The Telsla coil was rolled into place. The faraday cage of conductive mesh screening was already permanently installed in the back corner of the lab, though Orrin didn't plan on being inside it when the time came. Though it might protect him from the electrostatic charges of the coil, there was no guarantee it would protect him from the singularity he planned to create.

He'd been in his lead-lined office when the first Time Shift happened, and he couldn't risk any change now. His lightning laboratory would be empty at midnight. Hopefully, not for long.

Though he lacked tables and a few missing monitors, the vast majority of Orrin's equipment had been reclaimed by Phil and stacked up in the small space of the back office that had been previously a hive of books and research papers.

After he carried the last piece of equipment into the laboratory, Orrin returned to the dusty old Tektronic Oscilloscope under his desk. The machine was so ancient that it couldn't possibly have been considered useful. Even when his office was gutted, nobody thought it worthy to take. Orrin knelt, pried open the broken glass door and reached into the metal shell. As promised, a small hard drive sat inside. All his data would be on it, waiting for him to resurrect. Old Tek had once again, proved invaluable. Thanking Dimi under his breath, he inserted it into his laptop and began the arduous process of recreating his experimental protocol.

The original experiment had been designed over years and implemented over months. Now, Orrin worked quickly, relying more on muscle memory than he had ever done before. Energy measurements, wavelength frequency, sound and light monitors were set up. The few display screens he had, flickered with patterns and data.

His trolley of samples was missing, but there was no need for it today. The only natural element required was Ivy's amulet. He felt it growing warm in his pocket as he worked. As the energy fluctuations increased, the Moscovium responded. A single server whirred as he set up each machine. Hours passed without notice as Orrin worked in silence. There was no need to speak to anyone, no urge to eat. A single focus pushed him through the morning and into the afternoon. *Get Ivy back.*

He glanced at the arrangement of spectrographic equipment set up in the corner. He was missing an integral piece. The audio spectrum analyser that Phil had been caught stealing from another lab had never made it back here. Orrin ran his fingers through his hair as he silently paced the room, trying to think of a work-around. The machine was imperative for his ability to match the exact frequencies that he knew would resonate with the crystalline magnetite latticed around the reacting element. Without the spectrum analyser, he was at best making an educated guess, and at worst, a stab in the dark. With a sigh, he continued his ministrations on the other equipment. Brightly coloured graphs lit up one monitor, rolling in whips and plateaus as the electromagnetic fields in the room fluctuated. Earth's natural magnetic field kept a steady baseline underneath, telling the story of an increasingly volatile solar storm outside.

5pm. The hum of voices outside his laboratory increased. Footsteps came and went more frequently. Though no-one was interested in his supposedly empty laboratory, Orrin knew that the foot-traffic to the penthouse suite above increased the danger that he'd be caught hour by hour. All it would take was a mistaken turn by a journalist, a disoriented visitor or one last sweep of security and he'd be discovered. As the hours ticked on, Orrin's eyes flicked to the locked door minute by minute. His shoulders were wound up like coiled springs, aching and tense. His eyes dry from staring at screens. Even his breath seemed too loud for the silent room. The daylight that seeped under the door began to fade and Orrin had no choice but to turn on the lights. He stuffed his jacket across the base of the door, hoping to mute any light that escaped into the hallway.

Orrin pulled a roll of aluminium wire from his pocket and uncoiled it. With a bouncing stretch, he lassoed it around the overhead ceiling fan, twisting the two halves together on either side so they met down at the level of his chest as a single rope. Gently, he twisted the metal ends together to form a shallow cup. It wasn't ideal, but after much deliberation, Orrin had decided the conductive wire was the most likely solution to entice the lightning of the Tesla Coil into the black centre of the amulet. Ivy had worn it around her neck, but Orrin couldn't risk being in the room when the coil discharged. He pulled the amulet from his pocket. The black stone was hot to the touch. If it had ever before felt alive, now it was positively humming. With a deep breath, he placed Ivy's amulet gently in its metal nest.

Bring her back, Orrin whispered to it, as he stepped back. *If anything I ever do is going to work, let this be it.* He squeezed his eyes closed. *Please.*

CHAPTER 36

NEIL

"*N*ee-el! Nee-el!" Atasi shook him. The delirium shifted slightly, and the young woman's face came into focus. He'd lost consciousness again.

She was speaking in a hushed whisper, desperately trying to explain something. Neil forced himself to listen. The previous night, they had shifted camps again. They were further up the eastern side of Kelimutu, hiding in a camouflaged dug-out in the undergrowth. Neil was as close to Ivy and the hobbits as he dared. There were more of them now, he and Atasi had seen hundreds travelling. It was almost impossible to stay hidden from so many, so Neil only moved at night. He was far too slow to risk the daylight hours. This morning, Atasi had disappeared before dawn to search for food and had returned with green shoots of some kind for him to chew. He didn't have the heart to turn them away but shoved them under some leaves instead. His jaw ached and his vision swam. Food was out of the question.

Atasi helped Neil sit up and forced water against his lips. The sweltering day had passed in mud and rain. It was nearly dusk, and night was riding in stormy and wild. Tonight, was the night. Neil had waited desperately for this moment since he'd first

Fallen into the jungle, but now that night was here, he wasn't sure he could do it. There was no question that the red head was going to try to escape, she had written it in her journal. *If I can just get through the vortex before she does, I'll make it*, he tried to convince himself. *I'll get to a hospital. They can pump me with whatever it takes. I'll pull through.* As if to adjust his expectations, his fingers faltered on the water bladder. It slipped, adding more water to his soaked body.

"Ebu gogo," Atasi kept repeating. She was trying to lift him to his feet. "Berap." *Volcano.* "Mutu." *Coloured lakes.* "Go! Go!"

"Alright, I understand." Neil sighed. "It's time to go." He reached for the bag Atasi has given him to keep his equipment in. She picked it up instead, then gathered his four copper rods and passed them to him as Neil staggered to his feet. For now, the rods were still bound together as a single walking stick. But tonight, he hoped to use them for what they were intended. Finding his way home.

Leaning on the young woman and rods for support, Neil began a slow trek through the darkening forest. The climb was steep. They slipped and slid under the rising moon. Finally, trees gave way to low bushes. The massive rocky craters of the coloured lakes sat churning and boiling under the storm. Diffuse white plumes rose fifty meters in the air, ghosting the volcano in a shroud. Lightning split and crackled through the sky above. Neil turned and collapsed back against a rocky edge. He needed to rest.

"Ebu gogo," Atasi repeated, pointing. After a minute, she pulled him back up and led Neil further north along the rocky edge of the pale blue lake. From their new vantage point, Neil could see the triangular plateau where the three lakes met. That place was where he needed to plant his copper rod. But the crest of Kelimutu was crawling with hobbits. Hundreds upon hundreds of them had gathered upon the peak in some kind of meeting. In the midst of them, Ivy Carter stood head and shoulders above the rest. The air hummed with noise and distant conversation. Neil looked up to the moon. He had maybe five hours until midnight.

"We'll have to bide our time," he murmured to Atasi. "Wait for them to clear off so I can plant the lightning rod without being seen." Now that so many of the little people were here, he didn't like his chances of getting through them unscathed. And he wouldn't risk Atasi's life if he could help it. He looked at her. The young woman was watching the hobbits with such intensity, he doubted that she heard him speak. He shuffled around in his bag and pulled out the black stone Atasi had found him. He was sure that it would work. All he needed to do was plant the lightning rod, hold up the stone and bang – *he'd disappear*. The lunar energy fields, the lightning, and the stone. That's all it would take. He was sure of it. And what about her? What would she do? Would she come with him? Or watch him leave alone. There was no future for Atasi on modern earth. He knew that. But until Charat was dead, there was no future for her here either. It was the one thing Neil hadn't been able to resolve. He hated the taste of unfinished work.

We have time. Neil lay flat on the ground in the rain. Together, they waited. The storm washed him clean. Humidity cooked his fever, then rain brought his temperature back down. He felt himself beginning to drift away.

"Nee-el!" Atasi was shaking him again. Neil wasn't sure how much time had passed, but the moon was slightly higher. "Ebu gogo. Go." She pointed. The moonlight silhouetted the top of the mountain which seemed to be moving. *No*, he realised, straining to see in the dark. *They're moving away.* A landslide of the hobbits were heading down the southern side of the mountain. A smaller group had broken off and were drifting back to the western forests where they had set up camp.

"They're leaving," Neil pushed himself up higher. "This is our chance." He watched as they all disappeared, an anxiety-ridden twenty minutes of craning his neck over the rocky ledge they were hidden behind, until he was sure there was no movement on the crest. "Atasi," Neil pushed himself up. The mud squelched between his fingers. For a moment, he felt the fog clear. Quickly he began to unwrap the bindings around the copper rods. "We've got to do it now. To make sure the lightning hits the right spot. Come on." Atasi helped him to his feet, carrying his bag. With hearts pounding, the two of them struggled across the wide rift that separated the blood red lake from the icy blue one.

Neil dropped to the ground at the place he had Fallen. It seemed like a lifetime ago that he'd been here. *Has it only been two months?* So much had happened. Every day had been a struggle to survive. He felt old. Carefully, he lay his four copper rods along the ground. Each was a metre tall, with one end tapered wider and the other beaten thin. He picked up the first, drew himself up to his feet and carefully tipped it upside down. Using the point, Neil began to roll the rod between his fingers, down into the rocky ground with as much pressure as he could muster. It was a delicate operation. Too hard, and the slightly malleable copper would bend. Too soft and he wouldn't break the surface of the rock.

"Atasi." Neil bent over, exhausted by his efforts. Atasi took over, copying his actions, grinding the copper rod deeper and deeper into the earth. The moon drifted higher. Time was passing too quickly. The ground was too hard. He took over again, pushing the rod down as he twisted it. When he began to waver, dizziness clouding his head, Atasi took the reins. Neil wondered if she even knew why he did it. She couldn't possibly have understood his intention to draw lightning from the sky. But still she helped him, as she had come to do, out of friendship and kindness and nothing more. As he watched her struggle against the rain and rock, he had never felt more humbled.

Finally, the first lightning rod was buried deep enough to support the remainder of them. With Atasi's help, Neil nested one rod onto another, thin end into thick hollow, until three teetering meters of copper stretched into the sky. Together, they lifted it, balanced carefully between them, slotting the length into its first, half-buried, fellow. Lightning cracked overhead and splintered across the sky. The storm was worsening. The lighting rod stood tall and thin in the darkness, barely noticeable against the deluge of rain. But lightning would be drawn to it like moths to a flame.

"Step back for a moment." Neil gestured to Atasi to move away from the rod. He lifted his arm up toward the moon. It wavered. His muscles were failing. Neil had never felt closer to death. "If the lightning strikes me instead of this rock," he puffed. "I'll die instantly. If it hits the rock first, then we'll get the best light show this island has ever seen." Atasi backed away a few meters. She threw an anxious look over her shoulder. They were still alone.

"Nee-el?" Her voice reached him through the storm. "Atasi? Go?" Neil let his arm drop.

"What?"

"Atasi. Go," she repeated, insistently. "Go. Nee-el."

"You want to come with me?" He stared, stunned. "You want to go?"

"Go!" Atasi ran forward again. She took his hand. With a look that spoke volumes, Atasi lifted his wrist high into the air. He stared in wonder as they stood together, lightning skittering above their heads. There was no expectation in her face. No promise of a better life in his words. The woman was decades younger than Neil, and there was not a thing he wanted to offer her but friendship. Not a thing she wanted from him, but the same. And for the first time in Neil's life, it was enough.

Together, they held the stone high, until their arms grew weak and began to falter. Together, they cried into the rain, staring up at the sky.

But no lightning came.

Something was missing.

The stone and the lightning weren't enough. An hour passed; the moon was nearly overhead. Finally, Neil collapsed into the mud.

"I got it wrong." His voice cracked in defeat. "It's over. Come away," he said, pulling her arm toward the western edge of the icy blue lake. But it was she who caught him as he stumbled and slid down the slippery ridge, unable to control his failing muscles. Atasi settled him in a rocky crevice only a meter above the raging water. Below them, a toxic cocktail of chemicals fed the crater lake, filling the lungs with the sulphuric odour of rotten eggs. Neil squeezed the black stone in his fist. With a cry of fury and despair, he flung it into the depths of the icy blue lake. He had failed.

CHAPTER 37

IVY

Breathe. Just breathe.

The souls of Ivy's feet flew over drenched peat. She leapt off a mossy log, her toes slipping as she sprung away, forward momentum landing her safely on the other side as she sped on through the forest. The canopy above was lit by foliage with silver edges. A diffused glow lifted the darkness of night to almost day. Tonight, the full moon was the brightest Ivy had ever seen, even through the deluge of rain. *Onwards, onwards.* Kyah's face swam in her mind. The bonobo had been so determined, so *resolute*, in her choice. *Run. Home.* Her formidable strength had not been used to fight back. Kyah's arms had propelled Ivy from the cave instead and thrown her, head over feet, into the storm outside. Kyah meant to face the Karathah alone. To sacrifice herself. But Ivy refused to accept it. She only hoped that she wasn't too late.

Nearly an hour passed. Shadows slipped by Ivy as she ran. Shapes of the *Homo floresiensis* hunters that seemed to melt into the forest. They travelled together, around, and above her, more than six hundred strong. But despite their numbers, Ivy rarely saw a single person cross her path. They were nature in human form. Camouflaged into the undergrowth, tiny bodies of olive skin and dark hair. Arboreal arms lifted them seamlessly into the trees to avoid obstacles. Bipedal legs bore their flight over land. As the hobbits ran, the low hum of a dusk song floated in the air alongside them. Intertwining notes of excruciating clarity followed Ivy down the southern face of Kelimutu and filled her with adrenaline. They sang a war cry, but like none she'd ever heard. There were no screams of intimidation. No promise of violent victory. The harmonic notes promised only unity. Each voice was part of a whole. Together they would live, or together they would die. So simple, but the power of it resonated within her bones.

The rain began again in earnest. Ozone and peat moss and the musty biome of wet forest filled her lungs. The earth jolted and rumbled beneath her feet. Her soles beat harder against it. Another volcano had awoken. A new wave of ash washed down from the clouds. Ivy rubbed her eyes as she ran, streaking black across her pale skin. Despite the rain, she was not cold. Fear burned inside her. Fear that she would arrive too late. Fear that Kyah could already be dead.

A familiar bird call sounded through the forest, and Ivy slowed. From nowhere, Xiou appeared at her side.

"Where?" He asked. Ivy looked around, trying desperately to find a familiar landmark through the drizzle.

"That ridge up there," she pointed, "Just beyond it is the cave where he found us."

"I lead from here then." Xiou pushed forward, staying in Ivy's sight. Another bird call told her that the hidden others still followed.

Within minutes, she was climbing the familiar bank of vegetation that led up to the cave mouth. Ahead, Ivy could see the body of the hunter she had killed, slumped in a heap at the side of the entrance. The spear was still in him. Rain washed the fear from her shoulders. Xiou gave a nod. Taking a deep breath, Ivy left

Xiou in the shadows and stepped forward alone. Behind her in the darkness, she heard a whimper. She knew that sound.

"Kyah!" Ivy's voice broke with emotion as she turned around. The bonobo was trapped in the thickly braided fishing net that the Karathah had brought, suspended from a high tree branch just beyond the cave mouth. "Kyah! I'm here!" The bonobo's head turned, scanning the dark. As soon as she saw Ivy, she began to screech. Her lips were pulled back in fear, her eyes wide. Weaving a single arm through the net, she gestured wildly. *Run.*

But Ivy had already made her choice. She was here to bargain. *Breathe. Just breathe.*

Water cascaded down the rock face above the dark cave, concealing its insides. With a decisive shout, Ivy faced the terror she knew was waiting for her within. "Come out! Come and take your damned stone. You want it? Come and get it from me."

A lone figure stepped through the veil. The red-beaded hunter grinned in smug satisfaction when he saw Ivy's arm extended, the black amulet dangling enticingly from her fist.

"Ey-vee." His lips barely moved. A string of unfamiliar words fell from them like honeyed venom. The man stepped down over the lip of the cave, closer. Ivy wondered at his empty hands. He had no fear of her at all. His right ear was hanging at a grotesque angle. Dried blood streaked his face and neck. Torn skin across his forehead formed dark lines under the moonlight. He had not washed the stains away after Kyah's attack. With all this rain, it felt deliberate, as if he had chosen to wear the blood as a trophy. Ivy shuddered. Fear crept back up her spine. She stepped toward the man, amulet still held aloft. Ivy pointed up to Kyah. "Release her first."

The man looked up at his hostage, amused. He gave a sharp call, and the two hunters that had attacked Ivy in the cave earlier emerged behind him. Their leader barked some instructions, and they skidded down into the vegetation. Ivy stepped back as they drew close, but they continued past her without a glance. Neither held a weapon. At the base of Kyah's tree, one of the men unwound a long rope. The net began to lower. Kyah's fingers gripped it tight. With a shout, the red-beaded hunter encouraged his men to continue. He held his hands up. The words he recited to Ivy were cajoling and calm. His movements measured and at ease. *Trust me*, his body seemed to be saying. But the moonlight reflected cold, dead eyes.

"All the way to the ground," Ivy gestured. The net lowered further. As the bundle of terrified ape hit the ground with a thud, Ivy's concern and attention spun toward Kyah. In an instant, the red-beaded hunter raced the distance between them, tore the amulet from her hand and gave a shout. Both men heaved on the rope, swinging its captive back into the canopy with renewed hysterics. The knot went taut as they bound it tightly back to the tree.

A stunning blow caught the side of Ivy's head. She crashed to the ground, reeling. The red-beaded hunter dragged her backward by her long hair, forcing Ivy up to her knees, then kicked her forward once more with an explosion of violence. His bare foot hit her spine and pressed her hard into the wet ground. Mud filled Ivy's mouth. The pressure on her chest was unbearable. Vomit erupted from her lips. In a haze of pain, the flight of a spear whipped past her head.

"Ebu gogo!" The hunter's war cry was one of insane delight. "Karum-pat-in-uchawa-ebu-gogo!" The man laughed maniacally, and Ivy could only assume that Xiou and the others had run forward to protect her. They were no longer shadows, but ready and willing warriors. Ivy struggled to raise her head from the forest floor. One of the Karathah holding Kyah's rope ditched sideways, the shaft of an arrow suddenly between his eyes. The other tied the rope off tighter, ensuring Kyah stayed aloft. Throwing his head back, the red-beaded hunter screeched again. In an instant, his call was answered. Hundreds of Karathah hunters streamed from the cave, splitting the watery curtain as they spilled into the forest below. The red beaded hunter had not remained idle while Ivy was gone. He too, had called an army to his side. And as each sapien fell upon the invading hobbits, each three times their size with weapons all the more formidable for it, Ivy knew a new war had begun.

"Get up, Hiranah!" Guntah was dragging at Ivy's arm as Kora and Setian joined Xiou in his attack against the red-beaded hunter. Ivy groaned and staggered. "Get up!" With his own brute strength, Guntah dragged her away from their battle. With vicious jabs, the sapien hunter was striking at each of her friends in turn. A long knife had appeared in his hand, no doubt hidden until he'd had need of it. Ivy caught a glint of copper in the moonlight. The summoned Karathah army dispersed into the forest deluge, searching for hobbits to kill. Arrows flew from the branches. Invisible bodies flanked their sapien adversaries from above. The hobbits were lethal in their precision, but the sapiens boasted weapons and size of brutal advantage. Though Xiou's tribe had an edge by sheer body count, the fight was equal in skill. Lightning flashed overhead. Rain soaked the battleground. Ivy struggled to her feet as Guntah raced away. A Karathah hunter stepped back into her and Ivy pushed him away, straight into the path of a spear. Kora whipped by, face bloodied and eyes dangerous. Ivy's vision locked on Kyah, still trapped high above their heads. She ran toward the bonobo, only to be knocked down again. Ivy wrestled and kicked, forcing her assailant back into the forest. An arrow from the dark took him down.

Forest animals fled in silence. Only humans, and their battle-cries corrupted the night. Humidity rose as bodies fell. The earth rumbled. A heavy roll of ash began to bury the dead where they fell, as the sky thundered and wailed above. Xiou now fought alone against the red-beaded hunter. His spear hit the sapien with a thud. A wound not deep enough to kill. Ivy watched in horror as the Karathah wrenched the short spear from his own shoulder, face manic with rage. Xiou stumbled back. Kora appeared by his side. Her own spear caught the side of the red-beaded hunter's face, stripping his torn ear clean away. He turned, rushing at the tiny woman with fists flying. Xiou descended upon him once again.

Ivy raced to the tree that held Kyah. Her fingernails split and slipped over the knots that kept her friend suspended. "I'm coming!" Above, Kyah lurched and swung in the net. To fall from such a height would mean death, even for the bonobo. "Keep still!" Ivy screamed. A sapien hunter fell at her feet, knocking her back. The man's mouth dropped open as he fell forward. Kari raced toward him, looking gratified as he retrieved his spear and ran back into the fray. Death lay under every tree. The branches were alive with revenge. Hobbit tribes were fighting back with more vehemence than Ivy could have imagined them capable of.

Ivy scrambled back to the rope tying Kyah's net. The knot was too tight and swollen with rain. Dodging blows and bodies, Ivy searched her hide skirt for the knife she kept hidden. *It's fallen out,* she realised. Desperately, she searched for another way to cut the rope.

"Hiranah!" A sweet voice called down to her from above. Ivy threw her head back. Barely visible in the canopy, little Trahg was waving down at her. Dread cracked like ice through every inch of her veins.

"Trahg, no! You shouldn't be here!" As if to drive home that thought, a shout nearby was cut short with a devastating gasp for air. Ivy spun to see Tica fall, her fingers stretched over a spear in her belly. Ivy ran and fell to her knees as the old woman's eyes found her own. A moment later, they stared like coloured glass into the rain. A brutal jolt tore Ivy's head backward. Bending over her, a Karathah man had grabbed Ivy's neck. He pulled her backwards away from Tica, a stone knife in one hand.

"Charat!" The man was shouting, dragging Ivy toward the red-beaded hunter. "Charat! Ju-raku-Ey-vee!" Ivy twisted and skidded through the mud, trying to regain her footing. She pushed up onto her knees, then launched herself into his arms. Grief and rage poured through Ivy's fists into his chest. She fought back against the man, backing him into the base of a tree. He was strong, far stronger than she. As his blade touched her throat, Ivy's knee found his groin. The Karathah man doubled over. Ivy twisted the stone knife from his fingers and slammed it into his temple. Stunned or dead, Ivy couldn't tell, but the man collapsed on her feet. Ivy turned. She ran, clutching the man's knife. All around, the forest was falling apart. A wretched groan deep underneath the earth, reverberated up into her bare feet. With a shudder, the ground began to sway and tip.

All around her, sapiens and hobbits alike grabbed rocks and trees for support. Ivy staggered across the forest floor, desperate to reach Kyah and Trahg. The cacophony of battle increased. Lightning split the air into slivers.

Crack! An enormous tree caught the strike. Its trunk split, showering undergrowth with spikes of bark as it came crashing down. The top of it smashed into Kyah's tree, wedging against high branches and swinging the netted captive wildly back and forth. Inside, Kyah screeched and cried with such terror that Ivy could hear nothing else. Her heart broke into a thousand pieces. She raced back to the base of it, clawing at the trunk, desperate to find a way up to save her. Further along the branch, Trahg clung to the underside of a branch like a spider, unconcerned by the danger it posed. Ivy could scarcely bear to watch him. With a heave of his wiry little arms, Trahg flung himself back on top of the branch. He skittered along, planting himself at the top of the knotted vines that made up the rope. With the skill of an acrobat, Trahg shimmied down and landed lightly on the top of the suspended net. He fumbled in his hide cloth for a moment, then began to saw at it.

"Ey-vee." The voice that caught the back of her neck made Ivy's skin crawl. She turned, slowly, blood thumping. The red-beaded hunter was standing only a few feet behind her. It was as if all other movement ceased. The fighting and death that surrounded them both fell away to inconsequence. With a nasty grin, he held up her amulet, letting it swing gently from his fingers. "Tsume-reduka-ebu-gogo," he said.

"You! Charat?! Is that your name?" Ivy screeched at him. "You want the Ebu gogo?! Is that it? Well, you have them! You have them all here, right now, fighting to save their own lives!"

The hunter shouted back at her in words she couldn't know. He threw his head back, laughing cruelly. The rain filled his mouth, open to the night sky, but he didn't care. "Ebu gogo," he spat, his arms wide. He kicked at a body by his feet. Ivy couldn't bring herself to look down. She didn't want to know who she had lost. Every member of her family was precious. Unnatural shapes on the forest floor told her dozens had already been lost.

"Is this what you stole my amulet for?" Ivy screamed at him. The torrent of rain strangled her blood-red hair and ran into her eyes. She was a woman possessed, mad with grief and anger. "You think it will help you kill them all?!" The hunter watched her in delight. "Well, you've already won!" Ivy shouted back at him. "They all die! I've already seen it! They will all die because of *what you are doing now*!" Ivy's chest was heaving, torn breaths drowning in torrential waves of emotion. A crack of thunder rent the air and tore her heart in two. With a furious roar, Ivy launched herself at the man. For an infinitesimal moment, he was caught off guard. It was enough to allow her a grip on her stone knife. She drove it into the right side of his chest. The knife pierced his flesh, but the wound was not deep enough. The hunter fought back. A mighty blow caught her chest, and Ivy reeled. There was no air to breathe. Her lungs screamed for release. She fell forward gasping, as he took her again from the back, punching her lung. Sparks of white split the darkness behind her eyes. *I'm going to die.* Death suddenly felt like a release. Noise faded away as Ivy's mind fell toward darkness.

Breathe. Just breathe.

It was Orrin who she heard as she drifted on the pain. Orrin's voice that forced her back to her knees. His face she searched for as the bloodied forest swam back into view. *Breathe, Ivy. Breathe.*

With bile in her mouth, and blood on her face, Ivy staggered back up to her hands and knees. She was behind the red-beaded hunter now. He had stepped forward, leaving her for dead, to search for his next prey. Her amulet hung from the leather strap, wrapped around his left wrist. It was so tantalisingly close. Ivy's palms pressed into the mud. She forced herself to her feet.

"Hiranah!" The sweet voice shouted down at her. "Look! I told you we were the best in trees!" Ivy struggled to raise her head. Kyah was beside Trahg, free on the branch, the empty net swinging impotent below them. With a mischievous giggle, Trahg launched himself toward a lower branch. Kyah was close behind.

"No! Stay up there!" But Ivy's warning had no substance. Her lungs still too raw. With horror, she saw the red-beaded hunter turn back to her, alerted by the little boy's call. The man moved fast. His grip caught Ivy's wrist and he wrenched her around until she faced the branches away from him, one arm twisted behind her back, bones on the verge of breaking. With his other hand, the man drew back, then pelted something up into the trees above. A rock caught Trahg hard between his little shoulder blades.

Thwack! The tiny boy tipped sideways, crashing down through the branches. Kyah's reaction was instant and fierce. She leapt downward, following in Trahg's wake of snapped twigs, screeching with fear. Before the child hit the ground, the bonobo caught him by one leg, and scooped him up.

"Run. Home!" Ivy shouted up at her, hands signing desperately. But Kyah didn't need to be told. Trahg was already safe in her arms. With a shrill hoot, Kyah clutched the boy to her chest with one hand wrapped tightly around him, then took off into the night forest.

"You bastard!" Ivy jabbed her free elbow backward, smashing the man's ribs and throwing him momentarily off balance. The Karathah hunter slipped, throwing out his arm. Out of the corner of her eye, Ivy saw the amulet fling off his wrist to disappear into the tangled mass of vegetation and mud. But his grip was quickly tightened. He threw Ivy hard against the trunk of the tree. Her back ricocheted off the wet bark, slamming cruelly with a sharp crack to the back of her head. Through a dizzying haze, Ivy saw the man step closer. He was talking quietly to her now, a hollow smile spreading across his face, the familiar glint of cruelty in his eyes as he moved. "You're a monster," Ivy choked out through the blood inside her mouth. "Why do you hate them so much?" She shuddered and choked as the tree behind lent her strength. *"What do you want* from them? Their food? Land? The very air that they breathe?" His answer came as a shattering blow to her jaw. Ivy reeled, falling sideways. The red-beaded hunter grabbed her hair, dragging her back up to her feet. "I know what you want from them," she seethed, spitting blood into his face. *"Power. That's why you're doing this. That's always why people like you always do this.* You need to feel *important."* Ivy crashed into the ground as another blow caught her shoulder. For a moment that felt like eternity, she stayed there, staring into the filth beneath her face. She clutched the leaves and ash in her fists, begging them to hold her tight. To stop the world from spinning. Pain became distant. Ivy's mind was drifting.

Until it wasn't.

I had a life, she remembered. *They all had a life.* Warmth began in her gut and grew and spread until every inch of her body was on fire. *Why should we die?* Rage, the likes of which she'd never felt in her life, set ablaze. *I held my breath too long. Lived in fear too long.* The fury rose. Ivy's face twisted as she forced herself up, staggering. The hunter laughed in surprise.

"You know what?" Ivy seethed, stepping closer. Her warm breath hit his face. His eyes flashed wide. "You don't get to do this," Ivy spat. "Because you're not special. No more than me, or them, or anyone else. *You're only human, just like the rest of us!*"

With a bellowing wail, Ivy launched herself at his body. Punching, kicking any part she could reach. Ferocious protection erupted from inside of her. Ivy fought for the lives of her beloved. For Kyah. For Trahg. For Xiou and Shahn and Gihn. The soul-crushing loss of all those she had loved, fell upon the red-beaded hunter through her fists. The weight of it was far greater than he expected. Ivy struggled as he gripped her, exchanging fierce blows. She pushed off his body as he fell to the ground. A slippery rock caught her underfoot, and Ivy crashed down again after him. She cried out in pain. The Karathah hunter pushed back up to his hands and knees, muscles coiled, ready to spring at her. But Ivy's fist was first. The wet stone that had tripped her was clutched tight in her palm. Ivy slammed it against his head with a resounding thud. The red-beaded hunter sprawled backward.

He didn't move again.

"That's enough!" Ivy screamed, pushing up to her feet. She raced toward a group of Karathah hunters. They had someone circled, and their adversary was fighting for her life. "Kora!" Ivy burst into their fray. She spun wildly, taking in each sapien that stood before her. She picked one, the closest, and addressed him directly. "No more!" She shook her head. Behind her, Kora was shouting at Ivy to move. But Ivy held her glare on the sapien man with his spear poised, reaching out to him. Imploring his humanity. Begging for him to be *humane.* "Please!" Ivy knew her words meant nothing. "No more! Look – Charat is dead!" Ivy pointed to the base of the tree where she had left the hunter's body. "He's dead!" The Karathah hunters all turned to follow her gaze. Whispers began to filter amongst them. "No more," Ivy begged. She raised her hand, gently pushing his spear aside. The man's fingers twitched reflexively around the shaft of his weapon. He looked at his comrades. The other Karathah exchanged glances. Their leader, the instigator of this violence, was dead. A heavy moment passed, and then the hunter slowly lowered his spear. With a look of disgust, he shouted to the other hunters. He shifted his spear as he stepped back, spitting at Ivy's feet on the forest floor. With a growl he threw his hand up, then turned and ran into the forest. One by one, the other Karathah hunters followed.

Ivy stared, slightly dazed. She hadn't expected him to leave so readily. Shouts seemed to be fading away. She blinked hard, wondering if the battle was really over. Xiou appeared at her side. His face, already a spiderweb of scars, looked more battle-worn than ever.

"Trahg was here," Ivy said. "He got injured. Kyah has him."

Xiou nodded, his eyes full of worry. "She knows what to do."

"Have you seen the others? Guntah? Setian?"

"No," Xiou replied, "But I see their efforts. Look, Hiranah." Ivy followed his line of sight through the soaked and ruined forest. "The Karathah have given up this fight."

"For now." The sad smile she offered said more than any words could.

"Yes," Xiou agreed. "For now. This war is not won."

"But they will not attack us again in a hurry," Kora said, appearing at Ivy's side. Her skin was bloodied and bruised. Ivy knelt and gave her friend a fierce hug. Ivy's knees sunk into the mud, and she lifted her face to the rain, letting it wash clean.

"I thought I'd nearly lost you," Ivy said, getting to her feet again.

"They had no chance," Kora replied.

"Just one look at you is enough to kill anyone," Setian added, stepping up to rub his forehead against that of his mate. Kora grinned.

Xiou put his fingers to his lips. His bird call echoed through the rain. From the shadows, his people appeared like ghostly apparitions. As overjoyed as she was to see each face, Ivy's eyes searched for those faces she knew best. When all seemed to have returned that could, her heart sank. She walked slowly through the forest, searching for Guntah. With so few remaining to save their species from extinction, there were far too many newly dead. With gentle arms, Ivy gathered up those they had lost to lay together in the quietude of the empty cave. Quiet sobs passed as others did the same. As she bent to shift a tree branch, a moan froze her hands.

"You're alive," she pressed her forehead against Guntah's, pulling back gently. One of his legs splayed at an unnatural angle.

"I battled a tree and it won." The man hadn't lost his sense of humour.

"Phren will take care of you," Ivy assured him as he wrapped his arms around her neck. "I will carry you home to her."

"You've done well, Hiranah." Guntah panted in pain. "And the red-beaded hunter?"

"Dead." Ivy stepped over Karathah bodies hidden throughout the undergrowth. There were far more than she expected. Revenge had taken its toll.

"And the Life Stone?"

"Lost somewhere in the forest." She looked away to hide the expression on her face.

When all the bodies had been accounted for, and the dead laid to rest in the southern cave with its waterfall entrance, Ivy began the slow trek home.

Her hobbit family had lost over one hundred. The moon hung high. In two hours, it would pass overhead and continue toward morning. Ivy carried Guntah with as much care as the stormy jungle allowed her. Kyah was alive and free. The tribe had driven their Karathah tormentors back for a time, and the *Homo flore-siensis* tribes had been reunited. Hope remained. But still, Ivy's heart was bleeding.

Victory had come a cost.

Her own freedom. Her old life.

Orrin.

CHAPTER 38

ORRIN

7pm. His body ached as he ran test after test. Orrin crouched on the floor, carefully cradling a microphone beside his mobile phone. The sorrowful timbre of Ivy's cello sang through the phone, was picked up by the microphone and fed into the software on his laptop. With each play, the electromagnetic fields flowing throughout the room increased.

9pm. The equipment was set up. Every test had been run, with the exception of discharging the Tesla Coil. Orrin's fears grew with each minute that passed. Without the audio spectrum analyser, he could not be certain that the fundamental frequencies that Phil had provided him were perfectly played. Deft fingers flew over his laptop keyboard, setting each of the frequencies in turn through a tone generator. Each note carried not only its purest pitch, but also a range of harmonics above it that each occupied their own frequency within the sound. Orrin desperately needed to see the interplay of those harmonics against his electromagnetic graphs, but the lack of his analyser left him short.

He sat down at his laptop, scrolling the news for a sign of what was happening in the penthouse floor of the physics department. There were articles detailing the fluctuating energy fields, and various interviews with environmental experts, but it seemed that Cassandra had managed to keep a lid on their night's exploits. He imagined that she was planning to release the information all at once, in whatever way served her best. Orrin scrolled back up and a Breaking News article appeared as the page refreshed. He read it, his stomach twisting in knots.

Three Arrested in Cosmitech Break-in.

Three protesters were arrested earlier today after an attempted break-in to pharmaceutical giant Cosmitech. It is believed the three infiltrated the building in an attempted burglary of animal resources. Two men charged are already known to police, with one also believed to be involved in the arson attack on the company's headquarters earlier this month. All three protesters have been detained and are expected to be held until a court hearing–

Orrin clicked the window closed.

Shite. They were caught.

He felt like throwing up.

11pm. Orrin rubbed his eyes under his glasses. He gave his head a violent shake to clear the fatigue. It felt like days since he'd slept. *Keep your head straight, boyo,* he chastised himself as he ran through his checklist one more time and secured the charging lead to his phone. *Can't risk anything going wrong.*

11.40pm. The electromagnetic fields in the room whipped and coursed. Shoulders hunched, eyes trained obsessively on the output graphs, Orrin watched as the moment grew closer. Ivy's amulet sat eerily still in its suspended nest. Orrin's fingers itched to switch on the Tesla Coil. *Not yet. Nearly time. Just a bit longer.* Once more, he checked the transformer and power source to make sure the coil would be ready to charge. Orrin double-checked that the tone generators were set at the half-dozen frequencies that Phil had identified. *If he's wrong about even one of them, it'll throw the whole thing out.*

Sweat dripped in his eyes and Orrin used the bottom of his shirt to wipe his face.

CHAPTER 39

IVY

*L*ightning spidered across the sky as Ivy and the hobbits traversed the hour-long trek back up to Kelimutu's peak. The coloured lakes shimmered black in the moonlight, the surface of each, churning beneath heavy rain. No celebration greeted them. Death was mourned with each face that did not return and the fragile families that remained fell into one another's arms in grief. As a people, they had chosen to fight to defend their right to live. As mothers and fathers, sons and daughters, their sacrifice felt almost too much to bear. Phren sought out Xiou among the procession as he arrived back.

"You must come with me," she called to him. The old medicine woman looked exhausted. She took one look at Guntah's broken leg and ushered Ivy along too. They descended slightly down the western side of the mountain where the elders and children had set up camp. Ivy lay Guntah under a copse of bamboo to help shield him from the storm. "This will heal badly," Phren said, quickly studying his leg. "I will prepare you something for the pain and do what I can. But first," she gestured to Xiou. "Trahg followed you down to the south caves. We did not realise he had gone until it was too late. When she found Trahg had gone after you, Shahn followed, desperately trying to find him. But Trahg was too fast. When we finally found Shahn halfway down the mountain, she couldn't go any further."

"Is she injured?" Xiou looked anxiously through the scattered hunters reuniting with their loved ones.

Phren's ancient face softened into a rare smile. "Not injured, no." She led the way through a thicket, pushing aside drenched branches. A makeshift ceiling of bent and woven bamboo had been laced between trees and beneath it, Shahn was sitting in a pile of leaves and hides. Trahg sat huddled beside her. In Shahn's arms, a newborn baby suckled and squirmed.

Xiou's face lit up like sunshine. "You are safe," he breathed a sigh of relief, kneeling down in front of his mate. Xiou rubbed his forehead against Shahn's, then touched the newborn's face. "Welcome child." He sat back, opening his arms to Trahg who climbed into them.

"I rescued Kyah from the Karathah!" Trahg said, proudly. Kyah was sitting close by. She gave a soft hoot and Ivy's heart leapt with relief. The bonobo loped over to Ivy, who picked her up and whispered adorations in her ear.

"And think perhaps Kyah rescued you," Shahn corrected Trahg. "And you were very naughty for going after the hunters." Despite her tone, Shahn couldn't keep the smile off her face for long. Serenity slipped back over her. "I have scolded him many times since Kyah brought him back." Shahn held her hand out to the bonobo. "This one. She is a brave person." Kyah dutifully climbed down from Ivy's arms and crossed the small space, taking Shahn's hand. "Thank you, Kyah," Shahn signed. Kyah leaned forward, so that Shahn could press their foreheads gently together. "My Trahg would be lost without you." A prick of tears sprung to Ivy's eyes. The love between the bonobo and hobbit child was breathtaking. Neither cared that the other was differ-ent. Kyah was Trahg's playmate, surrogate mother, and guardian angel. It seemed only right that he would never have to be without her now. The time remaining for Ivy and Kyah to return home was nearly gone. Less than an hour remained before midnight, when the moon would begin its slow decent and the energy peak would begin to wane. But Ivy's amulet was lost. And Kyah was safe.

The bonobo pulled back, eyeing Shahn's new baby curiously. With deliberate care, Kyah gently pressed the back of her long hand to the newborn's lips. Ivy blinked her tears away. Kyah had offered the same gesture of maternal love to Trahg when she had first met him, only months before. Now, it seemed this new baby already had her heart as well.

"What will you call your new baby?" Ivy asked. It was Xiou who answered.

"Kyah," he said. "Of course."

Ivy smiled. "Perfect."

CHAPTER 40

NEIL

*N*eil lay wedged in the rocks beside the icy blue lake, a deluge of rain hitting his side. Beside him, Atasi had her eyes closed, facing the sky. She had been as attentive as always whenever Neil needed it but seemed otherwise vacant. They had failed to get the lightning to strike. The copper rod and the black stone had not been enough to lure the lightning. There was something missing. Neil's mind drifted in and out of consciousness as he tried to imagine what he'd missed. Some other trigger. Some reactant he hadn't observed. *It makes no difference now. I threw the stone away.* Neil had never felt more childish. More devastated. Despaired. Every cell in his body burned in torment, but the young woman beside him had never looked so peaceful. He couldn't imagine what was going through her mind. *Is she glad we failed? Does she think I'm insane?*

Now, once again, there was nothing to do but wait. Neil's only chance of escape now rested with the red head. If she succeeded in opening the vortex, he and Atasi could follow her in. If she failed, Neil knew he would die here.

"Ey-vee." Atasi's quiet voice broke through his delirium. "Ebu gogo." Neil looked up, stretching to see over the crevice without giving himself away. Much closer than before, hordes of hobbits were returning up the southern crest of the mountain. Neil and Atasi both shrank back, hoping the rain and darkness would be enough to keep them hidden. Some passed only meters away. The red head was among them, carrying one of the little creatures in her arms. Even in the dark, it was clear there had been heavy casualties. Some limped. Others held wounds together. The hobbits trailed in for over half an hour, bypassing the peak where his lightning rod still stood in the dark, but instead, dispersing down into the western forests.

Neil dragged his hide bag closer and tipped it out, watching as his clay bowls rattled away down the rock face. None of it mattered now. Just the phone. He shoved his mobile back inside the bag, then added Ivy's journal too. The journal was leverage. A peace offering. The journal was whatever it needed to be, to save his life. Atasi watched him.

"Ivy," he said. He held up the bag, giving it a little shake. "Ivy."

Midnight inched closer. Neil's eyes grew heavy. Time drifted.

*

No one noticed the last hunter to creep out of the southern forest. He watched the hobbits disperse, trailing them silently, as only a skilled tracker could. Taking advantage of the blinding rain, he slipped past the hidden rocky crevice, his eyes on Kelimutu's peak. He ducked up the thin ridge that intersected the three coloured lakes. As he reached the peak, a flash of lightning passed overhead, highlighting the thin copper rod that pierced the rock. With a spit of fury, the man dropped to his haunches. He touched it gently.

"Nee-el," he spat.

The red-beaded hunter scanned the moonlit edges of the forest.

Narrowed his eyes against the rocky outcrops around the lakes.

Pulled the copper knife from his waistband and gripped it tight.

Carefully, systematically, the hunter began to hunt.

CHAPTER 41

IVY

*I*vy sat above the camp on a quiet outcrop overlooking the Sister Lakes. Beside her, Kyah quietly picked apart some fruit. They were both exhausted, but nothing could have persuaded Ivy to eat. She was lost. More lost than she had felt when she had Fallen here. Across the crest of Kelimutu and down into the western forests, Xiou's tribe were settling for the night. There were still tears being shed. Memories of lost loved ones being shared. The near-midnight sky cracked and split above her, but Ivy's face was impervious to the rain. She sat staring at the three lakes as they churned, imagining the future she had sacrificed as if it had slipped quietly into the inky water.

She had lost her chance at freedom.

The new life she was trapped in stretched out before her as an untrodden road. The island was perilous. The very survival of the *Homo floresiensis* tribes was still unknown. She had given them the knowledge they needed to survive the Karathah. To unite and to adapt to the changing world around them. Most importantly, she had given them hope. Xiou was a good leader, and the tribes were all united in their choice to follow him. It would be a difficult path, but Ivy felt the truth of it in her bones. They *would* survive. She only hoped the cost of sharing the earth with *Homo sapiens* would be worth it.

She searched the stormy night. Stars were almost impossible to see through the floating ash. Her own future was now unwritten. She would live and die here with the love of her new family. But it wasn't their love that she craved.

If I could write a message for him in the stars, what would it say? she wondered. *That I tried? That I know he did too?* Ivy dropped her head back, letting the rain wash away her regret. *That I'm sorry. That I should have loved him when I had the chance.*

Her shoulders broke forward with a shudder. Ivy's face fell into her hands. She had been everything to so many people, that she had nothing left to give. The weight of the world was too heavy. Ivy had carried it as long as she could. It was time to set it down and let Xiou and his people take up the mantle. Beside her, Kyah offered a gentle hoot of condolence. She brushed at Ivy's shoulder, then lay her head there.

"You have done enough, Hiranah," Xiou said softly. She hadn't heard him sit down beside her. He gave Ivy a sad smile. "It is time for you to return home."

Ivy sighed and looked out through the blearing rain. "This is my home now."

Xiou shook his head. "This has never been your true home." He lifted his hand, pulling her palm out toward him. He covered it with his own. Ivy felt the warm weight of something fall into it. "Your true home is where your heart belongs. Far away from here." Ivy opened her palm.

"You found it?" She gasped. Adrenaline shot through her heart. Her amulet was practically glowing. "How?"

"I felt it," Xiou said, touching his forehead. "You forget that it is part of this place. It called me."

"I cannot believe it. You mean – I can–?" A devastating rush of emotion smashed through her all at once.

"Go home." Though his eyes held sorrow, Xiou's words were

clear. "Go back to your life, Hiranah," he paused, an odd smile coming to his lips – "I mean, *Ivy Carter.*"

Ivy fell forward, clutching Xiou, sobbing as if he had handed her everything she had ever wanted, all at once, to keep forever.

"We don't have much time," he encouraged. "Come."

She stood up. Ivy turned around slowly, her mind struggling against the impulse to run, to make it happen. She took Kyah's hand in her own. Behind her, gathered at the peak of the dormant volcano, her family were already waiting. Not just Xiou's tribe, but hundreds – all of those that had come together to start a new life. In her solitude, Ivy had not heard them gathering. Now they stood united in the storm, faces turned toward her in compassion, ready to let her go.

Ivy searched the sea of faces. Leihna stood in the milling crowd, a radiant smile on her face. Beside her, the young leader from the beach-cave, Ko, drew himself up tall. *A new beginning.* Kora and Setian were at the front of the crowd, surrounded by the orphans of Dozu Dhalu cave. The tribe's future lay in their hands, and she could think of no better surrogate parents. Ivy rushed forward to hug them and push her forehead gently against each of their own.

"You understand though, don't you?" She implored Kora. Ivy stepped closer, allowing as many as she could to hear her speak. "You must stay together to survive the Karathah." She found Shahn's eyes in the crowd. They were sparkling. Shahn's new baby was held to her breast and by her side, little Trahg held Filhia's hand. Trauma and grief had overwhelmed the girl since the murder of her sister. Her hopelessness was epitome of Ivy's worst fears for the future of their people. Ivy knelt, taking Trahg and then Filhia by the hands. "Be strong, Filhia," she coaxed her. "Rinap's joy still lives inside you." A tear rolled down the girl's face and Ivy squeezed her tight.

"I promise that I will spend the rest of my life fighting for you," Ivy said, getting to her feet. "Together, you have a future, but I can't promise you a safe one. There *is* kindness in the Karathah, but it is often outweighed by many who simply do not raise their voice. If we were united, as you are, we could change our world for you. But me – I will try, but I cannot do it alone. I'm only one person. *I'm only human."*

"We are all only human," Xiou said gently. "And that is why we never give up." He took Ivy's hand and led her toward the peak of Kelimutu. As they walked, his voice rose in a pure, melancholic note. With each step, other voices joined in. This time, their Dusk Song was for Ivy alone. They had called her here, and now, the tribes were sending her home. As the Sister Lakes came together at the peak of the ancient volcano, hundreds of notes wove together, lifting music through the blinding rain, up into the night sky above. Harmony resonated through her bones. It felt as if the very air Ivy breathed was alive. Beneath her feet, the earth vibrated, as if it were answering a call from the heavens.

As Ivy stepped up to the place where she had Fallen, the amulet in her hand burned hot. A blue glow shimmered the edges of the stone. Spiderwebs of lightning coursed and splintered through the sky. In the dark, a thin shadow reached for the stars. But Ivy didn't see the copper lightning rod hidden in the dark. She only saw the lighting itself as it whipped and shattered around her.

Suddenly, a splinter of blue light shot upwards from the glowing black stone on her palm. Ivy held it out. This time, she had no fear of the pain she knew was coming. Her heart was bursting with anticipation. Midnight was only minutes away. She marvelled at the power in her hands. The amulet that had twisted time to bring her here, now promised to deliver her home again. *Fifty thousand years.*

"Wait," Ivy cried suddenly. "The amulet! The Life Stone must stay with your people, Xiou. It's the only way to ensure it ends up back in Liang Bua cave. I need to find it there, in my future – in my time. But that means–" Ivy's thoughts struggled to make sense of the possibilities. "I must leave it with you! So, when I leave here, it is yours again." The truth of it was throwing itself at Ivy almost too fast to glimpse.

"Then I will take it back to Home Cave, Hiranah." Xiou said.

"No! Wait!" Ivy's heart was suddenly pounding. "Don't you see? This means that you don't have to hide! You don't have to live your lives in fear of the Karathah! There is another way to survive," she said urgently. The idea had been percolating in her thoughts for days. But until this moment, it had never seemed possible. "You could *leave* this version of Flores," Ivy cried, "and find a new home through the shards!" She held the amulet aloft. "The Life Stone is *the key* to opening new worlds for your people. You saw the worlds I speak of – you know that I Fell from one of them to be here with you. You pulled me back when I almost Fell again. There are worlds out there without the Karathah. You can find them!" Ivy didn't just want to imagine a world where evolution had taken a different path. She had already seen it. One hundred times over. Every shard had held the possibility of a new beginning.

"Search through the shards, Xiou," Ivy insisted. "Find a world that you can all survive in – *no*, not just survive, but *thrive* in. Find yourselves a new home. Find a world where the Karathah do not exist, where the forest can belong to your tribe alone." The amulet glowed brighter. She was running out of time.

"Leave?" Xiou looked unsure. "But we are part of this forest."

"And *every* version of this forest," Ivy insisted. "The place calls to you because of what is beneath your feet and inside your head." Ivy had long suspected that *Homo sapien's* lost ability to detect the magnetic fields of the Earth were still functional in the hobbit brain. Cryptochrome proteins drove the migration patterns of many other animals across continents and allowed them to keep their bearing, even when no other landmarks were available to guide their way. An internal compass, as it were. Something about Kelimutu oriented the *Homo floresiensis* people in the same way. Their brains were wired to feel the magnetic fields inside. And correspondingly, Kelimutu oriented them. There was some elemental quality so intrinsically part of the volcano on which they stood, that it was unlikely to change, even across worlds. The volcano, and the Earth, were created billions of years before the species evolved. Their own evolution, there-fore, was built around its unique makeup, not the other way around.

"Find the Falling Place in any world," Ivy said, "and it will call you Home. Sing your Dusk Song. Wait for the full moon. You know what to do," Ivy implored. "Please consider it, Xiou, as an alternative to living with the Karathah." She looked around. The faces she loved, smiled back at her. Their voices rose stronger in harmony. "But once you make that decision," Ivy said, "remember that you may never be able to return. You will have to leave the amulet behind, as I do now. The Life Stone belongs in this earth. It must be buried here in Liang Bua cave. If you all leave," worry lined Ivy's face, "then someone must stay behind." Surely such loneliness would be fate worse than death.

"I will stay," a quiet voice said. Ivy looked around. It was Floni who spoke, the mother of dusty-haired little Turi, who had died in the cave fire. "I will return to Home Cave alone," she said. "I would rather stay with my lost child, than travel to a new world without him." The woman was tiny and resolute in her sorrow. "I will take the Life Stone back to his resting place. Together, we will belong to this world alone."

"Floni." Ivy eyes were brimming with unshed tears. "*Flo* – you *will* stay, won't you?" Ivy knew in her heart that the woman was already decided. Her bones were destined to lie with her child, no matter how many years it took to reunite them.

Floni gave her a sad smile. She nodded. "I will stay."

"Then you'll consider it?" Ivy begged, turning back to Xiou.

"Together, the tribes will decide," he replied. "But please, Hiranah. *You must go.*"

Ivy stepped forward. Every cell in her body felt on fire. The moon was at its highest point. Rain fell and lightning flicked like white veins across the sky. With shining eyes, Ivy held out her hand to Kyah.

"Ky, it's time to go home."

But the bonobo didn't move.

CHAPTER 42

ORRIN

ick. Tick. Tick.

11.50pm. A key turned in the lock. The laboratory door began to open. Orrin's heart nearly burst from his chest. He spun around wildly, searching for a place to hide. He was too far from his office door to make a run for it. As the door opened and a man pushed his way in, Orrin froze like a deer in the head-lights. The man looked around, searching for his bearings, then shuffled in, carrying a heavy silver box. He kicked the door closed behind him and leaned back on it, breathing heavily.

"I thought–" Dale looked at Orrin, shame-faced, "I thought you might need this."

"Dale?" Orrin struggled to find his voice.

"Well actually, your friend Dimitri gave me the idea," Dale said. "I think he suspected I wasn't entirely – *loyal* to Chancellor Thandi's request to contribute up there. He pulled me aside." Orrin stared at the machine Dale carried under his arm as if it were made of gold.

"Dimi gave you an audio spectrum analyser?"

"Well, no," Dale admitted. "But he told me where I could find it. Said *someone* really needed it for–" Dale looked around, "for getting *someone* back from *a place she shouldn't be.*"

"Dimi said that?"

"Yeah, it took me a minute to figure out what was going on," Dale gave a shy grin. "He's making a real mess of things upstairs for them. Cassandra doesn't realise."

"Well, I think she's about to!" Orrin laughed a little madly. He ducked across the room to retrieve the machine from Dale's arms. "Because in about eight minutes they'll all be in for a hell of a disappointment. Quick, help me get it set up!"

Dale turned back and locked the door behind him. "I've been watching his data calculations. They're all wrong and he knows it. He's a good friend, Orrin. A better man than me."

"What you've just done makes you a bloody good man, Dale. *Forgiven, forgotten.* Quick! Go grab a connection cable from the office." Orrin rushed over to his laptop, rearranging the placement of his equipment. He took a monitor from the floor, quickly shoving the cables into his laptop. As Dale reappeared carrying a connector, Orrin grabbed it off him and plugged the analyser in. He switched it on. The frequencies he'd set in his tone generator lit up the machine like a Christmas tree. Rows upon rows of horizontal bars danced high and low as the fundamental frequency of each note was displayed, cascaded by their unique overtones. The notes came through the laptop speakers, feeding back into the microphone over the melody of Ivy's cello. It was a perfect amplification of the resonant frequencies needed to vibrate the crystalline magnetite surrounding the Moscovium.

"That one's off," Dale said, pointing to a flicker of colour.

"Damn it, you're right," Orrin tapped the keyboard with lightning fingers. "It's not hitting the mark like the others." He increased the frequency by one Hertz at a time, carefully watching the electromagnetic fields dip and whirl on the other monitor until they peaked. "I think that's got it," Orrin said.

"We need to get out of here," Dale said. "It's about to get really hot in this room."

Bang! Bang! Bang! The laboratory door rattled violently as someone on the other side of it tried to enter.

"Security!" A grim voice shouted. "Open this door, Mr Brennan!"

Dale's face drained. "They must have followed me." He ran for the laboratory door as Orrin leapt up off the floor, sprinting for the Telsla coil. Dale backed up against it, pitting his feet firmly down against the intrusion. "We can't be in here when it goes off!"

"I know!" Orrin's sweaty fingers stumbled over the switches. "I just need one more minute!" The Telsla coil whirred into action as the capacitor began to accumulate charge. Blue electricity jumped between the spark gaps as the electrons raced for the secondary coil at high voltage. The ionised air around the toroid lit up with crawling flicks of white and blue. Orrin met Dale's eyes across the room. "Time to run!" Orrin skidded back to his laptop, increasing the volume of the tonal notes amplified through the speakers. His fingers slipped over his mobile, increasing Ivy's cello to its highest volume. The combined efforts of the music notes fed back into the microphone, amplifying the frequencies to the highest output he could manage. A thread of electricity grabbed the air above his head. Orrin scrambled to his feet. He ducked around equipment and took a flying leap over a monitor. Dale had already run. He was waiting at the internal doorway to Orrin's lead-lined office. Beyond him, the rattle of men pounding against the laboratory door grew.

There were tears in Orrin's eyes as the overwhelming suffocation of Ivy's cello filled his laboratory. In the centre of the room, a blue glow shimmered around the amulet.

"Please," was all he could manage, as he pulled the door shut behind him and collapsed on the floor.

CHAPTER 43

NEIL

*A*tasi's screams barely broke the roar of the thundering storm. Charat dragged her, one-handed, out of the rocky crevice. Neil's body wouldn't move fast enough. The man had appeared from nowhere, a terrifying apparition of bloody fury. Charat's body was covered in blood and soil and there was a gruesome hole where his ear should have been.

He was shouting into the squall, raging at them both. Trying to drag Atasi away. She kicked and fought for her life. Charat pulled her into his chest and pressed the knife in his fist against her neck.

"Leave her!" Neil threw himself forward, forcing every drop of his draining energy at the red-beaded hunter. He landed a heavy punch to the side of Charat's head. It was enough to knock him away. Neil scrambled to grab the copper blade that clattered into the rocks. Charat's fist found Neil first. Neil's head ricocheted back. His vision swam. He couldn't breathe.

"Go!" He choked out. "Atasi, go!" But the woman was pounding on Charat's back, trying to drag him off Neil.

The two men struggled, cracking their bones upon the rocks. Charat spun and threw Atasi hard against the sharp crag. The back of Neil's head was only inches from the edge that dropped away into the icy blue lake. Neil fought for each breath. Charat lifted Neil's head, hitting it back against the rocks beneath him.

"She's – not – yours." Neil's voice was weak. An eerie hum of song met the clash of the storm and lifted above it, carrying hundreds of voices into the night. Somewhere, someone had begun singing. No, not one person, Neil realised in his haze, but many. Neil struggled to push Charat off his body. The two men rolled dangerously close to the precipice. One man full of hate and revenge for power and a woman stolen from him. The other simply trying to stay alive at the edge of death.

Up on Kelimutu's peak, hundreds of bodies were moving in, filling the spaces across the crest between the lakes. The creatures looked west, waiting for something or someone to appear. No one noticed the battle raging on the edge of the icy blue lake. No one saw the two men fighting for their lives in the dark. Above the peak of Kelimutu, an eerie blue glow filled the sky.

Charat pushed up to his feet, leaving Neil struggling on the rocks. The red-beaded hunter turned back to Atasi, launching himself at her with the ferocity of man gone mad.

Neil's eyelids fluttered as he lay prone on his back. Lightning was raining from the sky. *It's happening,* he realised as he drifted. The red head had succeeded in drawing the lightning down to the earth. Neil's eyes were closing. This was his chance.

Get up on your feet, he willed himself. *Climb the rock. Reach the peak.*

Go home. It was time to throw himself back into the world where he belonged.

Behind him, Atasi screamed. Neil made his choice.

His fingernails scraped at the crevice of rock. He clawed at a glint of copper. He rolled over, scrambled to his feet.

Neil's fist slammed against Charat's back. Before the red-beaded hunter realised he had a knife buried within it, Neil had thrown him back to the edge of the icy blue lake. Charat fell, mouth open, eyes wide, into the churning water below.

Neil collapsed. Atasi threw herself down beside him. Gently, she cradled his bleeding head in her arms.

"The phone," was all he could say. "Ivy. *Go.*"

His chest fell and didn't rise again.

CHAPTER 44

IVY

"*K*yah, please?" Ivy begged. She backed away from Kelimutu's peak. Mud slipped underfoot. Ivy stumbled, her hand, and the amulet dropping lower. Suddenly, gravity no longer kept the world right-side up. The stars were falling. "Please, Kyah!" Ivy cried. "It's time to go home!" She held out her hand, but still Kyah didn't take it. The bonobo shuffled closer, then looked back at Trahg. Kyah lifted her hand, gently moving it downwards in a diagonal line as she shook her head.

No.

"*What do you mean?*" Panic gripped Ivy's chest. "You have to! We don't belong here, Ky. I need you to come home with me. To the university. To Orrin. Remember?" Ivy's voice was getting higher. Her throat constricted. "*We need to go home now.*"

No. Home. Kyah signed. The bonobo scooted forward. For an infinitesimal moment, Ivy thought she had won. But instead, the bonobo lifted her hands once more to sign. *Diagonally down. Her index fingers hooked. A gentle hill.* There was no denying her choice. Ivy had taught Kyah those words. And now, she was using them to say goodbye.

Kyah. Stay. Kyah. Home.

"But please—" the weight of grief hit Ivy so hard she could scarcely breathe. "I need you." She ran forward, lifting the bonobo up into her arms. She held her body tight, too devastated to look into her face. "Please come with me," Ivy begged. "*Please.*"

The amulet fell gently between their skin. No human words could do justice to the images that flooded into Ivy's mind. It was a gift, from Kyah, of all the thoughts and emotions that lived inside of her, and the words she didn't have the ability to speak. Distant memories cascaded one upon the other and Ivy saw Kyah's life as the bonobo had lived it.

A profusion of green leaves. The comfort of a warm breast. A mother's arms encircling her newborn body, and the soft press of a long hand to her lips. Images moved slowly. Life was serene. There were others – a family. The familiar whips and trills of jungle birds. Happy noise. Playful days, clutching her mother's belly as she moved gently through the treetops. Soft, leafy nests. Balmy nights. Each day a tiny adventure, never far from safe arms.

Until a day that shattered the jungle. Her mother screeching. Her family scattered. Bodies falling from the trees.

Confusion. Terror. And then the strong arms that had always held her went limp. Infant Kyah tumbled and crashed to the ground.

Rough hands. Hard cage. Fingers poking and prodding, forcing unpalatable food into her mouth.

Noisy markets. Dust that choked. Stinging eyes. Hungry stomach.

The longest journey.

One cage. Another. Another. Until eventually concrete walls stole the sunlight away.

A tiny cage that became both prison and refuge. Kyah studied her fingers wrapped around those bars for days, weeks, months. Years.

She grew older. Her hands bigger. Every day brought new suffering. Other animals screeched and rattled their doors. All were taken away. Some never returned. Those that did had hollow eyes. They stared but didn't rattle.

Her body ached. Figures in masks and white coats passed through

Kyah's memories, on and on. Faces. Eyes. Needles and sutures. Clamps and restraints.

So sick she could barely breathe. Then well.

Then sick as her body shut down. Then well.

Then so sick that she simply stared at the ceiling of her cage, waiting for death to bring relief.

Then well, as more needles forced her to live again.

Kyah's long fingers picked at her chest, numbing the pain inside with pain on her skin.

Ivy's heart was breaking. Memories passed through her as if she lived them herself. *Kyah's loneliness. Fear. The hopelessness of a life with no relief.*

Another journey. Another face. A bigger cage.

Screeching animals. Strange smells that burnt her sensitive nostrils.

Then Ivy saw herself through the bonobo's eyes. *Images and flickering memories half-forgotten over years. Her own fiery-red hair squashed flat and dank against the concrete wall as she slumped, waiting for the bonobo to react without fear. Weeks of silence and soft whispers as the woman pushed morsels of food through the wire cage walls.*

The woman was singing. Sleeping. Breathing.

The bonobo was watching. Listening. Healing.

And then a new memory broke through. One single moment, when fear finally gave way to curiosity. Kyah reached out, touching the woman's hand wrapped around the cold steel bar between them. The woman's eyes lit up. Overflowing with compassion.

Slowly, trust came. Moment by moment. Meal by meal. Touch by touch. The woman with the red hair became the sun. Kyah's heart leapt with each visit. Slow afternoons of peace buried her pain. Playfulness, that she'd long forgotten.

Years passed. New memories.

Looking up at the woman's face as they walked hand-in-hand. The woman's skin was warm. Her arms strong. Her smell soft. Her voice kind. Her touch gentle.

Others came and went, but none loved her as the woman did. She was sister, mother, friend. The woman with the red hair was the sun.

But each night, the sun went down, and Kyah slept alone in the leafy enclosure.

A cage, was always, still a cage.

Tears fell unheeded as Ivy began to recognise the bonobo's truth. A devastating rush of sorrow threatened to drown her. In all of Kyah's memories, something was missing. Even at peace, an ache lay beneath. She was missing that primal feeling she had lost in infancy. The fundamental keystone of a life lived with joy. Something that had been stolen from her. Until now.

Freedom.

"I have to let you go, don't I?" Ivy whispered. Even as she stumbled over the words, Ivy felt the truth of it. Back home, in the behavioural research laboratory, Kyah was still caged. Though her life was now filled with kindness and love, she would still never truly be free. Kyah's life was managed. She was a resource. An asset. Property. Others would always choose her fate for her, for better or worse. Here, with Trahg and Shahn and Xiou, she was loved as an equal, with the autonomy of choosing her own life. Here, Kyah made her own destiny. With a family by her side, she was finally free.

"I can't keep you, can I?" Ivy sobbed. "My precious girl." She lifted Kyah's face in her hands. The sweet little face she had fallen in love with years ago. "You're like moonlight. Slipping through my fingers. And I have to let you go." Ivy dropped her forehead against the bonobo, closing her eyes. She couldn't bear to leave. To lose her for good. It was Kyah who lifted away. Her soft brown eyes full of empathy.

Kyah. Home. The bonobo signed again.

"I know."

Go. Home.

"I will."

Ivy rubbed the tears and rain from her eyes. Grief felt like an abyss beneath her feet. She forced her chin up. "You'll never be lost to me, no matter how many years pass between us. Because I'll carry you home," she lifted the bonobo's long hand to her heart, "in here." With a heaving sob, Ivy buried her face in her friend's wet black hair once more and kissed her face. "Be safe, Kyah. *Be free.*" Gently, Ivy lowered the bonobo to the ground. They stood in the rain, hands entwined, one drawn to the future. The other destined to stay in the past. Even as lighting flicked around her, searching for its path, Ivy couldn't bear to let her go.

"Hiranah," Xiou said quietly. "Go home."

Ivy's hand slipped away. Behind Xiou, the voices of his tribe lifted again, above the rolling thunder and pelting rain. The Dusk Song grew bolder. Harmonies lifted.

Without taking her eyes off Kyah, Ivy backed toward the triangle of earth where she had once Fallen. Lightning shivered and cracked. With a shaking hand, she lifted her amulet high. A splinter of blue light coursed down from the sky, drawn to the thin metal rod that stood behind her like a sentinel in the dark. Electrons chased through the copper; leapt across the ionised air.

Connected with the amulet above her head.

Crack!

All sound disappeared, as if sucked from the night. An anti-thunder rolled and pierced her bones as it coursed through Ivy's body, hitting the earth beneath her feet. A wave of energy leapt away, dragging thick, opaque air above her head, closing over her like a dome. On the outside of it, Kyah shimmered through the invisible divide, her hand still held up in farewell. Voices hummed in harmonic suffocation. The Dusk Song grew louder.

Snap!

The dome shattered into dozens of shards that held their place in the air around her, throwing light into new worlds. Dozens of splintered windows. Each reality separated from the next by a thin hazy line like smoke. But there was only one that called to her. A tiny shard. Unnoticed before. Untouched. Ivy lifted her hand, transfixed. The amulet dragged her fingers toward its centre. *They touched.* The black stone splintered into a rainbow of broken colours in her hand.

The faces surrounding Ivy dissolved into a swirling blur of black and grey. Kelimutu was gone. No trees. No lakes. No moon. *Nothing.*

Ivy's pupils contracted, blinding her vision in electric blue light.

Crack!

A gut-wrenching shudder filled the air. It rolled against her body in hot, heavy waves. The blue energy ripped through her, from her fist that clutched the amulet and up through her arm, exploding through her body like a supernova.

Ivy gave herself to the pain, letting it flood her cells. Darkness and pressure strangled her senses. She was moving. Fast. Ivy searched for an anchor in the oblivion but found nothing. Her skin was raw and stripped bare, but the bone deep ache that had plagued her for hours after the first shift seemed somehow further away. She let it go. The fear. The grief. The loss. *I'm not afraid this time.*

Ahead of her, a pinprick of darkest black swirled as it grew toward her. The harmonic noise intensified. The sound distorted, deafening.

"Please," implored a man's voice. It sounded warped and distorted, as if from far away, but right ahead of her.

There was a drowning rush of air. Ivy screamed into it, her voice disappearing into the thick emptiness that swallowed her. She couldn't see beyond the swirling haze.

So, Ivy didn't see the sapien woman with the turquoise feathers in her hair, eyes wide in terror as she launched herself from the shadows of the icy blue lake and bolted toward the dome.

Ivy couldn't see the chaos that broke out or hear the shouts and threats as the young Karathah woman raced through the crowd of tiny people to reach the swirling dark where Ivy had suddenly disappeared.

She didn't see the copper feather catch the moonlight, as the Karathah woman flung something hard and heavy into the haze.

Ivy didn't see the spears raised at Atasi. Or the young woman's life risked to fulfil a promise.

And Ivy didn't see the despondent little girl beside Shahn look up, drop her guardian's hand, and race forward to save the woman who had once saved her own life.

As Filhia took Atasi's hand in her own, and cried out to protect her from harm, Ivy leapt forward into nothing.

The amulet fell from her fingers.

The black stone fell at Xiou's feet.

Existence was shred from Ivy's bones.

CHAPTER 45

IVY

*P*ainless.

She was floating.

The black void that enveloped Ivy felt like a soft bed. There was no noise. Only rest.

*

Ivy didn't want to move and didn't try. Perhaps she couldn't move anyway. Where she had come from, or where she was going, made no difference. She simply, *was.* Somewhere beyond the dark, a voice was calling. Ivy sank into the comfort of that voice. It was a quiet, safe place to hide.

*

She lay still, with closed eyes, slowly becoming conscious of her arms, her legs and her face. Ivy was curled on her side, with something hard under and around her. She was cool, much cooler than usual. A hand stroked her forehead gently. The soft fingers ran from her brow up into her hair, rhythmically. The hand was gentle. Love. She lay contemplating this new knowledge. *She was loved.*

Kyah loves me, she thought vaguely. Soft memories passed by her, too distant to catch. *Gihn loves me. Shahn and Xiou love me.*

She tried to surface, but the suffocating silence dulled her senses. Ivy struggled, sure that there was something important to remember. She couldn't move. Her eyes refused to open. The hand was still in her hair.

"Ivy."

Orrin loves me.

Behind the void pressing her into sleep, Ivy became aware of a distant hum. It was a whirring noise, like a fan. She latched onto it, letting it carry her out of the deep. The noise grew louder, slowly displacing the silence of her cocoon. A scent drifted over her. Coffee. Spearmint. Something was pressing on her arm, she thought, because it moved rhythmically with each breath. *Up. Down.*

"Ivy."

Orrin.

"Ivy."

She forced open her eyes. Blinding lights assaulted them. Shapes came slowly. The forehead that had been collapsed on her shoulder, lifted. Ivy felt her own head being cradled gently off the ground. A face slowly swam into view. It suddenly all made sense.

Orrin.

She was home.

"I got you back," he was saying. Orrin's pale face looked exhausted. His smile couldn't have been wider. "I got you back."

"Orrin."

"Take it slow," he said, offering his hand. Ivy carefully pulled herself into a sitting position, reeling a little at the effort. She looked around. She was in a laboratory, Orrin's, she assumed. All around her, loose pages of her journal were spilled across the floor. The book itself was splayed open, face down, surrounded by the photographs and notes that had been stuffed inside it. It made no sense.

"How did my journal get here?" Ivy asked, finding her voice in the quiet room. "It was lost–"

"It must have Fallen through with you," Orrin said, looking around at the papers. "I assumed you were carrying it."

Ivy shook her head. She looked at him, stunned by the simple fact that she was sitting there at all.

"I came back," she breathed, her heart finally catching up. A glorious smile lit her face.

Orrin lifted a hand, placing it against her cheek. He swept Ivy's unruly red fringe from her face, tucking it behind her ear and gave a lopsided grin. He looked at her critically, taking in her dishevelled appearance. She was covered in blood and bruises and filthy with mud. Her curly mass of hair had long-since sprung free of its tied leather strip, and her old green singlet top looked as if it had been through a shredder. Ivy's feet were bare. The wound that Charat had left her with a month prior, was now a nasty, jagged pink scar above the ivy-leaf shaped birthmark on her left thigh. Her hide travelling skirt was in tatters.

"Rough night?" Orrin asked. Ivy laughed, a little madly.

"You have no idea." Every inch of Ivy's body felt marked with the past months of survival. But she felt all the stronger for it.

There was a quiet cough. They both looked up. A young man was standing awkwardly at an internal door. His mouth was open slightly, his eyes not sure where to look.

"Ivy Carter," Orrin grinned, nodding up at the man from his place on the floor. "I'd like you to meet Dale Brennan – lab tech, PhD student, *friend*."

"Hi Dale," Ivy said, politely. Dale looked as if he was about to faint. It took a few seconds for his manners to find his mouth.

"Hi," he said. Dale flashed a rare smile at them both. "I've heard a lot about you, Ivy."

"He really has," Orrin threw his head back, laughing. "*You* have no idea."

Ivy looked between them, nonplussed.

"Dale," Orrin said, suddenly serious. "Could you check–"

"Yep, of course. I'm just going to–" Dale made a clumsy motion toward the room behind him. "I'm gonna – um, check on some things – give you guys a minute." He ducked back out of the room, pulling the door mostly shut behind him.

Orrin turned back to Ivy. They sat for a moment, just looking at the others' face. Remembering. Months of unspoken words hung between them, but for now, simply breathing together was enough. Now, they finally had *time*.

"Kyah?" Orrin looked as if he didn't want to ask but felt compelled to.

"She chose to stay," Ivy replied. She squeezed her eyes shut against a wave of fresh grief. "And if I'm really back when I started – if this all worked the way it was meant to – then I suppose Kyah lived the remainder of her life, fifty-thousand years ago. With a family that loved her. Free to make her own choices. Be her own person." Ivy took a deep breath. "She was happy."

He nodded. Squeezed her hand. There was nothing he could say to ease that pain.

"And you?" Orrin asked, searching her face for a hint of regret in leaving Kyah behind. "Are *you* happy?"

The question felt like a dream. Ivy lifted her hand and let her fingers drift slowly across Orrin's face. Through his dark hair, watching it fall aside her fingers. She traced the outline of Orrin's cheekbone, the soft gleam of his glasses, the bridge of his nose. Trailing the rough stubble on his jaw until the slide of his neck led her hand down to his shoulder.

"Never happier," Ivy said. She had moved heaven and earth to come home. Not just to her old life, but a better life. A life without fear of loss. A life lived fully. Her thumb brushed Orrin's lips with a gentle swipe. Ivy leaned closer, desperate to feel those lips against her own. "I'm not going to lie to you, Orrin," she said, leaning back a little with a wicked grin, her breath warm on his lips as she spoke. "I haven't brushed my teeth in two months."

Orrin let out a slightly delirious laugh. "You know what?" he said. "I don't even care."

He pushed forward, dragging his hand through the back of her hair, bracing Ivy's body against his own on the laboratory floor. Falling. Crashing. For the first time, Ivy knew she had nothing to lose. She leaned upward, sealing Orrin's lips with her own. Ivy deepened her kiss, searching for the soft intrusion of his tongue. Moments passed, or minutes. His strong hand on her waist, burning the skin between her hide skirt and torn singlet. Every nerve ending in her body ached for more touch. More of this new reality that seemed too impossibly good to be true. *I'm home.*

The past months of raw emotion and the struggle to survive fell away. Her eyes open, because she couldn't bear to miss seeing his face, after so long without it. Smiling as she kissed his mouth, knowing how it felt to think she'd never have the opportunity again. Never wanting it to end. But practicality eventually won. After a moment, Ivy pushed up to sit cross-legged on the floor.

Orrin groaned softly as she pulled away but followed her lead to sit upright.

Ivy traced the inner corner of his eye, wiping away a tear with her thumb. She leaned forward and cradled his face in her hands. Let her fingers follow the firm line of muscle in Orrin's chest, feeling his heart quicken beneath the cotton business shirt.

"I'm really back, aren't I?"

"It seems so," Orrin replied. "But – I really thought I'd lost you there."

"You nearly did," Ivy said. "I want to say – *thank you*, Orrin."

"What for?" he asked.

"For not forgetting me."

"I could never forget you. Though, there is a problem with

that." Orrin's voice was rough, lips curled slightly at the edges. "You realise you can never go anywhere without me again, right?" His fingers twitched, lifting to close over Ivy's hand, pressing it harder against his heart. "Because I'm not sure I can survive the fall-out when you leave."

"Surely it wasn't much," Ivy smiled. "Besides you, I doubt anyone even noticed I was gone." Ivy was joking, but Orrin's expression turned grave.

"The world fell apart, Ivy." He shook his head, as if willing away a thousand bad memories. "Your little friends, the *Homo floresiensis* people, were suddenly a part of this world. Whatever you did in prehistoric Flores, you gave them the opportunity to change the course of their own evolution forever. This–" Orrin looked around, "this version of the world, didn't treat them kindly. *Humans* didn't treat them kindly. They were mistreated. Used for awful experiments, as entertainment, as pets–"

"No!" Ivy covered her mouth with her hand, instantly nauseous. "I never wanted that. I was terrified this would happen to them! *What have I done?*"

"I'm sorry," Orrin said, "but *Homo sapiens* simply can't see another species as *human*. The hobbits were defined by their differences, instead of all the ways we were alike. Their survival has become a punishment to them. I did what I could, but I don't think I made a difference at all–"

Ivy jumped to her feet. "I knew it! I mean, when has humanity ever been *humane?*" she was like a fury, raging around the room. "I hoped that when people saw how similar we all are, it would be enough. Their intelligence and empathy. Their families! But it's never enough for humans, is it? We need to dominate! We need to *use*. Gihn insisted on being given the choice to fight for their right to survive, and I agreed with them. Now look what I've done! I mean, they deserved the right to fight for their own survival, didn't they?!" Ivy was raving now, pink-faced, and almost buzzing with anger. "I warned them what sapiens were like!" She groaned. "And they knew it too – they *lived* it! I warned them that our – our *imperfections* could lead to a life barely worth living for them. Our selfishness, our greed. I asked the tribes to leave Flores, I *begged* them to never let sapiens know they were there. I mean, perhaps it was inevitable they would be discovered if they hid in the forests, but I gave them the most specific instructions of where to go–" The thought that Ivy had facilitated their survival, only for them to be treated so callously by modern humans was almost too much. "I need to fix this!" She strode to the laboratory door.

"No! Wait a minute!" Orrin called out, scrambling to his feet. Ivy paused with her hand on the door handle. "Just wait! Wait – *Dale?*" Orrin called. He crossed the room to the internal office door, pulling it open. Ivy followed him. The young man was clicking furiously on a keyboard. "What have you found?" Orrin looked as though he was bracing himself for terrible news. But instead, Dale swivelled his head toward Orrin, a look of incredulity on his face.

"I've found *nothing*," he said.

"Nothing like – *nothing's different?*" Orrin pressed urgently. "Or *nothing happened?* Or *nothing will ever be the same?* Or – *you found nothing online because the internet won't work...?*" Now Orrin was raving. The success of the Time Shift, and Ivy's sudden return to the laboratory had almost made him forget the state of utter chaos the world had been in only moments before it happened. But now, the reality of it came crashing back down.

Security guards had been banging on his laboratory door moments before Ivy had returned. Now, it was quiet in the corridor outside. Orrin could scarcely hope to *hope*. But the laptop in front of Dale held the answers.

"Nothing, as in – there's no mention of *Homo floresiensis* in the news," Dale explained. "And a search shows nothing more recent that the archaeological excavations in Liang Bua cave. The hominid is listed as EXTINCT in any reference articles relating to their phylogeny."

"Extinct?" Orrin's mind whirred. "And the energy fields?" He asked, desperately.

"Again, nothing," Dale said. "Not a single article about the press conference and energy capture on the top floor. It's as if it never happened at all. I've used a dozen search terms – energy fields, CSIRO, government press releases, solar storms – *nothing*. There's just this one news report that keeps coming up – one of the staff from the CSIRO has gone missing while doing field research in Melbourne. But there's nothing on the solar storms or the environmental disasters that were all over the news yesterday." He looked up at Orrin, his eyes hopeful. "I think maybe, we fixed it?"

"The only way we could have fixed it," Orrin said, slowly. "Is if the hobbits didn't survive after all. No hobbits, mean no magnetite mining, no magnetospheric decay, and no solar storms to tear the world apart."

Ivy looked at him, horrified. "I feel like perhaps I've missed a lot."

"I don't even know where to begin." Orrin shook his head. "But I'll tell you everything eventually. But for now – no hobbits also means no experimentation on them. No ethical dilemma – at least *for that one species*. There's still plenty to be said about the rest."

"Right." Ivy turned away. The words didn't seem to want to sink in. "So, the hobbits didn't survive after all?" she said. The fury she was carrying just moments before melted into sadness. Despite what Orrin had told her of their fate, Ivy was gutted.

"It seems not," Dale looked at Ivy.

"So, I failed them." For a moment, no one spoke. "Unless they did survive," Ivy said quietly.

"But there's no reference to them at all," insisted Dale. "No record of their existence outside of bones."

"But what if they took my advice?" Ivy said.

"They stayed hidden from humans for that long?" Orrin looked doubtful.

"I told them never to let sapiens find them," Ivy said. "And you have no idea how incredibly well they can blend into their forest. She looked at Dale and gestured to the laptop. "May I?" Dale rose and shifted out of the way. Ivy began to type search queries into the browser.

"There's an ethnographer who claims modern tribes have seen them in the forests of Flores," she said, "but no one else can substantiate it." Ivy typed in a new search query. "A few stories by locals. Oral histories passed down about little forest people. But nothing you could put your finger on for sure. So, I suppose –" she pondered, looking at the screen but not really seeing it, "I suppose it *is* possible that their species is still out there somewhere, staying hidden for their own survival. Or perhaps –" Ivy sat back, a distant look in her eyes.

"Perhaps–?" Orrin repeated, when Ivy trailed off.

"Perhaps they took my advice and left Flores," she said, looking between the two men. "Perhaps they found an alternate version of the Earth to evolve within where they could fight only against nature, and not against man as well. Perhaps, they decided to forsake this version of reality and forge a new path on an Earth without *Homo sapiens* to dominate them."

"Through the shards?" Orrin asked, his voice hushed. Dale looked between them, not understanding.

"Yes." For a moment, all three contemplated the unresolved question. Ivy got up and walked back out into the laboratory. She began to pick up all the unbound papers that had fallen out of her journal. She shuffled them together, looking at the notes she had written over her months staying with the hobbits. Sketches of Liang Bua cave, their weapons and sleeping hearths, branching family trees with the names of people she had grown to love. Her heart swelled in affection and grief over the fact that she knew, whatever their destiny had been, she would never see Xiou, Shahn, little Trahg or any of the others ever again. *Or my Kyah,* she thought. Her heart ached. The love she had for them, could no longer be given. Instead, it built up inside, threatening to spill out in tears.

"You okay?" Orrin said quietly from behind her.

"I will be," Ivy smiled, clutching the journal to her chest. "I'm still not sure how my journal came to be here."

"Maybe there are things we'll never know," Orrin said. "One thing I do know though, is that you never showed up to that date we were going to have."

"Yeah, sorry about that," Ivy replied. "I got held up."

"You broke the world apart." Orrin corrected her, with an amused shake of his head. "But here we are." He pulled her into his arms. "And I'm going to hold you to it. Tomorrow night. Dinner at my place?"

"De ja vu?" She laughed.

"Spectacular view of Port Phillip Bay," he grinned. "Pretty sure I promised you pasta last time, and I'm deadly in the kitchen."

Ivy stepped closer, critically aware of the promise she was making.

"I *will* be there."

"Yeah?" Orrin looked as if he was almost too scared to believe her.

"Wild stegodon couldn't drag me away," Ivy said.

Together, Ivy, Orrin and Dale, left, pulling the laboratory door closed behind them. Orrin lifted his hand to give Dale a reassuring pat on the back as they left the building.

"See you tomorrow in the lab, boyo?" Orrin smiled.

"You bet," Dale replied. "Though I think I could do with a sleep-in."

"I think we all could." Orrin took Ivy's hand. "Late start, then. Phil can hold the fort for a few hours."

Dale grinned. "Since when has Phil ever been in before us?"

"Fair play," Orrin said. He shook his head. "But it's safe to say I'll never hold it against him again."

"No," said Dale. "Neither will I."

*

No one noticed the mobile phone, cracked and filthy, that had skidded across the floor when Ivy's journal had been thrown into the swirling singularity behind her.

No one had seen it skid across the floor, un-wedging from between the book's pages, and lodge itself under a heavy piece of equipment that was pushed up against the wall.

No one noticed when the battery on the device stuttered to an end and the screen went black.

*

As they walked toward the carpark, the sleek glass fountain outside the Physics building shot prisms of silver and gold under the full moon. The air was cool and clean. Ivy took a deep breath, filling her lungs with the new day ahead of her.

She was *home.*

CHAPTER 46

IVY

 *ne week later.*

Ivy pushed her fringe behind her ear, balancing the cello case on her foot. She pulled the door of the small tutorial room shut behind her and made her way to the elevator. Closing her eyes, she lay her head against the mirrored glass as it rumbled down to ground level. It had been just another normal day at the university. She'd given tutorial classes on the usewear analysis of Aztec pottery shards and the symbolism on ancient Egyptian Canopic jars, and then marked a dozen papers for Professor Ellery, who had been delighted to find she'd returned from a vacation that Ivy convinced him he'd been forewarned of. Her eccentric PhD supervisor had been so all-consumed in his own lectures and research in the two months of Ivy's disappearance, he'd taken her word for it.

"Vacation, was it?" Ellery bustled cheerfully into her small office. "I must have missed the memo. Had to get Stevens to fill in on your tutorials while you were gone and you know what a wet sock that one is. Students asleep with their eyes open. Glad you're back, papers are piling up." Professor Ellery unceremoniously dumped an enormous pile of undergraduate assignments on her desk, that he'd apparently allowed to accumulate in her absence. "Don't leave me again, Miss Carter. I need your bright young mind to stave off the collapse of civilisation in this department!"

"I'll begin marking right away," Ivy had promised.

She pushed through the door of the residue laboratory in the archaeology department and found Jayne still sitting behind a microscope, studying her laptop. Leaning her cello case against a corner, Ivy walked over to her. Jayne looked up with a smile.

"Seriously, I got so used to being on my own in here I started talking to the walls," Jayne said. "I'm *so* glad you're back."

"Me too. I'm drowning in work already," Ivy rolled her eyes.

Jayne scoffed, playfully. "Don't pretend you don't love it."

"Honestly?" Ivy said, setting up her microscope. "Yeah, I do. I missed this."

"How's Kyah?" Jayne asked. "It feels a bit odd not seeing her around campus. She was kind of part of the furniture, wasn't she?"

Ivy gave a sad smile. "Yeah, she was. She's going well though." Her story had been recited enough times now, that Ivy almost felt comfortable saying it. "The rehabilitation colony over in the Republic of Congo have released her with a small family of other bonobos. She's free – as free as she'll ever be, in any case. We were so lucky to get a place for her, they don't usually take ex-lab animals because of potential neurological damage. The chances of them surviving in the wild are so small. But Kyah was a special case. She's one-of-a-kind."

"You must miss her," Jayne said, her face full of sympathy.

"I do. I got to spend two months in the jungle settling her in with her new family though. Honestly, I've never seen her happier." Ivy took a deep breath. "I dream of her every night, you know. I miss her hugs. Those beautiful eyes. How well she knew me – better than I knew myself, probably." Ivy wiped away a tear and gave a bolstering smile. "But she was free. She has a chance at a new life. So how can I think of myself? It's all I ever wanted for her."

Jayne nodded, her eyes twinkling. "And Liam?"

"He's still pretty angry with me. He'll come around though; he's always had Kyah's best interests at heart." Ivy continued the familiar lie. It had taken some research and planning to explain Kyah's disappearance but was as close to the truth as she could make it. "Honestly though, I couldn't get onto Liam at the time, and I had to make a choice. He's the lab manager, but he's always allowed me direction over her welfare. There was no point going to the departmental board about it, they're so bureaucratic with these sorts of things. If I'd waited, Kyah would have missed the opportunity for freedom. Liam's all fire and fight, but he'll simmer down. He's already backdated the paperwork and submitted it. He knows I did the right thing; he just doesn't like the way I did it."

"Well, you did disappear for two months and not tell anyone where you were going."

"I told Professor Ellery," Ivy lied, "but he forgot. Orrin knew too."

"Oh yeah, the sexy physics lecturer." Jayne raised an eyebrow, waggling it suggestively. "Aren't you the little dark horse? One minute you're avoiding him in the hallways, and next thing you take off for months and he's the only one who knows anything about it. So, you guys are getting pretty close, huh?"

Ivy laughed, a joyful sound that filled her up and made her toes feel warm. "You could say that."

"Well, I'm glad to hear it. It's about time you got your eyes off the microscope and onto some of the fine-looking scenery in this place." Jayne winked and turned back to her laptop while Ivy flicked through the pages of her journal. She had been planning to continue the identification of residues on the stone tool collection that had been excavated from Liang Bua before she had disappeared. It almost seemed silly now. Shahn had taught Ivy to identify and cook the edible roots and shoots herself using stone tools like the ones currently on her microscope stage. The animals that Xiou hunted and butchered were going to be quick to identify with DNA analysis now that she knew the most likely suspects to narrow down her search. It was all a bit *too easy.* Laboratory research had become field experience of the most intimate kind. Instead of pressing on with her PhD project, Ivy was already thinking of ways she could expand it. Of course, she could never reveal her own experience. Instead, she now had to prove what she knew, through archaeological investigation alone.

After a few minutes of comfortable silence, Jayne looked up from her screen.

"I've got something a bit weird here. Wanna have a look?"

"Sure." Ivy walked around to stand behind Jayne's bench.

"I've been looking into ethnographic research surrounding the Liang Bua site and one of the archaeologists on the ground has sent me a few photos of nearby cave-art. Apparently the local community were unaware of this one until now, and it's a completely different style and pigment to their own indigenous prehistoric art. I mean, I dunno – *Homo floresiensis* have no record of cave art at all, but if prehistoric sapiens didn't create this, who did?" Jayne scrolled through a series of photographs that progressively zoomed in on a very faded image set against the rock of a limestone shelter.

Ivy's heart skipped a beat. Handprints, dozens of them, in long-faded red, gold and brown. Some were barely there at all. Ivy closed her eyes for a moment, remembering Gihn's brow furrowed in concentration as he ground the coloured clays into a fine powder, then mixed the umber, sienna and ochre with animal fat to form the thick paste they needed to paint their hands. Every member of the family had placed a handprint on that wall. Ivy touched the screen reverently, tracing fingers. She could almost pick the hand of each person.

"I mean, it's got be the little Flores hobbits, right?" Jayne said, her voice rising in excitement. "The size of those prints – so small, but too many to be only children. And then there's this one–" Jayne traced the screen, outlining Kyah's print. "Comparative morphology is completely different. Opposable thumb, yes, but definitely not human. I'd say an ape of some sort. Which makes no sense at all given Flores has no endemic primates. I just don't understand what I'm seeing here."

"Fascinating," Ivy said, noncommittally. "I have no idea." The lump in her throat forbid her to say anything more.

Jayne scrolled through a few more images. "I don't get this one at all." Two simple line paintings stood side by side. The first, a white figure, tall and simply shaped with a hint of face and faded red hair. Beside it, a black heart-shaped face with rounded shoulders and a hunched back, curling under its rump in a single unbroken line. It was connected by one hand to a smaller figure; a simple crossed body in dark umber. Tears sprang to Ivy's eyes. She knew without question that Trahg must have drawn it. What child could resist, once they had been taught?

The second line drawing featured the same dark-lined creature, but this time, it held hands with the simple crossed figure again, but grown. Ivy couldn't help the tears that dripped silently down her nose. Their love and kinship had spanned a lifetime. Trahg had left his mark, perhaps, so that one day, Ivy might see it and know that her precious ones were safe. No matter how the tribes had managed to keep their survival from the modern world, this one physical reminder of lives once lived, could never be completely wiped away. When Ivy left the residue laboratory a few hours later, she took a printed copy of the cave paintings with her.

Strolling through the cloistered corridors surrounding the

vast quadrangle, Ivy smiled up at the familiar gargoyles as she passed.

"Mendel... Darwin... Leakey..." She greeted them in turn, delighting in old habits. It still felt strange to be home. Every breath she took felt like a gift. Every precious moment, a revelation. As Ivy walked the familiar paths home to her apartment, Ivy vowed never to bury herself in isolation again.

*

Old Tom Chapman greeted her as the sun went down. He was pottering about in the garden, as he often did, with a handful of daisies set in a neat pile by the front door. Though her landlord wasn't related to her by blood, Ivy had long considered him family.

"Hi Grandpa Tom."

"Ivy love, did you have a good day?" She pulled him into a gentle hug. "I'm so glad you're home," Tom continued. "It was terribly quiet without you here. "For a while there I was worried that you'd – well, that you might not be coming back. I don't know what I'd do if you left."

A flush of guilt warmed Ivy's face. Tom was a widower, who had also lost his only son early in the young man's life. *Dishonourable discharge,* the official letter had said, on account of desertion while serving in the Vietnam War. Tom and his late wife Iris had refused to accept it. But no matter how many years passed, Sean had never returned home.

"We'll I'm not going anywhere again for a very long time," Ivy assured him. "I'm sorry I gave you a fright."

"Oh, the odd adventure is always a good thing, love," he said, patting her hand. "My boy Sean was always off on an adventure somewhere or other. He sent us letters from all around the world. You mustn't hold yourself back on my account."

"I'm perfectly happy to stay right here for as long as I can," Ivy said.

"You're still wearing the amulet." Tom observed, looking pleased. "He sent that to Iris you know, in his very last letter. She wore it every day."

"I know, Grandpa Tom." Ivy had heard the story before. She touched the amulet around her neck. Orrin had replaced the chain for her. Though it still drew her eye, the amulet had shown no signs of doing anything out of the ordinary since she'd returned home. It was as inert as any other rock and Ivy was glad for it. She'd had enough adventure to last a very long time. She took Tom's hand and walked him back to his daisies, gathering them up for a vase. She was ready for a warm bath, and the delicious comfort of settling into her pyjamas for the night.

The following morning, anticipation gave wings to her feet. She had a new class to inspire, a fresh wave of research ideas to explore, and a long-awaited dinner date to look forward to.

It was past midnight. Ivy stared out at the inky black water of Port Phillip Bay. Tiny sparks of light danced on the surface reflected from a thousand stars above. She shrugged a little tighter into the oversized shirt she wore, enveloping her tired body in the scents of oak moss and fir. Sleep evaded her, as it had so often since she'd returned. There was simply too much to think about.

A thousand sacred moments fluttered in her head. A thousand touches. A thousand words. Sometimes, Ivy almost couldn't believe it was she who had lived them. She closed her eyes, letting all too recent images appear in the dark spaces. The red-beaded hunter frequently occupied her thoughts. Why he was so singularly determined to destroy the hobbits was beyond her. Something had incited him into poisoning them before she had ever arrived in Flores, and her appearance afterward had only inflamed his fervour. Ivy wondered what it was about her that had accelerated his efforts into such genocide. Perhaps simply, the presence of someone willing to defy him was enough. He had clearly been a leader within his tribe. Ambition and bloodlust too often went hand-in-hand. Unanswered questions plagued her each night when her mind was still enough to unravel them.

Mostly she wondered, how the hunter, *Charat*, the other Karathah called him, had known her name? *'Ey-vee,'* he had hissed at her, with those cold, cruel eyes. Had he overheard it somehow and figured it out? But the hobbits had called her Hiranah, not Ivy, and Kyah could not speak her name at all. Ivy had lost her journal at the stegodon hunt, but Charat could not have read it. And how then, had her journal been returned to her? Had one of the travelling parties found it and carried it back to Kelimutu? She hadn't sent any of them on a route that passed the southern plains.

And who was the *Homo sapien* woman that Orrin said had been recovered from the Liang Bua excavation? Orrin admitted his terror that it was Ivy had only tempered when Jayne had determined that the skeleton was of Austronesian origin. She was a prehistoric indigenous woman native to Flores, buried in the same stratigraphic layer as *Homo floresiensis*. Ivy couldn't imagine that any of the Karathah would willingly join them, or that any would be welcome. Surely, the dates were wrong.

An image flashed unbidden to her mind of the young Karathah woman with the turquoise feathers in her long hair. Not all of the Karathah had been unkind.

But it was the hobbit bones themselves, that very first skeleton dug from under six meters of rock and living floor in Liang Bua cave, that most frequently returned to haunt her. A complete skeleton, LB1, only one metre tall. No chin, tiny brain case, narrow V-shaped jaws with paired roots on her pre-molars

– prehistoric features mixed with the Stone Age technology of quite modern humans. At the time, it was nothing more than an enthralling scientific puzzle to her. Now though, Ivy saw those bones refleshed in her mind's eye, with all the kindness, imperfections and hopes they were once imbued with. Now, the bones had a face.

LB1 was no longer a mystery. Ivy could no longer bear to classify the tiny skull with a number, instead of a name.

Floni, she whispered. *Dear Flo. I remember you.* Whatever the ultimate fate of the tribe, Flo had already chosen her own destiny, to live and die along-side her beloved Turi's bones.

And what of the others? Ivy wondered, staring out into the water. *Did Xiou lead the tribes to a new beginning? Or did they stay united and adapt to the challenges of their own changing world, hidden from all others. I suppose I'll never truly know,* she thought. Ivy let her mind drift to what she was sure of. *That I loved them. And they loved me. That I had a family like no other.* Her chest swelled with happy memories. Gihn talking to her by the river. Shahn rubbing her pregnant belly. Kora indignantly scolding her own dinner as she hunted it. Though Ivy was the only one who would remember them, their faces would never fade through the passage of time.

There was a soft noise behind her. Ivy turned to see Orrin emerge from the bedroom. He moved in close behind her, wrapping his arms around her middle and sending a shiver up the back of her bare legs.

"You alright?" He asked.

"I just can't sleep. I keep thinking about everything that happened and wondering what became of them."

Orrin was quiet for a minute. Finally, he dropped his head down to the side of her neck. His breath warmed her skin as he spoke.

"I think you gave them the opportunity to survive humanity in the only way you could. Or at least, survive our particular species of humanity," Orrin corrected himself. "As soon as I met Indah, there was no question in my mind that she was human. Just a different kind to ourselves."

"Humanity," Ivy smiled. "It's in our nature to categorise and find differences. It helps us makes sense of the world... make sense of ourselves..." She closed her eyes, leaning her head back into Orrin's shoulder. "But I think, finding all the ways we are the same, serves us better. To be *humane*, perhaps, would be a better definition of humanity to aspire to?" Ivy considered. "When we *value* life, and recognise parts of ourselves in other animals, we humans seem to open up to the possibility that perhaps, we aren't as unique as we'd like to think. All those emotions we once thought were ours alone – self-awareness, empathy, suffering, pain and love – are shared with other animals. And we're richer for knowing it."

"I like that," Orrin said. "The love bit, especially." Ivy smiled, her eyes still closed, her head resting easily against him. "There's no question that things need to change, though," he continued. "It feels as if there's so much about our world we're just beginning to understand. I mean, the physics alone – this last few months has blown my mind wide open. It'll be years of new research for me. A whole cascade of new projects. I want to really understand how this happened."

"Do you think it could ever happen again?" Ivy said, the thought suddenly occurring to her. "The Time Shift, I mean." She lifted her hand, feeling the warmth of the amulet against the bare skin of her chest. "The stone hasn't given me any indication that it might, but still – I wonder if it's possible?"

"I don't see why not," Orrin said. "If we track those energy fields from the moon to its highest level and then trigger the resonant frequency of the element at the right time. Just add lightning, and *boom!*" His voice rose. "All that Moscovium under the volcano seemed to act as a lens, amplifying the frequency from under the earth. But we ran multiple surveys and found the energy fields associated with large deposits of Moscovium in quite a number of places around the earth. All in areas of significant evolutionary importance. Under the right conditions, those shards could appear in any of them."

"Showing alternate versions of what we might have been?" Ivy pondered. "If evolution had taken a different turn? Like changes in the environment? Different pressures on survival or finding a mate? A different ice-age or keystone species taking hold? I mean, there are so many variables that shape how we evolve."

"Yeah, any of those, I imagine," Orrin agreed. "When I looked in those shards, I saw different versions of reality that existed at the same time. Just changing one evolutionary step, like letting the hobbits survive long enough for the sapiens to discover their connection to the magnetite in the earth, was enough to reset the status quo and flick us onto a new evolutionary path. It's scary how easy it was."

"Easy, was it?" Ivy laughed. "I don't recall you being chased by Komodo dragons and giant storks."

"Definitely not in my skillset," Orrin agreed. "You can have your jungles and I'll stick to being chased by police."

"Mmm," Ivy frowned. "I think I've had enough of jungles for a while, thanks."

"It is an incredible discovery though," Orrin said. "When you think of what we could learn from this Time Shift. I plan on doing some research into it – though a lot more carefully now that we know it has the capacity to destroy our civilisation in immeasurable ways. Ruining the world once was enough for me. I'll keep it all theoretical until I know a lot more about it. Maybe we can forge a new way ahead with this – a better future for everyone."

"Isn't the future built on learning lessons from the past?" Ivy smiled, twisting her head to kiss his lips.

"Well, that's you," Orrin kissed her back. "We'll learn those lessons together. You look at the past and I'll look to the future. We should be able to figure it out between us, right?"

"We're two sides to the same coin, I think." Ivy untangled herself. She took a deep breath and stepped forward, touching the huge expanse of glass with her fingertips. Far above, the glint of a satellite crossed the night sky. The world outside looked – *perfect.*

"I got so used to seeing an aurora out there," Orrin said, "it's almost strange to have it gone." He moved in beside her, taking her free hand in his. Together, they watched the stars dance across the surface of Port Phillip Bay. "I need your help with something, by the way," Orrin said.

"Oh yeah?" Ivy curled inward, wrapping her arms around his neck. "Anything you want."

"I want to throw a dinner party."

"A dinner party?" Ivy laughed, pulling away slightly. "Okay, not what I expected you were going to say, but sure."

"Next weekend. We've got some mutual friends – a geologist and an astro-physicist – that *really* need to meet each other. Trust me, it'll be like watching a symphony write itself. Those two were made for each other."

"Sounds wonderful," Ivy said. "A symphony, hey?" She pulled Orrin down, bringing his mouth softly onto her own. As it always did, gravity tipped, and she felt herself falling. There was no end to this, Ivy knew that now. Even fifty thousand years couldn't keep them apart. She ran her hand down Orrin's arm, tracing the muscles under his skin, feeling them tense, as he pulled her in tight. Fingers through his hair, her mouth on his neck. Ivy's whisper found him through a haze of desire.

"If they're a symphony, then what does that make us?" she asked, breathlessly.

Orrin kissed her eyes, his voice hoarse. "Stars colliding," he said, without hesitation. "From the very first moment we met." He fell into her arms again.

"Isn't it funny, how long ago that seems?" Ivy breathed. "So much has happened since then."

His fingers drifted down until they brushed over the ivy leaf birthmark on her thigh. Every nerve in her body felt like it might explode.

"Everything has changed," Ivy said. "Life seems so much more precious. Like I can't afford to miss a single moment of it."

Orrin pulled away. He looked into her eyes with nothing but love.

"The one thing we have plenty of now, is *time*," he said. "We have all the time in the world."

EPILOGUE

CASSANDRA

"*H*e's been missing two and a half months, and this is the last place he was seen," Cassandra's voice rose with each word. "Surely you must know something. A man doesn't just disappear into thin air!"

"I've already told the police everything I know, Miss Chevalier." Chancellor Thandi shifted the notepad on her desk in agitation, her voice dangerously low. It was almost dinner time, and her day had been particularly tedious. "I remember Dr. Crawford," she said. "I spoke to him myself and when he left me here, he was very much alive and I assure you, he was in full control of his faculties. Now, I don't know where he went after he left this office, and I am sorry for your loss and concern, but I'm getting very tired of your continued harassment."

"I've seen the police footage, Chancellor. *He never left this building.*" Cassandra's back straightened; her lips thinned as she threw her hand in the air. "We were tracking the energy peaks over this university for days. As far as I'm concerned, your department was under government investigation. If you did anything to him–"

"And why on earth would I do anything to a man I'd only just met?" Chancellor Thandi spat back. "The energy fields were determined to be a natural anomaly. The issue resolved of its own accord, and I've got nothing else to say about it! I'm the one who provided the police with our security footage. I have no reason to believe there is anything suspicious. Clearly, there was some sort of technical error with the camera. The man is not here."

"Then where is he?" Cassandra growled. "He had an apartment, a child – no one's heard a thing from him since the day he was here. How do you explain that?"

"I cannot!" The Chancellor took a deep breath, trying to calm herself. "There is nothing else I can do to assist you finding your colleague." The academic's voice was laced with anger. She got to her feet. "If I receive *one more* email, or phone call, or visit from you about this matter, I *will* be pressing charges for personal harassment. Now, I suggest you leave this matter to the police and get out of my office before I have to call security to escort you out."

The woman's tone left no room to argue. With a look of contempt, Cassandra Chevalier threw her long hair over her shoulder and turned on her heel. She strode to the door. As she stepped through, it closed hard behind her. Furious, Cassandra turned up the hallway and began to throw open doors.

They're hiding something, she told herself. *Neil Crawford may have been a lot of things, but he was never the type to walk away from it all.* Something had happened to him; she was sure of it.

Cassandra took the fire stairs to the first floor and made her way along the laboratories, throwing a casual smile at anyone who passed in hallway. By the time she pushed her way into Laboratory 179, most of the building had emptied for the night. She strode in. Like all the others, this one was sleek and neat, with long silver benches and walls mounted with monitors. Cassandra snooped for moment, then gave up with a huff. There was nothing here.

As she turned away, a metallic glint caught her eye. She paused, one impeccable high heel in the air. She lowered it again. *There's something under there.* Cassandra got down on her hands and knees, heart beating faster. Manicured fingers groped under a heavy machine sitting on a trolley. Something was underneath it, glinting against the back wall. She got back up to her feet, grunting as she took hold of the edge and dragged the machine out from its corner. With the toe of her shoe, Cassandra flicked the dusty mobile phone from behind it. She picked it up. The face was cracked but she recognised the shape and model. She'd seen it countless times before and had one herself. They were standard issue for senior staff. Reliable communication was vital. A chill ran down her spine. This phone belonged to Dr. Neil Crawford. Cassandra tried turning it on, but the battery on the device was dead.

She looked around, slipping the mobile into her pocket. She could charge it at home.

"Neil?" Calling out seemed a pointless but necessary thing to do. Of course, there was no reply. The laboratory was empty. Not a single thing out of place.

Cassandra Chevalier turned and walked out of the room, swelling with vindication.

This isn't over.

JOIN MY READER'S CLUB

There are more books to come!

HayleyCamille.com/subscribe

JOIN HAYLEY CAMILLE'S
READER'S CLUB
FOR EXCLUSIVE NEWS,
PRE-ORDER DISCOUNTS
& A FREE BOOK.

SCAN ME

LOVE IT? PLEASE REVIEW!

Your reviews are vital to the success of each book. Each book takes me months or years to research and write, so I'd really appreciate a few moments of your time if you enjoy reading them.

HayleyCamille.com/extinct-novel

Become a part of **#IvysTribe** on Social Media to tell us what you loved about this series.

ACKNOWLEDGMENTS

Thank you so much for becoming part of Ivy's journey by reading this book. It has been such a joy bringing her to you. Ivy evolved from my passion for prehistory, combined with the habit of disappearing into my imagination. I hope you have enjoyed her adventure.

Thank you so much to my sister Jasmine, who proofread this book for me, on a very short time schedule and with such kindness and encouragement.

Of course, the real-world subject of this fictional story is owed entirely to the archaeological discovery of LB1 (Flo) and her fossilised *Homo floresiensis* companions at Liang Bua in Flores, Indonesia by the late Dr Mike Morwood and his collaborative team of Australian and Indonesian palaeoanthropologists, archaeologists and inter-disciplinary experts. This was a remarkable discovery that really shone a new light on the reconstruction of our hominid family tree and continues to astonish and inspire us as new details are revealed. Thank you to all these scientists who reconstruct our prehistory and expand our knowledge with such excruciating care and detail – I admire your work and passion greatly.

Finally and above all, I would like to recognise the animals in cages, laboratories, servitude and entertainment all over the world for the suffering, grief, imprisonment and sacrifice they continue to endure for the sake of our species. In a battle that seems sometimes hopeless, your innocence gives us the strength to keep fighting for you. One day, we humans will see you. A change is coming.

ABOUT THE AUTHOR

Hayley Camille is the author of the *Ivy Carter* adventure series and multi award-winning *Lady Vigilante* crime series, as well as *The Ultimate Players Guide to Skylanders* gaming guides for kids.

Hayley loves dinosaurs, jazz, animals and all things vintage. She loves to collect teacups, though oddly, doesn't drink tea.

www.hayleycamille.com

Connect with Hayley at:

ALSO BY HAYLEY CAMILLE

The Ivy Carter Series

HUMAN

Archaeologist Ivy Carter holds the fate of humankind in her hands.

Ivy Carter is no stranger to losing the people she loves. She keeps everybody at arm's length, even Orrin James, the brilliant young astrophysicist falling for her.

But when she is stolen through time, and trapped fifty thousand years in the past, Ivy is tasked with the greatest challenge of her life; to prevent the extinction of a primitive human species against overwhelming odds. Determined to save them and desperate to find a way back home, Ivy reaches out across time and space, to the only person in the modern world who remembers her.

As Orrin uncovers Ivy's trail of archaeological clues to prove she existed, the modern world around him spirals into destruction. Every move Ivy makes in the past, puts future Earth in danger.

Each alone, they battle demons, inside and out, to prevent a genocidal war that could change the course of human evolution forever.

In a thrilling adventure that flips between modern world catastrophe and primitive survival, Ivy Carter holds the fate of humankind in her hands.

Available at: HayleyCamille.com/human-novel

EXTINCT

Two species of Human. Only one can survive. The choice is hers.

In the stunning sequel to HUMAN, modern-day archaeologist Ivy Carter begins a perilous journey across prehistoric Indonesia, at a time when volcanic eruptions, mass extinction and a genocidal war are tearing it apart.

Available at: HayleyCamille.com/extinct-novel

The Lady Vigilante Series

Mrs. Betty Jones: Lady Vigilante is the award-winning crime series that readers describe as "An EXPLOSIVE laugh-out-loud story!" with the indomitable protagonist, Betty Jones, as "a female Jack Reacher", "powered as all hell" and "Sassy, Smart and Deadly!"

"Lady Vigilante takes on the tropes of femininity in the 40's- the dutiful wife, gals who just want to look pretty letting their man do all the heavy lifting and thinking - and flips them on their head." - *ScreenCraft*

If you love ruthless revenge, kick-ass action and unforgettable characters, then you'll love Betty Jones.

SEASON ONE

As WW2 rages, a lone vigilante takes to the streets of New York to wage war against a powerful crime syndicate. She's the antihero the city needs, hidden in plain sight, with the perfect double life. Meet Mrs. Betty Jones.

Betty Jones has a dark past, which she paints away each day with Avon cosmetics and a bright smile. She has created a new life with her picture-perfect family, but old scars are beginning to itch.

When a series of heists leave a trail of dead soldiers and missing military cargo, Betty recognizes the calling card of her past demons. Blessed with gifts that make her more than human, Betty is unable to live with the continuing existence of the people who once ruined her, so she embarks on a cold-blooded vigilante mission to be rid of them once and for all. But the past is catching up to her, and Betty's perfect life is beginning to crack.

SEASON TWO

A gang war is raging in the underbelly of 1940s New York as a mysterious femme-fatale, known only as the Boudoir Butcher, leaves a trail of bodies between the sheets. When NYPD Detective Jacob Lawrence turns to Betty for help tracking down the serial killer, she can't refuse him. After all, Betty has always been drawn to old flames and open fire…

But will Betty's perfect life be engulfed in the raging blaze she stirs up?

Season Collections available at:

HayleyCamille.com/lady-vigilante-season-collections

The Shadows and Light series

Judgement

In the shadow of Mortwood Forest dwells the most prolific murderer of the Kingdom. The curse he carries, however, may also make him their saviour.

In a world where magic has been lost and innocence is stolen, a prophesy begins. The darkest intentions hidden within every man's soul are exposed, as Shadows and Light, and only one has the power to Judge them.

But he is not what you expect.

Free short story available at: HayleyCamille.com/judgement